THE HUNTED MAIDEN

SEEDS OF HOPE BOOK ONE

DOUGLAS S. PIERCE

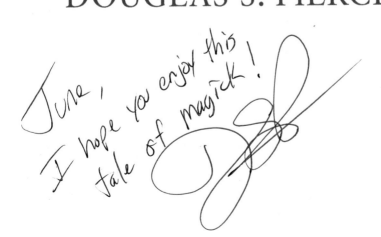

June,
I hope you enjoy this
tale of magick!

PRAISE FOR THE MAIDEN'S SONG

"…The characters were phenomenal! The story of Seldy and Rondel (Mouse) is completely unforgettable. I felt a royal connection to the characters right off the bat. The author spared no details making sure that we would never forget them and the struggles they suffered within this story. The adventure that Seldy and Rondel went through separately and together really made my heart hurt for them in some parts while in others, I was rooting the characters on… This was a powerful story from beginning to end. This story, and its characters, has taken a piece of my heart and hidden it within the pages of this book. I am so glad that I took that plunge into reading this book because this debut author has gained a new follower, and I highly recommend this read!"
—Five Star review by Jenny Bynum of Black Words—White Pages

"…It's nicely written and so very detailed that it pulled me into another world. Mouse and Seldy are interesting characters. They are the first two characters we get introduced to, and I wanted to know more about them and how their stories where going to intertwine. This one was a really good read."
—Five Star review by Amazeballs Book Addicts

"This is one of those rare times where I find myself frustrated in finding the right words for an amazing book. Truly a tale for the ages, *The Maiden's Song* will wrap you lovingly within its pages and keep you spellbound. A brilliant debut for what is sure to be a brilliant series. You'll want to curl up and lose yourself in a tale spun to rival the adventures in Narnia."
—Five Star review by Liliyana of The Faerie Review

"…The author weaves with intricate detail the journey to come. I can't say much without giving it away. The author did an amazing job of developing the characters and allowing their story to unfold organically. He mixed that with a host of interesting and vital supporting characters. Through his words, I could almost feel each scene and the emotions, especially the pain that was endured. I liked the fact that the author didn't just tell us of the personal growth, but it was demonstrated through action and the reactions of our primary character. While lengthy, the story did manage to keep me engaged enough to want to complete and find out what's next in this story. Mr. Pierce has set a high standard for himself that I hope is maintained in the sequel."
—**Four Star review by KayBee of KayBee's Bookshelf**

DEDICATION

This book is dedicated to the bright soul who gives me inspiration with every breath she takes—my daughter—Kerry.

I love you forever, kiddo!

ACKNOWLEDGEMENTS

No book is ever the accomplishment of a single person. I have had the invaluable assistance of innumerable folks, but there are a few who I would like to specifically acknowledge here.
Without the indulgence and countless sacrifices of my beloved wife, Patricia, this book would simply not exist. She is my North Star and guiding light. Her insight and input into the story and characters has been invaluable. Her patience with the immense amount of time I spent writing, editing, and thinking about it has been nothing short of heroic.

I would also like to extend a special thanks to Sherrie Dolby, my editor. She did a yeoman's work in whipping this monster of a manuscript into shape in a short time and while battling illness. She has a keen eye and a great sense of how to make the story better.

Each of the following people have also contributed to this book, in ways both great and small, and without them, it simply wouldn't be the story it has become. So, in no particular order, I would like to offer my thanks and appreciation to:
My brother, Dr. Steven J. Pierce, and his amazing wife, Lori; Dr. Jahn and Michelle Hakes; Alora Dana Cheek; the whole Cavanaugh clan at Crossing Hedgerows Farm — Daniel, Jean, Brennah, and Quinn; Rodelo Santos; the talented model and photographer Bunny Luna for being such a powerful muse for Seldy; Rebecca Poole of Dreams2media; and Rue Volley for being a great author-mentor!

AUTHOR'S NOTE

The Hunted Maiden and *The Seedling's Song*, Books One and Two of *The Seeds of Hope*, were originally published under the singular title of *The Maiden's Song, Book One of The Seeds of Hope*. Other than minor edits and formatting changes, there have been no significant changes to the story that was told in *The Maiden's Song*; it has merely been split into two books at the best possible break point so that each one can stand on its own within the larger series.

The Maiden's Song remains available as a special edition since it will always hold a special place in my heart for many deeply personal reasons. The choice to split that book into these two separate but deeply linked novels was made based on the recommendations of a number of folks, including my editor, Sherrie Dolby, and my dear friends Stephanie and Norman Hanley.

CHAPTER 1

Mouse

"Just don't look down."

Clutching the thick wood of the starboard wingmast with his knees, Mouse focused on the task at hand rather than the fact that he was perched on a relatively thin piece of wood that was the only thing between him and thousands of feet of open space immediately below. Fumbling against the biting wind, he jammed the end of the fraying rope through the second-to-last grommet of the tarp. His usually dexterous fingers had become clumsy and reluctant lumps of flesh in the frigid late Fanol wind. Tiny bits of ice clung to his eyelashes. Every inch of exposed skin burned as if a thousand bees were stinging him.

Another gust blasted up through the tight space between the mast and the side of the ship. It tore the edge of the tarp from his frozen fingers, yanking the end of the rope free of several hard-won grommets.

"By the Blazing Fires of the Fallen Star!"

Swallowing his frustration, Mouse tightened his grip and leaned out into the open air.

"Just don't look down."

The canvass snapped and popped in the howling wind,

dancing to its own wild music. Stretching further out over the void, Mouse snatched in vain at the flapping corner.

As quickly as it came, though, the wind died. The entire ship settled into an unnatural stillness. The normal creaking and groaning of the wooden hull faded into an eerie, uneasy silence punctuated by the soft slap of the tarp settling back into place. The sudden stillness in the midst of an oncoming storm could only mean one thing.

"Oh, shards!"

Mouse flattened out over the tarp and squeezed his eyes shut.

"Don't look down!"

He hugged the mast with both arms and legs.

With a screech that reminded him of the full-throated cries of a Slant-born whore being cheated out of her hard-earned coin, the wind washed over Mouse in an unstoppable wave. It slammed into the starboard side of the *Hunter's Ghost* with unimaginable force, sweeping the ship into the padded bumper-poles extending from the stone pier. The impact rolled through every board, mast, and line of rigging with bone-jarring force.

Above him, a dozen curses and cries of pain erupted as the rest of the crew scrambled to hold on in the higher rigging of the vertical masts or were knocked from their feet on the main deck. Beneath him, the wingmast bucked, flinging him several feet up into the air.

At the apex of his brief rise, a second, surging counter-draft caught the inside of Mouse's jacket, spreading the unbuttoned flaps to either side of his body like the wings of a bird in flight.

Time slowed. Movement ceased.

Suspended in the gap between the tip of the folded-up wing mast and the massive hull, Mouse couldn't help himself.

He looked down.

And in that single moment before he began to fall, the

breathtaking beauty of the view spooling out below and around him overcame the sheer terror gripping at his heart.

Extending both down and out to either side of his flailing bare feet, the cliffs of the island of Timos stretched as far as he could see. The uneven grey surface was pocked with ledges and crevices, and below each of them were streaks of shite from the countless generations of annoying shore gulls that had built their nests in them.

To his right, the wooden mass of the hull obscured his view of the stone docks and the port of Nashae beyond.

A towering mass of dark clouds loomed across the western horizon. The roiling formation was every bit as large and imposing as the stone cliffs that framed his eastern view. Lightning danced in dozens of places along the leading edge of the storm, creating images in the churning darkness that reminded him of faces — feminine faces — twisted into grimaces of unfathomable rage.

Blinking, Mouse shifted his gaze down towards the Untere thousands of feet below. The winding blue ribbons of water and the button-sized lakes dotting the landscape lacked the characteristic sparkle they had in the bright sun of a cloudless day. The verdant greens of the forests and the rich browns of the fertile soil were dulled by the shadows cast by the incoming storm.

I'm flying. Again.

The illusion of flight, however, evaporated as quickly as it came. Dropping like a stone through the narrow gap between the folded-up wingmast and the hull, Mouse reached out in desperation, flailing for the rope ladder. Twice the thick, rain-slicked hemp slipped through frozen fingers. But on the third try, he managed to keep his grip on the bottom-most rung. Jerked to a halt in mid-fall, his body twisted in the air. He slammed into the hull back first.

Whoomp!

The jarring impact sent searing waves of pain flaring out from each of the scabbed-over wounds that scored the length of his back. Convulsing in agony, Mouse nearly lost his grip. It took every bit of strength and determination that remained within him to push off with his left heel and flip his body around.

"Don't. Look. Down."

Gritting his teeth against the fresh waves of pain, Mouse began to climb.

It wasn't until he had pulled himself up several rungs on the ladder that the realization of how close he'd come to dying hit him. Intertwining his trembling limbs into the ropes, Mouse pressed his forehead against the solid warmth of the hull and gasped for breath. The relentless pounding of his heart against his eardrums obscured everything else until a deep and familiar voice called out from above, cutting through both the rushing wind and his hammering pulse.

"Mouse!"

Dalton leaned out over the railing. His long, forked beard flapped against either side of his otherwise bald head.

"What're ya doin' down there with no blasted safety harness?" The man waved a meaty hand. "Git yer land-lubbin' arse back up here!"

Mouse scampered obediently up the rope ladder until a pair of strong hands grabbed his collar and yanked him roughly over the railing.

"What in the blazes were ya thinkin', lad?" Dalton thundered over the swirling winds. "Doncha ever pull that shite again, ya hear me?"

Staggering under the combined onslaught of the storm's wind and the barely contained fury of Dalton's normally calm and steady personal song, Mouse raised his hands in futile defense.

"But Jigger said..."

"Listenin' to that fool'll git ya killed right blasted quick, son!" Still holding the lapels of Mouse's jacket, Dalton jerked him upright. "I can't watch yer scrawny arse and keep these bastards workin' hard 'nough to batten this ship down at the same blasted time."

"I'm nineteen years old and a deckhand on this ship!" Mouse bit back. He brushed the larger man's hands aside, stood up to his full height of just over five feet eight inches tall, and brushed his windblown brown hair from his equally brown eyes. "So I need to do my share, or they're just going to keep seeing me as—"

"I know, boy," Dalton cut him off. "I know ya mean well. But yer a bleedin' fool—"

Swept up in the power of the music flowing from the old sailor into him, Mouse lost track of what Dalton was shouting at him. His consciousness flowed instead into the stream of the man's raucous music as naturally as those annoying shore gulls rode the constant eddies and swirls of the wind bouncing off of the cliffs. He slipped past the strains that showed the deep concern the heavy-set man had for him and those that were focused on his responsibility to prepare the ship for the looming storm. His interest was captured, instead, by the vibrant images of a heavy-set, smiling woman and bright-eyed children gathering around Dalton as he returned home from yet another long voyage.

"Mouse!"

Strong hands found his shoulders, giving them a hard squeeze.

"Mouse! Wake up, blast ya!"

"Ah!" The fresh pain needling down his back jolted him out of his reverie. "Ow!"

"I'm sorry, son." Dalton dropped his hands from Mouse's shoulders as if they were on fire. "I didna mean to hurt ya…but sometimes…"

"I...uh..." Mouse sucked in his breath and leaned back, trying to avoid reopening any more of his still healing scabs. "I know, Dalton."

"What's happening to ya, boy?" Concern clouded the bald man's eyes. He pointed to Mouse's head. "Where do ya keep disappearin' to in there?"

"I'm sorry. I wish I could explain it."

"Whatever the reason, boy, ya need to stop daydreamin' so much or someday it'll land ya in more trouble than yer glib tongue can talk ya out of." Dalton sighed. "Never mind, I've got somethin' else for ya to do, somethin' that'll help more'n ya tryin' yer hand at any more of this here jib work."

"What's that?"

"I need ya to go into town," Dalton nodded towards the shore and pressed a small pouch of coins into his hand, "and get some grog for these thirsty bastards. They'll work harder if'n they know somethin' good's waitin' for them at the end of all this blasted effort."

Turning a corner on the cobbled streets of ancient Nashae, Mouse looked up and paused. Soaring high over the nearest buildings were the seven impossibly tall and thin spires of the Jalrun Conservatory of the Arts gleaming against an otherwise gloomy sky. The shimmering marble-faced towers dwarfed the squat stone and wood buildings of the small city that had grown up around it over the many generations of its existence as the premiere school for artists, musicians, and performers in the known world.

"Someday," he whispered to himself, "I'm going to study there."

Digging into his pocket, he thumbed the squared-off edges of the iron quads poking through the thin fabric of the pouch.

Maybe if there's some change left from the grog, he thought to himself, *I can buy a cheap flute.* He shook the thought from his head. *I'd be better off just stealing one...*

Mouse stomped each bare foot in place. He couldn't stop shivering. The soles of his feet were thick with callouses, but that thickened skin hadn't stopped his toes from going numb because of the cold. He pushed his hands into the pockets of his threadbare uniform jacket and pulled it tighter about his thin frame. Ducking his head inside the upraised collar, he forced one foot in front of the other, moving towards his assigned destination rather than the one that occupied his dreams.

"Ugh!"

Staggered by the bone-jarring impact with a hooded figure he hadn't noticed before, Mouse's backside landed hard on the rough cobblestones. He grunted at the fresh agony lancing up the scabs lining his back.

A massive figure loomed over him, unmoved by the force of their collision except for the hood of his cloak. The slipping fabric revealed the ruddy complexion, sharply-pointed ears, and thick-boned features of an orc. The orc narrowed his eyes and scowled down at him. In his far hand, he held an iron-tipped wooden staff as thick as Mouse's wrists.

"Watch where you're going, boy," the big orc snarled in a clipped accent through thin lips and pointed teeth.

Gulping, Mouse stared up at him. He was every bit as tall and broad through the shoulders as the captain was but with none of the fat that softened the familiar man's profile.

"I'm sorry, *ton'kul.*" Mouse held up empty hands.

The orc's eyes flashed. He spun on his heel, gripping the staff in both clawed hands as he took a menacing step closer.

"What did you just call—?"

A second figure emerged from the alleyway. He slipped between them with the easy grace of a trained dancer. The

7

still-hooded figure placed a restraining hand on the staff as he looked down at Mouse. The piercing blue eyes of a smiling, middle-aged human regarded him.

"Easy, friend. I'm sure the lad meant no insult," the man said in a deep, melodic voice. He offered his other hand to Mouse. "Isn't that right, son?"

"No, I mean, yes, sir!" Mouse reached for the offered hand without thinking. "I thought that *ton'kul* was the proper address for an...orc."

"It can be." The man nodded as his calloused hand gripped Mouse's. "If you're a warrior of equivalent rank and prestige as..."

Kerplunk.

The moment Mouse touched the man's hand, the unmistakable sound of a drop of water splashing into a pool somewhere — no, *some when* — captured his attention. The reverberating echo, however, was soon overwhelmed by the powerful music flooding into Mouse's consciousness.

The man's personal song thundered through the physical connection between them with all of the grace and subtlety of a military marching band rousing soldiers for battle. Drums pounded, cymbals crashed, and trumpets blared out in triumphant exultation, but those loud and brash instruments couldn't hide the quieter, deeper, and mournful melody of a single flute playing in the background or the soft strumming of a stringed instrument that he didn't recognize playing the hauntingly familiar notes of a long and tragic ballad.

Gasping, Mouse's eyes widened.

Kerplunk.

Mouse hadn't heard anything the stranger said as he was pulled back up to unsteady feet. It was only when he released his hand and stepped back that the music faded into the background.

"—right, son?" The man's eyes narrowed. "Are you hurt?"

"I'm fine," Mouse replied, shaking his head. "I'm sorry for getting in your way."

"No apologies needed, son." The man pressed the pouch, cold and wet from the puddle it had landed in, into his hand. "But I don't think you want to forget this."

"Thank you!" He flinched at the prospect of touching of the man's skin again but managed to close his fingers around the sodden pouch without any trouble. "Dalton'd have my hide if I lost this." He looked up at the man with relief and a great deal of respect in his eyes. "Where I grew up, I would've lost this for sure."

"Well, we can't have that now, can we?" The man stood up to his full height, somewhere north of six feet. He studied Mouse. "You're a sailor, aren't you?"

"Yes, sir." Mouse straightened up, pulling on the hem of his jacket, and made a point of looking the man in the eyes. "I am."

"What ship are you serving on?"

"The *Hunter's Ghost*, sir. A galleon serving out of Vander-mal on Dortyn."

Mouse sized-up the man for the first time. He was likely in his fifties but had aged well. His neatly trimmed brown beard was sprinkled with grey. His features were quite refined, but certainly not delicate. He had the weathered complexion of someone who spent a great deal of time outside. He was also, quite obviously, a man of significant means. A pair of well-kept dueling blades hung from sheaths held up by a thick, leather belt that was laden with other pouches and accoutrements. His black, knee-high boots were polished to a high sheen.

"Excuse me, sir," Mouse added. "But do I know you from somewhere?"

The big orc stiffened.

The man smiled.

"It's certainly possible, son." His eyes twinkled. "There's something that seems familiar about you as well, but I have a very good memory for such things, and I don't think we've ever met before." He winked. "I've learned, however, that the world is both much smaller than it seems and rather full of surprises. Perhaps we are destined to meet again?"

"Uh, maybe." Mouse blinked, surprised at the question. "But, I...uh...don't get out much."

"We should go," the massive orc grunted, "before the *storm* gets any closer."

The man ignored his companion and continued to study Mouse.

Tucking the pouch back into his pocket, Mouse noticed a long, thin leather case dangling from the man's belt. It reminded him of the priceless treasure that was lost when his mother had died.

Kerplunk.

"Sir?"

"Yes?"

"Are you...do you...happen to be a musician?"

The big orc's scowl deepened. He took a menacing step closer, but the man stopped him with a small gesture.

"I've played a few songs in my day." The man's brow furrowed. "Why do you ask?"

"I...uh..." Mouse cleared his throat. "Was wondering if you might know of a shop in this city where I could...uh...you know...uh...find...a practice flute."

"I doubt any shops will be open with this storm looming so close." The man's sharp gaze pierced him to the core. It was if the man could tell that he likely couldn't afford to buy an instrument and was considering stealing one. "Do you know how to play the flute?"

Mouse ducked his head, unable to meet the man's gaze.

"Yes, sir...I do...or rather...I did. My mom, well, she taught me to play when I was younger, and...uh...I would like to start practicing again." Pushing aside the ache in his heart, he cast a furtive glance over his right shoulder at the towering spires of the Conservatory. "If I can start playing again..." Mouse squared his shoulders, looked the man in the eyes, and puffed out his chest. "Well, one day I just know I'll be good enough to win a scholarship."

"We don't have time for this, friend." The orc's harsh voice cut through the quiet moment. His voice dropped to a pleading whisper. "The danger grows."

"Easy, friend." The man shrugged the orc's hand aside and took a step closer to Mouse. "There must always be time for musicians to talk about making music, or life would simply not be worth living."

Reaching inside of his cloak, he pulled out a long and thin object that was wrapped in a length of worn, blue silk. The man peeled the cloth back, revealing a simple but well-made and worn wooden flute.

His breath catching, Mouse's fingers twitched.

There was sadness in the man's expression that was reflected by the sorrow in his softening song.

Snorting, the orc tapped his staff on the cobblestones.

Crack!

The sharp report broke the reverie. The man plucked the flute from its wrapping and held it aloft with reverence.

"Son, take this." He presented it to Mouse with a flourish. "It was my first instrument, given to me by someone very dear when I was getting ready to study at the Conservatory, far too many years ago." His gaze grew distant. "She would've liked the idea of it going to another young student, I think."

"But...sir..." Mouse gulped. "I was just looking — hoping, really — to find something..."

"The ability to make beautiful music is a rare and precious gift." The man's jaw hardened. "Such a gift cannot truly be bought, sold, or *stolen.*" The man's expression softened. "Music has changed my life, son, very much for the better. Hopefully, this instrument will change your circumstances as well. Please accept it, from one musician to another."

"I—" Mouse shuffled back, waving his hands. "I can't."

The stranger stepped forward more quickly than he could retreat. Vibrant music washed over him as the man's song enveloped him in its powerful, triumphant notes. He smiled down at Mouse and pressed the flute into his hands. While his smile was broad, the tinge of sorrow never left his eyes.

Kerplunk.

"Take it." There was a hitch in his voice. "I had been saving it for my — well, someone very dear to me — but that person has since passed away." The stranger closed Mouse's fingers around the flute. "It would mean a great deal to know that an aspiring musician like I once was had it." The man arched a knowing eyebrow. "And someday, perhaps, you can return this kindness by giving the gift of music to someone else in their time of need."

Kerplunk.

With both of their hands wrapped around the precious instrument, the distant notes of another song slipped out from the furthest recesses of Mouse's memory.

The dream song! A hard lump formed in his throat. *But... how?*

The sweet melody of a single flute playing was as pure as it was beautiful. The deeper and more ominous drum beat hinted at a looming danger that threatened the bright innocence and boundless love captured in the melody. The contrast sent shivers racing down his spine.

He ached to hear more of the mysterious and familiar song

but even as he strained to hear it better, it faded back into silence. A single whispered word echoed in his mind.

...remember...remember...remember...

When the man's fingers slipped from his and he stepped back, Mouse stood there, trembling. The smooth, worn wood of the instrument was warm and reassuringly solid in his hands.

"Th-thank you, sir!" He looked up at his benefactor. "Can I have your name at least?"

"Perhaps when we meet again, son." His smile warmed Mouse to the bone. "Until then, it is best for each of us to be on our respective ways." Stepping back, he waved a hand in the direction from which Mouse had come. "That storm is coming. If you wish to accomplish your errand, you should do so before it arrives. This one looks to be a real screecher."

Mouse bobbed his head and hurried past man and orc.

"You take too many foolish risks," the orc whispered as Mouse brushed by.

The man's reply was too low to be heard, but Mouse didn't care. His attention was focused on the instrument clutched in his hands and on the bright future he might be able to compose for himself with it.

CHAPTER 2

Seldy

"Pull...Hold...Pull...Hold!" *Maestro* Banyan barked out his commands in a deep baritone voice.

With each call of 'pull,' Seldy renewed her grip on the rope and leaned back, adding all of her strength to the collective effort. With each 'hold,' she relaxed long enough to let her aching shoulders rest and repositioned her feet for the next command.

Her eyes remained fixed on Chad's broad back. His well-defined muscles grew taut beneath his loose-fitting cotton tunic with each pull, giving her a small thrill of anticipation for the next time she would be able to feel them rippling beneath her teasing fingers...

"Pull!"

The sharp command yanked her mind back to the task at hand. She dug her toes into the winter-hardened earth and threw all of her weight into the joint effort to lower the massive array of safety nets to the ground.

"Hold!"

Letting out a ragged breath, Seldy relaxed. Glancing around, she was glad to see that she wasn't the only one breathing hard.

Both Gregor and Talinn — each of them nearly as big as Chad — were struggling with the other line across the way. Chad looked back at her over his shoulder.

"We're almost done, Sunshine." He winked. "You doin' okay back there?"

Her heart fluttered. Seeing his chiseled features profiled in the flickering lamplight, Seldy was reminded of how lucky she was.

"You betcha!"

She beamed her brightest smile up at him, before brushing her silver bangs out of her eyes and re-gripping the rope.

"Pull!"

She couldn't help giggling when Chad struggled to regain his rhythm. Her smile had flummoxed him, again.

"Watch out below! And...release!"

There was a collective sigh when the rope was released. Seldy closed her eyes and turned away from the center of the ring as the mass of netting dropped the last few feet to the ground with a tremendous *whoomph*. A cloud of dust and grit billowed into the air.

"Take a breather!" *Maestro* Banyan's words elicited a few tired cries of relief until his next words cut them short. "But don't go anywhere! That storm's bearing down on us and *Maestra* Jhana expects this entire tent to be struck and stowed before it arrives!"

Chad grabbed her hand and pulled her away from the others before *Maestro* Banyan had even stopped speaking. He led her off into the shadows beyond the reach of the flickering lamps. She didn't bother to resist even though their friends — Lyna, Talinn and Gregor — rolled their eyes and began whispering to each other.

Soon they were surrounded by the stacks of crates containing many of the stowed props and equipment that the *kumpania* used in every performance. Once the others were out of sight, Chad pulled her in close.

He towered over her, standing over a foot taller than she did. Staring up at his mane of shoulder-length, curly, black hair and his gorgeous face, Seldy wondered, not for the first time, how she only came to notice how handsome he was in the last year or so. She had known him her entire life. They had been partners on the high-wire and the trapeze for years. Now, though, every time they were alone, her stomach fluttered, and she wanted nothing more than to melt into his arms.

"Have you told her yet?" His blue eyes were wide as he leaned in close. His breath warmed her cheek.

"Told her what?" Seldy tilted her head and batted her eyelashes, offering him a coy smile.

His eyes narrowed, but the corners of his mouth turned up.

"Oh, I see how it's going to be."

He pressed her back against the crates. They were so close she could feel the beating of his heart through the combined layers of her thin dress and his thicker tunic. Her heart raced in response.

"I've been waiting to do this all day."

He dipped his head, brought his hands up to cradle her face, and pressed his lips to hers.

All of her defenses melted away. Her heart pounded against her ribs as if she was running a long race. Her breathing quickened. Seldy allowed herself to become lost in the moment, wrapped in the warmth of his strong and steady presence. She slid her fingers into his thick mane, enjoying the feel of it almost as much as she delighted in his fresh, masculine scent. She uttered a soft moan and leaned into the kiss.

"Seldy!" Jhana's cry rang out behind them, cutting through the murmuring background noise.

"Shards!" She pushed Chad back with a muttered curse. "What timing!"

"You haven't told her yet, have you?"

"No," she sighed. "There just hasn't been time. With Tia's warning about the storm this morning..." She took each of his clean-shaven cheeks in her hands before sucking in her bottom lip in frustration.

"When are you going to tell her?"

"Where's my daughter, blast it?"

Seldy pulled Chad in for another kiss. It was a quick one, but it was full of promise and unfulfilled desire.

"Tonight," she whispered as she drew back with a gentle caress of his cheek. "I'll talk to her tonight, when we're all settled in to ride out the storm."

"Good." He gave her a wink. "Because I don't know about you, but I can't wait much longer."

Jhana was upon them before she could do anything more than offer a wistful smile in return. Chad slid back, creating a bit of separation between them as her mother rounded the corner.

"Oh! There you are, *rehla*!"

Stepping between the two would-be lovers with only a quick glance and a hint of a smile in Chad's direction, her mother bristled with a crackling, visceral energy. If she had any suspicion about what the two of them were doing only moments before, she hid it well.

Unlike Seldy, Jhana was bundled up, wearing a linen jacket over her traditional long-sleeved cotton blouse and a heavy woolen skirt that hung all of the way down to the tops of her booted feet. Her mother looked her up and down — from the thin, sleeveless dress that hung from otherwise uncovered shoulders and only came down to her knees, to her bare legs and feet — and arched a dark eyebrow at her.

"By the Shards of Luna, child, it's freezing out here! And likely to start snowing or spitting freezing rain at any moment! How many times do I have to tell you to put more clothes on?"

"Oh, Ma!" Seldy spun around, flaring the hem of her dress up around the middle of her thighs. "You know the cold doesn't bother me! I'm perfectly comfortable. Besides, it's easier to work without all that heavy clothing weighing me down!"

Jhana clucked her tongue in obvious disapproval. She cast a sideways glance at Chad, her grey eyes flashing.

"Chadraeg, have you tried to talk some sense into her about this?"

"Uh...um...no, *Maestra*." Chad took another step back and raised his hands. "She's eighteen now, so I can't boss her around like I used to. And frankly, I...uh...don't mind, actually." His cheeks flushed bright red.

Jhana's head snapped around at him.

"Of course you wouldn't," she huffed. "Men! You're all alike."

Seldy slipped up to her mother and rose up onto her toes. She planted a kiss on her weathered, brown cheek.

"Yes, they are. But that's why we love them so much, Ma!"

"I suppose you're right, Sweetling."

"Uh...I...should go, *Maestra*, to see if they need me to help with the netting..." He paused, backing up a step before adding, "...or something."

"Actually, Chad," she replied, freezing him in place with a glare. "I was looking for you as well, and I figured the easiest way to do that was to find Seldy."

"Uh...yes...*Maestra.*" He shuffled his booted foot in the dirt. "What can I..."

"The first thing you can do is drop this '*Maestra*' business," she snapped. "I've known you since you were a babe in swaddling. And since your mother passed away, you've eaten more meals at my fire than anyone else's." Her voice softened. "If you're as serious as the rumors going around the *kumpania* say you are about spending even more time with my daughter than you already do, you're going to have to start using my name."

Chad's cheeks blushed a deeper shade of brown. Seldy felt a surge of relief at hearing the tacit acceptance in her mother's voice.

"Yes, *Mae*...uh Jhana."

"That's better," Jhana said, giving Seldy's shoulder a tiny squeeze. "Now, take Talinn and Gregor and go check on the livestock and the horses. Make sure that the fences are solid and that the youngsters are inside their shelters. The winds are going to start getting bad soon, and I want all of you back before the worst of it hits us."

Ducking his head in acknowledgment, Chad cast a furtive glance and an awkward smile at Seldy. Stepping away, he called out for the others in a strong, confident voice.

"Yo, Gregor, Talinn! We've got new orders! Grab your jackets and gloves and come with me!"

Seldy sighed, her chest swelling with pride.

"I wouldn't be surprised to see him become *Baro*, someday." She flashed a grin at her mother.

"He's got the potential for it," Jhana acknowledged with a nod. She turned to face Seldy, her voice dropping to a hoarse whisper. "*Rehla*, can you please go check on Tiagra?"

"What's wrong?" Seldy gasped. "Is Tia okay?"

"I don't know. Ever since she made her proclamation about the storm this morning, she's been shut inside her *vardo* and won't let anyone come in, not even me." Her mother sighed, wrapping Seldy in a fierce, bear-like hug. "She didn't look well."

"Oh, no!" She tried to keep the worry from her voice. "I'll go see her right away!"

"There's something else." Jhana pursed her lips. "It's probably nothing, *rehla*. But Tia said something about the storm that I didn't mention to anyone else."

"What did she say?"

Her mother paused, visibly swallowing. Her hands trembled uncharacteristically in Seldy's fingers. Licking her lips, Jhana whispered,

"She said 'tis a *Fae* storm coming, a storm like no other.'"

"A *Fae* storm?" Her voice squeaked. "Like Dorel?"

Pressing her lips into a thin, tight line, Jhana nodded once.

The images of the devastation of that small coastal town were indelibly etched into Seldy's mind, even though it had been more than ten years. Every wooden structure in the whole town had been flattened. The vacant stares and the broken wails of the survivors that the *kumpania* had helped to dig out of the rubble still haunted her dreams.

For the first time in her life, Seldy shivered.

CHAPTER 3

Mouse

Grunting under the sloshing weight of the full torpedo keg on his shoulder, Mouse didn't see the missing cobblestone until it was too late. He stubbed his toes against the hidden edge and landed face-first in the slush. The wooden cask tumbled onto the cobbles, landing with a sickening thud.

The sixtel wobbled once before it began rolling downhill. Mouse scrabbled after it, ignoring the wrenching pain in his toes and the shock of getting doused in icy cold water. Muttering a stream of curses under his breath that would have made Dalton proud, he caught up to it and wrestled it to a stop.

Mouse held his breath as he tipped the barrel onto its end and inspected it, afraid of what he would see. Luckily, it was unbroken. He breathed a sigh of relief and settled back onto his knees.

"Oh, shards! My flute!" He plucked the instrument out of his sodden jacket with trembling fingers. "Please be okay!"

The dark wood of the instrument glistened in the fading light of the storm-laden day. Its lacquered surface was warm and smooth to the touch. In the process of examining it for cracks, his fingers fell into position over the holes as if he and the flute were long-time companions. Unable to resist the urge, Mouse pressed his lips to the mouth-hole and began to play.

He peeled back the corners of the blue silk wrapped around the instrument that his mother held and picked it up. It was bright silver, shining in the guttering candlelight of their small shack. She watched him, smiling, as he inspected it.

"Isn't it beautiful?"

"What is it?" He studied the gleaming tube. It vibrated softly in his hands. "It must've cost a fortune!" He looked up at her, wide-eyed. "How long have we had this?"

She smiled and set the silk wrapping aside.

"This is a f'leyn. It makes the most beautiful music. Your grandfather dug it out of the ground on one of his many expeditions. He believed it was made before the world was broken. Your father spent years restoring it and then learning how to play it before giving it to me on our wedding day."

"You mean this was made before the Sundering?" His eyes widened. "Wow!"

"Yes." She nodded, smiling. "Your grandfather studied antiquities like this and believed it was made by the Aelfani. The notes it plays are as sweet as any birdsong I've ever heard."

"But, Mom! If this...f'leyn...is that old, it has to be worth a fortune! Why haven't you sold it?" He turned the instrument over in his fingers, studying it. "We could leave this place and go somewhere better, someplace where you could wear pretty clothes again, like you used to. Someplace where there will always be enough food, and we can be safe!"

"No, Rondel." She drew back, her eyes glazing over. "I could never sell this!"

"Why not?"

"Because, other than you, this instrument is all I have left of your father's love."

Sadness filled his mother's blue eyes. She drew him into an embrace.

"It would be like selling a piece of my soul." She hugged him tight. "We have enough here. We are together. Meg makes sure that we have enough to eat. And the people here need me and my healing skills. The time will come when we will have to leave, but not for a while yet."

He continued to study the f'leyn as his mother spoke. It looked delicate but felt sturdy and unbreakable in his fingers. The silver gleamed in the dim light in their shack. But more than anything else, what captured his attention most was the hauntingly beautiful music that flowed into his fingertips from the instrument itself. It filled his mind with blurry images of a mist-shrouded forest that echoed with birdsong and the distant shouts of playing children.

"Besides," she added. "I have a sneaking suspicion that you may have inherited my family's musical talent."

Squirming against his mother's possessiveness, he held the instrument up. "Can you show me how to play it?"

"Sure." She wiped away the tears with a sleeve and sat up. "First, place your fingers over these holes, here and here." She demonstrated by moving his fingers over the cluster of holes at one end. "And bring this end up to your lips." She guided the instrument up to his mouth. "Now, take a deep breath, and blow."

The first few rusty notes that emerged from the flute were softer, slower, and deeper in tone than the f'leyn he grew up playing, but the music was beautiful and brought Mouse a peace he hadn't felt since well before his mother had died. He had only played a few stanzas from one of her favorite songs when the cold seeping into his knees and the tops of his bare feet reminded him that he was kneeling in the slush-covered street. He couldn't stop shivering. He pulled the flute away from his lips.

A frigid blast of wind doused him with ice-laden pellets of rain.

"Oh, blazes!"

Slipping the flute back into his jacket, he staggered to cold-numbed feet. Bending over, he hefted the cask back onto his shoulder and shuffled forward.

The winds continued to swirl, nipping at his heels and teasing at his soaked clothes, but the bulk of the rain held off. Slogging through the half-frozen, slush-filled streets, his mind kept drifting back to the notes and fingering patterns of all of the songs his mother had taught him.

Later.

Shaking his head, he focused instead on putting one frigid foot in front of the other. The promise of being able to practice in the warmth and security of the ship gave him the strength and determination he needed to keep moving forward.

It seemed like forever, but it wasn't long before he was standing outside of the crumbling stone wall separating the city of Nashae from the port of the same name. A remnant of the Great Riving — that dark time before the founding of the Guild Alliance over 350 years ago — the ancient wall was little more than a ruin, unlikely to be able stand up to even a single cannon ball. However, it was still tall enough in most places to obscure everything but the tops of the masts of the ships docked beyond it.

Where the guardhouse and a gate once stood, there was now a gap large enough for two wagons to pass through at the same time. A small wooden shack — serving as the customs booth for both cargo and people entering the city — sat lonely and forlorn in the middle of the space, its unlatched door swinging about on rusty hinges in the swirling winds. The bored officer who had been manning it earlier had likely returned to the safety and comfort of his own home. No more ships would be coming until the storm passed.

Slipping to a knee on a patch of hidden ice next to the shack, Mouse set the sixtel on the ground next to the booth and took a moment to catch his breath. Compared to the larger ports he'd seen in the Guild Alliance, the Port of Nashae was tiny and provincial with none of the tall cranes that loaded and unloaded cargo from the larger ships like he'd seen in those other places. Most of the quays were empty. The docks, comprised of equal parts of wood, stone, and metal, jutted out into the angry, storm-tossed sky. Three lonely ships strained against their anchoring ropes in the restless wind.

The *Hunter's Ghost* was small for a three-masted galleon, but it was easily the largest ship still in port. The other two were a pair of clumsy-looking coastal cogs, smaller merchant vessels that did most of their trading along the coast of Timos rather than traveling the open skies between islands like the *Ghost* did. Several other ships had left earlier in the day, when the storm was far enough away for them to slip out ahead of it.

Yer lucky, lad, to not hafta sail the open skies in ships like those coasters over there. Shivering, Mouse remembered Dalton's words from earlier. *I've sailed in plenty o'tubs like them, 'til I earned enough credit with the Guild to be able to sign on with the* Ghost.

Despite spending the last six months aboard the galleon, it was still disconcerting to see such bulky wooden vessels bobbing in the air, defying everything he knew about gravity. Massive ropes as thick as his arm connected each of the ships to various anchor points along the piers, but there was nothing but open sky and the sheer, stone cliffs of the edge of the island for thousands of feet beneath each of them. The massive islands of the Untere, far below, were obscured by the dark clouds of the oncoming storm.

Looking towards the *Ghost*, Mouse could just make out the shadowy figures of the crew swarming along the decks and rigging. They were too far away to pick out any distinct figures but snatches of Dalton's booming commands reached his ears.

"Pull like ya mean it, ya rotten bastards!"

"Tie down that tarp, Swain!"

"Jigger, get yer arse up there and secure the main; it's flappin' loose again!"

"No one gets outta this weather 'til erythin's right and tight!"

A bright flash seared through the gloom. Everything became a surreal contrast between black and white under the flickering illumination. For a timeless moment, everyone on the *Ghost* froze in place. Startled, Mouse jerked his head around just in time to see the tail end of a fork of lightning arcing across the sky. Without thinking about it, he ducked through the open door of the inspector's shack and slammed it shut.

Moments later, a massive boom rolled over him, rattling the shack like a drum being pounded on by a giant, playful child. Always sensitive to loud sounds, Mouse covered his ears, squeezed his eyes shut, and curled up on the floor. The wind picked up, howling its fury at being upstaged by its flashier companions.

Wind-driven sleet smashed into the sides and roof of the tiny building in great pelting sheets. The sound of so much water reminded Mouse of the stories his mom used to tell during storms when they huddled together in their tin shack in the Slant. Through those stories, she kept his attention riveted on those fantastic images of the world and how it was before the Sundering, instead of on the very real possibility of their home collapsing on them or being blow away altogether. She described great oceans of salty water that separated the lands from each other instead of the open skies. It was hard to imagine now that there ever was a time when there was so much water in the world that one couldn't see from one side of it to another.

Once, after watching him play with a couple of roughly improvised wooden ships in their rain barrel, his mom described how ships used to sail on top of water, instead of flying through the air like they did now. She also spoke of how the storms of that unbroken world would create huge waves that tossed those ships about like his toy boats were whenever he splashed next to them.

Pressed against the shaking walls of the booth, Mouse jerked up when a large piece of parchment peeled off the wall and fell on him. In the near dark, all he could make out on the paper was a pair of dark blobs that might be faces and the word 'Wanted' printed in thick black ink at the top of the page.

Sitting up with his back pressed against the damp wall behind him, Mouse strained to make sense of the images in the gloom. Lightning flashed again. He gasped. The pale light revealed enough details to recognize the two faces shown on it and for just enough time for him to read the names scrawled beneath each image.

Staring back at him were the intimidating orc he'd bumped into and his companion, the strange man who had given him the flute. Mouse's heart thudded in his chest.

The light was gone before Mouse could read anything further. His hands shook as he folded the poster in half and then in half again. He tucked it into his pocket, next to the flute.

His mind racing at the implications of his encounter, Mouse stood up, opened the door, and stepped out into the screeching winds and lashing rain. The storm outside paled in comparison to the maelstrom of thoughts and emotions swirling around inside of his own head. He hefted the sixtel onto his shoulder and staggered towards the ship. He wasn't sure how he would get back onto the ship in the middle of the storm, but he couldn't sit and stew in his own dark thoughts while waiting for a lull that was unlikely to come anytime soon.

CHAPTER 4

Seldy

Stepping out of the protective cover of the big top, Seldy looked up at the dark clouds overhead.

"Are you really a *Fae* storm?"

The only answer that came was a swirling gust of wind that messed up her unbound hair and toyed with the hem of her knee-length dress. Feeling more than a little silly for speaking out loud to the storm like it could actually answer, Seldy ducked her head and took off at a run, racing over half-frozen earth and patches of slushy snow in her bare feet. Despite the rough conditions, her steps were as light as they were sure, barely touching the ground.

The wind continued to rage, clutching at her in vain because neither the frigid air nor the snow bothered her. None of the bundled-up folk who watched her pass batted an eye. Everyone in the *kumpania* knew of both her immunity to extremes of heat and cold and of her acute dislike for wearing shoes of any kind, even in the depths of winter.

Uncle Tegger — who had brought her to the *kumpania* as an infant — said that her affinity with nature was due to her *Aelfani* heritage.

"There aren't many pureblood elves around for me to ask, Seldy, but I have heard plenty of stories about the elves of old being immune to the cold like you are."

"But why is that, Uncle?"

"Why, what?" He grinned at her, pushing a stray strand of silver hair back behind one of her ears. "Why aren't there many elves around? Or why are they immune to the cold?"

Seldy blinked in surprise before she flashed a bright smile at him and chirped, "Both!"

Chuckling, her uncle shook his head.

"I walked right into that trap, didn't I?"

She giggled. "Yes, you did!"

"Ah well," he shrugged, grinning. "I suppose I'll have to work my way out of it, then." He gave her a sly wink. "Luckily, the answers to both questions are related, so I can answer them with one story."

"Really?" She narrowed her eyes with suspicion. "You're not trying to get out of telling two stories, are you?"

"Such an accusation!"

"Uncle Tegger!" Seldy crossed her arms and pushed her bottom lip out in her best pout.

His expression softened. He brushed her lip back into place with a gentle thumb and then drew her in closer so that she was leaning against him. He began speaking in a soft voice.

"You're not quite old enough yet to hear the full story, Seldy, but I will tell you what I can now because it is important for you to know as much as possible about your heritage." He looked at her with a somber expression and piercing eyes, all of the humor from before was gone. "Do you remember your lessons about the Sundering?"

"Isn't that when the earth and moon were broken into pieces when the Dragonstar crashed into them?"

"Yes, that's correct." Nodding, he turned to face forward. He continued speaking. "Thousands of years ago — no one is really certain exactly how many years it has been since the Sundering — the world was whole and unbroken, and there was only one moon. She was called Luna."

Seldy leaned her head against her uncle's arm and listened, careful not to interrupt his story.

"The earth then was so full of magick and great wonders that we cannot even imagine them all today. But what is important for this story, is that long before the world was broken, there were two distinct and very different peoples living in our world — humans, or Umani as we are properly called, and the Faeani or, for short, the Fae."

"The Fae?" she squeaked. Shuddering, she wormed her way under the sheltering protection of his arm. "You mean like that terrible pirate, Sarlan the Red?"

He opened his mouth as if to say something but closed it again without speaking. Instead, he kissed the top of her head and continued.

"Yes, like Sarlan." His words sounded clipped, but that was to be expected when speaking of that terrible man and his people. "In that time long ago, the Fae were not feared and hated like they are today. In fact, they were seen as protectors of the natural world. They used their magick for many good things, like healing the sick and injured." He paused for a moment before adding, "The Fae themselves were immortal, meaning that they never grew old and died or fell sick from any disease."

"Wait." She furrowed her brow. "If there were only humans and the Fae, where are the elves in this story?"

"Patience, little one, patience." He stroked her cheek with a calloused finger. "I'm getting to them. As beings of pure nature, the Fae were varied in their shapes and sizes back then. Some of them looked like animals, while others looked more like small

31

people, except with pointy ears and dainty features, and yet others were beings of pure energy with no fixed form. It was said that some of them could even change their appearance and take on the shapes of other creatures. Some Fae liked the curiosity of humans and helped them with their magick. And some humans worshiped them as gods and goddesses of nature. Most Fae, however, were very shy and didn't like having to deal with mortals. And most mortals didn't believe they existed at all."

"You mean humans?"

"Yes. Humans." He nodded. "And you see, that caused lots of problems because humans are very curious about the world, and they try to go everywhere and see everything." He sighed. "Unfortunately, too many humans believed that they could own anything and everything they saw. This included those wild places that were sacred to the Fae."

"The Freeborn don't believe that!" Seldy interjected, her voice filled with pride for her people. "We believe that no one really owns the land, that it belongs to itself and that we are all just visitors!"

"That's correct." Her uncle beamed at her, nodding in agreement. "But the Freeborn are special; different than most other humans, aren't they?"

After she nodded, he continued.

"So, as humans grew stronger and more numerous, they also became bolder and greedier. And as they became more settled and civilized, the humans who once believed in them stopped worshipping the Fae. They began to lose contact with the natural world and became more self-absorbed. They built great cities, cutting down vast forests and hollowing out entire mountains to build them and to feed their growing appetites for things. By polluting the land with their farms and industries, however, they were destroying the lands that the Fae needed to survive."

"That's terrible," Seldy whispered, despite not wanting to interrupt the story. "What happened, Uncle Tegger?"

His expression was somber.

"The Fae *realized that they either had to fight a war against the much more numerous humans, or they would have to find a way to make the humans respect them and their special places. The rulers of the* Fae *were very powerful beings called 'Treemothers.'"*

"Treemothers?" Seldy cocked her head. "That's a weird name. How can trees have mothers?"

"That's a really good question, Seldy. I must confess that I don't know." He chuckled. "But returning to my story, if that's okay with you?" He arched a questioning brow.

When she nodded, he continued.

"The Treemothers got together and decided to send some of their daughters — called Treemaidens — out into the world of humans to find people who were willing to join the Fae *in protecting and preserving the wild lands. Not many came, but some did. Over many centuries, the people that the Treemaidens brought back to live amongst them in the forests and wild places changed, eventually coming to look like, and speak the same language as, the* Fae."

"You mean those humans became elves?"

"Yes, very good. Those humans, over a great deal of time and many generations, changed in appearance, developing long, pointy ears and bright eyes like the Fae *they lived amongst. And they came to learn some of the same magick as the* Fae. *They also developed the immunity to cold and heat and diseases, which helped them to live far longer lives than the humans from which they had descended. The elves were quite a bit taller than most of the* Fae *who they came to look like."*

"But Uncle Tegger, if the elves were tall, why am I so short?"

"Well, you're only eight, Seldy." He chuckled, mussing the top of her hair. "You've got a lot of growing to do yet. Besides, your birth mother was a small woman. Perhaps you will take

after her in that regard, even if you do look more elfin than she did."

"What was she like, Uncle?"

"She was one of the most beautiful women I've ever met, Seldy." His eyes grew distant. "She had long, golden hair and bright, blue eyes that sparkled like sapphires. Her complexion was pale, though not quite as pale as yours. Except for her eyes, she could have passed as fully human on a first glance. Her ears were much less noticeable since they were easily hidden within her curly hair. She wasn't very tall, maybe just a shade over five feet." He grinned down at her. "She was a kind and gentle soul. I only knew her for a little while, but she was so happy that she was pregnant with you. You were the most important thing in her life..."

Uncle Tegger stopped speaking when she sniffled.

"What's wrong, Seldy?"

"I love hearing about her." Seldy cast her eyes down towards the ground. "But I love Jhana-ma so much, and I don't want her to be sad because I'm so curious about my birth mother." Her shoulders heaved.

His fingers found the tip of her chin and guided her gaze back up to his intense, blue eyes.

"Seldirima." There was an undeniable power to the way he pronounced her formal name. "It's natural for you to be curious about your birth family. Jhana knows and accepts that. Her love for you is far stronger than any fear she might have of you learning the truth about from where you came."

"Still," she said quietly. "I'm glad we're alone right now."

"It shows how much you love her," he said. "That you don't want to hurt her feelings."

"What was her voice like, Uncle?"

"It was kind and warm, Seldy, but also strong and clear." His eyes grew distant again, as if lost in memory. "Whenever you

grew restless inside of her — which was rather often I might add — she would place her hands on her bulging belly, and she would sing to you, gently rocking back and forth. Her voice had a haunting quality to it..."

He fell silent.

"Was that when she sang my special song to me?" She stared at him, trying to wrest every bit of knowledge she could about her from him. "When I was restless?"

"Yes, it was."

His eyes misted over.

"That's okay, Uncle."

She placed a hand on his knee. Her touch brought him out of his reverie. He smiled, then cocked his head and gave her a quizzical look.

"Do you still hear her singing it to you in your dreams?"

"Sometimes," she sighed, looking away from him. "But it doesn't happen as often as it used to." She shook head. Tears formed in the corners of her eyes. "I can't remember very much of it anymore."

She sniffled. The first tears began to fall as soon as she stopped speaking.

His arms were around her then. He drew her onto his lap and cradled her like a babe while she cried unabashedly in his arms. He comforted her with quiet, soft words and gentle hugs.

When she stopped crying, he looked down into her tear-stained face and asked, "Would you like to know anything else about her, Seldy?"

Shaking her head, Seldy's lips curled into a mischievous grin.

"What about my father, Uncle, was he tall or short?" She giggled. "Was he an elf or a human? Was he..."

"Oho! You think you can get me so easily as that?"

He grinned down at her, his fingers finding her sensitive ribs and tickling her mercilessly. Still cradled in his arms, she *erupted in great peals of giggling, squirming laughter under his relentless assault.*

"Hey!...No...fair!"

She smiled as she raced across the open ground towards Ti-agra's *vardo*. Thinking of Tegger brought a smile to her lips, even if he used to distract her with tickling or funny jokes and stories whenever she asked about her father. She looked forward to seeing him every year — usually around her birthday — and so did the whole *kumpania*. His songs and stories about the world beyond their small island kept everyone both entertained and informed about what was going on in the larger world.

Tia told stories as well, but hers were different. While most of Tegger's stories were fresh and new, Tia's had an older feel to them. There was always a moral or a lesson that needed to be learned in her stories. There was no doubt who the better storyteller was, though. Even Tia admitted that the bard was a master of his craft who could always bring the audience to tears or get them laughing whenever he wanted.

Whoever the storyteller was, Seldy's imagination was easily aroused. She placed herself inside the setting of every story that was being told, old or new. It was her own special way to travel to strange, faraway places, to meet the handsome heroes who fought against grave odds to save beautiful princesses, or, even better, for her to imagine defeating the villains herself in order to save those brave heroes from certain doom.

But as much as she liked the idea of traveling and having grand adventures, she loved the daily reality of life in the circus even more. She was quite happy to enjoy all of the wondrous stories she could while remaining comfortable and content in the familiar routines of the *kumpania*.

Seldy's smile faded as she approached Tiagra's *vardo*. Hidden away at the farthest point from the main entrance to the great circle of *vardos* that surrounded the big top tent, Tia's home was intentionally secluded. But something in how the shadows draped over it felt off. The three bare oak trees surrounding the *vardo* didn't look like the trees in which she had spent much of her youth climbing and playing. They seemed to crouch away from the blackened sky, reminding her of the skeletal guardians of an ancient sorcerer's tomb from one of Tegger's fantastical stories. The bare branches rattled against each other in the howling wind. Her skin crawled at the memory.

Pausing at the bottom step, Seldy looked about. She couldn't shake the feeling of being watched.

"Tia?" she called out over the restless, howling winds. "It's Seldy. Can I come in?"

Caught up in a rogue gust, the dried leaves that had gathered beneath the open-faced steps swirled around her bare shins and arms. The leaves circled around her as if she were the center of the small vortex, crackling as they scraped against her skin. The rustling of the dried husks combined with the sighing winds made it seem as if the storm was whispering in her ear.

"He comes...sister..."

Shivers raced down her spine, making the small hairs on her arms, legs, and neck stand on end.

Thunder rumbled somewhere far away. Branches rattled against each other and scratched at the sides of the *vardo*. Leaves continued to spin around her, cackling as they broke apart from the force of the wind. Debris caught in her hair and clung to her dress.

"He comessss...for you....sissssster..."

"Who's there?" Seldy jumped back.

She landed a couple of feet behind where she had been in a patch of inch-deep snow. She dug her toes into the crusty snow to brace against the frozen ground. Crouched on the balls of her feet, she extended her arms to either side like when she balanced on the high-wire. Standing as still as a doe, Seldy's heart thudded against her ribcage.

The vortex, however, fell apart. The last bit of leaf litter was blown off into the night by another racing gust. The glorious sound of Bessie the Elephant's trumpeting call — accompanied by the welcoming cheers of the big-top work crew somewhere behind her — broke the fearful spell and silenced the last of the strange whispers.

"Stop imagining things," Seldy said to herself. "It's just the wind."

She picked the leaves from her hair and straightened the hem of her dress before bounding up the three steps leading to the worn door. She knocked loud enough to be heard over the storm, shouting once again,

"Tia? Are you home?"

When there was no answer, Seldy turned the brass knob of the door and gave it a good yank. The rusty hinges protested, but the door opened. She slipped inside the darkened *vardo*.

Seldy's heart continued to hammer against her ribcage like it wanted to bolt away. Pulling the door closed, she stood still, listening as her eyes adjusted to the unlit gloom of the interior. Outside, the winds continued to howl, but all was silent and still within, except for the sound of Tia's nasal snores coming from the back of the *vardo*.

Wrinkling her nose at the pervasive scent of dreamvine smoke hanging heavy in the air, Seldy took a hesitant step forward. Too late, she recognized the sweet and pungent odor from those few times she had cleaned up for the seeress after Tia had smoked the drug to help with her visions. *I should be holding my breath.*

Her eyes began to water. Seldy fought — and lost — the urge

to cough. Her head began to swim, and her limbs became heavy and clumsy. Her gut churned. Her lungs burned. Her thoughts grew fuzzy.

"Tia?"

Blinking through the thick haze of smoke, Seldy staggered towards the rear of the *vardo*.

She made it half-way to the rumpled bed before sinking to her knees, managing one more choked cry before the darkness closed in on her.

"Tia!"

Seldy's consciousness floated up toward a pulsing tunnel of swirling light and sound.

::I've been waiting for you, *rehla*.::

Seldy's eyes snapped open. Soft, diffuse light filled her vision. She blinked in confusion. As her sight came back, she saw that she wasn't inside of Tiagra's vardo *any longer. Instead, she was curled up in a bed of ferns in the midst of a beautiful forest.*

A light breeze tickled her cheek and ruffled her hair. Insects buzzed and birds chirped. The trees, full of leaves like it was high summer, swayed in the soft winds, whispering things to each other that only they understood. The pale light filtering through the canopy didn't have the masculine heat of the sun but was cool and feminine. The outline of a full, circular orb didn't resemble the irregular shapes of the Maiden, Mother, or Crone — the three Shards of Luna that she had seen all of her life. The orb's light illuminated the forest around her in an almost magickal glow.

"Tia?"

Blinking again, she scanned the underbrush, looking for the ancient seer.

"Where are you?"

::Up here. To your right.::

Pushing herself up with one hand, Seldy sat up and swung her head around.

"Tia!" She felt a sense of panic rising inside. "I can't see you!"

::Be calm, *rehla*, and open yourself to other possibilities. I am here. Look up into the trees.::

Taking a deep breath, Seldy shifted her gaze up. A pair of bright yellow eyes stared down at her. They were surrounded by an array of brilliant white and grey feathers as broad as a dish and joined by a hooked yellow beak strong enough to snap bones and sharp enough to sheer through feather, muscle, or tendons. She gasped.

"Tia?"

She stood up on trembling legs. She let her dress settle back into place before taking a tentative step in the direction of the owl.

"Is that you?"

The owl blinked and gave a soft cry, "Hoo hoo!"

"How is this possible?"

Moving a step closer, Seldy extended a hand.

"Where are we?"

::We are dreaming, *rehla*, yet also awake.::

The owl shifted its weight before spreading then closing its impressive wings again. It made no move to fly away.

::Here, all things are possible, if they can be imagined and your will is strong enough.::

"You're so beautiful!"

She stroked the owl's feathers, cocking her head to the side. After a moment's thought, she pushed her own thoughts towards the owl, like she did with her animals.

::But how did you know I could speak with animals like this,

40

Tia? It's a secret that Jhana made me keep from everyone, even from you and Chad!::

::It is a part of your birthright, *rehla*, just as this place is.::

The owl brushed up against Seldy's hands, cooing softly at her gentle touch.

::I brought you here tonight because it is finally time for you to start your journey of learning who you truly are and what you were born with the potential to become. You've been here many times before, *rehla*, during our naps together. But now you will be allowed to remember this place because you must return on your own in order to begin your lessons in earnest.::

::My lessons?:: *Seldy shook her head.* ::But what is this place? Where are we?::

::We are in the Dreamlands.:: *The owl blinked.* ::It is a special place. A magickal world that is a reflection of our waking world as it once was, long before it was broken.::

Seldy looked around in wonder, drinking in the quiet majesty of her surroundings. The towering oaks surrounding the small clearing were taller than any trees she'd ever seen before. The ferns that covered the forest floor stood nearly as tall as she did. She dug her toes into the soft loam beneath her feet, enjoying the rich feel of the soil against her skin. Drawing in a deep breath, she reveled in the fresh scents of so much vibrant life in the air.

"The Dreamlands! But I don't want the Sight, Tia! I don't want to be alone all of my life!" *Seldy shook her head again.* "I'm just a performer in the circus! I don't want to be anything else!"

As soon as the words escaped her lips, Seldy felt horrible. Everyone knew that those few gifted women among the Freeborn who became seers were doomed to lead loveless and lonely lives where they were both revered and feared by the gypsy kumpanias *that depended on the keen insights provided by their access to the Sight.*

41

If Tiagra took any offense to her words, though, she couldn't tell. Instead, the owl stood tall on its branch and regarded her with its unblinking gaze.

::Rehla, it is not your fate to be one of us who Sees, but rather to be the one who Does.::

"What?" Seldy blinked, trying to wrap her mind around Tia's strange answer. "I...I don't understand, Tia!"

::I have not brought you here to teach you the Sight, *rehla*. I brought you here to begin your real education.::

"I...I...I don't understand!"

::If you understood what was being asked of you, the burdens would be too great for you to bear. The choices that you face would be too painful.:: *The owl ruffled its wings.* ::But know this: whether you understand them or not, the choices you make in the coming days will affect the lives of many, both those that you love now and those that you will come to know and love in the future. I will help guide you for as long as I can, *rehla*...::

A distant rumble of thunder interrupted the owl's projected thoughts. Tia ruffled her wings. When the owl settled back down, she blinked, tilted her head, and continued.

::I am sorry. I thought there would have more time, but the storm has arrived in force. Remember to return here, and we shall speak again.:: *The owl spread her wings.* ::It is time to wake up, *rehla*.::

Before she could step back, the owl launched itself into the air, darting right at Seldy. At the very moment the bird would have collided with her, the world began to spin out of control. Everything fell away into darkness. She plummeted towards a tiny, green, glowing orb.

The orb pulsed brighter, and grew larger, with each beat of her heart...

...throom....throom...throom...

As she came closer, the orb began to resemble a giant seed. It glowed from within, giving off the same vibrant, emerald green luminescence she sometimes saw within her own eyes when she looked in a mirror. Each pulse of the light infused her with sensations that reminded her of a different season, from the dormant potential of a fallow field in winter to the youthful vitality of a spring meadow in full bloom, from the languid lushness of the forest at the height of summer to the exhausted, but bountiful harvest of fall.

Before she crashed into it, however, the seed was gone, and she was enveloped, once again, by darkness.

Startled awake, Seldy gasped. Two bony hands clamped onto either side of her head and pulled her up to the side of the bed with a surprising strength.

"It is time to wake up." Tiagra's voice sounded strained.

"But Tia, I am awake!"

Her tongue felt thick and clumsy in her mouth.

"The seed within still slumbers." The old seer stared at her while maintaining the grip on Seldy's face. "It must be awakened."

Seldy blinked. "Tia, I don't understand!"

The old seer's eyes glazed over and turned milky white. Tia's grip tightened, pulling Seldy closer to her withered lips. Distant, echoing words escaped her lips in a tortured whisper.

"The Enemy comes for you, child. A foe like no other. The night will be long and dark. The dangers will seem too great. But you must find your song, child, even when that seems impossible. In those darkest hours, remember this: you are not alone. Truth will set you free. Hope will be your beacon. But love is the source of your strength, *rehla*. Draw on it often. For only love and forgiveness have the power to redeem those who

43

have fallen into darkness and despair. Vengeance will only lead you deeper into the long night that looms ahead."

The seer's words made the hair on the back of Seldy's neck straighten, sending an electric tingle racing up and down her spine. She blinked several times, trying to make sense of her strange dream and Tia's even stranger words. Before she could say anything, the bony hands holding her close went limp, and the old seer's eyes fluttered closed.

CHAPTER 5

Mouse

Thud!

Mouse startled awake.

"Up and at 'em, Mouse." Dalton loomed over him. "Cap wanted another cell ready before he got back."

"Does it have to be tonight?"

His hammock swayed in time with the gusts of wind rocking the ship. Mouse groaned.

"In the middle of this blasted storm?"

"Bounty huntin' business, lad," the tall, bearded man replied with a shrug. Unaffected both by the deck pitching about beneath his widely planted feet and Mouse's resistance, Dalton remained steadfast. "Just followin' orders. Ya'd best learn to do that yerself."

"Yeah," he grunted. "I'll remember that."

Sitting up, the raw scabs on his back scraped against the ropes of the hammock. Grimacing, Mouse swung his legs over the edge. He looked up at the larger man.

"Which is it, cell or cage?"

"I already told ya — a cell, not a cage." Dalton glanced over his shoulder at him, "Don't dawdle around talkin' with that old orc or coddlin' that wolf ya like so much. Ya've got work to do."

"Yes, sir."

"Don't ya be insultin' me like that, now. I'm no officer," the old sailor grunted before his voice softened. "How's yer back doin'? Ya need any fresh bandages?"

"I'm okay," Mouse said softly, shaking his head. "It's scabbed up pretty good."

Mouse plucked the flute and the folded up poster from his personal shelf.

"What's that now?"

"Oh, this?" Mouse made a show of holding the flute up in easy view as he slipped the poster down his sleeve. "I got this in town today when I bought the ale."

"Didya now? Looks 'spensive." Dalton's eyes narrowed, and his brow wrinkled into deep furrows. "Where'd'ya get the coin fer sometin' like that?"

"I...uh..." Mouse dropped his gaze down to study the flute. "I..."

"Never mind, son. I don't wanna know." Dalton's voice dropped to a whisper as he pushed the flute back towards Mouse. "Just don't ya go stealin' anythin' from anyone on the *Ghost*, ya hear me? Neither I, nor Cap, could protect you from these scoundrels then." Clucking his tongue in indignation, the old sailor continued, "No crew worth its weight in iron will abide a thief in its midst. Ya hear me?"

"Thanks." Mouse swallowed the hard lump stuck in his throat. "I'll remember that."

"See that ya do." Dalton's eyes narrowed as he studied Mouse. Seemingly satisfied, the bigger man nodded towards the flute. "Ya any good with it?"

"I'm out of practice, but I used to be quite good with a very similar instrument."

"Huh." The bigger man chuckled to himself. "Well, with Chard and Pedar gone with Cap, we could use a little music to wait out the storm tonight. Why doncha bring that down to the Mess after yer done with yer tasks and join us for a few drinks and a song or two, eh?"

Mouse forced a smile to his lips. "Sure." He wrapped the flute in a spare cloth and slipped it inside his jacket before hopping down onto the bucking planks of the deck.

Staggering at first, Mouse was steadied by Dalton's quick hand on his arm. The big man released his grip when he flicnhed.

"One of these days, Mouse, ya'll find yer balance point. Then, just ya wait and see, it'll be smooth sailin' after that!"

"Thanks, Dalton. I sure hope so."

Leaving the crew bay behind, Mouse couldn't help but notice how much easier it was to find his footing on the swaying deck than it was to fit in with the crew on the *Hunter's Ghost*.

"What did I tell you about disobeying the rules, Mouse?"

The dark, bearded face of the captain loomed over him. The man was a foot taller than Mouse and more than double his weight. There was a hard look in the man's eyes and a determined set in his shoulders, but it was the strange softness in his personal song that caught Mouse's attention and gave him pause.

"Well, BOY?!"

The thunder in the man's voice quashed Mouse's attempt to puzzle out the deeper meanings of the softness in his song.

"Y-y-you said," Mouse stammered, "the punishment will be harsh, Captain."

"Did you think I was lying, boy?" He arched a bushy eyebrow. "Have I ever shown you that I was a man of idle threats?"

"No, sir." He tried to look contrite and apologetic. "You haven't."

The captain stood back, his huge, weathered hands clenched into scarred fists. He crossed his arms, looking from Mouse to the other members of the crew gathered on the aft deck of the Hunter's Ghost. Cook stood behind the captain, the usual sour look plastered on his sagging face. Haddock — the bald and heavily tattooed First Mate — stood to the right of the captain, bare-chested even in the cold Fanol winds. He had a hard look in his eyes as he fingered the coils of his ever-present whip — the Serpent's Tongue.

To the left of the captain stood a tall, thin, grey-skinned man, the captain's brother. Mouse shuddered. The rail-thin man's blood-shot eyes were as unfocused as his personal song was discordant and incoherent. Everything about the captain's younger brother felt wrong, but it was the seemingly random and broken notes that set his teeth on edge whenever he was close enough to hear it.

"Why did you do it then?"

The captain's hissed question hung in the air.

"I didn't really think about it, sir." Mouse ducked his head and swallowed. "In the Slant, no one pays much attention to the rules."

The captain threw back his head and laughed. None of the others joined him in his mirth. The big man stepped forward and clapped Mouse hard on the shoulder, staggering him with the force of it.

"You've got spirit, Mouse. I'll give you that."

As soon as the hand slid off of his shoulder, the captain loomed in close again, all humor gone from both his dark eyes and his song.

"But my rules are not to be broken. Not ever. I think you need a lesson in remembering that."

He was so close now that the spittle was spraying all over Mouse's face. The deadly seriousness of the captain's tone was matched by the pounding drum beats of his intense song.

"I tell you how much to feed the captives. No one else. I don't...ever...have to explain myself to you. Your job is to do what you are told and to do it quickly and well. You got that, boy?"

"Yes, sir." Mouse swallowed hard and nodded. "I do."

"Good."

The captain stepped back and nodded towards the First Mate.

"Haddock here is going to give you another ten lashes with the Serpent's Tongue to help you remember."

The captain narrowed his eyes and gave Mouse his hardest look yet.

"This is the last time I will be this merciful. Now, take off your jacket and get into position."

Licking his lips, Mouse shucked his woolen jacket and threadbare tunic, letting them fall to his side. He had no doubts about how serious the captain was when he stepped up to the thick timber of the aft mast and gripped the heavy rope. He leaned forward and spread his legs wide, assuming the all-too-familiar position for this form of punishment.

Blinding, muscle-clenching pain seared in a long line down his back from the right shoulder down to almost his trouser level. His knees threatened to buckle, but Mouse stood still, accepting his punishment as the justified price for his disobedience. That first lash was soon followed by the crack of the whip, the sound traveling a fraction of a second slower than the pain itself. Other than a single, muffled gasp at the first lick of the Serpent's Tongue, Mouse remained quiet throughout.

Mouse slipped into the darkened galley as quiet and meek as the creature he was named after. The bare soles of his calloused feet made nary a whisper as he slunk towards his goal. Raucous voices called out nearby — the sounds of drunken revelry — competing with the creaking and groaning of the ship being buffeted about by the raging storm.

Good, they're drinking. It must've been the right stuff.

Ducking down to avoid the single shaft of light filtering in from the Mess, Mouse sidled into the pantry. He stumbled when the floor beneath him shifted but caught the edge of a massive stew pot. That pot clattered into another. Cringing, he froze in place.

"Blast you, Jigger!"

Cook's curse ignited a round of riotous laughter from the others.

Hunched over, the long scabs on Mouse's back scraped against the rough fabric of his tunic. He bit off a hiss of pain as a warm trickle of blood seeped from a reopened wound.

Blast it! I need to get this done without leaving a trail that even Cook can follow.

Blinking away tears that filled the corners of his eyes at the all-too-fresh memory of his most recent whipping, Mouse pushed away from the cabinet. He slipped under the light and dropped to a knee in front of the pantry. He laid a pair of clean rags flat before opening it.

This is it. If I just get up and get back to my duties, I won't be breaking the rules again. I won't be risking everything.

Mouse stared down at the empty rags. His gut tightened into a hard ball of anxiety at the mere thought of letting the prisoners go hungry until the captain and his bounty hunting crew returned to change the current standing order to starve them into submission.

I can't do that. Mom, you taught me better than that. Rules that are wrong need to be broken. I just can't get caught.

Another round of raucous laughter from the Mess Hall reminded Mouse how close he was to being discovered. Opening the cupboard door, he yanked a pair of sausage links from the large coil of meat and pushed the rest back into place. He added a wedge of cheese and a big pickle to the rag before closing the door. He wrapped up the bundle of food and tucked it away inside his tunic, careful to keep it to the left side of his jacket, away from the precious flute and the disturbing poster.

Mouse slid over to the scrap pail next to the sink, dragging the other rag with him. He plunged his hand into the putrid contents. The odor was horrible but not nearly as bad as the Slant on a summer day. Nimble fingers soon found several large bits of gristle, a few strips of fat-laced meat, and a pair of slimy organs. He placed them in the second rag.

Wrinkling his nose, Mouse wiped the majority of it off on the edge of the rag, then wrapped that bundle up as well.

Another loud burst of cursing and laughter gave Mouse the cover he needed. No longer concerned with the need for stealth, Mouse scurried from the kitchen. His bare feet slapped the deck as he rushed towards the prison hold. It was past time to attend to his assigned duties.

It would not do to fail to get that cell ready in time for whomever it was that the captain was hunting in the midst of this storm.

CHAPTER 6

Seldy

The Enemy comes for you, child. A foe like no other.
Seldy's heart thudded against her ribs. She pushed back from the side of the bed and sank to her knees. Taking a deep breath, she tried to get the taut muscles in her shoulders and back to relax.

"What enemy, Tia?"

Her eyes narrowed. Thoughts swirled. Her stomach knotted, and her ears buzzed. She tried to make sense of the seer's strange warning.

"I don't have any enemies."

The ancient seer's only response was a soft snore.

Drawing in a deep and intentional breath amidst the lingering smoke, Seldy held her breath. She closed her eyes. Feeling her heartbeat slow from the renewed effects of the dreamvine smoke, she swayed back forth on relaxing muscles. The knot in her gut began to unwind.

No one is coming for us in the midst of a Fae *storm, so there's time to ask her what it all means later.*

She exhaled slowly before taking another deep and calming

breath like she did before performing on the high wire or the trapeze.

The important thing is that Tia isn't sick; she's just caught up in the Sight.

Opening her eyes again, Seldy regarded the ancient woman's sleeping face with a detached curiosity.

Did the Sight show you that I can talk to, and understand, the thoughts of animals, Tia? How long have you known?

"Seldy, come here."

Something in the way her mother's voice caught gave the seven-year-old girl pause. She stopped where she stood, still in her costume. She had been preparing to race off to feed her tigers after the show. She blinked up at her mother, surprised at the concern showing on her face.

"What's wrong, Ma?"

"I noticed that you weren't carrying the whip today when you performed with the tigers. Why is that?"

"Oh." Seldy relaxed, flashing a bright, cheerful smile. "Well that's easy, Ma. They don't like the whip."

"Of course they don't like it, Sweetling." Her mother pursed her lips. "But they've been trained to perform with it for years and know to fear and respect anyone who carries it."

"No, Ma." Seldy shook her head so hard that her ponytail flailed about. "The tigers know that the whip can't really hurt them. It just makes them mad." She beamed another proud smile up at her mother. "Besides, they like doing the tricks with me because I let them pick which ones they want to do!"

The furrows on her mother's brow deepened. Jhana-ma's eyes shifted, darting about before taking her hand and pulling her up the steps and into their vardo. She shut the door behind them, ignoring Seldy's squawk of protest until the door was closed. Sinking to her haunches, Jhana pressed her back against the door as if to keep the world away.

"How do the tigers tell you what tricks they want to do?"

"They just do, Ma." She shrugged, unsure why her mother found it so strange. "I can hear them when they want me to, sort of like talking except without using our tongues or lips! And they can hear me when I think words at them in a special kind of way. Just like Bessie and the horses and all of the other animals!"

Her mother stared at her, open-mouthed.

"That's why I don't eat meat, Ma," Seldy pointed out, helpfully. "Because I can feel and hear how frightened the cows, pigs, and lambs get whenever it's time for one of them to be eaten." She sighed, a deep sadness for all of the poor livestock animals that had been slaughtered over the years welling up inside of her. "Some of them understand why, but none of them like it." She shook her head solemnly. "Not at all."

Her mother gripped her thin shoulders hard and stared at her with an unreadable expression. Slowly her warm, strong hands worked their way along Seldy's neck until she cupped each one of her cheeks in a calloused palm. Her voice sounded hoarse.

"You can talk to animals like they're people?"

"Not all of them want to talk much, and some of them aren't very friendly." She shrugged with a frown. "The chickens are kind of mean to each other and to me. Lumpy, the old goat, tells all sorts of jokes I don't really understand. But it's not the same with people." Her tone became serious. "Because nobody in the kumpania can hear me when I think at them like I do with the animals, not even you or Chad, Ma. I've tried lots of times, too!"

Seldy noticed how quiet and still her mother had become. Jhana-ma's eyes glazed over even as her fingers caressed the back of her long ears lovingly. Finally, she shook her head and dropped her eyes to Seldy, staring at her with an intensity that she had never before seen.

"You've tried it with me?"

Seldy nodded.

"Don't try that again with other people, okay?"

"I don't understand, Ma." Scrunching her forehead up, Seldy squeaked, "Why not?"

"Seldirima." Jhana-ma almost never used her full name. There was a strange, fervent look in her eyes. "You listen to me right now. That's magick, real magick, and it will only bring trouble to the kumpania if the wrong people were to find out." Her fingers tensed as she emphasized her point. "You can't tell anyone about this. There could be real trouble. Do you understand?"

"But Ma, it can't be magick!" Seldy gasped. "It's as easy as talking to you!" Her insides churned at the idea that her special gift was some form of magick. Magick was bad!

"Seldy, it doesn't matter how easy it is for you. Other folk are not going to understand. If the wrong people hear about this and believe it, really bad things will happen to all of us." Her eyes narrowed. "Do you remember why people hate magick so much?"

"The Black Scourge." Seldy let out a high-pitched squeak. "I don't want anything bad to happen, Ma! I don't want to get sick or to get you or anyone else sick!" Taking a shuddering breath, she offered the unimaginable. "Maybe I should stop speaking to the tigers and Bessie?" Hot tears filled her eyes and began to stream down her cheeks.

Jhana wrapped her arms around her in a crushing hug.

"No, Sweetling. I know you and how much you love them. It would only make you heartsick if I asked that of you." Holding her tight, her mother continued. "But you've got to pretend that you don't talk to them. Even if it means that you have to carry the whip when you perform."

55

"Okay, Ma!" Her voice cracked.

Her shoulders heaved with sobs. Once her sobs subsided, Seldy pushed back from the hug. An idea came to her that filled her with hope.

"Maybe we should ask Uncle Tegger about it? Maybe it's not really magick but just something that all elves can do?"

"Shhh!" Jhana's eyes narrowed as she brought a finger up to her lips. "Don't talk about it again! Not to me, not to Gorman or Chad or even Tiagra! And especially not to Tegger!"

"Why can't we tell Uncle Tegger? He's so wise!"

Seldy felt her eyes filling with yet more unbidden tears.

"No. You listen to me on this. You can't tell him, not until I tell you it's okay. Promise me you won't tell him or anyone else. Promise me."

She held Seldy's hands in her own, her eyes beseeching.

Her sliver of hope crushed, Seldy nodded before answering. "I promise, Ma."

Seldy burst into inconsolable tears, sobbing like only a child could. Jhana gathered her up and hugged her tight until they were both cried out.

Blinking in the gloom, Seldy shook her head, only to have the *vardo* start to spin around her. Reaching out to the lacquered surface of the wooded cabinets on either side of her, she steadied herself.

Wow, no wonder Tia uses dreamvine for her Sight! This stuff is strong.

She licked her lips as the last vestiges of the memory sequence disappeared. Her eyelids began to droop. Her hands slipped from the cabinets to fall into her lap. Overwhelmed by fatigue, she tugged at the hem of her dress, pulling it up around her midriff as she contemplated shucking it and joining Tia in the bed, like she had countless times before. A nap would be so nice...

A strong gust of wind rocked the *vardo*, followed by the rat-a-tat-tat of hard and heavy rain pelting the roof, walls, and windows of the wagon.

The Fae *storm! Oh no, I've got to help! I can't go to sleep now!*

Calling upon the resolve and determination developed over years of performing night after night, even when she didn't feel like it, Seldy stood up on unsteady legs. She noted that the haze of dreamvine smoke was thinning above her, so she raised herself up onto her toes. Arching her back, Seldy stretched her head up and drew in several long and deep breaths of the cleaner air above.

Between the restless energies of the storm outside and being able to breathe clean air again, the buzzing in her ears began to fade. Seldy began to feel like her normal self again. She turned to regard Tiagra once more.

Seeing the goosebumps on Tia's skin and the bluish cast to the woman's lips, Seldy grabbed one of the seeress' spare blankets from the shelf overhead and spread it over her naked form.

"Sleep well, Tia."

She smiled down at the slumbering woman as she gathered the long, loose strands of her hair with well-practiced fingers. Seldy tied it into a thick pony-tail. The interior of the *vardo* was illuminated briefly by a series of flickering flashes filtered through the fine lace of old curtains, lightning arcing overhead, but the light was gone before the rolling booms of accompanying thunder rolled over them.

There was just enough light for Seldy to look around and ensure that everything was in its proper place before she pushed the creaky door open and stepped out into the storm.

Before long, her dress was soaked, and her hair dangled like a rat's tail. It slapped against her back as she bounced along.

Her feet and legs were soon spattered with mud, bits of leaves, and pine needles, but she didn't mind. She found the restless energy of the storm invigorating.

Like Tia's *vardo*, the large animal enclosure was away from the main circle of wagons parked around the big top. It was nestled into a small clearing edged by evergreens between the farther pastures used for most of the livestock and the circus itself. The less ornate supply wagons of the *kumpania* normally filled in the gaps between the trees in order to give Bessie and the tigers a semblance of privacy.

Many of those wagons, however, were missing. They had been moved to pack up the big top tent.

The front half of the clearing was marked by a makeshift wooden fence that only came thigh-high on Seldy — something that would hardly keep an elephant contained if she didn't want to stay put. A tall, open-faced shed stood at one end of the area, while a shallow, iced-over pond occupied the other end. The ground inside the ringed-in area had been trodden flat and smooth by Bessie's huge feet over the long winter.

The gate to Bessie's pen, however, was wide open, and the elephant was nowhere to be seen.

Stepping carefully through the muddy field towards the tigers' enclosure, Seldy approached the stacks of barrels and crates that separated the tigers' enclosure from Bessie's larger, open ring. She opened her mouth to call out to her tigers, but the sound of guttural voices carrying over the storm gave her pause.

Unsure of why she did so, Seldy ducked down behind the remaining crates and peered through a gap between them. Three tall figures stood on the far side of the enclosure, all of them looking in at the two pacing tigers.

Unable to make out enough details to satisfy her curiosity, Seldy projected her thoughts toward the tigers.

::*Amara, Layra, who is that visiting you?*:: She let a little of her concern for them leak through. ::*Is everything okay?*::

::*Seldy,*:: Amara replied. ::*The Bull-man is here with two strangers.*::

The irritation evident in her thoughts was matched by her impatient pacing about the enclosure. She bared her fangs in the direction of the three figures and let out a low, rumbling growl.

Amara's reference to her Uncle Gorman as the Bull-man wasn't meant to be kind. Nothing Amara did or said could ever be described as kind. She was the older, colder, and more calculating of the two tigers — the one who would escape to hunt her own meals once again if given the chance. And beef was — by far — her favorite meat.

::*Cubling,*:: Layra's softer, silkier thought-voice followed. ::*You should be in your own den on a night like this. There is something not-right about these strangers. Stay back.*::

Slipping behind a pair of rain barrels closer to the back of the enclosure, Seldy crouched down. She listened; glad for once for her pointed ears and the keen sense of hearing they gave her.

"...I don't know, friend Klard," Gorman slurred. "Theesh tigers have been in our circush for many, many years. Shince they were little more than cubsh, yesh?"

Seldy leaned her head around the nearest barrel, focusing on the two strangers.

One of the men was as wide through the chest as Gorman was but was even taller and heavier. He had a bushy, black beard that covered most of his face. What she could see of his face was scarred and tanned. He had a large, bulbous nose and small, close-set eyes that followed Amara as she paced about the enclosure.

The second man was just as tall as his companion but much thinner. The hood of his cloak was up, concealing most of his face. From within the shadows of that heavy cowl, however, a pair of red, faintly glowing eyes stared back at her. Transfixed by that malevolent gaze, Seldy was frozen in place. A cold shiver ran down her spine. The hair on the back of her neck stood on end.

Tha-throom.

Her heart pounded heavily against her ribs.

...The Enemy comes for you, rehla...*a foe like no other...* Tiagra's words echoed inside her head.

"Yes, I can see that they are well-fed and strong, *Baro.*" The bearded stranger's voice sounded cold and distant as she was pulled deeper into the gaze of the silent, hooded figure. "That's why I'm willing to pay such a good price. The risk, as they say, will be mine as to whether or not they prove to be good fighters and worth the investment."

Tha-throom.

The hooded figure did not speak or move as the bearded man and Gorman continued to speak, sometimes shouting at each other to be heard over the howling winds. The thin man's red eyes remained locked onto hers. Seldy tried to pull back, to close her eyes and hide, but she couldn't bring herself to move. Instead, it felt like she was being drawn down into a deep, dark pit.

Something, no...someone..., waited for her at the bottom of that gaping maw of darkness; someone who was both utterly foreign, yet completely irresistible. Thought-voices pressed against her consciousness; familiar voices, but her mind was closed to them. She was captivated.

Tha-throom.

Whatever the *Baro* and the bearded man were saying to each other was indecipherable, as if their words were distant echoes.

A different voice — a voice of consequence — called out his need for her. She couldn't make out what he was saying yet, but she could hear the pain in his voice. He was suffering made manifest...a noble being now banished into a shadowy and forlorn prison. He yearned to be free once again...but, there could be no escape...unless...

A snarling roar thundered above the storm, accompanied by Layra's orange and black striped mass splashing into the mud between Seldy and those captivating eyes. The great tigress reared up at the men and smashed her fore-paws into the bars of the enclosure. The whole structure rattled under the force of her fury.

Seldy collapsed onto her hands and knees, gasping for breath in the frigid slush. She shuddered at the dirty, oily feeling that enveloped her.

::*Cubling!*:: Layra's mind-voice pierced through fog in Seldy's mind. ::*Stay away from that one!*::

Scrambling until her back was pressed against the rain barrel, her chest heaving, Seldy closed her eyes and tried to regain her bearings as the noise of the tigers and the worsening storm washed over her. She lost track of how long she sat trembling in the icy mud.

Voices. Voices coming closer.

Seldy opened her eyes and turned towards the sounds. Two lumbering figures emerged from the gloom of the storm.

The *Baro's* steps were unsteady in the sloppy slush and mud, his heavy frame swaying like he was well into his cups. Everything about the usually dapper Gorman was drooping from the combination of wind and rain. His mustachios, which normally curled upwards in fanciful swirls, hung wet and limp on either side of his generous mouth. His heavy winter clothes were soaked through despite the fur-lined cloak wrapped around his shoulders.

Pushing to her feet, Seldy set her shoulders and clambered over Bessie's fence. She darted out, intercepting the men and blocking their way forward by planting her feet in the frigid mud. Her curled-up fists pressed against each of her hips. She did her best impression of Jhana's steely-eyed glare. The tips of her pointed ears quivered with pent-up rage.

Up close, the bearded stranger was even taller than she suspected, topping Gorman by several inches. He was bigger in the shoulders and stockier of build than her uncle, which was impressive enough. But there was something in the way he held himself that gave the impression that he was used to giving orders and having them followed. He bristled with weapons, from the pair of sheathed swords that hung from his belt, one from each hip, to the pair of handguns that were holstered in a bandolier across his chest.

Taken aback at seeing such weaponry so boldly displayed, Seldy fought the urge to flee.

The man's dark eyes widened and then narrowed. He made no attempt to hide the fact that he was studying her from head to mud-covered toe. There was an undisguised hunger in his eyes that nearly unnerved her.

"Ah, *rehla*, I am glad that you are here!" Gorman's voice boomed out over the storm. He waved towards the still agitated tigers. "Amara and Layra sheem to be upshet by the shtorm. Perhaps you can calm them, yesh?"

Before she could answer, the bearded man took a small step closer.

"*Baro*, is this the elf-girl you were telling me about earlier?"

"Yes, Mashter Dashtyr. I would like to introduce you to..."

"I'm Seldy." She spoke just loud enough to be heard through the wind. She didn't move as she stared up at the man. "And our tigers are not for sale!"

As he stepped closer, Seldy realized he was dressed in some sort of uniform. He wore a three-pointed felt hat with a massive feather that might have been impressive if the wind and water of the storm hadn't already ruined it. The bedraggled remains of the plume drooped off to the side. His dark blue overcoat was festooned with bright brass buttons and sported a set of matching triangular tails hanging down in the back. The glistening leather of shiny, polished boots came up to his knees and folded over.

He blinked in surprise at her pronouncement before turning an arched eye towards Gorman, as if seeking a different answer.

"Now, *rehla*, don't be rude. That'sh no way to shpeak to gu..."

She cut him off, her eyes never leaving the bearded stranger.

"These tigers are not for sale!"

A bolt of lightning arced overhead, followed immediately by a rumbling crack of thunder. Both Gorman and the bearded man flinched at the proximity of the strike. Seldy held her ground, unmoved by the spectacle.

It was only as the illumination provided by the lightning started to fade that Seldy noticed the cloaked figure standing a few feet behind and slightly off to the side of the bearded man. The hood of the cloak hung down over his face, so she couldn't directly see his eyes, but there was a faint red glow coming from beneath the hood. She felt the heat of that gaze. Frozen in place, she was unable to take her eyes off of the terrifying figure.

The bearded man was the first to recover. He shook the accumulated ice from his broad shoulders and clapped Gorman on the back, laughing.

"Well, friend *Baro*, I appreciate the drinks and the tour of your fine...uh...circus. But it seems that our business here is concluded for the moment."

Then he stepped closer, extending his gloved hand towards her.

"It was nice to meet you, Mistress Seldy." His smile didn't quite reach his eyes. "Someday soon, I hope to watch you perform. I understand that you and these tigers put on quite a show."

Startled by the big man's harsh laughter and sudden movement in her direction, Seldy's attention snapped back to him.

She ignored his hand and took a step back.

"If you do," she snarled. "We'll make sure to put on a special performance."

"*Rehla*!" Gorman barked out his disapproval at her. "I don't know what'sh come over you!" He nodded back towards the enclosure. "Go to your tigers and shettle them down, while I show our guests to their *vardo* for the night."

Not needing any further encouragement to take her leave, Seldy darted past the three men, heading towards the gate of the enclosure. In passing, she heard the bearded man reply,

"There's no need for such hospitality, my friend. We must return to Nashae."

"But shurely, you can shpend the night!" Gorman protested. "To travel in such a shtorm is madnesh!"

"I'm afraid we must..."

Their voices faded in the distance as they continued on. Seldy stopped outside the latched gate to the tiger enclosure. She paused to take a deep breath, trying to shake the feeling of foreboding that had settled heavily upon her shoulders.

Turning the latch and pulling the gate open just wide enough for her thin frame, Seldy stepped into the safest place she knew...

CHAPTER 7

Mouse

Pausing to take his last, deep breath of clean air, Mouse opened the door to the prison hold. The stale air reeked of animal waste and unclean bodies. Gathering his buckets, he stepped over the threshold and tugged the door shut behind him with a well-practiced motion of his left foot. He exhaled, breathing through his mouth to avoid the worst of the hair-curdling odors.

It helped, but not enough.

Once the wan light of the hanging lanterns in the hallway was gone, the gloom of the hold descended again. The narrow beam of weak, flickering light leaking through the round portholes high above the cells came from one of the hissing gas lamps that lit up the docks at night. The storm obscured any light that might have come from the Shard of Luna known as the Ugly Sister or the stars.

Even before his eyes fully adjusted, Mouse turned to dip his buckets in the open water barrels beside the door. The grunting, squealing crash of a boar throwing himself against the door of his crate shattered the relative silence of the hold. Mouse jumped, sloshing water from his second bucket even though he had been expecting it.

"Settle down, Gretch!" He tried to make his voice sound stern and commanding but cringed instead at how scratchy and whiny he sounded to his own ears. "Back away from the door or I'll skip you."

Gretch was a nasty, brutish creature. The massive razorback boar was destined for a gladiator arena somewhere in the Guild Alliance. Mouse would've felt bad about the creature's ultimate fate, but the beast tried to hurt him every chance he got. The boar slashed his curved tusks into the iron bars repeatedly, snorting in defiance. Tiny, deranged eyes stared out at Mouse, daring him to get close enough.

"Suit yourself." Mouse slipped down the narrow passage within the hold. Gretch's cage was by far the foulest. "Shadow won't mind eating yours, too."

Shadow was as different as night and day from the boar. Where Gretch was loud, smelly, and obnoxious, the huge, black wolf was quiet, clean, and grateful. The wolf's cage was three empty crates down from Gretch, as far away as was possible within that row.

"Hey Shadow," he said just loud enough to be heard over Gretch's ruckus. "I brought you a little something."

Two bright, yellow, lupine eyes opened amidst a pool of darkness that was curled up in the back of the cage. The wolf's jaws stretched open in a yawn to reveal sharp fangs as long as Mouse's thumb. Then he was on his feet, shaking himself.

Mouse pulled out one of the two kidneys in the sack and slipped his hand inside the cage.

The wolf sniffed the offering and wrinkled his snout before wuffling.

"I know, it isn't the best stuff, but it's the best I could do without it being missed."

Shadow took it from Mouse's fingers with his customary gentleness, then backed up and gulped the organ meat down in two quick bites.

He was already reaching for another bit of meat when he heard the shuffling in the cell just down the hall and across the way. Mouse glanced over his shoulder, towards the last cell in the row behind him.

A pair of ruddy hands clasped the bars of the cell. A small, wizened face pressed into the space between the bars.

"Is it morning already, lad?" The orc's gravelly voice was more than welcome. "It seems you were here not long ago."

"No." Shadow took the second kidney from his fingers. He lowered his voice now that the Gretch had fallen into a sullen silence. "I've been sent to get another cell ready."

While the wolf gulped down the second kidney, Mouse emptied the rest of the sack into the iron bowl near the front of the cage.

When the wolf bent down to get to the scraps, Mouse reached in and stroked the thick black fur of his strong neck and shoulders. Shadow tensed at the contact but, after a brief pause, resumed eating.

The wolf's song was as mesmerizing as it was haunting. The melody of howling voices crying out to each other sparked an undeniable yearning for freedom and community that was so powerful and clear that it made his heart ache every time he listened to it.

"Have you ever seen a wolf in the wild, lad?"

"No." Mouse pulled his hand out of the cage, his concentration broken. "The only animals in the Slant are the two-legged kind."

"Are we still docked in Nashae?"

Ignoring the sharp stabs of pain coming from his back, Mouse picked up his buckets and moved to stand in front of the orc before replying.

"Yeah, the storm's too strong to sail in, and the captain and his hunters are away, chasing a bounty, I think."

Setting the buckets down, Mouse pressed the package of stolen sausages into the orc's hands.

"Eat this quick or hide it. I don't know when your next meal might be coming or when they will get back." He shrugged. "With this storm, it could be a couple of days."

The orc took the package and regarded him for a moment. "Thank you, lad."

"I'm going to get this cell ready while you eat." Mouse waved to the cell behind him. "Once we're both done, maybe you can tell me another story of your time in the Marines."

"And maybe you will tell me your real name?" The wizened orc offered him a small, crooked smile. "I'm pretty sure your mother didn't name you 'Mouse.'"

"Maybe, Tra'al. Maybe."

Mouse shrugged out of his jacket and hung it on the latch of the open door before turning to face the empty cell across the small hall. He sighed, opened the unlocked door, and stepped inside.

"Lad, you're bleeding."

Opening the cell door, Mouse ignored Tra'al's observation. Instead, he retrieved his bucket of water.

"You've been whipped." It wasn't a question.

"Yeah, so?" Mouse shrugged his shoulders and bent to the task at hand.

"Was it for bringing me extra food like this?" The orc held up the still wrapped package.

"It wasn't just for you." Mouse looked up from his scrubbing, nodded over at Shadow, and shrugged again. "I broke the rules and got caught."

"That's against the law in the Guild Alliance." Indignation filled the orc's voice. "That bastard has no right to do that."

"Yeah, maybe." Mouse looked up at the incredulous orc. "But I'm not in much of a position to argue the law. By those same laws, I should be dead."

"What? Why?"

"I...I..." Mouse dismissed the questions with a wave of his free hand. "I need to get this cell clean."

Tra'al fell silent. Mouse returned to scrubbing the floor. After a few minutes, the orc's deep voice broke the awkward tension between them.

"Your spirit is too gentle to be a bounty hunter. Whatever drove you to enlist on a ship like this?"

"Enlist?" Mouse choked out that word. "Who said I enlisted?" He regarded the orc for a moment with serious, searching, brown eyes. "Besides, have you ever been inside the Slant?"

"I can't say that I have," Tra'al spoke through the food in his mouth. "I spent my time in the Marines scouting, fighting in various wars, and training recruits. I've only seen the Slant from atop the walls."

"Then you wouldn't understand."

The orc turned his attention back to his food and fell silent again. Mouse bent back to his work, glad for the silence.

"You know, lad, you don't sound like someone from the Slant. Your diction is too refined."

"If you've never been there," Mouse arched an eyebrow, "how do you know what we sound like?"

"I've served with my share of Slanters in the Marines," Tra'al chuckled. "And none of them sounded more educated than orcs recruited fresh out of the Untere. So what's your story, lad? The real story?"

Unable to meet the orc's steady gaze, Mouse dropped his eyes back toward the floor he was scrubbing.

"My mom wasn't from the Slant. She wouldn't let me use the Cant like everyone else did." Mouse forced his reply through the lump that formed in his throat. "She taught me to read and write, too."

"Where is she from?"

"I don't know." Mouse avoided the orc's gaze. "She died. She never told me where we..." His shoulders tightened. His fingers clenched against the brush. "I don't want to talk anymore."

The orc nodded, dropping his eyes back to his meal.

Mouse bent back to the task at hand, trying to work through the tears that blurred his vision.

The jolt of the ship slamming into the stone pier jarred Mouse out of the mindless cleaning routine into which he had fallen. He was on his knees, scrub brush in hand, having cleansed the last of the dried blood from the wooden floor of the cell. He blinked in the gloomy darkness of the hold, looking to his left. Tra'al was standing at the door to his cell, a worried look on his wizened face.

The ship shuddered again as another powerful gust of wind thumped it back against the pier. Tra'al stumbled, wrapping his fingers around the iron bars of his cell to steady himself. He regarded Mouse with dark, hooded eyes. He looked as if he were about to speak but was instead wracked by a heavy bout of coughing that bent him over. His shoulders shook with the effort, his breath coming in ragged gasps between coughing fits.

"That cough isn't getting any better." Mouse's eyes narrowed with concern. "Are you sure you don't have the Scourge?"

Tra'al waved the hand he used to cover his mouth, standing back up.

"Nay, lad. 'Tis not the Scourge. 'Tis something else wrong with me. These lungs of mine have gone bad, I'm afraid. They've been getting worse every winter for a while now." The orc offered a wan, fang-filled smile. "My days of scouting would seem to be over."

He regarded the orc's pinched face. His naturally ruddy skin, wrinkle with age, had weathered to an even darker shade of red from a life spent outdoors. His short, coarse hair — where he still had any at all — was grey. His eyebrows, and the rough stubble on his face, were also grey. His right ear was missing its tip. Both of them, however, were badly scarred. Like almost all his folk, Tra'al's nose was broad and flat with large nostrils. A long scar traced down the side of his head, from the missing tip of the right ear to the edge of his nostril. He had a small chin and thin lips that couldn't quite cover the protruding fangs that poked out from his bottom jaw. But despite all of it — the scars, the missing piece of his ear, the fangs that stuck out, and the weathered, hard look to his face — Mouse was comforted by the presence of the old orc.

Groaning, he pushed himself up onto knees and stretched his aching back. The floor of the cell was as clean as it was going to get. He tossed the brush into one of the buckets of dirty water and closed his eyes.

"Lad," Tra'al called out softly. "Before you go, we need to talk."

Exhausted, but still curious, Mouse cracked his eyes open and turned to regard the old orc. Ignoring the buckets, he stood up and padded out of the empty cell. He pulled his jacket back on and moved to stand in front of the orc.

Tra'al was easily the shortest orc he had met. They were roughly the same height: a little over five and a half feet tall — far shorter than normal for his folk. The old orc was well past his physical prime, even without considering the persistent cough and the badly healed wounds from the beating he had received when he had been captured a few weeks ago. His loose-fitting leather tunic was faded and torn in places, revealing a tough and leathery hide beneath it. His woolen trousers were as old and battered as his tunic. For his obvious advanced age, he still had a muscular frame, with shoulders and arms that were still thick with bunched muscles. Like Mouse, the old orc was barefoot. But Tra'al's long toes ended in sharp claws. Mouse had seen him dig into the wooden flooring of the cell with those claws, leaving marks in the cured wood.

The orc's toothy smile revealed all of his sharp teeth, as well as the gap where one of his upper fangs should have been.

"Do you know why I'm here?" He arched a grey eyebrow. "In this cell?"

The question caught Mouse off-guard. It had been a subject he had been curious about, but he had learned to be careful with the questions he asked of the prisoners that the captain and his team of bounty hunters brought onto the ship. All of the previous prisoners he had served had been hardened criminals who had been tracked down, captured, and brought back to the Guild Alliance so that they could face justice. He wondered what Tra'al had done, though, since he didn't act like any of the others.

"No. I don't."

"Do you want to know?"

Mouse nodded.

"Good. You do have some curiosity about you, then..."

Tra'al's voice trailed off as he went through another spasm of coughing that only ended when he bent over and hocked out a red mass of phlegm and blood into his waste bucket near the door. When he recovered, Tra'al looked into Mouse's eyes and spoke, his voice hoarse and thick with mucus.

"I'm in this cell because I was concerned for an old friend of mine, someone very dear to me. I heard your captain asking a loose-lipped bartender about my friend, and the information he received led me to believe that he was about to kidnap an innocent person in order to lure my friend into a trap." The orc shrugged. "I tried to stop him and failed. So here I sit."

"What?" Mouse couldn't keep the incredulity from his voice. "There's got to be more to it than that, Tra'al. The captain's a bounty hunter. He tracks down wanted criminals and brings them to justice. He's not a kidnapper! He is a man of honor."

"You speak of honor like you know what it is."

Tra'al pushed back from the bars separating them and spat on the floor. The orc drew in a couple of raspy breaths. When he spoke again, his voice was strained.

"Having honor is not the same thing as being honorable, lad. There have been a lot of unspeakable crimes committed in the name of honor."

"I don't understand."

The old orc's head dropped. He rested it against the bars, sighing.

"No, I don't suppose you do."

"Then help me to understand." Mouse pressed closer but was careful not to touch the orc. "How can someone have honor and not be honorable?"

Tra'al looked back up into his eyes. Standing up straight, the orc released the bars and placed his hands through them to rest lightly on Mouse's shoulders.

The familiar pounding drums of the orc's song flooded into his consciousness. Too curious as to what Tra'al had to say, Mouse fought the nearly overwhelming urge to follow the sounds of the orc's music to gain yet another glimpse into the man's mysterious life. Narrowing his eyes, he blocked out the music and focused instead on his words.

"It's hard to explain this in human terms, lad. The word 'honor' in the Trade Tongue translates into two very different concepts in my native language, 'kul and 'naq. In va'areshi, 'kul represents the sacred concept of a certain kind of accumulated respect, or honor, that warriors amongst my people earn through their deeds and accomplishments of note. Warriors spend their whole lives doing brave and often foolish things in order to acquire it and increase their standing in their clan and tribe..." He paused to collect his breath. "...But what can be gained in this way can also be lost. A warrior's place in the war band is determined by the amount of *'kul* they are perceived to possess."

Sparked by Tra'al's words, Mouse opened his mouth to speak, but the orc continued.

"*'Naq* is different; it refers to how one conducts oneself. It is a way of being, a life code, if you will, that is similar to what you think of when you consider someone to be honorable — their word is true and they do not cheat in games of chance or in affairs of trade. Thus, having honor, lad, is not the same thing as being honorable. Unfortunately, that's as true among humans as it is with my people, even if your language doesn't easily recognize the difference."

"Wait, Tra'al." Mouse furrowed his brow. "I remember you telling me that *ton'kul* was the proper address for an orc warrior. It means 'one of honor,' right?"

"It is the proper address from one recognized warrior to another, lad." The former Marine's dark eyes narrowed. "Why do you ask?"

"I...um...used it today with an orc I...uh...bumped into." Pulling his hands back from the bars, Mouse ran his fingers over the corners of the parchment folded up in his pocket. "I remembered your stories and wanted to be respectful, and since it was my fault that I wasn't watching where I was going and... uh...he was really, really big and mean looking..."

And I didn't even know he was a wanted fugitive!

"Lad, you've got to be careful! *Va'areshi* is a confusing language with many, many rules." Tra'al made a clucking sound with his tongue against his fangs before shaking his head. "By addressing an orc with that term, you were stating that you considered yourself equal to him in terms of your accomplishments as a warrior." The orc chuckled as his eyes traveled up and down Mouse. "He must have restrained himself, however, because you are here in one piece."

"Oh!" Mouse's eyes widened. He swallowed the lump in his throat. "I...uh...no, his companion, a man...I mean...I was lucky, I guess."

"Companion?" Tra'al's hands wrapped around the bars again as he pressed his misshapen and scarred face between them. "Describe this orc and his companion to me."

Mouse backed away from the orc's intense gaze.

"Why does it matter?"

Tra'al's eyes focused on Mouse's hand. His voice was low and breathy. "Lad, it matters."

He debated turning away from Tra'al and returning to his duties. The last thing he needed was for Haddock to find out that he had met the man who was the one bounty that the captain wanted more than any other.

And worse yet, I accepted a gift from the man!

But there was a burning intensity to Tra'al's gaze that broke down Mouse's resistance. Pulling the parchment out, he stared down at the folded up poster in both hands. He raised his eyes to meet the orc's.

"I...uh...I'm going to show you something." He spoke in a quiet voice, glancing both ways down the narrow, dark hall before staring back into the old orc's eyes. "But...you can't say anything to anyone, okay? No matter what!"

Tra'al regarded him for several long, quiet moments before nodding and placing a clawed hand over his heart.

"On my *'naq*, I promise."

Pressing the parchment into the orc's hand, Mouse stepped back and leaned against the bars behind him, watching as the old Marine unfolded the crackling paper and studied the images on it.

"That's the orc I met," Mouse croaked out his reply. "And

his...uh...companion." He was afraid to even say their names out loud.

The orc stood still, staring at the images on the poster. The parchment trembled in his claws.

"By the Blazing Fires of the Fallen Star!" The former Marine's whispered words were only audible because, for the moment, the storm outside had grown quiet. "Perhaps it's not too late..."

"Too late for what?" Mouse pushed off of the bars and took a step closer.

The orc's head snapped up as his claws tore into the back of the parchment.

"It's not too late to save her!"

"Hey, don't destroy that!" He snatched it back through the bars, cringing at the sound of tearing paper. But the bigger shock came when those same claws grabbed the front of his tunic and yanked him up against the bars separating them. "Let me go!"

"Be quiet and listen, lad!" The orc hissed his words. "I need you to take a message to Tegger Dan, tonight!" His breath smelled of sausage and cheese.

"I...I can't, Tra'al! I don't even know where they are. I met them on the street!" Mouse struggled in vain against the orc's strong grip. His heart thudded against his ribs, his breath came in short gasps. "But even if I did, it would be treason! I would become a criminal just like he..."

"Don't. Even. Say. It." The orc's claws dug into the worn fabric of his tunic. Tra'al's eyes flashed. He pressed his face between the bars, snarling. "Tegger Dan. Is. No. Traitor!"

With that last word, Tra'al was overcome by a fit of coughing. His grip weakened. Mouse jerked himself free. He staggered backwards until he was well out of reach.

Still bent over, Tra'al's shoulders heaved with each hacking cough. When the orc looked back up at Mouse, his eyes were wet with tears, and strings of mucus hung from his mouth and nose.

"I know...how...to...find...them. They...need to...know... about the...girl! They...can...save her!"

"What girl? The captain's not hunting for any girl, Tra'al; he's hunting Tegger Dan!"

Once he realized that he was shouting about things that were best not overheard, he took a deep breath and exhaled.

"Will...you...at least...try?"

"I can't!"

"I'm...sorry...my...friend..." Tra'al's shoulders dropped. He stared down at the floor. "I've...failed...you...again."

Unsure who the orc was speaking to, Mouse followed his gaze. The parchment had fallen between them. It lay, partially crumpled, on the floor. A tiny sliver of flickering light from above illuminated the face of the infamous bard.

Drawn in by the uncanny resemblance of the image with the real man, Mouse couldn't help but be transfixed by how that image stared back at him, accusing. The flute grew heavy in his pocket, weighing him down with even more guilt. He tore his eyes away from the poster.

"Are you okay, Tra'al?"

The orc turned away. But before he turned his back fully, Mouse saw a look of profound disappointment in his eyes.

He watched Tra'al stagger to the back of his cell before bending over to pick up the incriminating evidence of both his treachery and his cowardice. His shoulders heaved in a bitter sigh.

What can I really do? Mouse grabbed his buckets and shuffled out of the hold, turning that and several other questions over in his mind. *Who's this girl that Tra'al thinks is in danger? What don't I know about Tegger Dan? Why does an outlawed former noble mean so much to that old orc?*

And why do I care so much about disappointing him anyway?

CHAPTER 8

Seldy

Leaning into the swirling winds of the storm, Seldy paid more attention than usual to her footing. The frigid temperatures had frozen the slush and mud of the circus grounds solid, turning them into a minefield of ruts with sharp, icy ridges and small, snow-obscured troughs. Even though the cold didn't bother her, the footing was still slippery and treacherous, especially in bare feet.

Her racing thoughts kept returning to the two strange men that Gorman had been showing around. Each of them troubled her, but in different ways. The bearded man made a big show of being amicable towards both the *Baro* and her, but there was something off in his demeanor, as if he was deeply angry about someone or something. And the very idea that he thought he could ever buy either of the tigers...

How could Gorman-da even listen to such ideas? They're family! You can't sell family!

Both Amara and Layra had rubbed up against her as soon as she had entered their enclosure. She snuggled up to each of them in turn the way that she had done as a child. True to their individual personalities, her time with Amara had been spent rubbing and scratching the tigress' favorite spots before feeding her some of the choicest bits of raw and bloody beef from their food bin. Layra, however, had been more interested in keeping her close and thoroughly groomed Seldy with her rough tongue, scraping all of the dirt and debris from her exposed skin, purring deeply with each throaty exhalation.

Remembering Layra's gentle ministrations, Seldy smiled. She always felt safe and protected in her presence. That smile faded, however, as Tia's voice echoed in her mind.

The Enemy comes for you, rehla. *A foe like no other.*

But why would anyone come for me? There was no answer to her question. *I don't have any enemies!*

Unbidden and unwanted, the thin stranger's glowing red eyes forced their way into her consciousness. Seldy shuddered. She hugged herself as she walked, trying to make sense of how that man's gaze had kept her frozen in her place.

...A foe like no other...

The distinct crunch of a nearby boot on ice-crusted snow cut through the background sounds of the storm and snapped her out of her own thoughts. Blinking in surprise, Seldy stopped and listened, trying to narrow down where the sound was coming from.

She took a cautious step backwards when a second crunch came from just beyond the storage wain ahead of her.

"Hello?" she called out, trying to keep fear from creeping into her voice. "Who's there?"

She was in the very center of the camp, standing on ground that had — until this evening — been protected from the ravages of winter by the big top tent. She was surrounded by the dozen or so wagons that had been moved from Bessie's clearing.

Loose tarps snapped and popped. Heavy springs protested the buffeting pressures of the wind pushing against the wagons with incredible force. Rope ends dangled, only to be whipped around to slap against wooden crates or to snap into the spokes of the massive wheels. Thick flakes of snow swirled with each twisting gust — some swept up from the ground — but most of them falling fresh from the sky. Between the blinding snow and the random noises from wagons, she couldn't see who was nearby.

Seldy's heart raced faster. It wasn't like a fellow gypsy to not answer a friendly call in the dark of night. Boots crunched in the snow, but a sudden squall of wind created too much noise to pinpoint the echoing sounds.

Swallowing down the bile that threatened to come up, Seldy squared her shoulders and set her jaw.

I have nothing to fear! This is my home!

"GOTCHA!"

A large gloved hand clamped down tight over her mouth while a strong arm wrapped around her and lifted Seldy from the ground. Reacting purely on instinct, she thrashed about, kicking her heels backwards and clawing at the thick leather of the glove with her short, blunt nails.

Her assailant let out a choked grunt when one of her heels found the bunched muscles in his inner thigh. The grip around her midsection loosened. He staggered backwards.

As soon as Seldy's feet were on the ground, she pivoted on the ball of one foot with all of the speed and accuracy of the highly trained dancer and acrobat that she was, looking to deliver an even more powerful kick to her foe. Recognizing the voice behind the muffled grunts as Chad's, however, she softened and redirected her kick so that it landed on the meaty part of his upper arm instead of the original target of his head.

"Hey! Ow!"

He staggered under the impact of the blow.

"Chadraeg!" A surprising amount of anger seeped into her voice. "You scared me!"

She slapped her open palms against his bulky winter coat, driving him further back with each blow.

Collapsing against a stack of crates, Chad raised his hands.

"Easy, Sunshine! I surrender!" he gasped under the on-slaught. "I'm sorry!"

Seeing the clear apology written across his features, Seldy melt-ed. She threw her arms around him in a desperate, trembling hug.

"Whoah," he whispered into her ear, wrapping his strong arms around her shoulders. "I didn't mean to scare you this much, Seldy!"

"Shut up!" She choked back a sob. "And just hold me!" She buried her face in his chest.

"Whew!" Chad wrinkled his nose. "I can tell where you've been! Those tigers need baths when it gets warmer."

Despite his complaint, Chad held her close for several quiet moments before yanking his gloves off and cradling her cheeks in his warm, strong grip. He guided her eyes back up to his.

"Hey now, what's wrong? Are you okay?"

Looking into the eyes of the man she loved, Seldy's thoughts raced ahead of her tongue. The words tumbled from her lips in a confusing jumble that didn't even make sense to her, but she couldn't stop the flood.

"It's just...the storm...and Tia...and dreams...and enemies and strangers with glowing eyes...and wanting to buy Layra and Amara and...our lives changing forever..."

He tilted his head and pressed his lips to hers, interrupting the flow of her words.

Sighing into the kiss, Seldy closed her eyes, wrapped her arms around his neck, and surrendered. She took delight in the taste of his lips on hers and how his strong, masculine scent filled her nostrils. Little by little, the anger, confusion, and worry that had been clouding her thoughts faded as the delights of the moment pushed everything else aside.

She had no idea how long they stood there kissing in the midst of the storm, but when he pulled back and grinned down at her, she was able to muster a tentative smile in return.

"That's my Sunshine, right there."

Seldy's smile broadened. She opened her mouth to reply but was interrupted by a flash of lightning that lit up the sky. The crackling report of the accompanying thunder reverberated through the air, rattling the wagons and crates around them.

"Oh wow!" Chad's eyes widened. "I don't think I've ever seen thunder snow before!"

"Don't tell anyone else," she whispered, pressing in close. "But Tia told Ma that this was going to be a *Fae* storm."

He gave a low whistle. "I remember Dorel." Seldy felt him clench his hands into fists behind her. "Blast it! I hate the *Fae*! I'll sure be glad when the last of those nasty creatures are all dead and buried!"

"Chad!" Her stomach tightened at his harsh words. "That's not very nice!"

"Hey." He clenched his jaw. "They caused the Black Scourge, and they throw storms like this at us just because they can! And look at all of the havoc and hardship that that stupid pirate, Sarlan the Red, caused when he was still alive." His voice was thick with anger. "The world will be a better place when they're all dead and gone."

"I've heard all of the same stories." Her stomach churned. She pushed free from his embrace and regarded him. "But we don't know that they are all true! And besides," she added. "I don't think the answer for anything is for folk to die!"

"Sure it is, Sunshine." Chad tried to close the distance between them again. "If they're dead, they can't make any more diseases or send storms like this at us, can they?"

"No!" Seldy brushed away his hands and took a step back. "Killing people is never the answer!"

"But Seldy, the *Fae* aren't really people, are they? They're monsters!" He stopped trying to get closer, reaching down to pick up his snow-covered gloves. "That's why they keep trying hurt us." He shook the snow off of his gloves before slipping them back on.

"Tegger says that they haven't always been bad!" She planted her fists on her hips and stared up at him. "The *Fae* and the elves used to be close allies. And I'm an elf, in case you hadn't noticed!"

"Whoah, Sunshine!" He held his hands out in front of him. "It was a long, long time ago when elves and the *Fae* were friends. Besides, you're one of us now, a Freeborn gypsy, and you're the prettiest gypsy girl there ever was at that!"

He stepped closer, clearly hoping to end their argument with something sweeter than the loud and angry words, but Seldy slipped back out of his reach.

"Oh no you don't! I'm going home now! Good night!"

Seldy fought against the tears that threatened to overwhelm her. Unable to hold them back — and afraid that she might say something she would regret — she turned around and strode away.

Seldy didn't stop until she reached the steps of her home — the *vardo* she had shared with Jhana since the day Tegger brought her to the *kumpania*.

The storage crates and barrels that were usually scattered around the *vardo* for ease of access were all closed up and tucked away beneath the undercarriage. The only barrels left out were the ones placed directly beneath the eaves to catch the rain and snowmelt from the roof.

All of the shutters were closed, preventing any heat or light from leaking out. Looking up, Seldy noted the curly tendrils of smoke escaping from the cylindrical metal chimney, only to be scattered by the swirling winds. She took a deep breath and tried to calm her fraying nerves.

"I can't believe I had a fight with Chad tonight! And over what? The stupid *Fae*?"

Seldy trudged up the steps and pulled the door open. The wind snatched it from her grasp, whipping it into the railing with a startling bang.

Warmth, soft light, and the welcoming aromas of home spilled out into the night. Jhana, already in her nightgown, stood in front of the stove stirring a pot of jasmine tea. Her head snapped around towards the loud crash while the candles guttered from the rush of cold air.

"Brrr, *rehla!*" Jhana waved her inside. "Close the door before that blasted storm decides to come in and stay as well!"

After wrestling the door closed, Seldy turned to face her mother.

"Oh Seldy! You're soaked to the bone!" Her mother's tone was sharp as she placed a strong hand on each shoulder. She crinkled her nose. "Phew! And you reek of those tigers and elephant dung!"

Before Seldy could open her mouth to argue, Jhana waved towards the small watercloset next to them.

"Get out of those wet things and get yourself cleaned up! There should be enough warm water left in the tank for tonight, anyway, and then you can have some tea to take the chill off."

Knowing better than to argue with her mother, Seldy bobbed her head. Biting her bottom lip to help stave off the unbidden tears, she dropped her head and shuffled obediently towards the closet.

"Wait a minute." Jhana's voice softened even as the hand on Seldy's shoulder tightened. "What's wrong?"

Sniffling, Seldy wiped her cheek with the back of her hand. "It's...nothing."

"Oh no you don't, *rehla*."

Taking each of Seldy's hands in one of her own, Jhana drew her to the wooden bench beside their table.

"Come, sit down. Let's talk."

Seldy didn't resist being pulled down to sit. As soon as she did, the last of her meager defenses crumbled. Her shoulders heaved with sobs. Hot tears joined the rivulets of melting snow trailing down her cheeks and dripping from her sodden dress onto the bench and, eventually, onto the floor.

Jhana pulled her close, simply holding Seldy while the sobs prevented her from being able to talk. Her mother leaned over and kissed her on the forehead.

"When you're ready, *rehla*," she whispered,. "Tell me all about it."

Her first words were halting and jumbled like they had been with Chad, but Jhana just listened in that intense way of hers that didn't miss anything. Taking a deep breath, Seldy started over.

"It all started when I reached Tia's *vardo*. When I stepped inside, there was so much dreamvine smoke in the air that I began to feel kind of funny..."

She told her mother about everything, from the drug-induced dreams and mysterious warnings she received while checking up on Tia to the strange visitors that Gorman was entertaining. She repeated the disturbing conversation about selling the tigers. She described the weird, glowing eyes of the thin, silent visitor and the boiling rage she felt within the bearded man. The mood lightened when Seldy spoke of how she was able to calm the tigers by spending time with each of them, and then helping to get Bessie settled when she returned from helping take down the big top tent. She didn't slow down until she reached the part where she and Chad had fallen into their first argument. Her words became halting and were interspersed with choked sobs and a fresh round of tears.

Her mother never once interrupted, although her facial expressions flowed from compassion and love to anger and then back again at all of the right places. When Seldy fell silent, Jhana kissed her again.

"I love you, *rehla*." She offered a small smile and a compassionate squeeze of her fingers. "That sounds like a rough night. Why don't you take a few moments to get cleaned up and changed as I prepare you a nice warm cup of tea. We can talk as I brush your hair, like we used to do."

"I'd like that," Seldy smiled, returning the fond squeeze with one of her own. "Thank you, Ma!"

Freshly scrubbed and wearing her most comfortable night-dress, a faded and worn silk gown that Tegger had brought her for her sixteenth birthday, Seldy settled carefully into place on the big, comfy bed she often shared with her mother.

In the time that she had taken to get clean, the storm outside had intensified. The *vardo* shook from side to side as renewed blasts of wind hit it. Thick pellets of ice pelted the roof, walls, and windows. For Seldy, it was an oddly comforting sound, as it reminded her of the spring rains that surely weren't that far off now.

Sipping from her steaming cup of jasmine tea, Seldy let the flavors of the honey and tea swirl around on her tongue. The combination of the warm, flavorful liquid and the fragrant aromas soothed her jittery nerves. She set her cup and saucer on the table beside the bed and settled back into her mother's welcoming embrace.

They cuddled in silence, mother and daughter, for several minutes before she was ready to talk.

"Do you really think this is a *Fae* storm, Ma?"

"I don't know, Sweetling, but a shiver went up my spine when Tiagra said it. That only happens when she has Seen true."

Her fingers strayed to one of Seldy's ears. She stroked the outermost edge lightly, lovingly, like she often did.

"She is right far more often than most seers I've met."

The Enemy comes for you, child...

Tiagra's strange words echoed in Seldy's memory. Warm and safe in her mother's arms, those warnings sounded even stranger than they had when Tia had uttered them.

"Ma, what about the things Tia said?" She shuddered at the memory of how Tia's eyes had turned white when she had spoken. "Should we be worried?"

"I don't know, *rehla*." Her mother's voice was huskier than normal. "But I will speak to her in the morning, once the storm passes."

"What about those strangers? Do you think they'll convince *Gorman-da* to sell..." Her voice caught. "...Layra and Amara?"

"No." Her mother's response was so sharp and so immediate, that Seldy was both surprised and relieved at the same time. "He's a *Baro*, not a dictator."

"What does that mean?"

"It means that he can't make a decision like that — something that would impact the whole *kumpania* — without getting the consent of others." Her mother's voice dropped a level. "Me, in particular. As the Mistress of Coin, I have a lot of say in what assets are bought or sold." Her voice became hard as steel. "And I won't allow it."

"Layra and Amara aren't assets!" Seldy straightened up and pulled out of her mother's grasp, turning around to look at her. "They're family!"

"I know that, *rehla*." Her mother sat up and reached for the ivory-handled brush on the bedside table. Her voice softened.

"But remember, no one else knows that you can speak to them or any of the other animals. And no one can know about that, remember?"

"But Tia..."

"Tia's different, Seldy." Jhana reached up and gently turned Seldy's head before bringing the brush to bear against the mass of long, unruly, and still wet hair. "Do you remember that saying about seers and their secrets?"

" 'Secrets are like coins to seers: they're quick to hoard them and loathe to spend them...'" The familiar words slipped easily through Seldy's lips. The same could not be said for the brush that her mother was trying to work through her thick hair. "Ow!"

"I'm sorry, *rehla*!"

The pressure on the brush let up as her mother reached a thick tangle. Jhana's fingers worked their way into her hair, her tongue clucking against the roof of her mouth.

"Such hair, child. Do you know how lucky you are?"

"I don't feel so lucky right now!" Seldy couldn't help giggling through the pain.

They both fell silent as her mother continued to work through the knot of tangles. In between the rough patches, Seldy sipped her tea and tried to make sense of everything that had happened in the last few hours. Her thoughts kept circling back to how she was going to broach the subject of Chad and his proposal.

"So, when were you going to tell me the big news?"

"What?" Seldy snapped her head around. "How did you know?"

"That Chad had asked you to be his *consyrta*?" Her mother flashed a grin. "I'm your mother; it's my job to know these things!"

"But how?"

"Well, let's see." Jhana teased. "It could've been the way

you've been dancing around on moonbeams with your toes barely touching the ground since the moment he asked you." She ticked off each item on her fingers. "Or it might've been the way the two of you have been finding ways to slip away to steal a few private moments together for months now, and then there's the way you two look at each other when you think no one else is watching."

Seldy's jaw dropped as her mother continued.

"Or perhaps it was the fact that Talinn was moving his things from Chad's *vardo* earlier today, grumbling about how he had to 'make room for the lovebirds.'" Jhana closed Seldy's mouth with a gentle push of her fingers, grinning the whole while. "It hasn't been the best kept of secrets, *rehla*."

Before Seldy could say anything, Jhana leaned forward and planted a kiss on her forehead.

"Besides all of the that, the clincher was seeing how upset you were at him just a little while ago." She cocked her head to the side. "Your argument hasn't soured your plans, has it?"

"No, Ma. Not at all."

"This is a big step, *rehla*. Are you sure about this?" Those grey eyes regarded her. "Do you think you are ready for the responsibilities of being a *consyrta*?"

"I think so." Seldy didn't blush under this scrutiny. "When he kisses me, I get all jittery inside, like right before the first performance of each touring season. I love him!"

Her mother continued to watch her for a moment, then nodded. The brush began to move through her hair again.

"You're an adult now with an adult's responsibilities both in the *kumpania* and the circus." Her tone was gentle, reassuring. "Chad's a good man. He works hard and is responsible. He'll be a good *consyrtu*, I think. But there is much more to being *consyrtae* than breathless kisses and loving each other. You two will have to figure out how to share the chores and responsibilities of your new household. Who's going to cook the meals and clean up when you are both sore and tired after a long day of practice or performances? Who's going to get the water and the fuel for the stove? Who's going to do the laundry? It isn't easy living with someone you care about so much." Jhana paused before continuing. "When you live together, you see every aspect of that person, especially those parts of themselves that they try to hide from others." Jhana's eyes bored into Seldy's. "Are you prepared to see Chad in his worst moments?"

"I think so, Ma." Her nod became more forceful. "I'm ready, Mother." Her expression grew more serious as she sat up straight. "I need to apologize to him for snapping at him tonight!"

"That's something that can wait until the morning, *rehla*." Her mother laid a hand on her shoulders. "He scared you and then said some inadvisable things." There was a strange catch in her mother's voice, but she continued. "Let him stew on things a bit tonight. He'll appreciate you more in the morning for having to sleep on it."

"I don't like fighting." Seldy hugged herself, trying to calm the butterflies that kept churning inside. "Is it always going to feel like this when we fight?"

"When fighting with someone you care about doesn't make you feel terrible," her mother snorted, "you'll know the love between you is either withering or dead. That'll be one of your clues to bring an end to the *consyrtium*."

"If...if...things don't work out between us, can I come back home?" Her bottom lip quivered.

"Of course, *rehla*." Jhana wrapped her in a strong hug, whispering fiercely into her ear, "You're my daughter, and I love you more than life itself! Don't you ever forget that! You will always have a home in my *vardo*."

"Oh, Ma!" Relief flooded through her.

"I'm proud of the person you've become, Seldy. You and Chad will make a great couple."

They embraced for several long, quiet moments, rocking back and forth with the gentle swaying of the *vardo* from the howling winds outside.

"Have you been drinking *sarbat* with each of your moons?"

"Of course I have, Ma!"

Seldy tried to sit still as her mother resumed brushing her hair but couldn't quite manage it. She squirmed as Jhana worked out another knot in her hair.

"Neither of us are ready to be parents yet. But besides, we haven't gone that far...yet." She stressed that last word. "I've taken the tea during each of my last three cycles, so it...we... should be safe...when we do...get to do...that." She giggled again as she thought about how soon that might be.

"You better be!" Jhana's hands were gentle, yet firm, as she brushed her hair. Her voice became quieter. "Sex isn't just about making babies, Seldy. It is how two people connect on the deepest levels. I just want to make sure that you're ready for it. Chad's been like a brother to you, and now you will each care for each other in new and different ways. Once friends become lovers, things change between you forever."

Seldy sat still and quiet, thinking about Jhana's words before answering.

"I'm ready, Ma."

"It seems like only yesterday that Tegger brought you to me, Seldy."

Jhana set the brush down and wrapped both arms around her, pulling her into a warm embrace.

"How quickly the time has gone by." She squeezed her tight against her body. "I'm going to miss this."

"I'm not going anywhere, Ma!" Seldy turned her head to

look up into her mother's eyes. "We'll still be able to spend time together!"

The wind rocked the *vardo*. Thunder boomed overhead, and bursts of lightning lit up the dim interior of their home.

"Ah, but not in the same way, *rehla*. Indulge your poor, old mother," Jhana whispered as she bent down and placed a soft kiss on her forehead.

Leaning back into her mound of pillows, Jhana gently pulled Seldy back with her. Her fingers brushed aside the long silver bangs that fell in front of Seldy's eyes.

"Let me enjoy one more night of you being my little girl."

"I'll apologize...in the morning." Seldy yawned. "And let him know that you're okay with our *consyrtium*."

Jhana smiled and snuggled in even closer.

Exhausted from the day's events, Seldy's eyes grew heavy with sleep. She let all of her cares slip away. Her mother would speak to Tia and find out more about those strange warnings in the morning and *tiger-mas* weren't going to be sold.

Seldy was safe in her mother's arms. And no storm, not even a *Fae* storm, could ever change that.

CHAPTER 9

Mouse

Mouse shut the door to the small storage hold behind him and leaned against it. He closed his eyes and tried to stop from trembling.

Will...you...at least...try?

I can't.

The room was dark and quiet, sheltered from the sounds of the storm raging outside. The stale air of the cramped hold reeked of new canvas, raw hemp, and lamp oil. Hidden away beneath the forecastle, the small chamber appeared to have been designed as a cabin for passengers but was instead packed full of sailcloth, rope, replacement blocks for the rigging, and operating gears for the ship. The quiet was comforting. It was about as far away as he could get from everyone else on the ship.

Sinking down into a pile of coiled up rope, Mouse couldn't help remembering the look of bitter disappointment in Tra'al's eyes. He pressed the palms of his hands against his eyelids and rubbed them.

Will...you...at least...try?

"Don't you understand?" Mouse whispered back. "I'm no hero. I don't know how to fight! I run away and hide! That's who I am."

Outside, something pounded dully against the hull of the ship. The slow and steady rhythm of the pounding reverberated through the frame of the ship and into his body. Taking a deep breath, Mouse relaxed. He slumped down towards the floor.

"He's here!"

Mouse opened his eyes when a pair of grubby hands grabbed him. They wrenched him out of the tight space so hard that something on the back of the furnace ripped through the only tunic he owned and bit into his skin.

"Sorry, Mouse." The heftier and older of his pursuers, Bertie, pulled him out into the open. "But it's you or us, and it ain't gonna be me that suffers."

"Yeah, you shoulda jes stabbed that old guard like Lefty wanted, Mouse," Sunny chimed in, placing his hands on his shoulders. "He cheated us and was due fer gang justice!"

Mouse struggled for a moment until his captors moved to either side of him. Without warning, he went limp, sinking bonelessly to the stone floor. It was a move that neither of the bigger boys expected. He slipped from their startled grasp.

"Wha-" Bertie exclaimed as he staggered forward, leaning down to get his hands back on the fugitive.

Sunny stumbled, smacking his head into Bertie's chin with an audible crack that staggered them and left them both crying out in pain.

Scrambling on all fours, Mouse crawled beneath Bertie's widespread legs and took off running. He burst out the door and took off at full speed, racing through the muddy streets.

His toes dug into the wet mud, giving him better traction

than the other two because of their shoes. Mouse pumped his arms as he ran.

"There he is!" Chany cried out in her hoarse voice. "He's heading downslope!"

He tucked his head down and redoubled his efforts.

It didn't take long for the wider streets of the warehouse district to become a fading memory as he returned to the twisting, narrow alleyways of the Warrens, his home turf. Unfortunately, it was also home to the Alley Rats — his former gang.

The Warrens was a sprawling, packed maze of shanties, shacks, and ramshackle buildings shot through with clogged alleys where thousands of people were crowded so close together that there were no real streets.

His pace slowed as he dodged through hanging laundry and around packs of small, mud-spattered children. Urchins scatted from their games of hide and seek, shrieking as Mouse crashed through, playing the same game but for much higher stakes.

The people of the Warrens were used to the Alley Rats and their violent way of settling differences. It didn't take long for them to realize what was happening. The gang was calling for the head of one of their former members in a ritual that was as familiar as it was likely to end in bloodshed. The normal buzz of conversations — of laughing and playing children, of arguments between husbands and wives, and gossip between neighbors — died down to an expectant, worried hush.

Women who had been busy chatting gathered in their precious laundry, grabbed their too-curious children, and blocked their make-shift doors, hoping that the trouble would pass them by. Men who had been smoking, drinking, and playing cards threw down their hands, gathered up their meager stakes, and slunk back home. Children who were too old to be clutching their mother's skirts but too young to have been drawn into the gang life, ducked inside at the whispered commands of worried parents, only to find ways to peek out with furtive interest through the slats of their shanties, hoping to catch a glimpse of the entertainment.

Skidding around a corner, Mouse caught sight of a young boy who was maybe ten. The child watched him from behind a rain barrel, wide-eyed and open-mouthed. He wanted to shout out to the boy, "Stay away from the gangs, kid!" But he lacked the breath and time to do so. He could only hope that the look of sheer terror on his bloodied face was enough to scare the kid off of that path.

The kid was probably as doomed as he had been, however. It wasn't like Mouse had ever aspired to be an Alley Rat. He had watched similar scenes from the shadows when he was younger; yet, here he was anyway: fleeing for his life at the age of seventeen.

With renewed determination, Mouse raced past him, unable to spare another glance.

"Come in here, Mouse!" Blind Meg called out to him in her raspy voice.

She was as blind as the day was long, but she always knew who was coming or going around her shop. She was also one of the few people who wasn't afraid of the Alley Rats. A pang of regret stabbed through his heart for not taking her up on the offer she made when his mother had died.

"Don't be a fool, Mouse! I can protect you!"

Mouse knew better. He passed the entrance to Meg's shop, ignoring her entreaties. The last thing he wanted on his conscience was to bring Lefty's wrath down on her.

His heart raced as turned the corner and slowed. He stumbled to a stop just outside the entryway to the alley that led to the meager shack that his mother had somehow made into a home. The precious, hidden space between Meg's shop and their home was where his mother had grown so many of their herbs. He yearned to return to it, one last time.

Catching his breath, Mouse debated slipping back there, until he saw the dirty face and wide eyes of a child peeking out at him from the corner of a tattered curtain. With a mumbled curse, he took off running once again.

As he ran, he couldn't help wondering how many other folk truly knew what was going on. There were few secrets in the Warrens. His flight through the alleys of his home, fleeing from his own gang, would likely be whispered about in a hundred shacks. For a few days at least, folks who had not seen the chase would wonder where Mouse had gotten off to, until they heard the rumors. Then they would nod knowingly, sadly, saying nice things like, "That's too bad; he was a nice one, that one," and "I wonder what he did to earn that fate?" or even "Well, that's one less of them leeches to mooch off the rest of us!" But after a few days, he would be forgotten, just like Liddy and Fat Tom and Sarid before him.

With the normally crowded alleys clearing of people, Mouse picked up his pace but so too did those who pursued him. He heard the whistles, shouts, and banging behind and on either side of him as the gang spread out. They were combing through the Warrens in pursuit, winding down each passageway and ensuring that their quarry could not double back on them to escape. They knew this territory as well as he did, and they knew all too well just how slippery he was.

The only sounds he made were the squelching splatters of each muddy footstep and the huffing of his breath as he continued racing downslope. He wracked his brain, trying to think of a route he could take that would allow him to cut across the grain of the slope and eventually get back to higher ground, but that was going be harder to do the further down he went.

Seeing the opportunity presented by a drainage ditch oozing with thick, dark, muddy water and reeking of urine and feces, Mouse heaved himself across it. He landed on the bank of the far side with a grunt on all fours, just above the waterline.

"There's the git!" Chany's deep, yet still feminine, voice called out behind him. A chorus of whistles and cries followed her exclamation.

A rock splattered in the mud next to Mouse's head while another splashed harmlessly into the stream of filth behind him as he scampered up the slick bank. He was up and running again, passing a couple of shanties of folk who were so poor that they only had three walls; tattered blankets hung from their tin roofs to cover where the fourth wall should have been.

There was a huge splash and loud cursing as someone jumped and missed their mark. But others were coming, so Mouse had no time to enjoy even that small victory. He turned and continued slipping and sliding downslope, knowing that his options for escape narrowed with each slippery step he took.

More whistles. A chorus of angry voices called after him.

"Give it up, Mouse!"

They were getting closer, and some of them were on the same side of the ditch as he was.

Following the twisting, turning alley until it rejoined the banks of the drainage ditch, Mouse headed towards the one place that every Slanter feared — the Edge.

The Edge was where both the island of Dragon's Reach and the Slant ended. It was also where the runoff from the late summer rains and the sewage from this section of the miserable slum spilled off and went tumbling, unfettered and unfiltered, down into the Untere, thousands upon thousands of feet below. Every monsoon season a few of the poorest of the poor — those who had no choice but to build their shacks too close to the Edge — were washed off the slope and sent tumbling to their doom. But that wasn't the only time that people went over the Edge. It was a common enough fate for those who were on the losing side of the many gang wars over the muddy turf of the Slant.

That wasn't Lefty's style, though. He preferred to see blood.

Approaching the end, Mouse made his way through the last line of huts and hovels. Beyond that lay an open expanse of brown, muddy ground that ended with the open sky.

On his right, were the hovels of the truly downtrodden: worn out and scarred women too old and ugly to sell themselves any longer, men too crippled to earn an odd pent or two here or there with their labor, and those others who were so tired and destitute that they welcomed the inevitability of being washed away to oblivion. Most ramshackle buildings didn't have full roofs, and many lacked a front wall. With the commotion of the chase by the Alley Rats pursuing him, the inhabitants cowered in the back corners, hoping that he didn't involve them in gang business.

To his immediate left, the drainage ditch was full and wide, the water flowing faster, even as the smell grew worse from the added sewage from other, smaller ditches feeding into it. Beyond the ditch was another stretch of poor homes, called the Ramparts. It was named after the massive stone wall that separated the slums of the Slant from East Port just beyond it. That wall was tangible proof that the inhabitants of the Slant were completely unwanted, if not forgotten, by the privileged folk of Ventraxis proper. It came to an abrupt end at the Edge where a single, tall tower stood sentry against both invaders from beyond and any poor Slanter who dared try to breach the sanctity of the vast and wealthy capital of the Guild Alliance.

The Ramparts, which was only slightly wealthier and slightly less cramped than the Warrens, was strictly off-limits to the Alley Rats because another, more powerful, gang — the Daring Dawgs — controlled it. There had been bad blood between the two gangs for as far back as anyone could remember.

The sounds of the ongoing chase brought out the scouts of the Daring Dawgs. They stood at carefully chosen locations along the far side of the ditch. They clutched makeshift weapons and watched, impassively, as Mouse fled for his life towards the Edge. They didn't care why he fled from his own gang; they just wanted to make sure that all of the Alley Rats, including Mouse, kept to their own side of the canal.

There would be no safety found there.

A rock whizzed by Mouse's ear, splashing in the mud ahead just as he broke through the last line of shanties and found himself in the featureless, muddy expanse of ground that led up to the Edge. There was a hundred feet of open, soggy ground in front of him. The expanse continued off to the right for as far as he could see. To his left, the ditch had become more of a stream. It flowed right up to the edge, spilling its contents in a rush of brown, foul-smelling water that tumbled into the open space beyond.

There was a short stretch of more open space beyond the stream, but that ended at the massive wall that led up to the tall, fortified tower looming at the Edge. Its imposing bulk served as a stern reminder about how much the fine folk of Ventraxis wanted to keep the scum of the Slant from soiling their pampered and perfumed lives.

Sunlight glinted off of a steel helm from up high in the tower. Armed sentries stood watch, likely paying little heed to Mouse's plight below.

He was halfway to the Edge before he stopped running. His fate would be decided soon. Slowing to a walk, he moved forward as all thought of his pursuers fled his mind. He drank in the view of the world beyond the Slant.

"Might as well see a bit of the world...," he gasped. "Because it looks like this'll be my last chance."

It was a rare, cloudless, late summer day. Sunlight drenched the panoramic view, stealing his breath away as he soaked it in. Looking east, he had a view that represented all that remained *of the world after the Sundering — all three teres of islands, the blazing fires of the Fallen Star burning bright beneath them all, and even a small slice of Free Air, the vast expanse of open sky where the air was too wild and dangerous for any ship to traverse. He stood as close to the very edge of the known world as he was ever likely to get.*

Mouse was transfixed by the endless vista laid out before him. Thousands upon thousands of feet below his bare, muddy toes, the vastness of the Untere spread out before him. Unlike the island of Dragon's Reach, the islands of the Untere were huge. Sunlight glinted off of snow-covered mountains that strained, in vain, to reach up into the Midtere. Snaking ribbons of blue sparkled in the bright sunlight, while larger pools that must've been lakes caught his eye. Some bodies of water appeared to be larger than the whole island upon which he now stood. There were dark green masses that might be forests and lighter patches that were likely some of the fabled farms and ranches of the Downlands from where most of the food consumed by the elites of Ventraxis came. Many of those farms were worked by men and women formerly of the Slant, folks who had been gathered up in the occasional raids by the Grey Cloaks of the City Watch and deported to provide the never-ending labor required to keep the rich folk fat and happy.

What drew his eyes next, though, was not anything in the Untere itself, but the reddish glow that came through the yawning gaps between the islands and the deeper orange that was visible beyond the farthest edge of the eastern-most island below — the Fallen Star!

Mouse traced the gaps between the islands of the Untere with his eyes. He leaned into the stiff updraft in order to get a better look at the land immediately below. Something strange and wondrous caught his eye below.

The slimmest glimmer of hope.

"Mouse!" Lefty's voice called out behind him. "There's nowhere else to run now."

He turned around.

Lefty stood there, not more than twenty feet away, flanked on either side by a half dozen members of the gang. All of them held weapons, mostly clubs and knives. Chany held her trusty, iron-headed mace, cupping the head of it in the palm of her left hand.

"I'm not going to fight you, Lefty. I don't want to hurt anyone."

Lefty threw back his head and laughed. The others joined in, some of them more readily than others.

"Oh, I'm not worried about you hurting anyone, Mouse. You had your chance to show that you had the teeth to be a true Alley Rat. You failed." Lefty shook his head. "If only you would've learned to fight. You're too old to just be a pick pocket and scout anymore. I need fighters. And people who will follow my blazing orders."

"Let me go, Lefty," Mouse implored him. "I'll leave the Warrens. I'll find somewhere else to go. You don't have to kill me."

"That's where you're wrong, Mouse." Lefty took a step forward, a dagger gleaming in his left hand. "That's what you don't seem to understand. If I let you live, others will challenge me, too. That's how all of this works; only the strong survive the Slant, Mouse."

Mouse backed up until the mud beneath his bare heels slid away beneath him. His toes dug in deeper as he leaned forward, trying to avoid falling to his certain death.

"It doesn't have to be like this, Lefty! There must be another way!"

"It's too late, Mouse. You've broken your last rule." The gang leader looked to his left and then to his right. "Sunny, Chany, bring him back to me. We'll throw his body over soon enough, but I want to bleed him first."

Sunny gulped but stepped forward, club in hand. Chany smiled.

Mouse swallowed and stood up to his full height, relaxed now that his decision had been made. Before either of the two chosen assailants could close the distance to him, he gave a small wave to the only family he had had since his mother had died seven years ago.

"Good bye." He stepped off of the Edge, plunging towards what would almost certainly be his death.

The crack of the ship slamming against the ropes that held it securely in place jolted Mouse back to the moment. He shuddered at the memory of the sheer terror he had felt in that moment.

I need to stop trying to fly.

Leaning his head back against the door, Mouse wrapped his arms around his knees and drew them into his chest. A shiver of pain shot across his back as another half-healed scab tore open. He was past caring about the stains on his tunic as the familiar warmth oozed from the unhealed wound.

"What's wrong with me?" His voice sounded whiney and childish to his ears. "Why can't I just follow the stupid rules? Why can't I stand up for myself and fight back like everyone else?" His voice cracked. "Why do I always run away from every fight?"

The ship shuddered again as the winds changed direction, tilting to the left. The tiny porthole near the very front of the packed space rattled under the renewed assault of wind and water. Jarred loose enough to allow some of the elements inside, a small puddle had formed on the ledge beneath it. A single drop developed at the edge, dangling for a moment before falling in slow-motion. It landed on the metal lid of a can Mouse hadn't noticed.

Kerplunk.

A high-pitched, hollow whistle followed the resonating echo of the drop, filling the small room with an eerie music. It was a mournful song that reminded him of something, something he needed to remember.

The hair on the back of his neck stood up on end. His arms felt cold. The strange wailing song sent him reeling...

It was dark and scary.

A low moaning filled the air with a haunting, hollow song.

In the distance, there was the harsh sound of metal clanging against metal repeatedly.

Voices. Familiar voices — feminine voices — whispered. They were moving farther and farther away from the harsh metallic sounds.

Warm arms — familiar arms — held him close, keeping him safe. A blanket was wrapped around him, but he still felt the warmth of her neck pressed against his cheek.

He was being carried.

"How much farther?" A soft feminine voice whispered close by, a gentle hand caressing his head. "He's shivering!"

"It's not far now," the other voice responded in a strange lilt that was both alien and familiar at the same time. "We're almost there."

"Are you sure about this?"

He recognized the voice now — Mama! She sounded worried. "What if we're caught?"

"We won't be," the other voice answered, sure and strong. "But if we are, I will deal with him. He loves me. And he knows that I love him."

Mama shuddered, her arms tightening around him.

"How can you love that monster?" his mother sobbed. "He killed...Randil."

"I don't love the monstrous mask that he wears nor do I love the things he has done while wearing it. But I love the man beneath it, Mara." The other voice softened further. "I know that you cannot see beyond it, my love. Nor would I ever ask you to do so."

His mother stopped and turned. The other voice came closer, whispering her soft words.

"Nothing can bring your husband back, but from such sorrow we can sow the seeds of hope. And from those seeds a future may blossom for your people and mine."

"How?" His mama's voice was thick and heavy, like it cost her a great deal to speak each word. "How can we do that? We're both prisoners!"

Hearing the fear in her voice, he cried out.

"Love, Mara, and Truth."

The other voice was still close. A warm, tingling hand touched his head. A gentle calm settled over him. He remembered that touch. It belonged to the Shining Lady.

"Our love for each other and the boundless love we each have for our children, combined with the ability to show them the truth of things is what will make it all possible."

He was no longer cold or scared with the warmth of the Shining Lady's touch on his head. Then it was gone, but the warmth and calm remained as his mother turned again and resumed carrying him.

The harsh sounds faded, to be replaced by a constant but quiet song that filled the air with long, mournful notes. It was a song that honored the dead while celebrating life, hinting at deeper mysteries yet to be discovered.

The ship jolted again, ending the wind's song and shattering the strange memory or dream into countless shards.

Disoriented, Mouse stood up on unsteady feet, feeling for the flute in his jacket.

"Whoah!"

Mouse's tongue felt as thick as a woolen blanket. Remembering Dalton's earlier invitation, he fingered the flute sitting heavily in his pocket.

"I think I need to start playing again."

And, he added silently, *I could really use a drink.*

CHAPTER 10

Seldy

Sweetling, wake up."

Bleary-eyed, Seldy stirred from a fitful sleep. She lifted her head from the pillow.

"What is it, Ma?"

"Shhh." Jhana pressed a finger to Seldy's lips. "Quiet now." She spoke in a hushed tone. "I heard something."

The worry in her mother's voice brought Seldy fully awake. She clutched reflexively at the covers.

Her mother pushed her portion of the covers aside and swung her legs over the side of the bed. Pausing, she opened the top drawer of her nightstand and removed a sheathed blade. In a well-practiced motion, she slipped the blade quietly from its sheath.

Seldy sucked in a quick breath and bit down on her bottom lip to keep from asking any questions. Instead, she shifted her focus from her eyes to her ears.

The storm lashed against the *vardo*. Thick, heavy drops of sleet pelted the roof, creating a comforting sound for sleeping but now that she was awake and listening, it made it harder to hear anything else. After straining for several moments, Seldy looked at her mother and shook her head, unsure if she should be relieved or not.

A loud thump against the door made them both jump.

"Who in the blazing..." Jhana cursed and rose into a crouch.

Seldy pulled the covers tighter against her body.

Her mother was already moving by the time the door rattled a second time. She approached it cautiously, holding the naked blade low in her right hand while clutching the leather sheath high in her left.

Seldy's heart thudded in her chest. Her breath came in ragged gasps. She hoped that something had just been blown against their *vardo* in the storm — a thick branch from a tree, perhaps, or someone else's wind-blown chair or table that hadn't been secured properly.

"Seldy..." Her sharp ears picked up on the soft voice calling her. "...help me..."

"Ma, it's Chad!" Seldy flipped the covers aside and streaked past her mother before she could be stopped. "He's in trouble!"

Turning the inner latch, she pushed on the door.

It didn't budge. Something heavy was blocking it. She put her shoulder against the door and pushed harder.

Her mother called out, "Seldy, wait!"

The weight on the door shifted enough for her to push it open.

"Chad?"

Seldy's face crumpled as soon as she saw him. A wail escaped her lips,

"Chad!"

"I'm...s-s-sorry, Sunshine..." He clutched his stomach with blood-drenched hands.

"Blazing Fires!" Jhana was a step behind Seldy.

He staggered forward, his lips moving again, but no further

sound came forth. Red froth flecked his lips. Seldy reached out as he stumbled forward and collapsed into her arms, dragging them both down to the floor. The door slammed all of the way open as the storm followed Chad into the *vardo*.

Warm blood seeped through Chad's fingers and onto her.

Seldy tried to cry out, but her voice failed. Pinned beneath his larger and much heavier frame, she could only stare into his fading blue eyes and clutch at his cheeks with blood-smeared hands.

Jhana dropped to a knee beside them, her face pinched with worry.

A massive figure filled the doorway, blocking the pelting sleet and the howling wind. Klard Dastyr stared down at Seldy with dark, beady eyes and a snarl on his lips. He held a curved sword in one hand, its wicked gleam dulled by her *consyrtu's* blood.

Pinned beneath Chad's bulk, Seldy tried again to scream out, but her voice died in her throat as a second figure peered over the shoulder of the bearded man. A pair of glowing red eyes captured hers and stilled her cry before it could form.

The blade descended. Her mother reacted with impossible speed, twisting to the side and raising her dagger in defense. Sparks flew. Steel scraped on steel. It wasn't enough — strength and surprise overcame speed and determination.

The thick metal guard of Dastyr's blade smashed through her mother's defenses and into her head with a sickening crack. She grunted once before collapsing bonelessly backwards into the cabinets. The dagger clattered to the floor.

Unable to scream, Seldy could only watch in horror until the massive man loomed over her, cutting off the hold that the red eyes had on her tongue.

"Whhhyyyy?" she sobbed.

Klard Dastyr glowered down at her as he grabbed Chad's jacket at the collar and snatched him away from Seldy's scrambling, sobbing grip. The brute tossed her beloved's limp and bleeding form aside like he was nothing more than a doll. The man stood over her, his curved sword dripping blood from both the blade and hilt.

Seldy crab-walked backwards on hands and feet until her fingers brushed against her mother's bare leg. Both her coordination and concentration failed. She collapsed against her mother.

The second, thinner figure remained in the doorway — a chill, stark form that sent a shudder through Seldy's entire being. A loose cough wracked his hunched shoulders. He leered at her with eyes that no longer glowed.

Kneeling beside her, the bigger man grabbed the front of Seldy's nightdress with his empty hand and yanked her up into a seated position with very little effort. The worn silk of the thin gown ripped under his rough handling. He drew her close enough to smell the wine on his breath.

"Quiet now, girl. They both yet live but if you scream again, I'll make sure neither of them ever draws breath again. Their lives depend on you." He shook her. "Do you understand me?"

All Seldy could do was whimper in reply.

The man shook her again, tearing the collar of her dress even further. "Do you understand?"

"Y-y-yes," she squeaked.

"Good. Now, I'm gonna set you down and take care of a couple of things. Don't you move and don't you dare scream, girl, or you'll doom both of them."

When he released her, she scrambled back to curl up beside Jhana. She slid trembling fingers through Jhana's blood-matter dark hair to feel how bad the damage was. She bit her lip to keep from crying out in dismay at finding the thick knot on her mother's skull.

The grim-faced man wiped the blade of his sword ruthlessly

on Chad's tunic and sheathed it. He tore down a towel and calmly ripped it into several strips, staring down at her all the while.

"Come away now, girl." He held out his hand to her. "Come away quietly and no one else has to get hurt."

"N-n-no!" She clutched to her mother's unconscious form, her hands wet and sticky with blood. "No, pl-pl-please, no!"

The man grabbed her torn and bloody nightgown again with one hand and smashed his fist into the side of her face with the other.

There was an explosion of pain. Darkness descended.

It's time to wake up, rehla...

Seldy groaned. Her head hurt. A lot. She tried to open her eyes but only one of them obeyed, and the blurry images she saw didn't make any sense. The floor of the *vardo* was far below her. And it was moving. Her mind reeled.

Her legs were unnaturally stiff; tied together at the ankles, she realized. Her arms were twisted painfully behind her back, bound at the wrists. Something was stuffed into her mouth. She tasted cloth. Her tongue was dry.

What's happening?

She saw her mother, bound and gagged as well, lying on the floor. That was followed by a glimpse of Chad sprawled out on his face, bleeding and broken, the fletching of an arrow sticking out of his back.

It all came crashing back to her. She was being carried from the *vardo* and into the storm.

The Enemy comes for you, child... Tiagra's voice rasped in her mind. *A foe like no other.*

Her head throbbed. Tears blurred her one good eye. Her stomach churned, threatening to empty itself, even though the gag made that impossible.

I have to be strong, she thought to herself. *Both for Ma and Chad.*

Her captor moved out into the storm, bounding down the steps of the *vardo.* Hearing the sounds of both men and animals — horses, she realized — Seldy felt a flash of hope, thinking perhaps the *Baro* or some of the other men had come to her rescue.

"Bring me Bulger, blast it!" Dastyr's harsh voice boomed out from beneath her, cutting through the sounds of the storm and reverberating throughout her body. "We need to get out of here before anyone else comes!"

"Aye, sir! Here he is!"

Seldy chanced opening her good eye just a sliver. All she saw, however, was a moving slice of snow-covered ground, big hooves, and the back of her captor's boots and trousers as he carried her towards an unseen destination.

Desperate, she focused her thoughts and reached out to the minds of the horses nearby.

::Hoof-brothers and hoof-sisters, please help me! I am being taken from my home by these men! They've hurt me and my family!::

The only response was a sense of surprise among the horses. She didn't recognize any of their minds.

A timid, halting response came from a nearby gelding.

::Who...who are you?::

There was a nervousness, a skittishness, coming from the mind of the horse that replied. They were unhappy to be out in this storm and quite nervous.

::My name is Seldy! This circus is my home, and I am being taken by these bad men! Can you please help me?::

She sent a series of vibrant images of the circus, especially of the animals that she loved — Bessie and the many dogs and horses of the circus that she worked with. She was careful to avoid showing the tigers, knowing from experience how skittish horses could be about such dangerous predators.

Before the gelding could respond, a strong, aggressive, and unmistakably male presence intruded.

::*Ignore her! She is a captive.*::

A stallion, the strongest of the six horse-minds she felt nearby, responded with more force than she was accustomed to.

::*There is no help for you among us.*::

Seldy wanted to plead her case, but her concentration was broken from the jarring motion of being lifted from her captor's shoulder and thrown roughly over the hard saddle horn of the very same creature who was refusing to help. The wind was knocked out of her lungs. Her already throbbing head knocked against something hard. She lost the focus needed to project her thoughts.

A heavy hand held her in place as someone swung up into the saddle behind her. Pinned down between the unyielding saddle and the relentless pressure of the hand on her back, it was all she could do to stay conscious and present.

Fighting through the pain and a growing sense of panic, Seldy gathered her thoughts and redoubled her efforts with the horses. She included images of both tigers in her projections.

::*If you don't help me now, you will be in great danger! I will call on my other animal friends to help and when they come, it will be very dangerous for you all! I don't want to see any of you get hurt!*::

::*We fear no beasts of prey!*:: The stallion retorted. ::*Neither wolf nor great cat nor even scaled serpents! We will trample any who try to help you beneath our mighty hooves!*::

Reeling from the flood of graphic images of violence that the great stallion sent in reply, Seldy gave up.

"Alright, let's get out of here! It'll be a hard, cold, and wet ride back to the ship." her captor called out again. "Keep your weapons loose and ready! Cut down anyone who tries to stop us! Don't let anyone stand in our way, boys!"

Seldy's heart fluttered at those words. A cold pit of dread formed in her gut. But she didn't let it control her. Instead, just as *Maestro* Taryk and her mother had taught her, she channeled that fear into renewed strength and a determination to help herself as she explored the knots binding her wrists.

Remember, rehla, her mother's admonishment all of those years ago rang loud and clear in her memory, *if you wish to perform on the high-wire with the others, you have to learn to tie and untie all of your own knots.*

All of those countless hours of practice under *Maestro* Taryk's stern but patient tutelage came rushing back.

She used the horse's rough, sloppy stride to cover the small movements of her dexterous fingers as she began working at the knots. Seldy was stronger and far more flexible than her captor had assumed. Thanks to the *Maestro's* tutelage, she understood the weaknesses in the knots that bound her.

While she continued to work the knot, Seldy reached out to the only friend who could possibly hear her and find help.

::*Bessie! Help! I'm being taken by some bad men riding on horses! Jhana-ma and Chad are hurt! Please hear me!*::

Silence.

Hot tears burned down her cheeks. Seldy felt helpless and alone, unable to stop what was happening to her and unable to help either Chad or her mother. Everyone and everything that she had ever loved was being taken from her.

Then, despite the rushing winds, the pelting rain, and the pounding hooves, she heard it — the distant, yet unmistakable, trumpeting of an enraged elephant.

CHAPTER 11

Mouse

Heya, Mouse. Where ya been?" Telly jeered. "Dippin' yer wick with dem dock whores while all us real sailors were bustin' our humps?"

Mouse's cheeks flushed red.

"Aw, Telly. Lookit! Ye've embarsed da poor boy!" Jigger's voice cut through the laughter, only to spark a louder round. When it, too, died down, the thin man called out in a more serious tone, "Where *have* ye been to, Mouse?"

"Yeah, boy! Where have you been?"

All eyes turned towards Mouse, even the small beady eyes of Cook, the largest man in the room.

"You better not have raided my larder again to feed them beasts of yours, or you'll be lucky to only have the Serpent's Tongue feasting on you."

Mouse looked up sheepishly, opening his mouth to answer, but Dalton interjected.

"Leave the boy alone, laddies." The tall, broad-shouldered sailor commanded respect with both his voice and his bearing. "It's him who got the ale yer drinkin' before the storm set in.

Then he had orders from the Cap'n hisself." He silenced the dozen or so other hard men in the room with a challenging gaze before turning back to Mouse. "Are yer tasks done?"

"Yes, sir." Nodding, Mouse offered a nervous smile to the gruff man.

"Ha!" Telly gave a shout and punched Dalton in the shoulder. "You hears dat, boys? Ol' Dalt here's done ben promoted!"

The room erupted in fresh laughter as sailor after sailor called out variations of Mouse's answer.

"Yessir!"

"Yes, sirree!"

"Aye aye, Cap'n Dalt!"

"Yes, Master Dalton!"

Dalton remained quiet, letting the ribbing roll off his thick shoulders. When the noise died down again, he nodded and pointed at the familiar barrel set up on a table in the far corner of the room.

"Get somethin' to wet yer whistle, son, and relax a bit."

Shuffling over towards the keg, Mouse was glad when the attention of the others shifted onto other things. The Mess was one of the largest rooms in the ship, easily big enough to accommodate the entire crew of thirty-odd enlisted sailors — not that such a thing ever happened while the ship was sailing.

The captain and a few select others — Valk, the navigator, his apprentice Trevend, Haddock the first mate, and the rest of the professional bounty hunting crew — took their meals in the smaller, but more refined, State Room near the back of the ship, one deck above.

By comparison to the fine, polished wood of the State Room's table and high-backed chairs, the long wooden benches and tables of the Mess were crude and uncomfortable. The tattered curtains that normally hung loose and ill-fitting over the two man-sized portholes were tied back, revealing the raw fury of the storm raging outside. Rain and sleet washed against the windows, illuminated ever so often by spectacular flashes of lightning. The majority of the light in the dim hall came from the flickering flames of oil lamps that hung over each of the four large tables.

Nearly half of the crew was seated around one of those tables, either playing the card game that had recaptured their attention or watching and making fun of those who were playing. Dalton and Telly sat next to each other, their backs to Mouse, each of them guarding his cards from the leering eyes of the other. Cook sat across from them, his huge girth and nasty disposition making it impossible for anyone to sit next to him. The obese man glowered at everyone suspiciously, his heavy jowls rolling and bouncing as the ship was rocked by the buffeting winds of the storm.

Mouse was surprised to see Trevend, the young navigator's apprentice, leaning against the wall near the keg. While the young man was the only other person within five years of his own age aboard the ship, the two of them had nothing else in common. As an apprentice in one of the most powerful guilds in the Guild Alliance, Trevend was on track to become an important and well-respected member of Ventraxian society. The young navigator-in-training was dressed for the part. His freshly shined black leather boots gleamed while his white, cotton trousers and ruffled, white silk shirt were pressed and pristine, unstained by the sweat of any of the labor that kept the *Ghost* in flying shape. His short, black hair had been slicked back into place, and his face — like his manicured fingernails — was freshly scrubbed and clean.

True to his training and station in life, Trevend didn't acknowledge Mouse's presence as he approached the keg and filled one of the tin mugs sitting next to it. Instead, the young navigator regarded the boisterous antics of the rough crew with a look of sheer disdain, which marred his otherwise unblemished face.

Taking a sip of the bitter ale, Mouse ambled back towards the rough and tumble sailors gathered around the table. Hailing from the poor working classes of the many disparate islands of the Midtere and Untere that made up the Guild Alliance, their accents and appearances were as mismatched and worn as their clothes. Most of them were barefoot, just like he was. They all sported at least one tattoo, but most had several. A few, like Dalton, maintained long, scraggly beards while shaving their heads bald. Both Telly and Jigger had multiple piercings in their ears and noses, but they weren't alone in that. Some even pierced their cheeks with rings of silver or gold.

It seemed that each of the sailors strove to look different from each other; yet, in the aggregate, they all ended up looking similarly outlandish and rough. Without exception, they were larger and stronger than he was, their muscles honed by years of hoisting sails and working the lines on ships like the *Hunter's Ghost*. Uniformly, they had the heavy callouses, strong hands, and thick fingers of those who made their living working with their hands.

Approaching Dalton and Telly from behind, Mouse saw the cards in Dalton's hand. He didn't know enough about the game of Shipmates to know whether it was a strong hand or not, but if the satisfaction evident in Dalton's personal song was any indication, it was.

Shipmates began with one person dealing out a card to each of the players, who then made bets, trying to drive the other players to place more coin into the community pot. Each player tried to build a winning hand of cards that would win the combined totals of all of their bets. He had seen it played often enough to know that the best players won as much or more by bluffing the others than by how good their cards really were. In the middle of the table stood a small pile of coins consisting of more than two dozen pents and a few quads — enough to make a respectable haul for whoever won it.

Cook had the deck of remaining cards in his pudgy hands, his thick fingers poised on the top card as he regarded Telly with a baleful glare.

Telly ignored Cook's gaze as he added the finishing touches to one of his infamous stories.

"...so dere I was, runnin' wit my trousers 'round my ankles, my wee-Willie swingin' in da breeze, fleein' fer my life as I tried to escape dat damn doxie's husband! If'n t'weren't such a gods-be-damned big-arsed blade, I'da turnt 'round and shown 'im a good whatfor wit me fists..."

"We've all heard dis story before, Telly," Dalton's thick voice cut through the smaller man's story. "Yer always gettin' in trouble by beddin' some married woman. So ya bettin' or what?"

"Yeah, it'll be two pents each for you prigs to see what I'm packin.'" He emphasized his words by grabbing his crotch with his empty hand.

Taking another sip from his ale, Mouse let the rhythms of the crew's banter wash over him. He tuned out the details of the bidding and the half-serious jibes being thrown around. Having grown up in the Slant, the rough and chopped language spoken by the crew of the *Ghost* was easy to understand. The Slanter's Cant he grew up with was very similar to the version of pidgin Trade the crew used amongst themselves.

Slipping deeper into his reverie, Mouse kept listening as hands were played and pots were won and lost, losing track of time. He didn't care who won or who didn't; instead, he was fascinated with the interplay between the invisible songs that each man possessed and the outward bursts of guffawing laughter and cutting insults at one another's expense. The incredible and complex symphony of sound washed over him describing each man and the role he played within the crew and, in some way Mouse was still trying to grasp, the larger world. It seemed impossible that this was something that only he could hear and appreciate.

"Mouse!"

Dalton's voice snapped him out of his reverie. He blinked, trying to focus his eyes. He hadn't noticed that everyone was looking at him.

"Yeah?"

"Are ya gonna play for us or not?"

"Sure." His right hand was already reaching into his jacket for the flute. "What do you want to hear?"

"First," Cook snapped, irritated. "Let's hear if'n you're any blasted good. 'Cause I don't want to be bothered if'n you suck."

The corpulent man glared at Mouse as if he doubted that there was anything good or decent about him.

"Mebbe it'd be best if he sucks," Telly smirked. "He is pla-yin' a flute aft'all! The only flute I like being played is hangin' betwe-"

"Enough!" Dalton's one word command silenced the snickers. "Go ahead, son. I'm curious to see how ya sound."

"It'll be a minute before I can play a real song; I need to loosen up."

Mouse ignored the derisive laughs coming from Telly and Cook's snort of disgust. Staring at the instrument, his fingers naturally settled into place around the holes as he brought it to his lips.

Pushing everything else aside, Mouse closed his eyes and focused on getting familiar with the flute. He ran the instrument through the scales his mother had taught him. After the third time through, he opened his eyes. Everyone in the room was looking at him with wide eyes.

"What? Am I that bad? It's been a whi-"

"No, son," Dalton cut him off. "Yer a good sight better'n we've heard in quite some time." He nodded and waved. "Go ahead and play us a real song now."

Several other men nodded, adding encouraging words of their own.

"Yeah!"

"Play it, son!"

"Just wait til Chard and Pedar hear 'im!"

Cook's beady eyes narrowed further as if he were trying to figure out how Mouse would be using this success to get out of doing real work, while Telly's expression became thoughtful.

Mouse brought the instrument back to his lips and began playing one of the first songs he had ever learned, one that could be heard coming from just about every inn and tavern at some point in the evening: "The Maiden's Dance." It was a fast-paced, lively piece that usually lifted people's spirits and got them moving.

Becoming lost in the joy of making music again, Mouse only peripherally heard the clapping and stomping of the men as they were swept up in the infectious beat of the song. He found himself moving about the room, tapping his toes, and swaying in time to the rhythms of the song. Since it was a short one, Mouse restarted it at the beginning. The third time through, he ended with a flourish and came to a full stop.

The room erupted in applause the moment his song ended. Big hands clapped him on the back. Men crowded around, calling out their favorite tunes.

"Heya, Mouse! D'ye know 'The Merry Widow?'"

"How 'bout 'The Sailor's Lament?'"

"I want t'hear 'Three Mugs and a Keg!'"

Dalton saved him, stepping in with his massive bulk and shielding Mouse from the crush of his admirers.

"Enough, lads! Give 'im some air!"

Beaming, Mouse didn't want the moment to end. For the first time in the six months since he had been discovered as a stowaway, he had at last found a small measure of acceptance amongst these hard men. Even Cook's distrust had visibly eased.

Grinning from ear to ear, Mouse held up a hand.

"I've got a great song for you guys! It's my favorite." He paused, licking his lips as he looked about. "I'm not sure how popular it is, but it is the best song I know. It's called 'The Nobleman's Fall.'"

An expectant hush fell over the mess. Men shifted and settled back into their chairs. Their card game — and the pile of coins in the center of the table — was, for the moment, forgotten.

Thinking of his mother and how much she loved this song, Mouse brought the flute to his lips, closed his eyes, and began to play.

It didn't take long to become lost in the varying rhythms and complex note sequences of the song. He no longer heard the crew clapping and stomping along with his music. Keeping his eyes closed, he focused on hitting the right notes.

This song, more than any other, reminded Mouse of his mother and how much she liked to watch and listen to him play the *f'leyn*. She had taught him many others, but this was the song that she held out to him as a reward for practicing hard and learning his notes and scales. Within a year of his first touching the instrument, he had mastered the song, despite the complex sequences and fast pace in key parts.

By the time he turned nine, Blind Meg would let him play as long as he liked in her slop shop, letting him keep whatever meager tips the wretchedly poor folk of the Slant could offer up in appreciation. In less than a year and half, he had gone from being a complete novice to someone who could play the instrument for hours on end. With his *f'leyn* in hand, Mouse never lacked confidence. No one bothered or harassed him, and everyone who heard him play spoke about what a bright future he had.

While the flute's music was nowhere near as good as that of the *f'leyn*, Mouse felt whole again for the first time in years.

"Watch out, Mouse!"

Dalton's thick, insistent voice cut through the notes of his song but before he could find a place to stop, someone hit him — hard.

"Blasted stowaway!"

A second blow to the side of the head knocked him to the floor. Stars splashed across Mouse's vision.

"Blazing traitor!"

The flute tumbled from his fingers and clattered to the floor beside him.

"Traitorous Slanter's git!"

Stunned, Mouse watched helplessly as a dirty foot kicked the flute. It rolled away from him, deeper into the tangle of bare feet and worn boots.

He reached out for the precious instrument, but someone kicked his arm roughly aside. A second kick knocked the wind out of him. He coughed, gasping for air.

"Let him be!" Dalton thundered. "Ya rotten bastards!"

Men shouted and struggled above him. They cursed, pushed, and shoved at each other. Punches landed with meaty thuds amidst muttered curses. Through it all, Mouse's blurry eyes remained focused on the flute. It was an instant away from being crushed, and with it all of his dreams of making a life for himself as far away from this ship and the Slant as he could get.

Curled up into a ball, Mouse tried to stem the tears that threatened to spill out. Big hands grabbed the lapels of his jacket and hauled him roughly to unsteady feet.

"Mouse!"

Blinking through the tears, Dalton's battered and bloody face swam into view. The big man shook him.

"Pull yerself together and git outta here! Now, blast ya!"

Dalton pushed him away just as something crashed into the big man's back. The sailor ignored the blow long enough to wave at Mouse and shout, "Go!" before falling to his knees in obvious pain.

Mouse stumbled out of the Mess and into the hallway. When he glanced back at the cursing, struggling mass of drunken men, he wasn't looking at Dalton or Cook or Telly, but on the floor beneath them all, straining to catch a glimpse of his flute.

Unable to see it, however, Mouse did what he always did when things got violent.

He fled.

CHAPTER 12

Seldy

The stallion thundered to a stop. Tendrils of pain jolted through Seldy's already aching skull. She tried not to flinch when her captor bellowed.

"Blast it! Chard, Jansen! Get down there and see if that blazing tree can be moved!"

Other voices, equally harsh, answered as the stallion danced sideways on nervous hooves.

"Aye, Cap'n!"

"Yes, sir!"

"Whoah, Bulger. Easy does it!"

Her head covered by a sodden blanket, Seldy could only listen. The shrieking wind and pelting sleet made it difficult, but there were still clues as to where she might be. Branches creaked and clattered with each gust of wind. Horses stamped in the mud, nickering with impatience. Rain pelted down onto a carpet of crackling leaves.

Her hands were free. She had worked the last knot loose just before the stallion jerked to a stop. Her fingers tingled as blood flooded into them.

It was a struggle to stay still and keep quiet.

::*We are here, Cubling.*::

::*I see you, Seldy!*::

::*Layra-ma! Amara-ma!*::

She fought the urge to jump for joy at feeling the familiar touch of her tiger's minds.

::*Oh thank goodness! Where's Bessie?*::

::*She comes,*:: Layra responded. ::*But she is large and slow and very not-fast; she must clear her own way through the trees.*::

::*Seldy.*:: Amara sounded concerned. ::*Why are you with these men and not warm and dry in your wooden cave?*::

Her captor shouted something, but Seldy ignored him. She responded to her tigers with a series of images, showing them what had happened. Once the last images were sent, she added,

::*I have freed my hands and can probably get away if I try, but my legs are still bound. I won't be able to run yet; I will need a moment or two to loosen that knot.*::

::*The only way we can help you, Cubling,*:: Layra replied, her mind-voice solemn, ::*is to shed the blood of these manlings. But we don't want to break our promises.*::

::*These men are not of the* kumpania,:: Seldy replied, her stomach churning at what she was about to say. ::*They attacked us and hurt both Jhana-ma and Chad. You will not be breaking any promises.*::

::*We will taste the meat of these bull-men this night, Seldy.*::

Amara's anger was mixed with a fierce hunger. Seldy's stomach lurched.

::*We will distract them, Cubling! Seek your escape when the confusion begins!*::

Simultaneous images of what each of the tigers saw flashed into her mind. Disoriented, Seldy struggled to make sense of seeing the same scene from two different perspectives. Layra was stalking them from behind, moving stealthily towards the last rider in the group. Amara, however, was hidden in the needles of the fallen evergreen tree that blocked the road.

The power of the raw emotions bubbling through her shared links with the tigers gave Seldy pause. Amara's adrenaline surged as the tigress leapt from the fallen tree and shredded a dismounted man who never saw her with both tooth and claw. The flavor of warm, coppery blood invaded Seldy's taste buds.

Layra's muscles were bunched with anxious energy as she approached from behind. She gathered herself for a leap at the rearmost rider.

The scream of Amara's first victim faded into a gurgle as he died. Other men, including her captor, shouted in surprise.

The stallion jerked to the side, his massive hooves splashing in the mud. Seldy was ready for the moment when the man holding her down removed his hand.

She flung her arms wide, casting aside the sodden blanket. Calling upon years of acrobatic training, she kicked her feet back, tucked her chin to her chest, and bucked forward to tumble, head-first, towards the muddy ground.

Bracing for impact, Seldy pulled her arms in to her body as she fell, tucking her chin to her chest. And just as she had practiced hundreds of times before, she rolled onto her back in the icy mud, slapping both hands into the churned mud to disperse her momentum.

A heady rush of strength came flooding into her tired, aching limbs. The pain in her head faded. Her connection to each of the tigers deepened and sharpened. Instantly, she sensed where each tiger was. The ground shook with each of Bessie's approaching, but still quite distant steps. The panic of the horses crashed into her mind. She shut them out.

Slipping blood- and mud-spattered hands down to the knot that bound her ankles, Seldy loosened it, kicked her feet free, and stood up. She ripped the gag from her mouth and took a deep breath. Panicked horses stamped and whinnied as they jostled into each other.

::*Bessie comes!*::

::*Thank you, Bessie!*:: Seldy's spirit soared. ::*Thank you Amara and Layra for helping!*::

A loud explosion split the air above and behind her. Whipping her head around, Seldy's gaze settled on her captor towering high above her. He was aiming a smoking pistol in Amara's direction.

::*Amara, watch out!*::

The bullet had already missed, but Amara yowled in pain when something else thudded home with tremendous force, sinking deep into the flesh behind her shoulder. She stumbled sideways, her jaws ripping the arm of a second man from his torso.

Amara's pain flashed through their shared connection. Seldy's knees buckled. She clutched at her ribcage, shooting pain radiating from the spot.

::*I am sorry, Seldy! But I can fight no longer!*::

The fletching of a crossbow quarrel stuck out of the tigress' side, a growing stain of blood surrounded the wound.

::*Oh, Amara! Get away! Be safe!*::

A white-hot rage flared up within her. The rage fed on and consumed her pain, like kindling being added to a campfire. Every jangled nerve bristled with rage.

::*We are here, sister!*:: A chorus of whispering female voices spoke to her. ::*Call upon us, and we will answer!*::

Seldy didn't recognize them or understand what the voices meant, but it didn't matter. Her mind shrank back from the raw and bloody carnage taking place as a deeper, more primal part of her roared up to fill the void. Fueled by anger and fear, it saw the world through a prism of danger/not-danger. It only cared that she and her animals were under attack, and these men were responsible.

The chaotic energies of the storm further fueled her rage. The fury of the howling winds bolstered her strength and honed her determination to help herself and her animal friends. Calling upon that rage, Seldy blasted images of wolves and tigers racing in for the kill at the big stallion that loomed over her, threatening to trample her into the mud.

The stallion, however, brushed off her attack and lurched forward, closing the distance between them.

Another man screamed in pain as Layra leapt up from behind and knocked the man who had shot Amara from his horse. The tigress followed him to the ground, ending his pain. Through their connection, Seldy again tasted the warm, coppery rush of blood as it gushed into Layra's mouth. Instead of being repelled, however, she felt a strange and terrible satisfaction when the tigress' powerful jaws severed his spine.

Her bearded captor tried to rein in his stallion as he turned in the saddle towards Layra, drawing a second pistol from his belt.

"NOOO!!!"

Darting forward, Seldy focused all of the energy surging through her body into the tips of her fingers. She touched the stallion's chest, her fingers spread in a wide arc.

Her fingertips burned into his hide with a crackling pop. The odor of scorched horse hair and burning flesh assaulted her nostrils.

The stallion's eyes bulged. He reared up in pain and shock, flailing about with his plate-sized hooves.

Surprised as much as the stallion was at the intensity of their sizzling connection, Seldy danced out of the way. Her lips twisted into a feral grin of triumph, however, when her captor tumbled from his saddle. The huge man landed in the mud with a splash. His pistol slipped from his fingers, still unfired.

Free of his rider, the stallion lurched away from her, his eyes wide and white with fear.

Seldy stood over her captor, defiant and angry. Rage churned inside of her. She stared down at him wide-eyed and wild-haired as the flimsy fabric of her torn and blood-stained nightgown fluttered about her thin body.

"You hurt my family!" She growled down at him. "I will end you!"

::*Yes, sister!*:: The chorus of feminine voices cried out. ::*End him now!*::

Deep within her psyche, however, the terrified young woman who had been snuggling with her mother and talking about her future with Chad cowered. She ached to crawl back into her mother's arms and have a good, hard cry.

Neither her primal mind nor the pulsing rage within her, however, cared about such things. The deadly energy pressed against the backs of her eyes, seeking its release. She bent down on one knee, extending her fingers towards his chest as he stared up at her.

Helpless, his deep-set eyes were wide and white with terror. His lips twitched. He tried to speak but failed.

Her fingertips still smoking, Seldy leaned in closer.

Frozen in place by the intensity of her gaze, he didn't move.

::*Seldy, watch out!*::

Seldy blinked as the elephant's thought-speech came crashing into her mind.

::*Bessie comes!*::

Bessie's warning snapped the hold her primal self had on her attention. Seldy jerked her head around to see the gaunt man with glowing red eyes looming up out of the shadows right behind her.

That stare. Those eyes.

She stood transfixed.

He reached for her.

Layra crashed into the man from the side. Both man and beast went flying.

The man snarled and spun in mid-air. A blade flashed in his hands. They tumbled to the ground in a tangle of limbs, biting, slashing, and kicking at each other in a fierce battle that should have been over before it began. No man had the strength and speed to survive an ambush from a fully grown tiger.

Seldy watched in horror, however, as the gaunt man rose up from the mud first and plunged his heavy blade into Layra's neck. A geyser of blood fountained high into the air, covering him in her gore.

Pain lanced through her neck and towards her heart, dropping Seldy to her knees. She was frozen in place as the shock overwhelmed her. Almost as quickly as it came, however, the agony was consumed by the rage erupting within her.

"NOOOOO!!!!!!" Her screech cut through the noise and furor of both storm and battle.

Surging to her feet, Seldy lifted her arms towards the sky and called out to the storm. The energy that had been coiling within her, ready to end her captor's life, leapt from her fingertips and arced upwards. At that same moment, a bolt of lightning crackled down from the clouds overhead, splitting into a dozen luminous branches. The largest of those branches met her energy and merged with it.

::YEESSSS!!!:: The chorus of countless feminine voices echoed through her mind, shouting their words in unison. ::STRIKE HIM DOWN!!!::

A brilliant green light illuminated the night with the intensity of a thousand burning suns, writhing down her upraised arms. Engulfed in the essence of the *Fae* storm, it felt like every fiber of Seldy's being, from the quivering tips of her pointed ears to the soles of her mud-caked feet, was on fire. She crackled with the combined energy of the storm and her own incandescent rage. Every strand of silver hair stood on end and sizzled.

As the power swept her away in its swirling vortex, an image flashed into Seldy's mind. A great, glowing seed covered by an unbreakable shell filled her vision — the same seed she had seen during the dream in Tia's *vardo* but much more distinct.

The outside of the shell was covered in bright green runes of a language she did not understand, strange shapes forming in the constantly shifting pattern of ridges. It pulsed with the same shade of luminescent green as the lightning, beating in time with the accelerated rate of her pounding heart.

Tha-throom.

Understanding dawned. The seed was inside of her, and it contained something profoundly sacred and unimaginably powerful. If she could only break through that shell, she would be truly complete. She would know, once and for all, who she was and where she really came from.

The image faded, however, only to be replaced by the sight of that gaunt man standing over Layra. He held a bloody blade in his hand with a look of triumph on his face. He turned to face her, his eyes blazing red.

Tha-throom.

The energy within her bucked and roiled, seeking its release. She was too small and fragile to contain it for long without being consumed. Dropping both arms towards him, she spread out her fingers.

A bolt of crackling, green-tinged energy leapt from each of her fingers. A foot away from her, the ten individual strands began to twine around each other like filaments of rope, merging into one enormous bolt that lit up the night as it leapt towards the gaunt man.

Tha-throom!

It crashed into him with a thunderous explosion of light and sound that seemed to sunder the world anew. The red glow faded from his eyes the moment before it hit him. Those dull, lifeless eyes widened in shock and horror as the bolt slammed into his chest and threw him backward as if he were no more than a discarded doll.

Seldy staggered to one knee, feeling weak and drained. Her trembling muscles felt like they did after she had performed several grueling high-wire routines in a row. But she also felt more connected to everyone and everything around her. One cherished connection, however, consumed her thoughts as the primal mind faded, its power spent.

Tha-throom.

A fading heartbeat.

Layra-ma's heartbeat.

::*Seldy*...:: Layra's mind-voice was weak. ::*You will always be my little Cubling. Be strong and fierce but remember that your greatest strength is your ability to find and give love, not your anger.*::

It took more strength than she thought she had left, but Seldy stood up and stumbled over to Layra.

"Layra-ma! No!" Seldy shouted as she buried her face in the tigress' thick, bloody fur.

::*Don't leave me!*::

She reached for the wound in Layra's neck with trembling fingers. The blood was no longer spurting, only oozing. The tigress' heartbeat continued to fade.

Tha...throom.

Desperate to find a way to help her, Seldy tried to call on the same energy that she had used to blast the man with the glowing eyes, but nothing came. Instead, deep in the recesses of her mind, she heard a vaguely familiar strain of sweet, yet powerful song.

Music! Why?

The notes reminded her of that special song, the one that Tegger said that her mother sang to her before she was born. Long ago, it had infused her dreams as a small child but had since receded to only faint echoes that were quickly forgotten again when she awoke.

Sensing power in that song, Seldy tried to pull it closer, to hear and understand it fully again. But the harder she tried to listen, the more distant it became.

::Remember...to...love...Cubling.::

Tha...throom.

Everything became still and silent. The winds calmed. The driving sleet stopped falling. The light in Layra's eyes fell dark as she exhaled her last breath. Seldy hugged the neck of the great tigress with all of her remaining strength.

The moment of silent stillness grew into a yawning gulf of emptiness that threatened to extinguish love from her heart much like the rage had consumed her pain. Without looking up from her beloved tiger-ma, she felt the presence of others all around her — from Bessie lumbering towards them to the pack of skittish horses and the surviving wounded and stunned men who had attacked her and her family. But, for the first time in her conscious life, she could only feel the thoughts of one tiger nearby.

The silence was too much. A single keening note welled up from the very depths of her being and expanded until she could no longer hold it in, even if she had wanted to. The sobbing wail that escaped her lips was laden with all of the grief and loss she felt.

Other voices joined with hers. Amara's terrifying yowl split the night air, while Bessie's trills rumbled so low that she felt it in her bones. Even the elusive and mysterious chorus of whispering voices joined in the mourning.

Seldy was so lost in grief that she didn't care when her

would-be captor approached her from behind. Something slapped against her shoulder, something metallic and alien and evil.

Indescribable pain erupted throughout her body, more pain than she had ever felt in the entirety of her life was concentrated in that one horrible instant before she was plunged into a deep, dark, frigid void where there was nothing.

No connection.

No warmth.

No love.

CHAPTER 13

Mouse

Mouse tumbled head over heels towards the distant ground, thousands of feet below. The rushing air pushed into his open mouth and filled his lungs, making it impossible to exhale. But instead of looking at the ground or worrying about the proximity of the jagged rocks zipping past, Mouse searched for the tiny glimmer of hope that he had spotted from above.

There!

A small tree, no more than a sapling, stuck out from the dull grey stone and brown mud that dominated his view — a welcome speck of green life bursting from the cliff-face of the Edge.

Twisting himself around, Mouse made a desperate grab for the tree. He clutched at the springy trunk of the sapling the moment his fingers brushed against it. The willowy little tree bent over double but, luckily, it held long enough to swing his downward momentum sideways into the face of the cliff.

There was a flash of pain as a bone inside of a finger snapped.

Stars danced in front of his eyes; tiny motes of brightly colored lights buzzed past his face.

Swallowing the shriek of agony that tried to escape his lips,

Mouse managed to keep both hands on the trunk of the sapling. His shoulders throbbed; his arms had nearly been wrenched from their sockets in the effort of stopping his fall. What little breath remained in his body had been blasted from his lungs by the jarring impact with the stones and packed dirt of the cliff-face. Yet, improbably, he held on, and so too did the sapling. Blinking away the tears, Mouse wished that those strange little lights would go away, but they persisted, flitting about the corners of his vision and buzzing in his ears.

No, they're singing!

Their sweet and simple song was so quiet that he could barely hear it above the punishing wind and the pounding of his own heart. The faint music spoke briefly to him of forgotten songs, hidden seeds, and the need for a beacon of truth and light to shine forth against a looming darkness.

A strong earthy smell filled his nostrils. Clumps of soil and small rocks loosened by his impact crumbled and tumbled down the face of the cliff.

"By the Fires Below!" he gasped.

A few leaves — loosened by his hands slipping down the trunk — danced and fluttered with the glowing lights in the surging updraft. The sapling shuddered, forcing him to focus on his own survival.

"Thank you for saving me, little tree."

The sapling shuddered, its ruined trunk cracking under his weight. He slid a few inches down the side of the cliff. Scrambling, Mouse probed the surface behind him with his feet. Finding a tiny ledge, he wedged his left heel into a small crevice and straightened up. That took some of the pressure off both the damaged sapling and his aching shoulders.

It was only a momentary respite, however. Shutting out the throbbing pain in his broken pinky finger and the agony of what were likely torn muscles in his shoulders, Mouse craned his neck around from side to side, trying to judge which side offered the best prospects for handholds so that he might eventually climb back up to the Edge.

A surge in the updraft sent a fine, but pungent, mist into his face when he turned to the left. He closed his mouth and eyes against the rank odor of human waste wafting in the mist. It was the discharge from the sludge-stream flowing off of the cliff above.

The sapling shuddered again.

This thing isn't going to hold me for much longer.

Turning back to the right, he scanned the cliff with a growing desperation.

A half dozen feet to his right and a few feet below, he spotted a ledge that stuck out sufficiently from the cliff around it. A deep shadow hinted at an indentation just above it. It was illuminated by a contingent of the strange, singing lights that were now dancing over there instead of around his head.

If only I could reach that...maybe that's an entrance to one of the smugglers' tunnels Lefty was always talking about...

But before he could gauge the distance, the narrow crevice he was lodged in gave way. Slipping free of what little support he had, all of his weight dragged on the failing tree.

Roots tore loose. His fingers slipped down another few inches. His heart thudded in his throat. He started to sway in the constant wind. More leaves fluttered away as his sweaty hands slipped, and he slid a little further down and closer to his doom.

"By the Blazing Fires, I'm not going to die!"

There was little hope, however, that the sapling, or his aching hands, would last much longer. Kicking hard with his left heel against the slick, muddy surface of the cliff-face, Mouse pushed himself to the right and into the swirling winds. The sapling creaked and cracked but held as he swung to the right and then back again.

"Come on! Just a little bit more!"

He kicked out his heel again, harder this time, pushing himself and the sapling with all of the strength he could muster. His momentum gave him a little extra distance. He twisted his body further to the right so that he was closer to facing the cliff.

Now!

Releasing the sapling just as it tore loose from the rocky soils of the wall, he dove towards the ledge.

For the second time in just a few minutes, Mouse felt the rush of air on his face. He turned as he fell, reaching once again for salvation in the face of near certain doom.

Jolting awake, Mouse smacked his forehead into a low-hanging beam that shouldn't have been there.

"Ow!"

Groaning, he fell back down into a nest of coiled rope and spare tarpaulins. Rubbing the newest sore spot on his already battered body, Mouse took a moment to get oriented. The space he was in was dark and cramped, with only a sliver of light filtering in through the covered porthole to his left. The room had the all-too-familiar smell of musty canvas and hemp.

"Wha...why am I here again?"

The pain and confusion of last night's chaotic conclusion came rushing back with all of the force of the sucker punch that had knocked him down last night.

"Oh! The fight...my flute!"

Desperate fingers searched the pockets of his jacket and his immediate surroundings as his heart leapt into his throat.

"Shards! It's gone!"

Mouse gasped. His head throbbed, both from the fresh knot on his forehead and from last night's blow to his eye. The scabs on his back had torn loose again. The fresh, stinging pain of each wound reminding him of all of his failures.

But there was an even deeper pain — something that hurt far more than any mere physical pain — that added fuel and urgency to his self-recriminations. He had tasted music again. After seven long and hard years without having an instrument to play, he had been reminded of his deep and abiding love — no, his need — for making music. With that flute in his hands, he had been alive again for the first time since his mother had died. And now it was gone, likely smashed to bits in the struggle that had sent him fleeing back to the secret hiding place he had survived in for weeks after sneaking aboard the *Ghost*.

Mouse set his teeth and clenched his hands into tight fists. Pain — whether it came from the aches and bruises of his body or the sorrow in his heart — was a familiar foe. Pain meant that he was still alive. It was proof that he hadn't given up.

Not yet, anyway. He sighed.

Steeling himself for the agony that would follow, Mouse clambered carefully out of his sleeping nest and stood up. Looking around in the dim, filtered light of the tiny hold, he wondered if it wouldn't have been better to have remained in hiding all of those months ago.

I could've slipped off of the ship at the first port of call, and none of them would've ever known I had been here.

That had been a terrible, lonely time — endless days and nights of silence filled with dread at the possibility of getting caught for something as innocuous as going to relieve himself, let alone when he stole into the galley to find some crumbs of food. It was only after observing the captain for several days — and sensing the soft spot in his otherwise aggressive and dominant song — that Mouse decided to take a chance and reveal himself.

There were so many stories in the Slant of the terrible things that happened to stowaways on ships. They almost always ended in some form of gruesome death, whether it was being thrown from the deck of the ship to fall to their death in the Untere or getting crucified high up on one of the masts.

Shaking such thoughts from his head, Mouse let himself out of the cramped space. He had been taken before the captain to answer for his crimes and had been offered the choice of working off his debts by serving as a cabin boy or by being sold off to fight for his life in the gladiator arenas.

That was the easiest choice I've ever made.

Life aboard the *Hunter's Ghost* wasn't all that different from his time with the Alley Rats, except he ate better, and it was easier to keep clean. But just like in the gang, he was the lowest ranking member of the crew, and he was given all of the dirty and thankless jobs that no one else wanted to do.

Padding down the narrow hallway of the lowest deck, Mouse noted how quiet the ship seemed. None of the rest of the crew were up yet, except perhaps Cook.

Climbing the steep stairs, Mouse paused at the landing with the closed hatch that led to the second deck.

I wonder if my flute is still in the Mess? He shook his head and continued climbing. *It's not worth the risk of getting caught by Cook; he'll just think I'm coming to steal more of his food.*

He paused again at the top of the stairs, listening for any activity beyond the door.

Except for a gentle patter of raindrops, all seemed quiet. A soft, pale light leaked through the gap between the warped door and the frame. He pulled it open and stepped out into the grey light of dawn and a light rain.

Even after six months on the ship, he was still impressed by both the size and complexity of the *Ghost*. Topside was broken into three distinct decks, each one representing a distinct area of responsibility. The mid-deck was the lowest and largest of the three and was where the majority of the work took place, especially while the ship was in port. The massive mainmast rose from the center of the deck to a towering height above. It was easily the tallest and thickest of the three vertical masts. The fore and aft decks each had their own shorter and thinner masts, while the wing masts — which extended out from the sides of the ship when it was flying — were maybe as long as those but were even thinner.

Mouse pondered the confusing array of ropes and pulleys above him that were used to deploy and control the two huge sails that were currently furled up beneath the two crossbeams called "Yards." The closest yard was half-way up the mast, while the smaller one was near the top, just beneath the small basket at the very top.

He shuddered at the thought of climbing into the crow's nest. It was a duty generally given to the most junior members of the crew, especially those who were agile and limber like he was, but Haddock had made it very clear that he didn't trust him for that essential duty. Jigger and Sadro, who usually pulled that duty, grumbled that he should have to learn the hard way. The first mate, however, held firm.

His eyes were drawn towards the smaller aft-mast. It's single yard was high up, and the mass of cordage — the ropes and cords of the rigging — hung down loosely from it, likely having come loose during the storm. His eyes trailed down the smaller mast until they reached the hand-holds that were all too familiar.

The whipping post.

Three times. He couldn't help hissing through clenched teeth. Three times in six months. *I wonder how much of my blood is stained into those boards?* His back muscles twitched, adding fresh pain to the agonizing memories of being whipped by Haddock. Wave after wave of indelible pain washed over him. His breath caught in his chest. His fingers balled up into tight fists.

You've been whipped. Tra'al's gravelly voice echoed in his mind. *That's against the law of the Guild Alliance.*

Fat lot of good that does me.

Mouse swallowed the lump in his throat.

But it's not going to happen again.

The sense of grim determination settling over him surprised Mouse. He forced his fingers to unclench and took in a deep and calming breath.

I'm going to get my flute back and get off of this blasted ship, one way or another.

"Boy!" The captain's voice bellowed out from the docks nearby. "Ring that blazing bell. Roust those lazy layabouts from their beds and extend the gangplank! Blast it all!"

His head snapped around. The captain, Haddock, and Valk were all dockside, waiting to board the ship.

Captain Dastyr's best cloak was ripped and caked in mud. His bushy beard was plastered against his raw face and streaked with dirt and with blood. His weapons — the two pistols that were always stuck through his belt and the two blades he was constantly honing — were all caked in mud. Several buttons were missing from his jacket. Mouse had never seen the man look so disheveled and out of sorts.

As bad as the captain looked, however, his brother was even worse. The strange man was leaning heavily against the captain, unable to support himself. His weird eyes were glazed over, and his head lolled on his shoulders. His cloak and tunic had been shredded. He was coated with even more mud and blood than the captain and was visibly wounded, perhaps even mortally so, from long lines of deep claw marks scoring the left side of his face to matching gashes across his chest and abdomen. Valk's left arm dangled motionless from his shoulder; his right arm was draped over his older brother's shoulders and held in place by the captain's firm grip.

Mouse's eyes shot over towards Haddock, who looked good compared to the others. His cloak was clearly wet, but there were only spatters of blood and mud visible. A small form was draped over the man's shoulder; a pair of dirty feet dangled out of the blanket that was wrapped around the figure.

"Shards, boy!" Haddock barked at him. "Don't just stand there looking dumb! You best jump when the Cap'n gives you a blasted order! Now hurry the blazes up!"

Scurrying across the mid-deck, Mouse grabbed the rope to the brass bell hanging between the main-mast and the aft-deck and yanked on it repeatedly. The bell swayed wildly as its brash song disrupted the sleepy morning. He sounded it four times — the "All-Hands-on-Deck" command.

Dropping the rope, he rushed over to the port side of the ship and shoved the gangplank out through the slot in the railing until the weight of it tilted it down to the dock, several feet below. He locked it into place, opened the gate, and stepped aside.

Haddock bounded up the plank carrying the rolled-up form over his shoulder, using long strides that spoke of years of practice and no concern for the possibility of slipping. Once he reached the top, he smacked Mouse hard across the face with the back of his free hand.

Mouse yelped, more out of surprise than from the fresh pain spreading across his face.

"Next time, boy," the deeply sun-tanned man hissed, "you'd best not make either of us repeat ourselves!"

Mouse stood back up, wiping the trickle of blood from his mouth with a sleeve. He composed himself so as to not look defiant.

"Enough, Haddock," Captain Dastyr said in a tired, but almost kind tone. "We need him."

The heavyset man staggered up the gangplank, cradling his unconscious brother in his arms like a baby.

"At your service, Captain," Mouse said, ignoring Haddock's evil glare.

He swallowed hard at the overpowering odor of burned flesh and charred clothing. His eyes widened.

"Did you get that cell ready?"

The captain stared down at Mouse with keen intensity, his brother still cradled in his arms.

"Yes, sir!" He straightened up and saluted smartly. "It's clean and ready for the prisoner."

"Good." Was that relief in his voice? "Go get Bulger from the hitching post down on the docks and load him up. We will be leaving this shitehole of an island as soon as he is secure. Then, come see me in my cabin. I've got some instructions for you on how to care for this new prisoner." The captain glanced only briefly at the bundled-up form slung across Haddock's shoulder. "Do you understand?"

"Yes, sir."

His gaze followed the direction of the captain's glance, but he quickly shifted it back to the man who held his fate in his hands.

"What of the other horses? And the rest of the hunting party? Should I be expecting them as well?"

"They didn't make it, son. Things got a little rough." The captain shrugged his massive shoulders. "Go on now, get on with it. Come see me once Bulger is taken care of."

Pedar, Jamsen, and Chard didn't make it? What in the blazes did they run into?

It was hard to imagine any of those three falling to anything. They were all former Marines and long-time bounty hunters who had served with the captain for many years. It was even harder to imagine what had done so much damage to the captain's brother.

Several long strands of dirty, silver hair hung limp and wet from the other end of the bundle on Haddock's shoulder. Closer now, Mouse noted how small and delicate those dangling feet seemed.

Is that a child? Mouse kept his thoughts to himself and turned his attention back to the captain. "Should I bring my medical bag when I come see you, sir?"

"No need, son." The captain stared into his brother's face with a gentleness that Mouse had never seen before. "I'll tend to Valk, myself."

The captain's muttered words were almost lost in the stiff breeze.

"It's okay, brother. We're safe on the ship now."

The captain looked up from his brother, his eyes narrowing. He nodded towards the docks.

"Run along, now, boy." His posture straightened and his commanding presence returned. "The crew will be waiting to help you board Bulger and get him down to his stall. Take good care and get him settled properly; he's had as bad a night as we have. Give him an extra ration of oats."

"Yes, sir." Mouse saluted and then scurried down the plank.

By the time he reached the dock, he had pushed all thoughts of fleeing from his mind. He had duties to perform.

CHAPTER 14

Seldy

*C*old.
So cold.

Jolted awake by a sudden change in her position, Seldy let out a low moan as fresh waves of pain washed over her. The oily rag stuffed into her mouth absorbed the sound as easily as it soaked in all of the moisture from her mouth.

It felt like she'd been run over by a *vardo*; everything hurt. Her skull was pounding as if Serge was forging a new sword and using her head as the anvil. Her wrists and ankles were bound so tight that they were scraped raw. She'd lost feeling in her fingers and toes hours ago. Her gut was sore from being slung across the saddle horn and then someone's shoulder for what seemed like hours. The long muscles of her arms and legs were cramped and stiff from being bound in place.

Worst of all was the ice cold, yet burning, sensation around her neck and on the back of her shoulder. She'd been hit by something — something that had sent her spiraling into a deep, dark place devoid of form, warmth, and connection. She'd been slipping in and out of consciousness ever since.

Seldy shivered. She couldn't see anything through the blind-fold, but her senses of smell and hearing were unaffected. A sharp, masculine musk reeking of sweat and fear assaulted her nose.

"We oughtta be killin' this cursed witch," the man grumbled. "Insteadda bringin' her on board our ship."

Strong arms supported her beneath her shoulders and bent knees, but she was being held out away from his chest at arm's length, as if whoever was carrying her wanted to be as far away from her as possible. There were other voices in the distance, but she couldn't make out anything that was being said over the clomping of hard-soled boots on a wooden surface.

"This is beyond crazy," the voice continued to mutter as a heavy door was opened, and they began descending. "Wild ti-gers, rampagin' elephants, and witchcraft!"

Each jolting downward step sent fresh sparks of agony shooting throughout Seldy's body.

She would've welcomed the blissful ignorance of sleep if she didn't fall into that strange, frigid place devoid of all sensation each time she lost consciousness.

Her captor heaved her back onto his shoulder, ignoring her grunts of pain as he slung her around like a sack of potatoes. A door opened and closed. Her nostrils were assaulted by the fetid stench of cold iron, unwashed bodies, and the pungent scent of excrement from both animals and people. She fought the urge to cough through the gag and failed. Her whole body convulsed.

The person holding her stiffened.

"Shards!"

Keys rattled and metal clanked.

"You're not gonna use nonna your blasted magick on me, you rancid witch!"

Magick? I'm no witch!

Hinges shrieked in protest. Seldy was thrown. For a moment, she was suspended in the air, weightless and formless.

"Now you stay put, little rehla, *Gorman-da has to check on something, eh?"*

Seldy giggled at the way her uncle's funny face-hair tickled her nose as he spoke to her. She reached for it to see if he would squeal again when she pulled on it, but he was too fast for her, extending his arms so that her target was just out of reach.

"Aho! I see you're up to your little tricks again!" He laughed as he bent over to set her down in a small ring of boxes and crates. "Now don't you go anywhere, you little wiggle worm." He waggled a big finger down at her. "Or your mother will kill me! I'll be back in a few minutes!"

At three-years-old, Seldy understood what was said to her, even if she never answered. But, of course, she had no intention of staying put. There was just too much to see and explore in the big, wide world.

Once he was gone, Seldy shimmied out of her restricting dress. Naked as the day she was born, she clambered out of her small enclosure and scampered through the knee-high grass towards her favorite destination: the pen where the giant orange-and black-striped kitties lived.

She had only seen them from a distance, but the great cats fascinated her like nothing else. Dancing from one pudgy foot to the other, Seldy giggled with delight as one of the big kitties moved restlessly through the area beyond the iron bars that separated them.

Hearing her, the cat stopped in its circuit and turned its great head to stare at her with unblinking eyes. Those mesmerizing eyes were so pretty. *Giggling again, she reached a tiny hand through the bars towards the kitty.*

The cat's lips curled away from each other as it stalked towards her, revealing massive white teeth longer than her hands. The black nose of the beast twitched. It sniffed her hand, its eyes narrowing. The cat towered over her.

Waves of emotion — feelings of profound sadness, of aching loss, and of deep-seated anger — rolled off of the great beast and touched Seldy's heart. She ached with sympathy for the creature, sensing its frustration at being kept inside of this big playpen and, worse yet, when it was forced into the tiny cage on wheels whenever the kumpania moved from place-to-place.

Staring up into those sad but fascinating eyes, Seldy just knew that she had to do something to help the kitty feel better. The bars of the enclosure were close enough together to keep the kitty from escaping — and from anyone big from getting in — but she was tiny. Careful to avoid touching the nasty iron of the bars — the metal smelled bad and burned her skin — she slipped in between them.

The kitty snarled and fell back into a crouch, but Seldy wasn't scared. She knew just what the poor kitty needed: loving. Rushing forward, she wrapped both of her tiny arms around the great creature's thick neck and buried her face in its warm, soft fur.

A tentative voice pushed against her mind.

::What are you doing, little Cubling? The masters will fear for you. They will worry that I will eat you! They will bring their pain sticks and hurt me!::

Blinking in surprise at hearing the voice of the kitty in her mind, Seldy — for the first time in her short little life — tried to respond. Screwing up her forehead, she thought out the words that she had not yet spoken to her Ma or any of her many uncles and aunties.

::I'm Seldy!::

The words came out haltingly at first, but the kitty's reaction told her that she'd been heard.

::Why kitty so sad?::

The great cat rubbed its head against her.

::My cubs, little one, I miss them every day.::

::Baby kitties?::

Seldy pulled back to stare into the kitty's eyes, though she left her pudgy hands on either side of the kitty's massive head, her fingers trailing through the soft fur. She glanced around.

::Where baby kitties?::

The tigress didn't respond with words but with images and emotions. Blurry images of two young tigers staring down at her from high above. They were at the edge of a great pit dug into the earth, trying to find a way to come down safely so they could join their mama. They mewled down at her in fear. The mama yowled in return, warning them to stay back. She paced restlessly about the bottom of the pit, seeking a way to escape.

The images were accompanied by waves of sorrow and loss, making it clear, even to a three year old, that their mama was mourning them. The big kitty closed her eyes and let out a heavy sigh. She dropped to the ground.

Seldy hugged the mama kitty with all of her strength. She ran her fingers through her fur and sent feelings of love back to her.

::I'm sorry.::

Her own thoughts were choked with sadness for the big mama kitty. A blurry memory of her own bubbled to the surface, of a beautiful face staring at her with bright, sparkling blue eyes, and a hard truth became clear to her.

::My first mama gone too. Maybe baby kitties have new mama to love them like I do?::

The tigress accepted her loving touch.

::That is not the way of tigers, Cubling.::

The kitty's sorrow reminded her of the sadness she remembered in the bright blue eyes of her first mama. Seldy knew that

*she was loved by her Jhana-ma and that there were many others
in the* kumpania *who loved her like a mama should.*

::I know! You can be my kitty-ma! I like having lots of
mamas!::

*The kitty began to groom Seldy with her massive pink
tongue, tickling her with its roughness and purring with each
exhalation of her great lungs.*

*Giggling with delight at each rough pass of that tongue, Seldy
felt the cat's heart opening up to the love that she was offering.
Soon, she was curled up and snuggling between Layra's massive
forepaws in the tiger's makeshift den within the enclosure. The
other tigress, Amara, paced nearby. Layra glowered protectively
over her little 'Cubling.'*

A deep, unbearable sadness overwhelmed Seldy as she hung
suspended in the air. The precious memory lit a spark to the
dried kindling of her grief.

Oh, Layra-ma! I'm so sorry!

The memory dissipated as she slammed into an unyielding wooden surface. Her legs hit first. Still bound and gagged,
she was helpless to do anything to arrest her fall. Seldy's head
smashed into the same surface. There was a flash of fresh stars
and a mix of pain, both new and old. Darkness came for her
again, swallowing her up.

She returned, crying and broken, to that nameless, formless
void.

CHAPTER 15

Mouse

The ship swayed as Mouse padded down the broad hallway of the aft deck, making his way to the captain's quarters. The once strange feeling of the ship in flight was now familiar and welcome. Just as the captain had promised, the crew had been in place and waiting for him when he brought Bulger through the lower entrance into the rear-hold. The large space at the rear of the lowest deck in the ship had been converted into a stable for the steeds of the bounty hunting crew long before Mouse joined the *Ghost*.

There were a lot of sullen looks amongst the crew as he led the stallion aboard, and more than a few black eyes and bruised faces, but no one said anything to him — about the fight or anything else.

Even stranger was Bulger's behavior. This was the first time where the beast was docile and compliant instead of his normal cantankerous self. He had snorted in relief at the familiar confines of the stable hold and allowed Mouse to tend to him without once snapping at him or trying to stomp on his toes. His feistiness only returned when Mouse tried to inspect the five small scorch marks burned into his chest.

"Blast that orc's thick fucking skull!" The captain's voice came loud and angry through the closed door to his office.

Orc? Pausing outside of the door, Mouse held in his breath. Instead of knocking, he leaned in close and pressed his ear to the door.

"Help me wrap these knuckles, Haddock."

Haddock's voice was lower, subdued far below his normal boisterous level.

"Aye, Cap. I'm glad you put his mouthy ass down, that's for sure. I'd've paid good coin to see that beat down."

"Yeah," the captain gave a sharp laugh. "It did feel good, especially after the night we had."

"Cap, are you sure we need to keep that witch around?"

"Of course we're going to keep her, you fool! She's worth a blazing fortune!"

"I don't know, Cap. Dan's bounty should be rich 'nough."

Someone snorted, but Haddock continued in a plaintive voice.

"I ain't ever seen anyone do what she did to your brother! She's one of them witches they talk 'bout! If any of the crew find out what she is...or what she's capable of..."

A witch? Mouse's eyes widened. *The new prisoner did that to Valk?*

"Dammit, Haddock! How many times do I have to tell you? She's worth a fortune! And it doesn't have anything to do with that bastard Tegger Dan! Not anymore!"

"Wait a minute, Cap." Confusion was clear in Haddock's voice. "I thought we snatched her up in order to lure the bard back to Vandermal because she was someone he cared about?"

"It was, Haddock. It was." Klard sucked in his breath sharply. "Ouch! Be careful, blast you!"

"Sorry. These knuckles are a mess."

So Tra'al was right; they did kidnap someone. Mouse bit his lip. *And Tegger Dan was in town all along!*

"So why are we going to keep her, Cap, if we don't need to trade her for the bard?"

"She's worth more than this whole blasted ship and all of the cargo and prisoners we've ever captured, that's why!" The captain's voice sounded triumphant. "We're killing two birds with one blasted stone here! I left Dan a note, so once he finds out she's been snatched, he'll still come crawling on his belly to us to trade for her, all right. But when he does, we'll take him and collect his bounty! Then we'll turn her in to the High Seeker and collect the reward for finding this prize. We'll be heroes of the Guild Alliance and filthy stinking rich besides!"

Both men erupted in laughter.

Mouse fought the overwhelming urge to retch.

"Why's she so valuable, Cap?"

"Are you daft, Haddock? You saw what she did to Bulger and to Valk! I just know that she was doing something with those blasted animals. She was controlling the—Ow!"

"Hold still, boss!"

She hurt Bulger, too? Mouse blinked. *Controlling what?*

"Be careful! That fat bastard of a gypsy was going on and on about how she cared for those blasted tigers and that blazing elephant, which was why he couldn't sell any of them. She's got magick, Haddock. Real blazing magick!"

Magick!

Every hair on Mouse's body stood on end. His hands began to shake. He couldn't stop shivering. He wanted to flee back down to the stable, but he couldn't peel himself away from the door.

"It all makes sense now, Haddock!" The captain continued in a booming voice. "That witch is the Wilderling woman that the Supreme Seeker is looking for! That traitorous bastard has been hiding her in plain sight on that backwater of an island all these years, letting her pretend that she's some blasted elf!"

She's a Wilderling? A Fae? Mouse's shivering became a violent shudder. His stomach churned. *I guess she's not so innocent after all.*

It's never wise to judge someone by the word of others, Rondel. His mother's voice whispered deep in his memory. *Make your judgements based on your own intuition.*

Conflicting emotions of fear and shame waged a war inside of his roiling gut. With effort, he focused back on the conversation taking place behind the door.

"...her magick is what I'm worried about, Cap! What if she does to that cell what she did to your brother? She might send us all to our deaths!"

Mouse gulped.

"Stop being such a ninny! You saw what my Seeker's Circle did to her." The captain's voice boomed. "I've fought the Wilderlings on Aerhythia, Haddock. I've been a *Quaestidor*. She may have magick, but she's got the same weakness as all the rest of those miserable creatures. That's why I put that iron collar on her. The *Fae* can't abide iron or lodestone, so she won't be able to break out of that cell. This ship was designed to hold them, after all. Besides, I've got something you don't, Haddock. Faith. I've seen the power of the Seekers firsthand. The Seekers saved Valk when he was dying of the Scourge, and they'll keep us safe from that girl and her magick."

"Whatever you say, Cap." Haddock didn't sound like he was reassured.

"Ouch! Dammit, be careful, arsehole, or I'll break my other hand over your blasted head!"

"Sorry, Cap! I'm almost done. Hold still."

There was some quiet muttering that Mouse couldn't hear, even though he strained to do so.

"So what are we gonna do with that orc, Cap? He might've fetched a decent price in the arena before, but you busted him up pretty good. He's probably not gonna be worth much now."

"I'm not worried about him any longer." The captain gave a harsh laugh. "He was just insurance. He's outlived his usefulness. If he dies, we'll just chuck his carcass overboard and send him back to the Untere where orcs belong. If he lives until we get back home, I'll amuse myself by paying him back for all of the shite he did when I was a recruit."

He's going to kill Tra'al?

"So it's true then? What he said about training you in the Marines?"

"Yeah, it is." The captain laughed. It was a deep and harsh sound. "That puny runt was one of my instructors in the Marines. Dan and I both served under him. If he hadn't reminded me, though, I wouldn't have remembered. I've tried to block a lot of that shite out. But it keeps coming back."

"There, that should do it for your hand."

"Thanks." There was a quiet pause, then the captain's voice grew louder. "By the Shards of Luna, how long does it take for that boy to care for a single blasted horse?"

Uh oh!

"I don't know, Cap. But I'll go find 'im."

"Wait, Haddock." There was a shifting of weight beyond the door. "Keep all of this about the witch — and what we saw her do — to yourself. Don't answer any questions from the crew about her. As far as they're concerned, she's just an elf with a bounty on her head." There was a slight pause. "And if anyone asks about the others, just say there was more resistance than we expected."

"I hear ya, Cap. Best for them not to know about her or what happened to the others, that's for sure. It'd only bring trouble. I'll go find that blasted stowaway."

Mouse backed away from the door, timing it so that it appeared that he was just coming up from taking care of Bulger.

Haddock stepped out into the hall. His eyes narrowed when he saw Mouse.

"What's taken you so long, stower?"

"Bulger was hurt, sir." Mouse forced himself to look Haddock in the eyes. "So I took some extra time in brushing and getting him settled."

"Cap's waitin' on you, boy." Haddock's expression relaxed. He pushed the door open and motioned for Mouse to enter. "Best you get in there and listen to what he's got to say. Screw it up, and you'll feel the Serpent's Tongue on your back again." There was an evil gleam in the man's eyes. "If you're lucky, that is."

Suppressing a shudder, Mouse slipped past the man and into the nicest suite of rooms on the whole ship.

Sunlight bathed the room, reflecting off the lacquered surfaces of expensive wood. Mouse had no idea what kind of wood it was, but it was dark and rich and polished to a high sheen. There were lines of gleaming silver and a bone-white material inlaid throughout the etchings on the desk and matching wood panels. Full bookcases lined the walls of the room, easily containing more books and scrolls than Mouse had seen in his entire life. Another door, nestled in the aft wall, led to a small hallway and the private quarters of the captain and his brother.

Enjoying the feeling of the lush carpet on the soles of his bare feet, Mouse lingered, waiting for the captain to notice him. He resisted the urge to dig his toes into it, but only barely.

The captain stood with his back to him, staring out through the large bay windows set in the starboard side of the hull. His right hand, heavily bandaged, was being held by his left. He was dressed in a clean, dry uniform. Blue trousers were tucked into gleaming, knee-high boots. The tails of his matching blue jacket hung straight down. White cotton ruffles peeked out from beneath the end of each sleeve. His dark hair was brushed back into a short pony tail, and his beard was its normal, bristling self again.

"So how is Bulger, son?" The captain's voice sounded thick and tired, like he hadn't slept all night.

"Spooked, sir. He's got a set of burn marks on his chest that he didn't like me touching, but they don't seem too serious." He swallowed to keep himself from saying anything further.

The captain didn't immediately respond. He just stood watching the view through the window.

Mouse remained at attention like Haddock had taught him, facing the captain's back, waiting to speak only when spoken to. His gaze shifted to the view he had missed before: of the sun-dappled landscape of Timos through the pristine windows. Except for the gleaming spires of the Conservatory, the tiny buildings of the city of Nashae looked like a set of child's toys. The port sat at the very edge of the city; the two remaining cogs bobbed up and down in the light breeze.

Without turning around, the captain said, "It was a rough mission, much tougher than we expected."

"Yes, sir."

Mouse wanted to ask how the woman had hurt Bulger, but he knew better.

"But I understand that things also got a little bit exciting here on the ship." The captain's voice was low and even. He didn't move. "Is that correct?"

"I...uh...yes, sir." Mouse's cheeks bloomed bright red. He cleared his throat. "There was a fight in the Mess last night, sir."

The captain let go of his bandaged hand and reached into his jacket for something.

"So, I hear that you are a bit of a musician." His voice became quiet. "Is that true?"

"Yes, sir." His throat tightened. Mouse shifted his weight onto the balls of his feet.

The captain turned around, his face a stone mask. His black, beady eyes focused on Mouse. He held the flute. It looked small and frail in the big man's thick fingers.

Mouse's heart swelled at seeing the instrument again, whole

and undamaged. Something in the captain's bearing, however, gave him pause. He remained quiet and still.

The big man then held it out towards Mouse.

"Show me."

"What do you want me to play, sir?"

"Play the last song you performed before the fight broke out."

Taking the flute, Mouse moistened his lips and put the instrument to his mouth. Glancing up, he noted that the man was watching him like a vai-hawk staring down its prey. He took a couple of deep, shuddering breaths and closed his eyes.

He began to play.

CHAPTER 16

Seldy

*I*t is time to wake up, rehla."
The soft words echoed in the darkness, a familiar-sounding voice, a distant memory. Shivering, the young woman clutched her thin arms about her frigid body, huddling against the damp stone wall. She couldn't recall how she had gotten in this strange place or even who she was.

She was cold despite her nightdress. It was wet and clammy against her skin. Something hung around her neck, something that was...binding her.

The object was heavy and cold and yet it somehow burned and chafed against her skin. She brought her fingers up to tear it away but gasped in pain and jerked her burned fingers back. The heavy iron collar weighed her shoulders down. When it bumped into the stone wall behind her, the impact sent waves of agony searing throughout her body. Her cry of pain echoed in the darkness.

Rocking forward, she sobbed, trying to remember who she was and how she came to this horrible place.

Images and sounds flooded her mind: lightning crackled, the smell of wet men and horses moving along a forest road, the creak of worn leather, the rain spattering on cloaks and gear, the echoing strains of a beautiful song - the notes of it now obscured, a chorus of disembodied voices crying out for violence, then silence, deafening silence and undiluted darkness.

"I...am..." The name was on the tip of her tongue, but it eluded her as even more images came rushing back.

...of painted wagons and smiling people with dark hair, tanned skin, and bright eyes...campfires in the night surrounded by happy people singing and dancing and joking...a giant tent made of canvas and adorned with colorful silks...

...there were animals...horses and mules who pulled the many wheeled vardos of her people...something massive, with tough grey skin and thick ivory tusks and a warm, ticklish trunk that could pick her up and twirl her onto its back...B-b-b...

"Bessie!"

The name rolled off of her tongue, filling her with hope as her memories returned.

"Amara! Layra!"

Blurting out their names caused a rush of warm memories of the two tigresses to come flooding back into her mind — their soft orange and black fur, the way that their purring reverberated through her whole body, and the joys of cuddling up and napping with them, cradled snug and safe amidst a tangle of massive paws.

Those thoughts dissipated as quickly as they came, however, as another image of Layra — one of her bleeding to death alongside an ice-rimed road in the midst of a storm —slammed home.

"Oh, Layra!" she called out, reaching in vain towards the fading image of her beloved tiger with outstretched fingers. "I miss you so much!"

Metal clanked against metal, pieces of her collar brushing against each other as she rocked back and forth.

The tigress' eyes flashed as the last vestiges of the image faded.

::Be strong, Cubling.:: Layra's mind-voice whispered against Seldy's consciousness. ::And remember...member...ber...::

Her name came rushing back to her with all of the power and ferocity of a tiger's deep, rumbling roar.

"I am Seldy!"

She sat up straight, swelling with pride and determination.

"I am Istimiel Seldirima, daughter of Istimiel Jhana, Mistress of Coin of the Kumpania Istimiel, the best circus in all of Timos!"

Her strong and lilting voice echoed in the darkness, the lyrical sound of her words imbued with the musical quality of the Gypsy Cant of the Freeborn.

Surging with confidence, Seldy pushed herself away from the slick stone and sat up on her knees. She thrust her hands out away from her body, trying to get a sense of this strange, dark place.

The temperature began to drop.

Shivering, but determined, she continued to explore her immediate surroundings. There was no light and no noise other than her own ragged breathing, but she had the distinct sense that someone, or something, was nearby and coming closer. She pulled her arms back.

"Hello? Is there anyone here?"

She couldn't stop her teeth from chattering.

Something changed in the air. It thickened. Her words were swallowed by the gathering shadows. Shuddering, she inhaled, preparing to call out again.

The hair on the back of her neck stood on end. Despite her nightgown, she felt terribly exposed. Hugging her arms to her torso, Seldy fought the urge to shrink back against the wall. A cold breeze ruffled her hair, the chill raising goosebumps all over her body. Her teeth chattered.

"Hello? Who's there?"

The silence was profound, the darkness absolute. She didn't hear any footsteps or feel anyone's breath. She couldn't see anything. Nothing physical was touching her, other than the cool and damp stone. But...the looming, frigid presence...drew closer.

"It is I, my precious Seldirima." The hissing voice grated against her nerves like a rusty iron gate being opened and closed repeatedly. "I have found you, my bride, at long last."

The darkness thickened. A dreadful presence coalesced nearby and drew close enough to touch her. Seldy's stomach roiled, threatening to empty itself. Despite that, she sat up taller and threw her head back in defiance.

"Who are you?" She tried to sound strong and sure, but her words sounded small and weak against the terrifying power of the presence. "And where am I?"

"Don't you remember me?" An ice-cold tendril of darkness brushed her cheek, teasing loose strands of her hair and exposing her ear. The whispered reply wormed its way into her ear. A pair of red glowing eyes opened in front of her, piercing her heart.

"You were at the kumpania!*" She tried to look away from those eyes, but she couldn't. She was frozen in place just like she had been the very first time she saw them. "Why?!?"*

"I came to bring you home, my sweet Seldirima. Finally." Each word was drawn out, spoken slowly and with clear relish. "I have known you since long before you were born, when you were promised to me. Come with me now. Surrender to me, and I will show you the way home. We shall be together forever, as we were always meant to be."

"I was home!"

Anger flared inside of her. She sat up even straighter, pushing against the pressure the creature was trying to exert with his glowing red eyes.

"I don't know what you're talking about! I'm not going anywhere with you! And I'm not your bride! I love Chad!"

As soon as she said his name, the image of her dear, sweet consyrtu *falling into her arms came rushing back. Her heart leapt into her throat even as her shoulders sagged. She covered her face with her hand, a massive sob escaping her lips.*

"Oh Chad!"

Like a predator, the presence pounced. The voice somehow came closer, so close that it spoke directly into her mind, just as she did with her animals.

::Forget that mortal man, my bride. He is unworthy of you. Love, my dear Seldirima, is a mortal weakness. Join with me and experience what it is to have true power.::

The presence thrust itself into her very being, invading her mind and spirit. Repulsed, Seldy shuddered.

...Love is the source of your strength, *rehla.* Tiagra's whispered words echoed softly in her mind. Draw on it often...

Desperate for anything that might her help resist the invading presence, Seldy clutched to her memories of Chad and hugged herself, curling up into a ball. She pushed back hard at the presence invaded her mind.

::Stop! Leave me alone! I'm not going anywhere with you! Get out of my mind!::

Green, living energy surged inside of her, pulsing outward from the very core of who she was, the energy adding its strength to her improvised defenses. At the center of that energy was the same hard-shelled seed she had seen when she had somehow called the lightning from the storm and sent it into the creature when he struck down Layra. Glowing runes covered the outer shell of the seed, shifting with each pulsing heartbeat. She grew stronger, and the runes brighter, with each pounding beat.

Tha-throom.

"*You should welcome me, Seldirima!*"

Pushed from her mind, the oily, serpentine presence enveloped her both physically and psychically in tightening coils of inky, slithering darkness. He pressed harder against her mind, seeking a way through her new defenses. The image of those mysterious eyes was burned into her consciousness so even when she managed to close her own eyes, she still saw him staring back at her.

"*I can free you from the mortal prison that binds you,*" his grating voice whispered in her ears. "*Let me in, my bride, and I will show you how to unlock your true potential!*"

"*NO!*" she shouted her reply, uncurling her body and pushing against the pressure he was applying with all of her might. "*Get away from me!*"

The irresistible force of his implacable evil contested with the unmovable object of her determination, neither one giving or gaining against the other for what seemed like an eternity. His frigid, serpentine coils constricted, but the seed within her continued to pulse, giving her the strength to resist.

"*To surrender to love is to embrace weakness! He cannot save you from my wrath! I shall find and destroy this Chad, just as I slew that cursed beast of yours!*" The voice grew louder, echoing off of the stone walls all around her. "*I will destroy everyone and everything that you love until you relent and accept your fate! You WILL become my bride!*"

He began to bombard her with terrible visions — images of the people and animals she loved being slaughtered by nightmarish creatures...vardos laying broken and overturned, some of them burning...of naked, scared children being captured and led away in chains by leering, armed men...of Bessie lying torn and bloody on the ground, being fed upon by a fearsome, dark-winged serpent with glowing red eyes and a long, coiling tail that ended in a wicked, barbed stinger...

"NOOOO!" The scream tore from her throat as she fought to push those visions from her head. The horror, however, ate away at her defenses. Her walls began to crumble.

"My minions are legion," the voice whispered in her ear again. "And my hunger for you is insatiable. Now that I have found you, my bride, I will have you — in every way that you can be had."

The coils tightened further, constricting around her chest, stealing her breath. She couldn't even cry out.

"Submit to me, Seldirima. You have been abandoned by everyone who has ever loved you. No one can save you from your fate. You are all alone. And alone, you cannot hope to defeat me by yourself."

The walls closing in around her, Seldy collapsed to the stone floor, hugging her thin arms to her body. She curled up into a fetal position. The coils reached for her throat, becoming one with the iron that shackled her. The metal burned with an icy fire. She tried to scream, but no words came.

Turning her gaze inward out of sheer desperation, Seldy saw her Jhana's grey eyes staring back at her. Her mother's fierce, whispered words resonated throughout her being.

You're my daughter, and I love you more than life itself! Don't you ever forget that!

Tha-throom.

The glowing seed pulsed with each reverberating echo of those words, growing stronger and rebuilding her defenses with each beat. Struggling with the weight of the world on her shoulders, Seldy straightened up once again. She staggered to her knees again as her mother's undeniably fierce love filled her with its impenetrable strength.

"NOOOO!!!" she cried out, forcing out the words. "I am Seldirima, daughter of Jhana."

Energized, Seldy surged to her feet, standing straight and tall and proud. Her defiant words echoed the lessons that had been instilled in her for as long as she could remember.

"I am Freeborn! We bow to no one!"

All at once, the pressure dissipated, leaving Seldy gasping, exhausted, and weak-kneed. But for the moment, at least, she was free of the suffocating pressure.

"Very well, my bride." The grating whisper sent chills down her spine as it came right next to her ear. "But remember, this was your choice. You shall bear witness to the costs of your recalcitrance."

Something cold, agonizingly cold, touched the back of her shoulder.

A kiss.

Excruciating pain exploded outward from that point.

She cried out as the frigid shadows swallowed her whole.

CHAPTER 17

Mouse

The first note Mouse played had started as a tiny seed planted long ago by his mother in the fertile bed of his imagination. Through the years since her death, that seed had been watered by countless tears. The cherished memories of those special evenings in their humble shack in the Slant had sustained him through many dark and lonely nights as a reluctant gang member and then a desperate stowaway.

His breath flowed through a real instrument once again, allowing that orphaned seed of hope to sprout and blossom into the haunting song that reminded him so much of her.

While Mouse couldn't remember the exact words to the song, his mother had spoken often of the story it told. The light and airy pace at the beginning sent shivers down his spine, as it reveled in the youthful innocence of a pair of noble twins — a brother and a sister — fresh out of childhood. Fairly early in the song, however, their idyllic existence was shattered when the girl was raped by a much older man in the gardens of her family's estate. Capturing the tragic power of that event with the requisite jangling and discordant notes the song needed was especially challenging. It wasn't the violence of that night that made the story behind the song so interesting, however, but how the theme of each of the twins changed after that terrible event.

The song followed each of them in alternating stanzas as their lives took different turns. The girl is isolated from her family and sent off to a far-away temple to give birth to the child created that night. That child is taken from her and raised by others, but she eventually finds redemption, love, and purpose in her life — and, for a brief time at the end of the song, she is reunited with her grown daughter.

The boy's side of the story, however, turns darker with each stanza as he becomes driven by the need to take revenge upon the man who had wronged his sister. He grows into a twisted version of the bright and talented young man he was before, turning manipulative and resentful. As the song progresses, he descends into a kind of madness that leads him to avenge his sister in such a terrible fashion that two families — and many lives — are irrevocably shattered.

Closing his eyes, Mouse became lost in the music. His mother's image filled his thoughts. She smiled at him like she used to do so often, swaying back and forth to the early upbeat rhythms of the song. Her sun-kissed skin radiated with health and beauty, and her blue eyes sparkled with life once again. Her long blonde hair, normally tied back into a pony tail, was unbound and hung loose about her shoulders — a golden-halo illuminated by the dying rays of the sun. His heart skipped a beat at the vision of his mother in all of her glory. Her beauty didn't need any makeup or any adornment; she was perfect.

Tears squeezed through Mouse's closed eyes and trailed down his cheeks, but he didn't stop playing the song that evoked her until the flute was ripped from his fingers.

"Blast it, boy!" The captain's roar filled the chamber. "I said enough!"

Mouse staggered backwards, disoriented and blurry-eyed. "Wh-wh-what?"

The captain loomed over him, staring down at Mouse with wild-eyes, his chest heaving. He clutched the flute in his bandaged right hand, his other hand clenched into a fist that was cocked and ready to be unleashed at the smallest word or movement.

"What's wrong, sir?" Mouse took a half-step backwards and raised his hands to show that they were empty and harmless. "Am I that bad?"

Captain Dastyr closed the remaining distance between them in one step. He snatched the front of Mouse's tunic with the same hand that still held the flute, jerking him off his feet.

"It takes some roarin' big balls to play a blasted Tegger Dan song on my blazing ship, let alone THAT blasted song!"

Mouse flinched as the captain's voice rose to a thunderous crescendo.

"I didn't want to believe you were that stupid, boy!" His other fist quivered.

Mouse felt several scabs tear under the rough pressure on his back from the now taut fabric. Wet warmth oozed from his back in a dozen places.

"I don't understand, sir!" His voice squeaked like the animal he was named for. "That was the song you told me to play!"

He couldn't meet the captain's eyes for long. He dropped his gaze down to the protruding end of the flute tangled up in his tunic. He couldn't help but hear the powerful beat of the captain's personal song. The strongest theme that emerged from the multiple strands of complex music was that of being wronged — of the need to seek vengeance for an unspeakable crime committed against him and his family. There were hints of other themes — buried deep down — that matched notes he'd last heard when the infamous bard had given him the flute. One faint echo reminded him, achingly, of his mother.

"Did you know that was one of his songs?"

Spittle flew from the captain's mouth into Mouse's face. Black, bristly whiskers brushed his cheeks. Mouse could've counted the tiny little blood vessels in each of the man's eyes if he hadn't been so scared.

"No, sir! I didn't!" Mouse squeaked. "My mom taught it to me. It was her favorite."

The massive man blinked, his glare reflecting doubt at Mouse's words.

"I would never willingly play one of that traitor's songs, sir!"

His feet were soon touching the carpet again. The big man let go of his tunic and stood back.

Captain Dastyr pointed with the flute towards a pair of cushioned chairs in front of his desk before moving around to his own side of the ornately carved monstrosity.

"Take a seat, son."

He laid the flute down on the desk before grabbing the wheeled chair behind the desk and lowering his bulk into it with a sigh.

Still trying to comprehend what had just happened, Mouse stood rooted in place, his mouth agape.

"Sit down, boy," the captain snapped. "Don't make me repeat myself again. That won't be good for either of us."

Mouse slunk over to the nearest chair. He lowered his backside onto the front edge of the cushioned seat. His eyes darted between the flute and the captain.

"How old are you, son?"

"Nineteen, sir." Mouse swallowed. "My birthday was earlier this month."

The captain picked up the flute and studied it. He arched a big, bushy eyebrow.

"And you've been on my ship for what, six months now?"

"Yes, sir." His precious flute was small and delicate in the big man's scarred and calloused hands. "It was the beginning of Seddin...when I was brought on board."

"Don't you mean, when you snuck aboard?"

Unable to keep his eyes off of his flute, Mouse replied sheepishly. "Yes, sir." He cleared his throat. "But, sir, I didn't have any idea what ship that crate was going to get loaded on. I just knew I had to get away from Eastport before I was discovered."

"That was rather foolish, you know." The big man leaned back, his chair creaked in protest. "Those Grey Cloak prigs can't do anything to you compared to what the captain of a ship can do to any stowaway he finds..."

"You don't know what it's like in the Slant, Captain..." Mouse blurted his reply, interrupting the captain in mid-sentence. Thunderclouds formed on the captain's forehead. He ducked his head. "I'm sorry, sir. Haddock taught me better'n that."

The captain's deep rumbling chuckle caused Mouse to look up again. A small smile broke through the nest of tangled black curls surrounding the captain's thin lips. There was a brief flash of gleaming white teeth.

"I like you, son. I can't really place my finger on why, but I like you." The big man shrugged. "Maybe it's because you remind me of Valk when he was your age." The smile disappeared as quickly as it had formed. "You know, I've never made a habit of tolerating stowaways on my ship."

The big man's thick eyebrows knit together, forming a single, bristling black bush.

"But I've let you work off your debts as a cabin boy, which flies in the face of the tradition and the rules of the Mariner's Guild." The captain cleared his throat before continuing. "If it'd been up to Haddock and the rest of the crew, you'd've been strung up and hanged or thrown overboard. You know all of this, right?"

"Yes, sir." Mouse replied. "Dalton explained it to me."

"Up until a few moments ago, I had hoped that you might become a halfway decent sailor and maybe earn your wings as a full-fledged member of this crew." The captain's tone had grown somber.

Mouse's palms started to itch. His stomach lurched.

"But I'm afraid that's not going to happen now. Not after what I just heard."

Mouse's throat tightened. "But, sir..."

The captain's upraised hand cut him off, then dropped back down to finger the flute.

"It would be a waste of my time and good coin, boy, to make a sailor out of you."

Mouse's heart thudded in his chest. His world came crashing down around him.

"But, sir..." He dropped his head in defeat. "Where will I go? What will I do?"

"Mouse, look at me."

Reluctantly, he looked up at the captain through blurry eyes. The captain's lips pressed into a thin, white line.

"When even a wool-headed fool like Dalton can see that you've got the raw talent to do something better with your life — well, I would be an even greater fool to let you waste it by becoming a blasted sailor."

As soon as he finished speaking, the captain's eyes trailed down to the flute in his fingers, giving Mouse a moment to recover. The captain pointed the end of the flute at him.

"Now, I can't stand that blasted song or the shite-eating bastard who wrote the blazing thing. And I'm no fan of bards in general or the other kinds of fools that hang out at that Conservatory."

He swung the flute around to point at the rapidly dwindling city of Nashae, beyond the windows.

"But you're talented enough — and still young enough — to gain admission to that school."

"I don't know how I can ever hope to go there, sir, especially if you won't let me stay on to earn a living." Mouse ducked his head again to hide his tears. "My mom always dreamed that I might someday study there, but that dream died when the Scourge took her." He remembered how beautiful she still looked, even after that terrible disease had ravaged her body.

"My mother died of the Scourge as well."

The captain's quiet, somber words broke the reverie that Mouse had fallen into. He looked up again. He stifled a sniffle.

"How old were you, sir?" he blurted out the question before adding in, "I was ten when my mom died."

If the captain took offense to the most junior member of the crew asking him such a personal question, it was hidden behind a mask of his own sorrow.

"She died when I was but a child and Valk was a toddler."

Mouse sniffled as he sat up.

"I'm sorry, sir, for your loss."

Captain Dastyr straightened up, his emotions back in check.

"Yes, well, it seems we have that in common." He cleared his throat and regarded Mouse. "But back to the business at hand." He paused, studying the flute in front of him. "I could sponsor you...for a price."

"Sponsor me?" Mouse blinked. "To the Jalrun Conservatory?" His voice became higher pitched at the mention of that school. "But...how? Why...?"

The captain leaned forward, his eyes blazing.

"Do you know who and what the Wilderlings of Aerhythia are, young man?"

The intensity of the captain's gaze caught Mouse off guard. He scooted backwards in the seat.

"Yes."

The big man's expression became deadly serious.

"Good. I need your help with that new prisoner, Mouse. She's a Wilderling who escaped Aerhythia and has been hiding amongst the good folk of Timos." The captain's knuckles cracked from the pressure he put on them by pressing down on the desk. "If you help me to get her where I need to take her, I'll see to it that your mother's dream for you is realized by sponsoring you, and I'll pay all of your necessary living expenses until you graduate. How does that sound?"

"What about my flute, sir?"

Captain Dastyr gave him a feral smile. He picked up the flute. Mouse's heart soared until the man took out a key chain and selected a small key on it. He opened a drawer in the desk, slipped the flute down into it, and then locked it shut.

"You won't be needing that until we've completed our mission, son." He arched an eyebrow. "I can't have you riling up the crew or getting distracted from our shared purpose." The big man leaned forward, staring at Mouse. "Do you understand me, boy?"

The hollow feeling in his gut deepened. Mouse gulped.

Peering through the gloom, Mouse could just make out a small, huddled figure lying in the exact middle of the cell he had cleaned. Her back was to him, so he couldn't discern any more details than he had seen before. She was covered in a mud-caked blanket but despite the covering, she was shivering so much that he could hear her teeth chattering together. As he watched, one of her feet twitched.

Mouse turned his attention to Tra'al. He set his buckets and supplies down in the narrow hall between the cells. Both Gretch and Shadow were unusually quiet. The rhythmic groan and creak of the ship in flight was barely noticeable above Tra'al's raspy breathing and the muted clicking of the Wilderling girl's teeth. Shadow lifted his head from his paws. He whimpered once before turning his lupine gaze back towards the new prisoner.

"Tra'al? Are you okay?"

Mouse fumbled for the key to the cell. The orc was shrouded in the deep shadows of the back wall of the cell.

"I've got some fresh bread for a change."

Tra'al's only response was a soft groan.

With a click of the lock and a squeak of the rusty hinges, Mouse opened the door to the cell. About half-way to the orc, he slipped in a puddle of sticky liquid and fell to a knee. Something sharp stuck into the meat at the heel of his left palm.

"Ow!" Mouse winced and jerked his hand back. "A tooth? Oh no, Tra'al! This is one of your fangs!"

Plucking the shard from his flesh, he darted the last few steps to reach the groaning prisoner.

"What happened? Why did they do this to you?"

Tra'al cracked an eye open. His whispered words were labored and breathy.

"Dastyr...has...always...had...a...problem with...being told...the truth."

Blood seeped from several small cuts on the orc's puffy face. His mouth was a bloody mess. The missing tooth was one of his bottom fangs. Its absence changed the whole structure of his lower jaw. There was a gaping wound on the left side of his bottom lip. Mouse set the fang down on the rear bench and fetched his supplies. Kneeling down again next to Tra'al, he dipped the rag in the cool water and pressed it to the orc's mangled lip.

Tra'al flinched and hissed at the pressure, raising a hand in protest, but Mouse held it off easily.

"Relax for a moment."

Mouse took on the calming, controlled tone his mother had

used so often when she treated the people who had come to her for help.

"I need to clean this out a bit. I don't want your wound turning sour on me."

The hand fell away. He dipped the rag and wiped away the blood and pus to get a better look at the wound. Once he was satisfied with its cleanliness, he brought up Tra'al's hand to hold the rag in place.

"Keep some pressure on this while I check out your other injuries."

Mouse's mother had been the closest thing that the Warrens had to a healer. She took in folk who had all manner of injuries, from broken limbs to bad cuts and even fatal illnesses. She cared for them with whatever rudimentary and primitive supplies she could find. The appreciative folk, or their families, would bring small gifts of coin or food or clothing, whatever they could afford. But just as often, those poor folk could only thank her with kind words and a hug.

As soon as he had been old enough to help, whether that was to go out in search of the right supplies or to help hold a patient still, he was tasked with doing so. In the process, Mouse learned how to tend to and diagnose most common and minor wounds. As he grew to understand his musical gift, he was able to help his mother even more by listening to the personal songs of the patients and discerning what they revealed about what was truly ailing them. Between the skills he learned and developed from her and what the patients' songs revealed to him, he became quite the valued helper.

After she died, those skills made him particularly useful in the gang, as there was always someone in need of being stitched up or of having a broken bone set. It was one of the reasons he had been allowed to stay alive so long without having to fight — because the gang needed someone who could patch up those who did do the fighting. He never spoke about his secret gift to any of them, however, as that would've been seen as witchcraft and would've led to a certain and gruesome death.

He examined Tra'al's head before moving down to the orc's chest with careful, probing fingers. Listening to his friend's muted song, Mouse furrowed his brow. By all outward appearances, Tra'al had only suffered a busted tooth, a minor concussion, and a few major bruises. The only cut that might benefit from stitches, though, was the mouth wound, but that was a tough area to stitch up, even if he had had the right supplies to do so.

His song, however hinted at something that was much deeper — the possibility that one of his previously broken ribs might have shifted and punctured a lung. The orc's breathing was more troubled than it had been. It hadn't been very good before the fight; now, it was sounding even worse. He looked into Tra'al's eyes.

"Can you cough?"

The orc shook his head, his dark eyes clouded with pain.

Mouse pressed his lips together. If a lung had been punctured, there was nothing that he could do. Listening again to the old orc's song, it was significantly weaker than it had been. He tried to hide the worry from his eyes.

"I will see about getting you something for the pain."

"Ale..." Tra'al gasped the word out.

"I don't think that would be a good idea."

With surprising strength, Tra'al reached out with his left hand and gripped Mouse's forearm.

"Where...are...we...going?"

Mouse's mouth went dry.

"Vandermal, on Dortyn."

"How...long?"

"A week, maybe a little more." He shrugged. "Depending on the winds and weather along the way. Why?"

Tra'al nodded weakly in the direction of the other prisoner.

"The...new prisoner..." he gasped. "What...to...do...with... her?"

Mouse found himself looking down, unable to meet the orc's eyes. The silence between them drew out until the orc squeezed his arm again, insistently.

"Tell...me."

"The captain said she was a Wilderling, and that she has magick — real and dangerous magick. He said that someone in the Church — the High Seeker, I think — is looking for her and will pay more money than they've ever seen for her." He swallowed again, finding it hard to speak but feeling like he needed to get all of it out. "Tra'al, I'm scared. The captain wants to keep her a secret from the rest of the crew, and he promised me that if I take care of her and you — and keep his secrets — that he'll..."

Tra'al cut him off with a shake of his head and another desperate squeeze.

"Help...her..."

"I am...I mean...I will...I'm supposed to take care of..." His voice trailed off when Tra'al's claw-tipped fingers tightened.

"...escape!...Help...her...escape!"

"She's a Wilderling!" he gasped. "Three of the men who went out for her didn't come back! I heard him and Haddock talking about how she controlled animals and hurt Bulger and Valk with her magick! Haddock is scared of her, and nothing scares him!"

The old orc's face hardened into a look of determination. He squeezed Mouse's arm so hard that he started to lose feeling. Tra'al's voice had the same edge and determination that his face showed.

"If you don't help her, lad...all...of...our...sacrifices...will... have...been...in...vain."

"Whose sacrifices? What are you talking about? I don't understand!"

Droplets of blood and spittle flew in equal amounts from the orc's ruined mouth.

"Help...her...escape!"

Tra'al's song strengthened just like his grip on Mouse's arm: the thunderous beats of war drums mixed with a distant echo of a sweeter melody, one that reminded him of the song he heard when the flute was offered to him by Tegger Dan.

There's something about that song...something I'm supposed to remember...

Mouse shook his head.

There was so much he wanted to say to the old orc — about how deadly serious Captain Dastyr was about taking the young woman to this High Seeker and about how dangerous the Wilderlings were.

I have a chance to be trained at the best school in the world! He struggled to keep his selfish thoughts to himself. *How could I give that up for any prisoner, especially a Wilderling?*

Before Mouse's inner conflict was resolved, however, Tra'al's strength gave out. His chest heaved with a wet gurgling breath. The orc's left hand loosened and slid from Mouse's forearm while his right hand slumped to his side, dragging the blood-soaked rag with it. Tra'al's good eye closed as he slipped into unconsciousness, leaving him all alone to wrestle with his concerns for the orc and his fears about the Wilderling.

Mouse stood up and turned around to face the direction of his next duty. A maelstrom of conflicting emotions swirled around his heart.

"Why would I help her escape?" Mouse's whispered words were too soft to be heard by anyone else. "Wilderlings killed my father."

CHAPTER 18

Seldy

Seldy jerked back from the scalding pain on her shoulder. Desperate to escape the monster and his foul kiss, she flailed her arms and kicked out with her leg. There was a jarring impact from her heel connecting with something real and solid.

"Ooof!"

Someone collapsed behind her. A male voice choked out a low moan.

Panicked, Seldy scrabbled forward on hands and knees, pushing free of the confines of the woolen blanket. Her head smacked into something solid. Fresh pain from the throbbing ache at the top of her head competed with the lancing agony from the back of her shoulder and the burning sensation around her neck.

She sought to draw on the strength of her mother's love and on the pulsing energy of the seed inside of her, but those things were gone. She was hollow and empty inside, a shivering husk of a person, alone and forgotten by everyone except the monster who sought to claim her for his bride.

Seldy curled up into a tight ball and huddled against the

rough-hewn wood of the wall. Her heart hammered against her ribcage; her breath came in ragged gasps.

Remembering the monster, Seldy opened her eyes. Spotting the sodden blanket first, she snatched it and pulled it up to use as a shield between herself and her tormenter. A strange man — still doubled over and groaning in pain — knelt less than five feet away.

"St-st-stay away from me!" She tried to sound strong, like she had when she defied the creature before, but her chattering teeth and squeaky voice betrayed her. "I'm not your bride!"

In the shadowy, filtered light of the dark space, she couldn't make out many details about the man or the place in which she was. The floor and the wall she was leaning against were both made from wood, instead of the frigid stone of her memory. A wooden bench or bed of some sort jutted out from the wall just ahead of her and beyond that, there was another thick wooden wall. Behind the groaning man stood a series of thick iron bars across the front of the chamber with the heavy frame of an iron door — also fashioned out of close-set iron bars — set in the middle. A couple of feet behind her, there was another open wall fashioned solely from iron bars with more open space beyond that. Seldy's stomach churned.

"A cell," she squeaked. "I'm in a cell!"

Her whole body trembled uncontrollably from the cold. She dug her fingers into the wet wool of the blanket, pulling it tighter about her body.

"Unnggh!"

The young man struggled to push himself up onto all fours, coughing as he did so.

"That...was...uncalled for," he gasped. "I was only trying to clean your wounds."

His voice was vastly different than the cold, serpentine voice of her dream. His tone was breathy, frustrated, and entirely human. When he turned his face up to her, her breath caught in her throat. She was staring into a pair of warm, brown eyes framed by a mop of unkempt, curly brown hair, all set in the earnest-looking face of a young man who had to be fairly close to her in age.

A massive purplish bruise covered the upper right side of his face. His right eye was swollen and he moved as if other injuries troubled him.

"Oh! You're not a monster!"

His eyes widened. He pushed himself up to his knees, straightening up slowly with a grimace.

"No," he said in a quiet and somber tone. "I'm not a monster." He closed his eyes and shuddered. "At least...not yet."

A silence fell between them as the young man opened his eyes, settled back on his knees, and studied her with an intense gaze. Other than showing her that his hands were empty, he didn't move.

He had a strong nose and a prominent chin. His lips were soft and full. His face was unshaven and covered with stubble that was at least a couple of days old. He had the tanned complexion of someone who spent a lot of time outside. It was his soft eyes, however, that kept pulling her gaze back. Something about him seemed familiar.

His gaze was focused on her own eyes and ears initially but kept drifting down to the collar around her neck. He looked discomforted by its presence; yet, he remained still and silent. As she watched him, his eyes glazed over as if he were listening for something, his brows knit together in consternation.

The stiff collar burned hot against her neck, but the blistering heat didn't provide her with any comfort. She was so cold that her arms and legs were trembling.

This young man was nothing like the horrible men who had come for her during the storm. Despite the clear signs of having recently suffered from violence, he didn't carry himself like either a hardened warrior or a victim. There was a kindness and warmth to his eyes that reminded her of Chad.

Oh Chad, my love!

Blinking back tears, Seldy pushed her worries for Chad aside and instead focused on the young man before her. That he reminded her in some small way of her *consyrtu* had to be a good thing.

Her eyes shifted down from his face. He was wearing a faded blue overcoat that had seen better days. It was a little too big on him, hanging loose over a thin, but athletic frame. The buttons of the coat were of different sizes and colors, as if each one had been replaced over the years from different sources. The fabric of the jacket had been torn innumerable times, but each tear had been stitched back together with a patient hand. Whoever had repaired it was someone who took great care in their work. Beneath his jacket was a worn cotton tunic that might once have been white but was now dull beige.

His woolen trousers were probably meant to match the color of the jacket but had faded at different rates, leaving them darker than the jacket. A thin leather belt that was far too long for his thin frame was drawn through the loops of the trousers; the end of it dangled half-way down his right thigh. Without that belt, the ill-fitting trousers couldn't have remained around his waist for long, since they were clearly made for someone far heavier than he was. Tucked behind him, his feet were bare.

"Miss," he finally broke the silence between them. "Are you okay? You have a nasty burn wound on your shoulder that I was trying to clean up."

He nodded towards a wet rag that had fallen to the floor, but he didn't make any move to pick it up or come any closer to her. A wooden bucket filled with water stood just beyond the fallen rag, and a pair of lumpy burlap sacks sat nearby, the nearest of them was larger than the other.

Before she could respond, the building lurched down and to the right, throwing Seldy off balance. Her shriek of surprise was lost amidst the groaning creaks of the wood all around and the rattling of the iron bars within their brackets. Falling forward, she caught herself by dropping the blanket and bracing herself against the floor with both hands. She looked up, her eyes wide. She was surprised to see the young man still sitting as he was, seemingly unperturbed by the fact that the whole room had just tilted, dropped beneath them, and continued to sway for several moments afterward. A dark stain grew around the base of the bucket, proof that the sudden lurch hadn't been in her imagination.

"What's happening?" Her voice was tiny and frail. "Where are we?"

She pushed herself back up to her knees and pulled the sodden and muddy blanket back up to cover herself, despite how little warmth it provided.

The young man's expression remained serious and calm; his eyes met hers. They were filled with both concern and compassion.

"We are in the hold of a ship," he said. "The *Hunter's Ghost*, to be precise. It is captained by Klard Dastyr."

"A ship?" Seldy gasped. "Wait, Klard Dastyr! He was trying to buy our tigers!"

The tall, bearded man's face flashed in her memory: his small, dark eyes studying her with far too much interest at the tiger's enclosure. That image was quickly replaced by another image of him: his eyes wide with shock as he lay sprawled and stunned in the icy mud. She was reaching toward him, intent on ending his life with the strange energy coursing through her body.

A fresh wave of memories crashed over her, each one more powerful and painful than the last — Chad's shocked face as he fell into her arms, trying to staunch the flow of his life's blood as it gushed past his fingers; Jhana being smashed in the head and crumpling to the floor, unconscious; of Layra dying on the side of the road, her heart failing as blood spurted from the terrible wound in her neck; a pair of glowing red eyes as a harsh, disembodied voice promised destruction and death for everything and everyone she loved.

Seldy looked at the only person who could possibly give her any answers. She croaked out a single word laden with all of the confusions, fear and misery she felt.

"Why?"

The young man looked into her eyes for a long, hard moment and swallowed.

"I can't answer that question, miss. But you are a prisoner on this ship, I'm afraid." He dropped his gaze again, as if he were unable to bear looking at her after saying those words.

She shook her head in disbelief and frustration. That single, small movement sent fresh waves of pain through her as the iron of the collar chafed against skin that was already raw and inflamed. She couldn't keep the small cry from escaping her lips. The room began to spin. Her heart thumped against her ribs, seeking to escape the prison of her body. Her whole body was trembling with cold and pain. The walls of the already small room began to close in on her. The iron bars beyond the young man began to warp and shift, dancing in their brackets as they jeered, laughing at her pain.

"Miss, I wish I could answer all of your questions, but I'm not allowed to."

His quiet words and sober demeanor became her anchor, giving her something to grasp onto, to steady herself. The room stopped spinning, and the iron bars of her prison became stationary again. For a moment, at least, the pain in her neck subsided, even if her shivering did not. Swallowing hard, she teetered on the precipice of utter despair. Yet, somehow, she forced herself to keep talking.

"Why? Are you a prisoner, too?"

"No, ma'am." The young man shook his head, his lips pressed together. His tone was apologetic. "I'm a member of the ship's crew. I've been assigned to take care of you, to tend to your wounds and make sure that you are fed and otherwise okay." He paused, looking down at his knees for a moment. "One of my jobs is to take care of the prisoners for as long as they are on this ship."

She opened her mouth to ask another question but closed it again before speaking. The way the room echoed when the wooden walls creaked and the iron bars rattled with each swaying movement of the ship told her this was a much larger room than she could initially see, drenched in gloom as it was. The only light in the chamber came from the narrow rays of sunlight streaming through narrow slits set high up on the wall behind her, far above the ceiling bars of her cell. An unlit lantern swung from a hook above the door to her cell.

Unable to see much, Seldy concentrated on the information that her other senses could provide. The rank odors of old animal wastes hit her with a palpable force. In the circus, she had dealt with more than her share of such things, so it wasn't something that normally bothered her. But her animals had sunshine and open air, and their offal was dealt with on a regular basis. She wrinkled her nose in disgust. Her ears picked up the obvious sounds of movement towards the other end of the long chamber, something rather large and heavy was pacing in a confined space, banging against the bars of a cell or cage, grunting and huffing as it did.

Turning her head in that direction, Seldy was startled by a pair of yellow eyes staring back at her from the inky darkness of a large cage on the other side of the empty cell adjacent to her.

She scooted backwards, her heart thudding heavily in her

chest at the sight of those eyes, the horror of her nightmare returning full force. But then the eyes blinked, and she refocused and saw that it was just an animal — a wolf. He was a massive male wolf with black fur that made it easy to miss him in the dark shadows of the hold.

Fascinated by the intelligence in those eyes, Seldy tried to reach out with her mind to the wolf, but the collar grew hotter around her neck. Gasping at the sudden agony, she lost the concentration needed to project her thoughts. Blinking away the fresh tears of pain, she felt a familiar tingling sensation in her mind.

An image flashed into her head of the wolf loping through the forest, late at night with his pack, howling up at whichever of the three Shards of Luna was in the night sky at the moment. Then she was one of them, a powerful she-wolf racing through the darkness, hunting for prey with her pack, her family. She was wild and free, full of life and joy. She howled, adding her voice to the collective song of the pack in a fierce celebration of freedom. The wolf closed his eyes. The vision ceased and the harsh reality of their joint captivity slammed back into her.

Wiping away the tears with the back of one shaking hand, Seldy turned from the wolf back towards the front of her cell. Beyond the bars with their door, there was a small hallway that separated her cell from another set of iron bars with their own door and lock. She saw the slumped figure of another person in that cell along the far wall. The figure was too far away, and the shadows too thick, to make out any details.

The sounds of movement, coming from beyond the silent, shadowy wolf, led her to believe that there was another cell or cage beyond his that was occupied by a rather large and quite restless creature. She turned to see what it might be, but the distance was too great, the gloom too thick. The collar prevented her from reaching out with her consciousness.

Drawing in a deep, shuddering breath, Seldy turned back to

the young man. He hadn't moved, other than to shift his posture as he let her absorb her surroundings. His eyes remained focused on her, his expression unreadable.

"I...I see." She tried to put on a brave face, but she couldn't stop her bottom lip from quivering. "And what's going to happen to me? To all of us?" Her darting eyes included all of the prisoners and captives in her question.

Her question appeared to catch him off guard. His eyes fell to the floor between them.

"I...uh...that's for the captain to say, miss."

She watched as he swallowed hard before looking up at her again.

"But I can tell you that I'm called Mouse, and that I will try to make your time here as comfortable as possible."

A dull pain throbbed through her neck and shoulders, a pain that grew sharper each time she moved her head from side to side or up or down. She was cold and wet. Fear gripped her heart.

I'm a prisoner.

But as terrible as that thought was, she couldn't stop worrying about Chad and Jhana and the rest of her family. The terror of that cold dark place and the foul monster who threatened the whole *kumpania* continued to gnaw at her. Her gut churned.

Overwhelmed, Seldy just wanted to curl up and cry. She yearned to wake up from this nightmare in Jhana's warm, cozy bed. She needed to check on her animals after the storm. And more than anything else, she was desperate to leap into Chad's welcoming, protective arms and kiss him until all of this horror was washed away by his love, forgotten as the bad dream it surely must be.

How long will this horrible nightmare last?

Despite all of the confusion, loss, and pain she was feeling, Seldy forced a small smile to her lips and replied in the only way she knew how.

"Thank you...Mouse."

CHAPTER 19

Mouse

Those eyes! They're so striking, but why do they seem so familiar?

Sparkling emerald green eyes stared back at him from behind a tangled shroud of mud-caked and blood-spattered hair. What little he could see of her battered face was expressive; emotions flitted unfiltered across her features. Fear, uncertainty, and confusion were all evident as her pupils darted about like a caged animal.

Well, we are in a cage, and she has been collared like an animal.

The iron collar was too big to fit tight against the skin of her delicate neck, so it shifted whenever she moved. Angry red welts marked her bare skin wherever the metal had touched it.

It took a great deal of effort to peel his eyes away from the evidence of her captivity and focus his attention inward. He leaned forward and listened for the hidden music that should give him clues about who and what she really was.

Why can't I hear her song?

Mouse frowned. At this distance, and with as much time as

he had taken to discern it through all of the background noise of the creaky hold, he should've been able to hear her song. But there was only a pained silence. He had never met anyone without a personal song, and it was more than a little disconcerting.

What if the Fae *don't have songs like the rest of us?*

As if in answer to his unspoken question, the young woman moved. She pushed the curtain of dirty and bedraggled hair aside, fully revealing her face.

Where it wasn't covered in mud or dried blood, her skin was pale and delicate. She had a relatively narrow face with a prominent nose, high cheekbones, and a slightly rounded chin. Her mouth was wide. Her lips might be considered generous but, at the moment, they were blue and pressed into a thin, forced smile that didn't quite reach her eyes. The features that gave away her heritage more than anything else were the long, pointed ears that poked through the unruly mass of tangled grey or silver hair. They stuck out far enough from the side of her head that he wondered how she could sleep on her side without damaging them in some fashion.

Without the benefit of listening to her song, Mouse could only rely on his eyes and other senses. He studied her bruised and battered face as she huddled against the back wall of the cell.

His gaze kept returning to those mesmerizing emerald green eyes. Even though one eye was surrounded by a massive bruise, her eyes glowed with an interior light that caused them to sparkle like precious gems in the gloom of the cell.

Staring into them, he remembered who else possessed eyes like that...

Kerplunk.

Kerplunk.

The rhythmic movements came to a stop. He nestled deeper into Mama's neck, whimpering softly. The warmth of the blanket and the feel of her soft breath against his ear made him sleepy.

A low and gentle whistling sound filled the void between the steady dripping that echoed all around him.

"It's so beautiful, Anna!"

The wonder in Mama's voice drove him to open his drowsy eyes. His vision swam with countless tiny lights in a dizzying array of colors swirling through the air.

"What is this place?"

Kerplunk.

"It's called the Mistmother's Womb, Mara."

Hearing the Shining Lady's voice, he turned his head to see her profile in the soft illumination of the dancing lights. She was even more beautiful — and more shiny — than usual. Her blue eyes sparkled with an inner radiance that was enhanced by the glittering reflection of the other lights.

"This cavern is sacred to my people because it is the very place where the Mistmother sacrificed herself for us and gave birth to her last child in the process."

"The Mistmother?"

Mama shifted her position, cradling his bottom in one arm while using the other to stroke the hair on the back of his head. With the shift in position, his tummy rumbled. He grasped the annoying fabric between him and her breast and pulled, seeking to reach the meal that always awaited him there.

"Yes. It is her shroud of protective mists that make it possible for the Fae to survive here on Aerhythia." The Shining Lady's words echoed throughout the cavern. "Without her, we would have no chance against the endless hordes of settlers."

Kerplunk.

"Well, I think your lover is doing a pretty good job of that, isn't he?"

193

There was bitterness in Mama's voice. He turned his gaze back to her, although his fingers still sought their way through the offending cloth.

"He and his crew have killed hundreds, maybe even thousands, of innocent people."

"He is desperate, Mara. He's fighting a war that cannot be won, against a people that should be allies, instead of foes." *The Shining Lady stepped closer, touching Mama's face. Her lilting words were soft.* "The real enemy is hidden from view, sowing the hatred and ignorance that fuels this endless war."

Kerplunk.

"But..." *Mama began to object, then shook her head before looking down at him with sadness in her eyes.* "He's hungry, Anna. I should feed him before he grows too restless."

"No, not yet." *The Shining Lady's fingers touched his ear and stroked his cheek, filling him with warm, fuzzy feelings.* "He will eat soon enough; it is part of what we must do. But there is much to be done in preparation."

"What exactly are we doing here?"

Mama's nervousness unsettled him, but the Shining Lady's continuing touch comforted him. He stared up into those eyes, entranced by how they glittered with the reflection of the dancing lights in the vaulted chamber.

Kerplunk.

"We are going to give our children a chance to grow into the kind of people who can make a real difference. Perhaps, they will even help to heal this broken world," *the Shining Lady whispered as she kept stroking his cheek.*

"What?"

Confusion filled his mama's voice as she offered him her thumb to suckle on. He took it into his mouth greedily.

"How can we do that here?"

"By doing something." *The Shining Lady's voice grew even*

quieter. "*That's only been done one other time since the world was broken. We will be calling upon the* Na'amweh Ta'ir.*"*

There was a moment of utter stillness, as if those last words had somehow swallowed all of the echoing sounds of the shimmering cavern.

The silence ended when Mama spoke up.

"*Calling upon the what?*"

"*The* Na'amweh Ta'ir. *In your language, Mara, it is the Song of Creation.*"

Kerplunk.

Lost in reverie, it took Mouse a moment to realize that she had spoken to him.

"You're welcome, miss." He pointed to one of the burlap sacks. "There's food in that bag if you're hungry. But I should really look at the wound on your shoulder first. I would like to clean and bandage it, if I may?"

The *Fae* woman's smile disappeared at his words, her eyes darting about the small cell as if she were looking for any hidden dangers.

"I won't hurt you. I just want to help. I don't want any of your wounds to turn sour."

He remained rooted in place, watching the emotions flit across her features. She was scared and unsure of him and this place but, eventually, she met his eyes and nodded.

Mouse raised his hands slowly and straightened up.

"I'm going to bring the bucket and rag over to you first, then grab my supplies. Okay?"

Still more than a little sore from where she had kicked him, he shuffled forward gingerly. As soon as he started knee-walking towards her, he heard a low, rumbling growl coming from his right.

Mouse turned towards the noise.

"What's wrong, Shadow?"

The wolf stared at him. Hs lips pulled back from his massive fangs as his growl turned into more of a snarl.

The woman's eyes bounced between him and the wolf, uncertainty writ plainly across her expression. Clutching her blanket even tighter, she pressed herself against the back wall of the cell before the collar shifted on her shoulders.

"Easy, Shadow." Mouse was surprised both by the sharpness of his command, and the way that the wolf quieted down. "I'm going to help her." He turned towards her. "I hope he's not scaring you, miss. He's not normally like this."

She blinked up at him, her expression neutral for the first time.

"You can talk to him?" Her teeth chattered with each word.

"Sure." He offered her a tentative grin. "I talk to him all of the time, but he has yet to say anything back to me that I can understand."

Her demeanor brightened at his first statement but quickly crumpled with his attempt at a joke. Her shoulders slumped as she ducked her head, sobbing into the blanket wrapped around her body. She twitched in obvious pain every time one of her sobs caused the collar to shift around her neck.

Mouse bit his tongue, unsure of why his joke had failed so badly. With a soft sigh, he moved in closer, peering at the circular wound burned into the pale flesh of her right shoulder. He sucked in his breath at the blood seeping around the edges of the circle of inflamed, burned flesh.

Whoah! That looks just like a Seeker's Circle!

"*Do you have any questions, boy?*" Captain Dastyr's normally gruff voice was softened by the fatigue that was evident on his face.

"Yes, sir. If the Wilderling is so dangerous, how will I protect myself from her if she tries to hurt me or to escape?"

"That's a good question."

The captain leaned on the desk in front of him and pushed an object Mouse hadn't noticed before forward. It was some sort of pendant, attached to a leather thong.

"Have you heard of the Seekers?"

Mouse nodded. Everyone knew of the Seekers. They were the fanatical followers of the most powerful and dynamic religion in the Guild Alliance. His mother had taught him basic history, so he knew that their religion — formally called the "Church of the Found" but often referred to simply as the "Church" — was much younger than the Alliance itself, having arisen from a little known cult to become the preeminent faith within the Alliance in only the last hundred years. He didn't know much more about the Church, other than it had gained enough strength to have replaced the Tinkerer's Guild on the Grand Council of the Guild Alliance after Tegger Dan's disgraceful actions brought that once proud and powerful guild to ruin.

"Do they have any churches in the Slant?"

"No, sir."

"I didn't think so. The circle is our holiest symbol, Mouse."

He picked the pendant up and showed it to him. It was a plain, black circle of forged metal. The band of metal was as wide and thick as his pinky, creating a perfect circle that was slightly bigger than his palm.

"It represents the everlasting life that all true believers seek; a reward that only the Found God can grant. The best Seeker's Circles are made from lodestone, like the stuff keeping this ship afloat." He picked up the pendant and handed it over the desk to Mouse. "This Circle is made from the next best substitute — good, hard iron. If the witch gives you any problems, any problems at all, you just show her that circle, and she'll behave.

If she doesn't, touch it to her skin, and she won't be able to give you any more trouble."

"But I'm not a Seeker, sir." Mouse furrowed his brow. "How will this help me?"

The big bearded man chuckled as he sat back. For a moment, his eyes glazed over as if remembering something wondrous. When he focused on Mouse again, the captain's demeanor became deadly serious.

"Perhaps that is something we can work on, son. Connections with the Church can do a lot of good for you, beyond saving your soul. But fear not, for Wilderlings cannot tolerate the touch of iron to their skin, whether you're a Seeker or not."

Listening to the captain's words, Mouse's attention was drawn to the ominous change in the captain's song. The more the captain spoke of the Seeker's and their church, the darker and deeper the tones of his song became. In the back of his mind, Mouse heard the faintest hints of that haunting song he had first heard when he held the flute for the first time. The moment he touched a curious finger to the cold, smooth, iron band of the circle, however, those wispy notes evaporated as if they had never existed.

Staring down at the wound on the sobbing woman's shoulder, the pendant weighed his pocket down like an anchor. His stomach churned.

But Chard and Pedar and Jamsen are dead because of her. She nearly killed Valk!

Pushing aside those nagging doubts, Mouse dipped his rag into the cold water of the bucket and wrung it out. The Wilderling gasped in pain when he pressed the rag to her wound, but she didn't resist.

Remembering a technique his mother had often used when treating her patients, he spoke to her in a quiet voice.

"Miss? Would you like to hear a story?"

When she didn't respond, Mouse continued working in silence until the wound on her shoulder was clean. Rustling about in his bag of supplies, he looked up to see her puffy, tear-stained eyes studying him with trepidation. He held the jar up for her to look at.

"This is just honey mixed with some ground up willow bark. I'm going to spread it on the bandages. It will ease your pain somewhat and reduce your chances of getting wound rot." He offered her a tentative smile. He nodded towards her shoulder, "It would be easier if you turned your back to me instead of the wall. I'll be gentle, I promise."

After a bit of hesitation, the young woman nodded and shifted her position.

Her thin nightgown was wet and transparent. It clung to her feminine curves, leaving no doubt that there was nothing underneath the flimsy garment but her bare skin...

Pushing aside those improper thoughts, Mouse pulled out a fresh roll of gauze.

"What kind of story?"

Her voice was so quiet that it was almost lost within the constant creaking and groaning of the ship in flight.

"Pardon?"

"I like stories," she said, loud enough for him to hear. "What kind of stories do you know?"

"Can you gather your hair and remove the strap from your shoulder please?" He dipped the first strip of gauze into the honey and glanced up at her. "This stuff is pretty sticky."

She eased the strap to the side with trembling fingers, then gathered in her hair and pulled it in front of her left shoulder.

"Thank you, miss."

Leaning forward, he carefully pressed the honey-laden strip across the top portion of her wound. The girl stiffened and gasped at the first contact but relaxed when he smoothed it out with gentle pressure.

"I know a lot of different stories, miss. From scary to funny to heroic, if that's your interest."

"Nothing scary." She gave the smallest shake of her head. The collar shifted. "And I don't feel much like laughing right now."

From the hitch in her voice, Mouse got the distinct impression that was something she had never said before. He dipped the second strip into the honey.

"Have you ever heard of Archalon Dan? He was called the Sword of Mercy!"

"Uncle Tegger's last name is Dan." Her posture stiffened. "But he's a bard, not a warrior. Are they related?"

Tegger Dan is her uncle? How is that even possible?

His sticky fingers still knuckle-deep in the jar of honey, Mouse felt the pieces of her puzzle clicking into place.

That's why the captain kidnapped her!

Focused as he was on the task of helping her wounds, he had all but forgotten that the infamous outlaw was a direct descendant of the greatest hero in the history of the Guild Alliance. His first instinct was to scoff and to make some sort of derisive comment about how the traitor had nearly ruined the Dan family name but after the way Tra'al had defended him, Mouse hesitated.

And...he gave me the flute.

"I think so, yes." He swallowed. "Archalon Dan was the founder of House Dan. Have you ever heard any stories about him? He was a great man; the greatest warrior the Guild Alliance ever produced."

"No, but I would like to." Her whole body shuddered. She pulled her knees up to her chest and wrapped her arms around them as if trying to conserve what little heat she had. "Brrr...I'm so c-c-cold."

"As soon as we get this wound covered, miss, I can get you a dry blanket and a clean tunic to change into."

Glad to shift the conversation away from his conflicted feelings about Tegger Dan, Mouse continued.

"Nearly a century and a half ago, a boy named Archalon was born in the Slant to a young woman who had to sell her body to men in order to make ends meet..."

"What's...the...Slant?" the Wilderling asked in a slurred voice, interrupting the story.

"Um...it's the place where I grew up," Mouse replied, applying the second strip to her back. "It's a huge slum composed of countless shanties and shacks that sits on the muddy slopes outside the walls of Ventraxis — the capital city of the Guild Alliance. It's a dirty, nasty place where lots of really poor people barely get by. It's ruled by gangs who steal from anyone who has anything to steal and kill anyone who tries to stop them."

"It sounds terrible!" She trembled beneath his fingers. "Wh-wh-why would anyone live in such a...pl-pl-place?" Her words faded until the last part of the question was so quiet that Mouse had to strain to hear it.

"No one would, if they had any real choice." *Except for my mom.* Reaching for the next strip, Mouse kept that bitter thought to himself. "But you see, everyone wants to live in 'Traxis, the big, beautiful city where there's always enough to eat and drink and where the living is easy. You have to be a citizen of the Guild Alliance, however, and you have to have money — a lot of it — to stay in the city. Those poor souls who don't have the money or the citizenship needed to stay in the capital are forced out into the Slant to try and earn a way into the city. Some hope to do so with their brains or their talent, others try to...steal it. Some succeed. But most don't. I was just lucky enough to escape the place with my life..."

His voice trailed off. He pressed the third strip into place, covering the last of her shoulder wound.

Her body was shaking non-stop, and her teeth were chattering. Her skin was cold and clammy to the touch. There was a ring of smaller burns around her neck, but Mouse wasn't sure how to do anything about those without causing her more pain.

Unless I remove it.

He took a deep breath and wiped the last remnants of grainy honey from his fingers using the rag. He shook his head.

I don't have the key, and the captain made it very clear that the collar protects us from her magick. It needs to stay on.

"Miss, the main wound is covered for now, but you'll have to be careful with the bandages; the honey is the only thing holding them in place."

She sat there, silent, rocking back and forth.

"Miss, are you okay?"

"I'm s-s-so c-c-cold." Her voice was weak and faint. "I d-d-don't kn-kn-know why. I n-n-never f-f-feel c-c-cold."

He pushed back up onto his knees and moved around to see her from the side. Her lips were thin and pale. She was staring ahead, unseeing. She clutched the wet woolen blanket to her torso as she continued to sway in place.

Mouse placed the back of his hand on her forehead. She didn't even seem to notice his touch. Her forehead was as cold and clammy as her back.

"Uh, miss...I think it's best if you were to get out of those wet clothes and get yourself into something warm and dry." He pushed the larger burlap bag up next to her. "There's food and a dry tunic in there that should easily fit you. I can get another blanket, one that isn't wet like this one." He stood up. "I'll leave the bucket of water and soap in case you want to wash up before you change."

She didn't respond to any of his words or even seem to notice him. Her lips were moving, as if she was trying to speak, but nothing was coming out.

She's in shock. That realization hit Mouse like a punch between the eyes. He blinked down at her rocking form.

"Miss?"

He touched her left shoulder, but her only reaction was to slump sideways. Her eyes remained open, staring at nothing until the pupils rolled upwards into the top of her skull. She began to convulse.

"Shards!"

Mouse tore the blanket from her limp fingers and tossed it aside. He didn't pay any attention to how revealing her dirty and torn nightgown was, focusing instead on trying to help her sit up. He jerked his fingers back when they grazed the collar. Searing heat burned into his skin.

"Ah!" he cried out. "How can that be so hot?"

Gathering her into his arms, he lifted her, careful to avoid touching the collar again. Scorching heat radiated outward from the metal, penetrating both his tunic and his jacket. He carried her to the center of the cell to the one patch of decent sunlight filtering in from above. Kneeling down, he held her against his chest with one arm while reaching into the sack containing his spare tunic with the other hand.

Balling it up with one hand, he carefully laid her down so that her head rested on the makeshift pillow and then stared down at the collar.

That thing's gotta come off! His heart hammered against his chest. The lump in his throat made it hard to breathe. *It's killing her!*

Mouse slipped his fingers into the deepest recesses of his jacket, seeking the small set of tools that he had promised himself that he would never use again, especially not on this ship.

"I'm not going to let you die," he whispered through pinched lips to the twitching, unconscious girl. "Not if I can help it."

Pulling out his picks, he selected the ones he thought would work the best and bowed down. Before touching the tips of his tools into the tiny opening of the lock, he hesitated, bracing for the heat that would certainly be transferred from the collar to his fingers through the metal of the thin tools.

"C'mon, Mouse," he hissed at himself through gritted teeth. "What are you afraid of? It's only pain."

CHAPTER 20

Seldy

*S*unlight sparkled off of the ice-coated trees zipping by at a dizzying rate far below her.

I'm flying. But why? And how?

Seldy could neither blink nor shift her gaze in order to answer her questions. Her field of vision remained focused on the breathtaking snowscape below. The world continued to shift and move, bobbing up, ever-so-slightly, and then back down in a mesmerizing and rhythmic manner.

Where am I?

The snapping rush of buffeting winds surrounded her, but she neither felt the bite of the winter air on her skin or the playful tug of it in her hair. She couldn't feel anything at all, neither pain or cold. Her mind reeled, trying to grasp this strange new reality.

What's happening to me?

A narrow road sliced through the forest below, a road full of gentle bends and oddly familiar twists. Despite the great height, the view was clear and steady enough that she could make out two figures running along the road in the same direction that she was flying. Cloaks billowed out behind each of them. Both figures were armed; the lead figure carried a long staff in one hand while the trailing figure wore swords sheathed at his belt.

Those men...they look familiar.

The leader pointed with his staff towards something ahead at the very edge of her vision — a fallen tree across the road. He came to a stop and pushed back the hood of his cloak, revealing the deep ruddy complexion and the lanky black hair of an orc. The second figure joined the first, pushing his own hood back. There was no mistaking the neatly trimmed salt and pepper beard or the strong profile. For the first time since her nightmare began, hope surged within Seldy. It was a hope so fierce that she couldn't help naming them.

Uncle Tegger! Paandokh!

::Ah, yes. The great Tegger Dan!:: *The all-too-familiar voice grated in her mind, crushing the tiny spark that had kindled inside of her heart.* ::How convenient!::

Before the being's words even began to register in Seldy's mind, her view changed. Black talons appeared on the edges of her vision as the world tilted. The view shifted up and backwards, showing her a flash of the cloudless horizon before a formation of several hideous, dark-winged creatures came into view.

Seldy had never seen or even imagined anything as horrible and fearsome as these creatures in her life. Their heads were shaped like wolves, except they had horns sprouting from their foreheads, and their skin was covered in dark scales instead of fur. Their gaping maws contained row upon row of sharp fangs. Great black wings sprouted from heavily muscled backs and with each heaving flap of those bat-like wings, the corded muscles of their squat and powerfully built bodies rippled beneath their scale-covered hides. Each of their four limbs ended in a massive paw that bristled with talons so dark that they absorbed the sunlight instead of reflecting it.

"Naksh'tu'ahl bru'ash!"

Four of the eight monsters in her immediate view turned their heads in response to the command before tucking their wings closer to their bodies and diving towards the unsuspecting men.

::No!:: *Seldy projected with as much strength as she could towards the voice behind her, even as her view shifted to follow the progress of the diving creatures.* ::Why are you doing this?::

She was helpless to stop the hideous beasts from plunging towards Tegger and Paandokh. She wanted them to look up, to see the danger that was heading towards them, but neither man noticed. Instead, they kept racing towards the fallen tree; the very place where Layra — and some of those vile men — had died.

::Because that insolent mortal dared to interfere in the affairs of his betters!:: *The voice reverberated with bitter vitriol, forcing her back within herself.* ::He dared to steal you away from me, my bride, and now he shall pay for that crime!::

::Stop calling me that! I'm not your bride!:: *She pushed back against him with all of the strength she could muster.* ::Uncle Tegger brought me to Jhana-ma after my birth mother died!::

::Is that the lie you've been told, my bride?:: *The voice softened and pulled back.* ::I shall teach you the truth of things. Once, that is, these culprits have been dealt with.::

::Watch out, Paan-da! Tegger-da!::

Unable to make her actual voice heard, Seldy could only hope that her projected mental warning would reach the men who seemed oblivious to the doom approaching from above.

::They cannot hear you, Seldirima, for you are bound in iron. So long as that is true, you see and hear what I choose to show you. You cannot save them from my wrath.::

The hard truth of his words bit deep.

I have to help them! **Her mind reeled.** *But how can I?*

...love is the source of your strength, rehla*...,* **Tia's remembered words were echoed by Layra's,** *...remember that your greatest strength is your ability to love...*

Those words rang like a bell through her mind, resonating with something trapped deep inside of her. Seldy stopped fighting the invasive voice and turned inward.

Love. My love for them. That's the answer!

Tha-throom.

Retreating to the center of her being, Seldy conjured up every loving memory she had of Tegger — each laugh, hug, and fond kiss on the forehead or cheek they had exchanged and every funny story of his adventures and her own life in the circus that they had shared. Each treasured moment added another tiny bit of nurturing energy to the small but growing seed of hope she built up amidst the mountains of despair that continued to obscure her outer thoughts.

Tha-throom.

She spoke his name into that seed, imbuing it with all of the love she had developed for him over the years. When it was so full as to be close to bursting, Seldy used all of the stubborn determination and willpower that had been instilled in her for as long as she could remember to hurl it towards the ground.

CRACK!

The seed shattered the moment it struck the invisible bounds that kept her spirit imprisoned. The impact reverberated through her entire being as red and green energy exploded around her. Power crackled. The world shook.

Tha-throom...

::NO! That's not possible!!!::

Somehow, a tiny sliver of the love she felt for Tegger escaped her iron-bound prison and shot towards the man who had brought her to the only home she'd ever known, the man *who'd sacrificed so much to give her a life filled with laughter and love.*

::TEGGER-DA!!!!::

The ironclad will of the voice closed around her conscious-ness like a steel trap. Seldy's vision began to fade. But before it went completely dark, Tegger's head snapped around to stare up in her direction — the same direction of the impending at-tack. His piercing blue eyes widened in surprise, making them somehow visible despite the great and growing distance be-tween them. His lips moved to form a single questioning word, a word she recognized from a lifetime of reading the lips of her fellow performers when the noise of the crowds made it too loud to be heard...

"Seldy?"

Seldy fought to keep from squirming as Tia worked the brush through her long hair. The ancient woman hummed a soft tune as she worked, clearly enjoying their quiet time together. It took every bit of her limited eight-year-old's patience to remain still and quiet. Keeping her bottom firmly rooted in place on the bed between Tia's legs, she stared down at her bare feet and wiggled her toes. Her shoulders heaved in a sigh.

"My, my, rehla, *aren't you the mopey one today."* There was more than a hint of a tease in the seer's cracking voice. The brush stopped mid-stroke. *"What's wrong, Sweetling?"*

"Oh, Tia," Seldy sighed again, her bottom lip quivering. *"I don't know."*

"Oh?"

Seldy understood what Tiagra was doing. The ancient seer always seemed to know what troubled folks long before they actually said anything about it.

"I'm sad because Chad misses Belynda, and so do I!"

"It's natural, rehla," Tia's voice softened, all hint of teasing now long gone, "to mourn someone who has passed from this world, even months or years later. It's a sign of how much love they shared with the world when others miss them so."

"It's not fair, though, Tia!" Her fingers tightened into small fists, clutching at the hem of her short dress. "She was so young and beautiful, and she was one of our best acrobats!" Her voice caught in her throat. "Chad still needs his Ma!"

Soft and warm arms enfolded her in a hug and drew back against the surprisingly stout frame of the ancient woman.

"That's right," the old woman whispered in Seldy's long ear. "Cry it out, rehla."

And cry she did. She curled up into a ball and leaned into Tia's comforting embrace. As she sobbed, the seer simply held her close and rocked her back and forth, humming a different, more solemn tune until Seldy's tears dried up and the tightness around her heart eased.

Wiping the tears from her cheek with the back of a hand, Seldy turned her face to stare up at Tia's wrinkled, wizened visage. Still sniffling, she finally spoke again,

"Tia, what happens to us when we die?" Her voice caught in her throat. "Are we gone forever?"

The old woman's arms tightened around her.

"Ah yes, I thought maybe it was time to speak of such things."

Tia stroked the outer edge of Seldy's ear, all the way up to the tip and back down to the base in long, slow movements.

A soft sigh escaped Seldy's lips as warm tingles radiated throughout her body with each loving stroke. Besides her mother, Tia was the only other person Seldy ever allowed to touch her ears. They were extremely sensitive to the touch, and she'd been mercilessly teased about how different they were by all of the other children for as long as she could remember. As the only elf in the kumpania, she couldn't help being self-conscious about how much she stood out from the others.

"We are much more than these mortal shells, rehla." The old seer smiled down at her as she continued to stroke her ear. "Every living being, from the smallest plant to the largest creature that has ever lived, has a spirit, or a soul, as some call it. And that soul is what makes each of us unique and special."

Seldy blinked, trying to keep from relaxing so much that she fell asleep. Tia had lulled her into dozens of unwanted naps with her fingers over the years.

"But how come we can't see our spirits?"

"Ah, rehla," Tia chuckled. "Some people can see or feel the presence of spirits." The crinkles around her eyes deepened as she smiled down at Seldy. "Do you know how you can sometimes tell whether a person is someone you want to get to know better just by looking at them and maybe talking to them for a little bit?"

She nodded, fighting off a yawn.

"Well that is because you are sensing something deeper about that person than the way they look. It is your soul recognizing something about the other that either fits with you or it doesn't. It is a deeper level of understanding about the world and everyone in it that comes from the very core of our being: the spirit." Tia bent her head down to kiss Seldy on the forehead before continuing. "Some people are much better at listening to their own spirit than others."

Perking up a bit, Seldy flashed a sleepy grin. "I'm pretty good at that. I feel things about other people all of the time, even when I can't see them and they can't see me."

"I've noticed that about you, rehla."

Seldy giggled.

"You know, there's an ancient story from before the breaking of the world that tells how some folk used to believe that our whole world is simply the physical manifestation of a great and powerful song."

"*Physical manifestation?*" She blinked again, frowning. "*What does that mean?*"

"*It means,* rehla, *that those folk believed that everything you see and touch and smell is actually created out of music. They claimed that we are all beings of pure energy who create the world around us through the special vibrations of our unique songs, and that everything you see and experience is a result of the great song that we create together.*"

Seldy stiffened in Tiagra's arms, panic tinging her voice.

"*But Tia, if that's true, what happens when we die? Does that mean our song ends...forever?*"

The old woman continued stroking Seldy's ear.

"*Oh no, Sweetling. Our spirits and their songs are eternal. When our physical bodies die, our spirits simply move on from this world to the next.*"

"*The next world?*"

Tia chuckled again, casting her eyes up and beyond Seldy before returning to stare at her with a mischievous smile.

"*There are worlds beyond this one, Sweetling. I know because I visit one often when I call upon the Sight.*"

"*You do?*"

The ancient seer's smile stretched to include her eyes.

"*It is a wondrous place,* rehla. *It's a place that everyone visits when they dream. It's the first destination of our spirits when our body dies until they move on to places beyond my knowledge. Sometimes they stay there for awhile, and sometimes they don't.*"

"*Why do spirits stay there, Tia?*"

Seldy stifled a yawn as Tia's fingers continued to work on her ear.

"*Each one has their own reasons, Sweetling.*" *The old seer shrugged her narrow shoulders, lifting Seldy gently in the process.* "*If they died unexpectedly like Belynda did, they may simply wish to visit with their loved ones during their dreams and tell them the things they didn't have a chance to before they died."*

"Spirits can do that?" Seldy gasped. "They can visit our dreams?"

Tia nodded.

"Chad has been dreaming about her." The yawn she'd been fighting finally escaped her lips. "Maybe...maybe she's been talking to him in his dreams? Telling him how much she loves him?"

She stretched inside of Tia's cradling arms and yawned again before snuggling even deeper into the old seer's welcoming warmth. Her own voice sounded distant and far away.

"Maybe my birth mother is...still...singing...my...song...to... me..."

::Awaken.::

That single word burned through Seldy, stirring her from the foggy haze she had fallen into. Disoriented, she tried to blink, but found that she couldn't. The image sharpened from an indistinct black blur into the clear view of a pair of glowing red eyes staring at her.

::Yes, my bride. That's it.::

The voice forced itself into her mind, brushing aside every attempt at defense she tried to raise against it. Unsure of what was happening, she fought to form coherent thoughts in reply.

::What's happening? Where am I? Why can't I feel anything?::

::Do not try to fight me, my bride, for you are fully under my power now. I have reinforced your bindings. There will be no more displays of disobedience.:: *The powerful presence of the voice enveloped her, wrapping itself around her consciousness.* ::I have brought you home, to your wretched *kumpania*. It is time for you to see the price of your defiance.::

Her view expanded beyond those piercing red eyes to show a close-up of the monster's face. It was a horrifying mix of the features of several different animals. The overall shape of the head was lupine, with a long snout and a gaping maw filled with rows of monstrous fangs. A serpent's tongue darted out between the fangs, tasting the air. A pair of thick ram's horns curled backwards from its forehead, looping around its ears until the tips pointed forward, just below and behind the base of those ears. The creature's whole head was covered in a fine mesh of dark scales that seemed to absorb light rather than reflect it.

::What kind of monster are you? Who are...?::

Seldy's question died in mid-sentence as her view continued to expand. The creature's upper body came into focus, and it was clear that it was no longer flying. Its enormous wings were folded up behind its back as it stood on its hind quarters. Lean, taut muscles rippled with every movement beneath the creature's scaled hide. That wasn't what drew her attention, however. She saw the familiar outlines of a vardo *behind the monster. Chad's* vardo.

::Do not be deceived by this horrid body.:: *The creature waved at its chest.* ::This is but a shell I don when the need for violence arises. I wear many faces, Seldirima, and when this necessary work is over, I will assume a form more pleasing to you.:: *The creature turned its head to gaze back at the* vardo *behind him.*

::Why are you doing this?!?::

His amusement flooded into her mind.

::Because you must know that there is no home to welcome you back, no family to come to your aid. You are mine and mine alone. There can be no alternative.::

::Please! No!:: *Helpless to do anything else, she poured all of her emotion into her plea.* ::I'll do anything you ask, just please don't hurt them! Don't hurt Chad!::

Her view shifted as the world spun around. Strangely, no one shouted out in alarm. No one screamed in terror. She watched as creatures stalked off in different directions before her view returned to Chad's vardo...her future home.

The voice didn't respond to her entreaties. Instead, a massive set of claws ripped the door from its hinges. The creature was so large it had to stoop to enter the small, dark interior. During that moment, Seldy's only view was of the familiar worn wood of the floor and several pairs of dusty boots and shoes lined up by the door. She recognized each pair, remembering happier times when she'd seen Chad in each of them.

"I've been waiting for you, Drak'nuul."

A shaky, but feminine, voice cut through the nostalgia clouding Seldy's mind. Her view shifted the moment the creature straightened up, revealing Tia standing between them and Chad's bed.

"Then you are a fool, old woman!" The creature's voice filled the tidy space of the vardo with vitriol. "Because you will die a bloody death."

::Tia! Chad!:: Seldy threw all of her strength towards trying to reach either of them, but her warning crashed into the unassailable walls of iron and crystal that bound her, unheard.

"I have been gifted with the Sight, Skinwalker." Tiagra stared directly at Seldy, her grey eyes boring into whatever object kept her from escaping. "I am here to offer you a choice."

The creature took a step forward, towering over the diminutive form of the ancient seer. She remained rooted in place, unfazed and unimpressed.

"You have no choices to offer me, fool! Your feeble witchcraft has no power over me!"

There was a slight shift in Seldy's view as the creature raised a wicked claw in preparation to strike Tia down.

::NOOOO!!!! Don't hurt Tia!!!::

The only move that Tiagra made was to straighten up, shifting her gaze so that she could continue staring at Seldy. Her eyes turned milky white, and her voice grew loud and distant.

"The seeds of your destruction, Skinwalker, have already been sown."

Tiagra's voice echoed when she spoke, filling the crowded confines of the *vardo* with a brilliant, pulsing power that Seldy never suspected the old seer possessed. Light flared from each of the woman's fingertips, bright as the noon sun.

"Yet, it is not too late. Release the girl, call off your servants, and return from whence you came...and you may yet survive, as undeserving and wretched as you are."

The creature staggered back under the unexpected onslaught, raising an arm to shield its eyes from the unrelenting white light.

"Arrgh! What is this sorcery?" the creature shouted in surprise. "No mortal can wield such power!"

For the briefest of moments, Seldy felt the walls of her prison weaken. Another mind pushed its way through the protective wards and touched hers. There was something comforting and vaguely familiar about the presence, someone from her earliest dreams. From within the blinding light, a single image formed: the face of a beautiful woman with glittering blue eyes and curly blonde hair framing a delicate elfin face. The tips of pointed ears poked through the curls. The woman beamed at Seldy, a smile so warm that it melted all of the fear she felt, transforming it to wonder and awe.

::Trust the Guardian, my daughter. You will know him by the scars he bears, scars that he earned serving others over himself. Only together will you have any chance of defeating the Enemy.::

::Mother?:: *As soon as she asked the question, Seldy knew the answer.* ::Mother! Help me!::

Her mother's face grew solemn.

::You must help yourself, Seldirima. Seek the answers to your questions in the Dreamlands. Call for your totems. Find your song. Discover the power of your own love and learn to trust in the truth that only the Guardian can sense. The seeds of your salvation have already been sown. You and the Guardian must harvest the fruits of our sacrifices. Your path will not be easy. Be strong for each other, however, and together you may bring forth hope into this broken world.::

Her mother's image began to fade, dimming with the light that emanated from Tia.

::Mother! No, don't go! Tia needs you! Chad needs you! I need you!::

Despite Seldy's desperate pleas, her mother faded further.

::I will wait for you on the shores of the Gloaming Sea in the Dreamlands, my daughter. Seek me there. I love you.::

Those were the last words she heard before the image and her mother's presence disappeared completely.

The iron will of her captor slammed back into place. The creature stood up to its full imposing height.

"Enough of this foolishness!" The monster's harsh voice grated in the near silence of the vardo. His arm drew back for the killing blow. "It is time for you to die, witch!"

Tia was small and frail and entirely normal again as she watched her doom approaching. She didn't flinch or move. Instead, she smiled up at the monster with unreadable grey eyes.

"You think you've won, Drak'nuul, but neither the hate you've sown, nor the fear you've instilled in others, will save you. If you slay me now, you will be taking your final steps down the path leading towards your own destruction." She smiled up at the creature that loomed over her. "This, I have Seen."

The talons slashed down, slicing across Tia's wrinkled face and neck with deadly efficiency. Blood fountained into the air. The ancient seer staggered backwards, trying to catch her balance with one hand while reaching out with the other gnarled hand towards Seldy. Her lips moved one last time as the light faded from her eyes.

"Remember...rehla..."

Tia slumped to the floor, lifeless and still. Seldy's mind reeled in shock and horror.

"Now, my bride, it is time to deal with this other distraction."

The creature stepped over Tia's body to stand at the side of Chad's bed.

The skin of his face was drawn tight against the underlying bones. A sheen of sweat covered his skin. Her *consyrtu's* eyes were closed, but his eyeballs were moving beneath his lids, as if he was dreaming. His lips moved, repeating a single phrase over and over again, "I'm sorry, Sunshine."

::Noooo!!:: Seldy's will crashed in futility against the iron walls of her prison. ::Please don't hurt him!::

A talon darker than obsidian traced a trail of blood along Chad's cheek before coming to rest against his throat. It was poised to end his life.

Chad opened his feverish eyes and uttered a single confused word through cracked and dry lips.

"Seldy?"

CHAPTER 21

Mouse

Mouse bit his bottom lip to keep from crying out. Pain lanced through his fingertips. Bent over the *Fae* woman at an odd angle in order to make use of the single beam of sunlight, he worked at picking the lock with trembling fingers.

How is this blasted thing getting hotter?

Sweat streamed down his face. His empty stomach gurgled at the enticing smells and sounds of sizzling meat indifferent, it seemed, to the fact that it was the aroma of his own flesh that it found so tantalizing.

Twice already, he'd been on the verge of turning the last tumbler inside the lock before the pain became too much to bear. Each time, he'd given up, dropping his tools with a curse. The first time, he pushed back into a seated position and debated whether or not he should continue until she convulsed again. Dipping the rag and his fingers into the cooling water of the bucket next to him, he cleaned the dirt and dried blood from her face until she relaxed. Then he tried again.

The second time, he clutched his burned fingers to his chest and asked himself a question: *Why am I suffering so much to help her?*

Looking down at her battered body, Mouse was reminded of his mother and her last few conscious moments...

"My song is almost over, Rondel..."

Rondel's heart nearly burst. He squeezed her nearest hand tight in his.

"No, Mom! Don't say things like that!"

Even as he denied it, Rondel knew the truth. The peaceful melodies of his mother's song were fading towards their unavoidable finale. It was a terrible thing to know with certainty that the person he loved more than anyone else in the whole world was dying, and there was nothing he could do to stop it. He had never hated being able to hear the songs of others as much as he did in this moment.

"You have a special gift, Rondel...one that you must...use wisely." Her breathy voice grew weaker.

"But I don't understand it, Mom!" Tears were streaking down his cheeks.

"You will, Rondel...you will...I'm so...proud of you, my son. You...have such a true...and good...heart. I wish that I could've lived to see...the man...that you will become."

His mother could barely lift her head from her makeshift pillow made of old, discarded rags, much like the rest of the nest that served as their shared bed. Her skin was pallid and blotchy, parts of her face taking on the stony grey color brought on by the Black Scourge. She coughed into her free hand, a hacking, croupy cough that brought up bloody bits of mucus into her palm.

Releasing her hand, Rondel dipped a clean rag into the bucket of cloudy rainwater and used it first to wipe her forehead before gently guided her head back down. Then he wiped away the bloody mess in her hand.

"Mom, don't give up hope! You have to keep fighting!"

He tossed the dirty, bloody cloth into a second bucket, one that was already half-full of rags that would need to be washed and boiled, just like she had done so many times when she had cared for others who had come down with the Scourge.

"You're gonna be okay! You've gotta be! I need you!"

Her blue eyes were bloodshot and dull but, for a moment, they became clear and bright, as if she was exerting all of her strength for one last rally on his behalf. Her right hand, so thin it resembled a claw, clutched his shoulder, bringing him closer.

"There...is...so...much to tell you...so little time..."

Her breath came in ragged gasps, each word she spoke a small victory in a great war, but it was a war that she was clearly losing.

"Mom, don't try to talk! It just weakens you." He grabbed her hand before her strength failed and brought it to his lips. Her skin felt rough and leathery to his lips. "Save your strength, please!"

Her eyes fluttered closed. Her head settled back. Before long, though, they opened again and tried to focus on him.

"You...reminded...me...of your...father...just now..." She turned her head weakly away to cough then, ever-so-slowly, turned back to look at him again. "You...have his...good and kind heart...he...would be...so...proud."

Her eyes closed again, and she fell into a light sleep. Her skeletal hand clutched his small, pink hands.

Her words had sent a chill down his back. She rarely spoke of his father because it brought her such pain to remember him and how he had died. Rondel knew the basic story of their short marriage but had no real memories of them together. His mother had been born to a wealthy noble family — that much was obvious, even though she flatly refused to speak of them. She only told him that she had been estranged from her family *when she had fallen in love with Randil Perth — his father, a merchant who dealt in rare and ancient artifacts that she had met while traveling. She spoke of how the two of them had gotten married in secret against her family's wishes.*

He watched his mother breathe, worrying that each hesitating rise and all-too-quick fall of her chest would be her last. Her eyes cracked open again.

"Rondel..." Her voice sounded so very weak. "I...love... you..."

"I love you too, Mom!" Hot tears streamed down his face, falling onto her cheek as he leaned over her.

Her dry, cracked lips stretched into a small smile. Her fingers squeezed his tightly.

"Always trust...your heart...and remember...her song. She... will need...you..."

That last word came out with a sigh as the last of her breath slipped through her lips. Her fingers went slack as she seemed to sink into herself in front of his eyes. Her eyes remained open.

Rondel slumped over his mother's now lifeless body, sobbing uncontrollably as he cradled her in his arms.

"Mother...help...me..."

Hearing the young woman utter those barely audible words, Mouse was filled with shame. He picked up his tools and bent back down to the task of saving her in the only way he knew how.

Pushing aside distractions, Mouse focused his attention on the feel of the tools in his hand and the way they interacted with the tumblers inside the lock. With one final twist of his fingers, the last tumbler clicked into place and the collar sprang open.

"Yes!"

Tears of relief and pain streamed down his cheeks as Mouse pushed himself back up to his knees and finally held his fingers up to the light.

He gasped. His picks were still stuck between the pads of his thumb and index finger on each hand, the skin around each of them was blistered and charred.

"By the Fallen Star!"

He shook the tools loose. Bits of skin tore free, sticking to the metal of each tool as they fell to the floor.

Trembling from shock, Mouse could only stare in disbelief as clear liquid oozed from the broken blisters on each hand.

"How am I going to explain this?" he hissed in pain. "Or do the work I have to perform?"

"Noooo!" The young woman's anguished scream ripped through the stuffy air of the hold and snapped Mouse out of his pain-induced stupor. "Don't hurt Chad!"

Her screams, however, were merely the first notes in an eruption of sound that hammered at Mouse from every direction. Shadow howled at the top of his lungs. Gretch squealed louder than ever before while thrashing his murderous tusks against the bars of his cage.

The physical sounds of the Wilderling and the animals, however, paled in comparison to the onslaught of inner sounds that crashed over him in successive and unrelenting waves. The first wave of pounding music to hit him were all songs that he recognized — Shadow's mournful song, and his desperate longing for the freedom of the forest and the thrill of a moonlit hunt; the steady, stately rhythmic drumming of Tra'al's song; Gretch's pounding, incoherent madness.

Reeling under the unexpected impact of so many songs hitting him at once, Mouse clapped his hands over his ears, cringing from the onslaught.

"Please!" Mouse cried out in anguish. "Make it stop!"

Instead, things got worse. In successive waves, new songs kept slamming into his mind until he was being bombarded with the notes of every person and animal on the ship — each of them washing over Mouse like a legendary tidal wave from the time before the Sundering. Individually, every song reverberated louder and stronger than any personal song he'd ever heard before. Taken together, they became an indecipherable cacophony.

Mouse's head throbbed. It began as a dull ache but quickly swelled into sheer, blinding agony. It felt like his brain was determined to hammer its way out of his skull. Sobbing uncontrollably, he screwed his eyes shut and collapsed to the floor in a quivering, helpless mass of jangled nerves. Something warm and soft pressed against him. Reflexively, he clutched to that warmth and held on to it for all he was worth.

Silence.

Blissful silence.

Kerplunk.

Kerplunk.

He opened his eyes. Nestled in his warm blanket, his gaze was drawn towards the myriad of tiny dancing lights above. He was no longer in Mama's arms but resting in a nest made from his blanket on the ground. He stretched his tiny limbs, pushing aside the loose fabric that covered him. His tummy rumbled.

Kerplunk.

"Anna," Mama's voice called out softly from the side, drawing his eyes towards her silhouette. "Are you sure that this is the only way?"

She pulled her tunic over her head, revealing the profile of her bare breasts in the shifting, scintillating light.

He gurgled with delight and smacked his lips in anticipation of a welcome meal.

The Shining Lady stood with her back to him, the multi-colored lights illuminating the bare, pale skin of her back and legs. Turning in response to Mama's question, her round belly and full breasts came into view. The two women were facing each other.

Kerplunk.

The Shining Lady extended her hands to Mama, her voice echoing softly throughout the chamber.

"I wish it weren't, Mara. But yes, I'm sure."

Taking the offered hands, Mama drew the Shining Lady down into the soft sand next to him so that they were both kneeling while facing each other. He reached towards Mama, but he was thwarted by the distance between them. He gave a soft cry of frustration.

"It's such a high price to pay, though!" *Mama's voice sounded strained.* "It's just not fair!"

Kerplunk.

The Shining Lady bowed her head, the soft golden curls of her hair shifting around her pointed ears. Her shoulders heaved. A sob escaped her lips. Mama wrapped her arms around, and held onto, the slightly shorter woman. They held each other as a shroud of quiet descended on the cavern.

Kerplunk.

The Shining Lady pulled back and offered a smile to Mama. She placed her hands on the stretched skin of her own belly.

"My daughter is so very special, Mara. She's worth every sacrifice that I must make." *Her voice was filled with awe.* "She's got such a beautiful spirit, and she has so much potential..." *The Shining Lady's voice tightened and caught in her throat as she turned her glittering eyes towards him.* "...and until you and Rondel came into my life, I despaired of ever finding a chance to save her."

Seeing that one of the women had finally noticed him, he

cried out in hunger, a fierce, demanding cry that echoed through the chamber.

"Oh!" Mama gasped at his cries.

She reached over, picked him up, and brought him to her breast. His lips found her nipple and latched on before he was fully settled into place. He began to suckle greedily, his hands opening and closing in rhythm to the flow of warm, sweet milk into his mouth.

Kerplunk.

The Shining Lady leaned in close, brushing her fingers across his cheek and head.

"Don't let him take too much, Mara. He will need to be hungry for the ritual to work properly."

"That won't be a problem; he's got a very healthy appetite." Mama smiled down at him.

The sound of their words washed over him, gentle and welcoming but without any real meaning to him. His attention was on maintaining the latch to her breast.

"He's got such a strong, pure heart. I couldn't ask for a better Guardian for my daughter."

"I still don't understand, Anna. What exactly is this ritual going to do? How will any of this help your daughter?" There was a brief pause as Mama's voice dropped even lower. "And what does it really mean for Rondel to become her Guardian?"

Kerplunk.

The Shining Lady's fingers moved from his cheek to Mama's as the two women looked into each other's eyes.

"Mara, place your hand on my stomach. Close your eyes and let yourself go quiet, as quiet and still as you can."

Mama leaned forward and laid a hand on the bulging tummy of the Shining Lady. Closing her eyes, she fell silent. He was content to continue suckling.

His eyes widened when the stillness of the cavern was

overcome by the sweet strains of soft music that flowed into him through his mother's body. It was a powerful and beautiful song that filled him with love and a vibrant, irrepressible energy.

Mama stiffened and started to withdraw her hand until the Shining Lady shifted hers to hold it in place.

"Tell me what you hear," the Shining Lady whispered in a reverent tone.

"Music!" Mama gasped. "The most beautiful music I've ever heard!"

"That is my daughter's ta'ir — her special song."

The woman's glittering blue eyes stared down into his as she smiled down at him.

"Look at how he is smiling, Mara! Rondel hears it too!"

She stroked his cheek again with warm, loving fingers. Her voice fell to a whisper as she spoke directly to him.

"Remember this song, little Guardian, remember it."

Her words resonated, wrapping themselves up with the song as it echoed throughout his being.

Remember this song...remember...

He gave a soft, plaintive cry when Mama removed her hand and straightened back up, ending the connection to the music.

Kerplunk.

Mama smiled down at him, her own blue eyes not quite as bright as the Shining Lady's. When he calmed down, she looked back to the other woman.

"That's beautiful, Anna, but what does that music have to do with any of this?"

"It has everything to do with it!" The Shining Lady leaned forward again. "All creatures, great and small, have their own individual ta'irs. Humans, Fae, animals of every kind, and even the plants in the forests and fields each have their own unique ta'ir, small and simple though they may be."

"How can that be, Anna? This is the first time I've ever heard

of such a thing, and my brother is a bard! He knows more about music than anyone I've ever met!"

Kerplunk.

"The Fae are born with the ability to hear and interact with the ta'irs of those around them. It is what separates the Fae from everyone else, Mara."

"Then how can we hear her song? Neither Rondel nor I are Fae!"

"Because of who she is and who she has the potential to become! Her ta'ir is so strong and so pure that even non-Fae can hear it if they really listen for it."

Mama sat back, pulling him closer into her breast. He felt the tension in her body, but the milk continued to flow, so he continued to nurse.

Kerplunk.

The Shining Lady continued, her words echoing with the sounds of the dripping water.

"You have a ta'ir, Mara, and so does Rondel. But I can only hear them when I am very close and I listen with my entire being. It takes more effort than it should because I am only part Fae. I have spent a lifetime living amongst those who tried to suppress my connections to the magick that is my birthright."

Mama looked as if she were about to speak, but the Shining Lady lifted a hand, silencing her.

"There is so very much to explain, and I'm afraid that we won't have enough time to do so. The short of it is that I can only hear your ta'irs because I was not born here on Aerhythia. I'm from a small island called Timos. I'm the last surviving descendant of a powerful Fae woman who perished in the Sundering. She was a Treemother, one of the female rulers of the Fae. The Wilderlings of Aerhythia lost their immortality — and their connection to the sacred music that comes with it — due to a powerful curse cast during a conflict long ago. All of them, that is, except for my daughter's father."

His mother gasped.

Kerplunk.

The Shining Lady continued, dropping her hands back down to her tummy and rubbing it softly.

"He is the only surviving child of a different Treemother, one who once ruled the Fae *of this island before she was mortally wounded trying to save it during the breaking of the world."*

A profound silence descended on the cavern while the dancing lights became still and dimmed. He shivered in his mother's arms and stopped suckling. He would have cried out, but something stilled his tongue, stole the breath from his lungs.

"As she lay dying, in this very chamber, with the whole world breaking apart around her, she found a way to save her land and her people from the devastation and death that claimed so many others. She gave everything of herself to give birth and then become the Mistmother." Her words echoed eerily in the unnatural silence of the cavern. "If the Treemother was willing to sacrifice herself for the sake of others, how can I not sacrifice whatever is necessary for my daughter?"

Mama shook her head in answer. Tears streamed down her cheeks.

"My daughter is special, Mara. I knew it the moment she was conceived, when the beauty of her ta'ir *overwhelmed both of us. I was so thrilled that such a powerful and vibrant spirit chose me to be her mother. In my dreams, I saw her silver hair and her emerald eyes and her gentle, loving soul, and I fell in love with her. I was so excited to be giving birth to a child who could help heal the world. She will be a Treemaiden — with the potential to become a Treemother — the first Treemaiden to be born since the world was broken." The Shining Lady choked up and fell silent for a few moments. "I was beyond ecstatic, until the Mistmother came to me in my dreams with different, more troubling visions — dreams that showed me the danger that she was in."*

Once the echoes of her words faded, nothing stirred in the cavern.

"What danger is that, Anna?" Mama's cracking voice shattered the spell.

"A danger," the Shining Lady whispered, *"that only a Guardian can help her to overcome."*

Kerplunk.

Mouse jolted awake. Blinking, he couldn't make out anything in the darkness that filled the hold. Though his eyes were blind, his other senses kicked in, flooding him with information.

He was on his side, curled up on the unyielding wood of the deck beneath him. The constant stream of gentle creaks mixed with the occasional groan of the wooden timbers told him that he was on the ship and that they were still flying. Something warm and soft —no, someone — was curled up inside of his limbs. His left arm and leg were draped over the other person, while the person's head rested upon his outstretched right arm, using it for an improvised pillow.

His mind still foggy, he inhaled deeply. His nostrils registered a strange, heady mixture of scents, ranging from a slight floral fragrance that he didn't recognize to the earthy smell of freshly turned dirt. A strand of the person's hair tickled his nose. He snorted, blowing it out of the way.

His whole body tingled with a warm energy that reminded him of something from his dream...but he couldn't quite place it. The tingling was strongest, he noted, all along the scabs on his back, making them itch in a way that made him want to squirm. The side of his face and the tips of his fingers were also tingling.

Mouse blinked again, hoping his eyes would adjust to the near total darkness of the room. The ship shuddered and groaned again as it caught an updraft. He felt the deck rise and tilt slightly, causing whoever was in his arms to give a small groan of his/her own. The person pressed tighter against him. The soft sole of the person's foot brushed against the top of his bare left foot.

He gasped at the warmth and softness of the skin-to-skin contact. He wracked his brain, trying to figure out who was cuddled up to him and why it felt so very...right. Everything came rushing back to him.

The Wilderling woman!

It took every bit of willpower he had to not jerk away from her. His mouth went dry, and his heart began to race. A lump formed in his throat. Hot blood pounded in his ears. Taking a deep breath, Mouse prepared himself to move. However, that resolve slipped away the moment he realized that the only music he was hearing was the soft, haunting notes of the song he remembered from his dream.

Remember this song, little Guardian, remember.

A pale, diffuse light filtered down from above, too weak to be the sun. The shaft of silvery illumination gave just enough light for Mouse to see a single pointed ear thrusting up through a tangled mass of long, straight hair. He felt the heat of her breath warming his right wrist with each soft exhalation.

Silver hair and emerald eyes...could that dream have been real? Is she the unborn daughter of the Shining Lady?

The soft strains of the song from the dream...the *ta'ir*... echoed through his mind, joined with the lilting voice of the Shining Lady...

Remember this song...remember...

He blinked again, trying to put the pieces of the strange puzzle together.

How can I remember something from when I was so young? I was just a baby!

The young woman stirred, mumbling something unintelligible in her sleep before pressing back against his abdomen and sliding the sole of her foot back across the top of his again. He gasped. Her movements sent tingling tendrils of warmth shooting throughout his body. He felt a stirring in his loins. The combination of the beautiful song echoing in his mind with the tingling warmth of her body pressed up against him was too much. He felt the urge to press in even closer, to enfold her in an even tighter embrace, to let his fingers roam and explore her enticing, feminine curves.

No! That wouldn't be right!

Disgusted by his own errant thoughts, Mouse disentangled himself from her as gently as possible. In slow, but difficult stages, he pulled his left leg and arm back and slid away from her backside. Each time she stirred, he paused, waiting until she became still and the steady rhythm of her breathing resumed before he moved again. Soon, their only point of continuing contact was his right arm, still stuck beneath her head.

Flailing out with his left arm, he managed to find the rolled up tunic that had been beneath her head. Ever-so-gently, he lifted his right arm high enough to slip the tunic into place before easing her head back down.

The moment he pulled his fingers back, he was assaulted by a wall of sound. All of the *ta'irs* of every man and animal on board the ship washed over and through him like the howling winds of a raging *Fae* storm on the loose.

Clutching at his ears, Mouse staggered blindly backwards until he crashed into the bars of the cell and slumped down to his backside. The music overwhelmed his senses and pushed everything else out of his mind. There were so many *ta'irs* — each of them uniquely vibrant and powerful — his skull felt like it would shatter under the myriad of pounding pulses. He had no way of blocking out any of them. Mouse had spent most of his life straining to hear and decipher the songs of the people he met, but he'd never been able to hear more than one at a time before. Now, he felt like a tiny feather cast adrift in a storm, buffeted from every direction by swirling winds that seemed intent on keeping him from finding a safe landing spot.

"Mama! What did you let her do to me?"

His voice was too soft to penetrate the sounds that assaulted him. With his head throbbing, it took everything he had to force his eyes open and look at the sleeping woman.

She hadn't moved. She was curled up in the middle of the floor of the cell, her head resting on the folded tunic. Her torn and tattered nightgown had ridden up, revealing more of the pale and bare skin of her backside than was decent. He would've turned his eyes away in shame but just looking at her lessened the raging storm of sound battering away at what remained of his sanity.

Deep inside, he heard the distant, sweet notes of the same song from his dream.

Her ta'ir. He thought to himself. *Only the song isn't coming from her — it's coming from me. How is that possible?*

The longer he watched, the stronger that song became, even as all of the other songs faded into a momentarily manageable background noise. Unsure of what he was doing, Mouse reached down and invited that song, that *ta'ir*, fully into his conscious mind.

It blossomed inside of him like a spring bud opening to the summer sunshine, filling him with warmth and love and a calm, reflective energy. Like pieces to a puzzle he never knew existed, all of the other songs fell into place, synchronizing in some way that he didn't understand to become what seemed, at first, to be a beautifully woven tapestry. Each song was a thread with its own distinct color and thickness; yet, when they wove themselves together, they formed images of both people and creatures. Some he recognized, but others seemed to spring from nightmares. The longer he studied it, however, the clearer it became that the tapestry was a single comprehensive image.

Mouse blinked, stunned at the vision that was unfolding inside of his mind. The overall image, however, was so dire, so terrifying, and so clearly foreboding of great danger that he was chilled to the bone.

"By the Blazing Fires of the Fallen Star! What does it mean?"

He stared at the images. Despite the horrors contained within it, he kept staring at it, trying to memorize every panic-inducing detail. When the young woman's *ta'ir* faded so did the images and all of the other *ta'irs* from which they had been constructed.

Using the iron bars for balance, Mouse stood up, trembling. He hadn't even noticed how his breathing had become shallow and ragged until he tried to take a deep, calming breath. His teeth chattered. Despite how cold he was, he slipped out of his jacket and laid it over her like a blanket.

She stirred briefly at the touch of the jacket, burrowing deeper into it.

Still trembling, Mouse gathered his bag of healing supplies, the pieces of the still-open collar, and his fallen lock picks before stepping back towards the door. It was only when he reached for the iron key to the cell that he noticed that his fingers were no longer bloody and burned. He stared at them in wonder, then realized that the pain from the freshest wounds on his back had faded considerably as well.

He shook his head in disbelief; the urgency of the danger pushed aside the need to understand how he'd been healed of his recent hurts.

"I've got to tell the captain!" His whispered words crackled in the stifling stillness of the hold. "But will he believe me? Will anyone?"

234

CHAPTER 22

Seldy

Wrapped in the strength of a welcome embrace, Seldy was safe and warm. Floating in darkness, she snuggled closer, clinging to her only anchor to reality in an otherwise formless and timeless void. The only sounds she heard were the soft, yet powerful, notes to a song that she didn't recognize. It reminded her of Tegger, especially in those treasured private moments that they shared when he came to visit.

"Uncle Tegger!" She cried out his name, only for it to be swallowed by the void as soon as it left her throat. "Please be okay!"

The music continued, unabated. The soothing notes eased the aches of her battered body and assuaged the pain of her horrific memories. The song had a gentle, mournful tone that acknowledged and empathized with her feelings of loss and loneliness. It was as if whoever was playing the song had a deep and personal knowledge of the pain that came from losing loved ones and had the same unrelenting fear of being left alone and unloved in a cruel world.

Seldy didn't recognize the exact instrument, other than it

was a small wind instrument of some kind. The music of the *kumpania* was made with drums and banjos and cymbals, instruments that drove her and the other young folk to dance and twirl with wild abandon around the fires on many a windblown night. The languid pace of this song calmed her frayed nerves and allowed her a moment of respite from the terror that threatened to consume her.

Enchanted by the beauty of the music, she forgot that she wasn't alone until she brushed the top of the other person's foot with the sole of her own. Warmth flowed into her body through that tiny bit of skin-on-skin contact, restoring her strength. The music originated from the person who was holding her.

She shifted her focus from the haunting music to its source.

In the utter darkness of the void, Seldy couldn't see him but from the unyielding firmness of the lean frame enveloping her to the strength of the person's grip, he was undoubtedly male. Each moment of their embrace brought renewed strength and vitality to her limbs. Every breath she took in his arms was less hurried and more relaxed than the previous one. The pounding of her heart eased as her sense of security and safety deepened.

The horror of witnessing Tiagra's bloody death began to fade. Comforted as she was by his presence and his soulful song, it seemed as if everything that happened to her had been part of a nightmare from which she might soon wake up.

The soft and steady rhythm of the man's breath warmed her ear and tickled the back of her neck. It reminded her of the times when Chad would wrap her in his arms and draw her in close as they sat around the *kumpania* campfire listening to the stories and wisdom of the elders. He would lean into her hair and whisper naughty things, knowing how much she loved it.

She didn't understand how Chad was producing the music that she had needed so much or how it was possible that he *could be here for her in this place that wasn't really even a place.*

"Oh, Chad."

She snuggled in closer. She delighted both in the feel of the rough texture of his trousers pressing against the bare skin of her backside and the wonderful sensations of brushing the sole of her foot along the top of his again.

"I don't want this dream to end unless I can wake up in your arms!"

Her voice, however, was swallowed by the strange silence of the void just as Chad's song began to fade. Physically, he began to pull away from her, bit by bit.

Seldy tried to cry out, but the sound never left her throat. She wanted to reach for him, but her limbs refused to move. When he pulled his arm from beneath her head and broke their last point of physical contact, the music stopped.

Silence engulfed her, swallowing her feeble protests like a hungry snake consuming a struggling rat. She was alone again, helplessly adrift in the featureless void, without a rudder or an anchor.

The clatter of iron on steel startled her awake.

The first thing she noticed was the absence of pain biting at her neck, followed almost immediately by how warm she was. She was covered by something that bore a strong, but unfamiliar, masculine scent and felt stiff against her skin. She was curled up into a fetal position on a hard, wooden floor.

Seldy kept still and listened. Wood creaked and groaned, the noises shifting with each rush of heavy wind against the outside wall, seemingly ahead of her.

The ship! She realized with a start. *I'm on the ship in a cell! It wasn't a dream after all!*

The diminishing sound of bare feet slapping against the floor pulled her from the despair that loomed like a sharp cliff, bringing her back to the moment. Someone had just shut the door to her cell and was rushing away, leaving her alone.

The slamming of that door threatened to overwhelm her in a swirling morass of fear and worry, but a lifetime spent as the daughter of Jhana, the Mistress of Coin of the Istimiel *kumpania*, had left its imprint on her.

What good does it do you to worry about that which you cannot change, rehla? Jhana's strong words came back to her in a rush. *It's better to stay alert, understand the situation, and be ready to act. Then you can take advantage of any opportunities presented that may arise.*

Seldy's thoughts turned back to the young man who had been in the cell with her before the darkness claimed her.

Mouse.

His warm brown eyes, earnest manner, and disheveled brown hair stood out in her memory.

What a strange name for a young man.

Drawing in a deep breath, Seldy oriented herself fully to her present circumstances. Her nostrils were assaulted by the acrid tang of old urine and the unmistakably pungent odors of porcine feces. Having tended to the needs of various animals all of her life, those things didn't bother her as much as the rank combination of blood, mud, and sweat emanating from her own body. She wrinkled her nose in disgust.

"Ugh," she muttered. "I need a bath!"

Water sloshed nearby in time with the steady movements of the floor, offering the promise of relief.

Shifting the stiff cover aside, Seldy pushed herself up into a seated position. Blinking, she allowed her eyes to adjust to the dim light provided by the single moonbeam filtering through the small window high above the iron bars of the ceiling of her cell. Looking up towards the source of the narrow beam of light, she realized that the collar that had caused her so much pain and suffering was gone. She explored the areas where the collar had burned her with tentative fingers. Bits of charred skin and thick scabs flaked away from the tender, slightly puckered skin underneath.

"Oh!" Tears of joy and relief spilled from her eyes and trickled down her cheeks. "Thank the stars!"

The grumbling from her gut and the urgent discomfort of a full bladder cut short her celebration. Looking around for one of the sources of the terrible odors filling the room, Seldy identified a round hole near the rear corner of her cell floor where she could address the second problem. She also noted the bucket of water and the burlap sack sitting next to her discarded cover.

After standing up, Seldy peeled the tattered remnants of her favorite nightgown and let it slip to the floor to pool around her ankles. She stepped out of the torn, blood- and mud-spattered garment, leaving it where it lay. It was only after she relieved the pressure on her bladder that she noticed the blue jacket that Mouse had been wearing had been her cover and that her pillow looked to be a bunched up tunic made of rough-hewn fabric.

Inside the burlap sack, she discovered a battered tin cup, a loaf of crusty bread, a wrapped hunk of pungent yellow cheese, and a single bruised and wrinkled peach. The cup reminded Seldy of how thirsty she was. She drained the cup three times before her thirst was slaked. Filling it a fourth time, she set it aside and moved the bucket to the front of the cell so that she could bathe without getting her small meal wet.

Her stomach continued to grumble as she bathed. Seldy, however, was so relieved to be getting clean that she ignored it. The bar of soap she found next to the sack was rougher and much less pleasant smelling than the floral scented soaps she was used to, but it served its purpose well enough, and the suds it produced were easy to rinse off with her rather limited supply of water.

In the midst of a second rinse of her hair — most of it pulled around to the front — a deep and gravelly voice shattered the illusion that she was alone.

"I see that the view from my cell has improved rather substantially since I was last awake."

Startled into a surprised yelp, Seldy pushed her hair aside.

The wizened face of what must be a truly ancient orc was staring at her. He leaned against the bars of his cell, watching her with amusement crinkling at the corners of his dark brown eyes.

"Oh, I'm so sorry."

Seldy dropped one of her hands down to cover her exposed sex.

"I hope I haven't offended you, *Maestro*."

"Nay, lass," he chuckled, arching a sparse eyebrow. "It is I who should be sorry for intruding so rudely. I shall turn around and leave you to finish with what little privacy we are afforded in this vile place."

"No need, *Maestro*." Seldy offered a relieved grin. She continued to wring the water from her hair back into the bucket. "I'm used to bathing and changing in front of others. We do it all of the time in the circus."

Before he could reply, the old orc broke out into a spasm of coughing that had him hanging his head and spitting out a reddish globule of phlegm and blood.

Forgetting about her sopping hair, Seldy scooted around the bucket and approached as close as she could without actually touching the iron bars. Having been freed of the iron collar, the last thing she wanted was to touch that foul metal again.

"Are you alright, *Maestro*? That cough sounds horrible!"

"Aye." The orc spat, then spoke in a hoarser voice. "It'll be the death of me afore long, that's for sure." He raised his head to regard her with rheumy eyes.

"I'm so sorry." Seldy couldn't help staring into his eyes. She was drawn to both the strength and wisdom she saw reflected in them. "I wish I could help you."

"You already have, lass, just by being here." His face broke out into a sad smile as he examined her in return. "Although I sincerely wish that you hadn't been kidnapped."

"Huh?" Sitting back on her heels, she offered him the brightest smile she could summon. "Oh, thank you." Then, remembering her manners, she added, "I'm sorry, I should introduce myself. My name is Seldy. I'm...I'm from the Istimiel *kumpania* on Timos."

Try as she might, she couldn't keep the sadness from tinging her voice. Her smile wilted.

"I'm Tra'al, lass." The sadness in his voice matched hers. "And I'm afraid that I am the one who owes you an apology."

"An apology? Whatever for?"

"It was my job to keep you safe whenever your circus performed near Sa-Vang." His eyes dropped to stare at the floor between them. "And when your *kumpania* moved on, I was supposed to keep my ears and eyes open for anyone seeking you out."

"What?" Seldy gasped, straightening up. "How...why... where?"

The questions kept coming, half-formed and abandoned as soon as they escaped her lips. She pressed her face as close to the iron bars as she dared and focused on making sense.

"But *Maestro*, we've never met before! How could it be your job to protect me? And from whom?"

The orc's shoulders heaved in a great sigh that devolved into a hacking cough. When he stopped wheezing, he looked at her with unreadable dark eyes. The hard set of his grizzled features told her of his frustration and disappointment with someone or something.

"You don't remember me, lass, because you weren't even supposed to know that we were out there, watching over you in every town and city. At least one of us was supposed to be there at every performance."

His clawed fingers tightened around the iron bars in a grasp, his knuckles cracking in protest.

"But why?" Seldy tried to wrap her mind around what he was saying. "I don't understand why would anyone need to watch out for me? I'm just a simple performer in a circus! I don't understand!"

Even as those words slipped from her lips, Seldy couldn't help thinking of the creature who kept claiming that she was to be his bride. She shrank back from the iron bars, her thoughts spiraling until the orc's gravelly voice brought her back. His dark eyes were focused on hers.

"Any *Fae* child would be in mortal danger, if folks..."

Tha-throom.

Fae.

The word echoed inside of her heart like a gigantic bell being tolled. Goose-bumps erupted all over her body. Seldy shuddered violently as every hair on her still wet body — from the ultra-fine, nearly invisible hairs on her arms and legs to the roots of the long silver hair on her head — bristled at that word.

Tha-throom.

"*Fae?*" She gasped out the word in the form of a question before adding, "I'm not *Fae*! I'm an elf!"

He fell silent and regarded her for a moment. He shook his head gently.

Tha-throom.

"You're *Fae*, lass, whether you want to believe it or not. And speaking as someone who has fought against them in their own lands, you're more *Fae* than any other that I've ever met — save one."

"No! I can't be!" Her mind reeled at the possibility. "The *Fae* are evil! Everyone knows that! They're unspeakably cruel! They're responsible for the Black Scourge with their dark magick!" Her voice rose with each exclamation. "And...and I don't have any magick!"

Tha-throom.

She yelled those last words, trying to make them true by sheer will alone. Yet, even as she rejected the very notion that she was *Fae*, niggling reminders of just how different she was than anyone else she'd ever met kept popping into her mind — talking to animals with her mind...being able to walk barefoot in the snow on the coldest winter day...always knowing whether a strange new plant or mushroom she found in the forest would be safe to eat or not and what medicinal uses they might have...calling on the lightning in the middle of that storm to strike down that terrible man...

Tha-throom.

"I'm sorry if you never knew, lass, but that's the truth of it." Sympathy filled his eyes. He shrugged his shoulders. "But more important than the fact that you are *Fae*, is the possibility that the wrong people have put the pieces together to figure out who your father was..."

Again, the orc's words cut through her confusion.

"My father?" She blinked. "You know who my father is?"

"Aye, lass. I do."

Tha-throom.

Seldy studied her companion with all of her senses. The answer to her question — based on his solemn expression, his calm demeanor, and his serious composed posture — was clear.

He knows!

"Who is he?" she demanded, leaning forward. She dropped her arms down to her sides, balancing with her fingertips on the wooden floor. She was as close as she could get to the foul-smelling iron without getting burned by it. "I have to know!"

"I shouldn't be the one to tell you about him, lass."

His eyes shifted, scanning her from head to toe as if seeing her for the first time. He pointed his claw towards the items behind her.

"Why don't you put on the clothes Mouse brought for you? It seems we have much to discuss, and I don't think I can manage to do that properly for much longer with you in that...uh... state." The corners of his mouth tugged upwards in the smallest of grins. "It's been far longer than I would like, if you know what I mean." Winking, he added, "Not that I don't appreciate the view, mind you."

"Oh!" The amusement in his eyes broke through the anxiety that had been building inside of her. She giggled. "Of course!"

He turned his gaze up towards the single small window, high above the roof of her cell that let in what meager moonlight they had to see by.

Standing up on wobbly legs, Seldy turned and staggered back to where her supplies of food and dry clothing were. She wasn't used to the way the ship constantly shifted beneath her feet, first one way and then the other. Her empty stomach churned and gurgled in double protest.

Seldy unrolled the tunic she'd been using for a pillow. The rough-spun wool of the sleeveless garment was scratchy against her skin, but the hem of the tunic reached the mid-point of her thighs. Jhana would've clucked her disapproval at how much of her could be seen through the overly large arm- and neck-holes, so Seldy picked up Mouse's jacket and slipped her arms inside of it. Unused to the bulk of so much clothing, she shifted it about until it felt more comfortable. Her movements caused something to crinkle inside the jacket, perhaps a piece of paper in an interior pocket.

Before she could satiate her curiosity, the food she had laid out earlier caught and held her attention. Her stomach gave a fierce rumbling growl, reminding her yet again of how empty it was.

"Oh *Maestro!*" she called out over her shoulder. "Do you mind if I eat a little something while we talk? I'm famished!"

"Of course not, lass. You're going to need all of the strength you can find when you hear my tale."

Swallowing the hard lump in her throat, Seldy pushed aside the doubts that started to creep in. She bent down to gather the food and her cup of stale water. She paused, however, when she saw a pair of yellow eyes staring at her from the midst of the wolf's cage, not far away. She felt the brush of a vaguely familiar mind against her own.

::*I am called Shadowfang. Now that the firestone has been removed from your neck, I can speak to you properly,*:: a deep, masculine voice whispered inside of her mind. It reverberated inside of her like a wolf's cry in the crisp night air. ::*I will guard your sleep tonight, Leafsister, so that you may seek the answers to you questions in the land of dreams.*::

Seldy blinked, stunned by the power of the wolf's connection to her mind.

::*Leafsister?*:: she thought back to him. ::*Why do you call me that? My name is Seldy.*::

::*It is the proper term for one of your kind, Leafsister. Just as I am a Fangbrother.*::

::*One of my kind?*::

::*Yes.*::

A series of blurry images flooded her mind, images of beautiful young women dancing in a clearing in the forest. They were naked except for belts of greenery tied around their waists, wrists, and ankles, and flowers were blooming amidst their hair. Long, pointed ears pushed through their wild hair and bright, crystalline eyes glowed with as many different hues as their varied skin tones.

::It has been many, many generations of the Pack since we have seen your kind, Leafsister. But we still remember. The Pack always remembers.::

His mind-voice, and the beautiful images he sent to her, were as soothing as they were surprising. Seldy was reminded of Layra. A pang of loss tugged at her heart.

::I am pleased to meet you, Shadowfang, and I welcome your friendship. But I don't know what it means to be a Leafsister. I've never met any others!::

"Miss?" Tra'al called out in his gravelly voice. "Are you alright?"

Realizing how it must look to the orc, Seldy turned her head and nodded.

"Yes, *Maestro.* I'm okay!" She nodded towards the wolf. "I'm making a new friend."

::I will guide you, Leafsister, when the time is right, to the land of dreams. Perhaps you will find others of your kind there.::

Seldy felt the wolf draw away from her mind as his eyes closed. She blinked and stood up, careful not to spill any of the precious water in her cup. Her mind was still reeling when she sat down again, this time facing Tra'al.

Who am I?

What am I?

Who is my father?

And why does everyone else I meet know more about who and what I am than I do?

CHAPTER 23

Mouse

Mouse's stomach grumbled as he approached the Mess. The inviting sounds of silverware clattering against tin platters and mugs thumping down with authority clashed with the blood-soaked imagery of the tapestry woven from the songs of the ship's crew.

Unable to put those images from his mind, Mouse stopped and slumped against the wall. He drew in a deep, shuddering breath. Every dip and rise of the ship was a reminder that they were drawing closer to the doom that seemingly awaited them.

I have to find the captain and convince him that we're all in danger. But what am I going to say? Who's going to believe me? I'm not even sure I understand it!

Ignoring his grumbling gut, Mouse leaned his head back against wall, closed his eyes, and allowed the strange images to wash over him again…

The tendrils of countless shimmering ta'irs coalesced into an image of the Hunter's Ghost. The ship — seen at a distance and in profile — was in grave danger. It was in the grip of massive serpentine tentacles that coiled around the hull. They were pulling it away from a mass of dark clouds dominating the right side of the image.

The storm clouds were laced with jagged bolts of lightning arcing in every possible direction and were pregnant with the promise of lashing rains and punishing winds. Between the crushing coils and the whipping winds, the tattered remnants of the sails whipped about, and the frayed ends of over a dozen ropes trailed behind the ship.

Mouse's eyes were drawn back to the left side of the image — the direction the ship was heading — which was dominated by the scariest and largest tree he could imagine. It stood impossibly tall and strong. The trunk of the tree was easily as wide as the ship itself, while the massive crown of strange leaves dwarfed the ship many times over. The leaves were blood red on one side and bone white on the other. But they weren't as strange as the bark — or the lack of bark. The trunk and limbs of the tree were covered in a hide that was in turn covered by sparkling and translucent scales.

Those tentacles, he shivered at the sight of them, *are branches of the tree!*

Mouse followed one of the many undulating branches reaching towards the ship. Remembering what he would find when he came to the end of the serpentine limb, he shuddered. Captain Dastyr struggled, red-faced and helpless against the monstrous coils wrapped around his mid-section. He was being lifted from the deck as if he weighed nothing. Stranger still, however, was that Valk's snarling face was staring back at his older brother with glowing, red eyes. His head was somehow attached to the end of the tentacle-like branch.

Dozens of tentacle-branches swarmed over the ship. Dalton stared down in obvious disbelief as the jagged jaws at the end

248

of one such serpentine limb erupted from his chest in an explosion of blood and gore that set Mouse's insides to churning each time he saw it. He would've retched, if there'd been anything in his gut to throw up. Dalton and the captain, however, were the exceptions. Haddock and most of the rest of the crew were gathered on the mid-deck, standing slack-jawed with their shoulders slumped in submission. They stood staring like marionettes, weapons dangling from limp hands as they ignored the plight of the captain and Dalton and watched, instead, the one remaining confrontation in a battle that was otherwise already decided.

Following their gaze, Mouse shifted his perspective towards the forecastle of the ship where a naked female figure stood in profile, her arms raised defiantly towards the looming menace of the tree. There was no doubt who she was. Her silver hair glinted in the sunlight, illuminated, like the rest of her, by a vibrant green energy that radiated outward from her tiny body.

The Wilderling witch was surrounded by four animals, three of which he had never seen before. The largest and fiercest of them was a huge tiger, larger by half than Shadow. The pale, almost white fur of the great beast was marked by a series of black stripes. It was rearing back on its hindquarters, the remnants of one tentacle dangling from its bloodied jaws while it slashed out at another with massive forepaws.

On her other side, the one closest to Mouse, stood a pale wolf — slightly smaller than Shadow but still strong and fierce. It snapped at another tentacle with its already bloodied jaws. The wolf's pale fur matched closely the light shade of the huge cat's main coloring — so pale that it might be considered white or even silver.

Flying above the young woman was a fierce owl with its wings spread wide. The bird's sharp talons were buried deep into the flesh of another tentacle of the tree, ripping great furrows into the scaled hide. The owl's feathers were as pale as the other two animals' fur, but they reflected the green light emanating from the woman better than its allies did.

Behind her, Shadow stood on all four paws, his head held regal and high as he watched the confrontation.

A swarm of tentacle-branches was descending upon the *Fae* woman and her defenders, some of them already torn and bloody from the battle, while others were fresh and unscathed. But the one that stood out was thicker and stronger than all of the rest, ending in another human head, much like the tentacle that had ensnared the captain. This one, however, was someone that Mouse didn't recognize. He was a young and obviously handsome man with tan skin, curly black hair, and chiseled features. Like Valk, however, his eyes were glowing bright red.

As confusing and compelling as the violent confrontation between the tentacle swarm and the witch was, Mouse was inevitably drawn back to his own image. There was a calm look on his face, as if nothing was wrong in what was happening around him. He simply stood there with his eyes closed on the opposite side of the forecastle, playing the flute as if he hadn't a care in the world.

What's wrong with me?!? He ached to call out to his own image. *How can I be playing something as trivial as music when everyone else is in mortal danger and fighting for their lives?*

Even more puzzling was the shadowy, incomplete form of Tra'al standing behind him. The orc had placed one clawed hand on the shoulder of Mouse's image as if the old Marine was trying to get his attention.

::WHAT IS THIS FALSEHOOD??:: The power of those words slammed into Mouse's mind like the head of a hammer driving a nail into his skull, shattering the image into thousands of tiny fragments. *::WHO ARE YOU?!?::*

Coils of darkness looped around his consciousness, threatening to suffocate him.

::ANSWER ME!!!:: the grating voice echoed throughout his mind. *::WHO ARE YOU?!?::*

"C'mon Mouse!" A thick finger poked him in the chest, hard. Dalton's harsh whisper cut through the fog of his thoughts. "Wake up, ya fool!"

"Ow!" Mouse groaned as he slammed into the wall behind him. Blinking away the last strands of his vision, he shook his head. "Why'd you do that?"

Dalton's thick black and grey whiskers bristled. The strident notes of his normally placid *ta'ir* reflected the expression on his face. His left eye was surrounded by purple and black bruising, and his lower lip was swollen to the point of near bursting. He didn't look happy.

The patterns of the big man's song felt wrong. For as long as he'd known him, Dalton's *ta'ir* had had a slow and steady drum beat mixed with long, somber notes from some sort of wind instrument and the calm, pleasant strumming of a lute. It was the kind of song that spoke of someone who possessed a great deal of patience and more than a small measure of kindness. Mouse sucked his bottom lip into his mouth and bit down. The fresh pain and salty rush of his own blood kept him from getting lost in the older man's song.

"Ya gotta stop this daydreamin', boy!"

The older sailor loomed over him, pressing him against the wall. He leaned in so close that Mouse could smell the remnants of cooked carrots, roast beef, and boiled onions on his breath.

"Where've ya been?"

"Tending to my duties with the prisoners," Mouse snapped. The accusing tone in Dalton's voice helped him to focus on the man's words, and away from his *ta'ir*. "Doing what the Captain told me to do! Why?"

"Do ya know what blasted time it is?" Before Mouse could reply, Dalton continued. "Both Cook 'n Haddock've been hollerin' for ya for the better part of two hours now!" The big man pressed two thick fingers under his chin. "Ya were so late that Jigger got drafted to take Cap's meal up and serve 'em." Dalton's eyes narrowed. "And you know how much Jigger hates pullin' extra duties! He's gonna find a way to take it out on yer hide, so ya better watch yerself!"

Mouse gulped, wondering if the change in Dalton's song was out of concern for what Jigger might do in retaliation.

"I'm sorry, Dalton. I lost track of time."

"It don't do no good to apologize to me, boy. I'm not the one those who's huntin' fer a reason to screw with ya. But I can't afford to be puttin' my arse on the line for ya anymore, either! Ya nearly got us both killed with that stunt ya pulled!"

"What stunt?" Mouse furrowed his brow. "You asked me to play some music, and that's all I did!"

Dalton balled up both meaty fists and pressed them into the wall on either side of Mouse's head.

"I didna ask ya to play no song like that!"

"What song?" He regarded the battered older sailor. "'The Nobleman's Fall?'"

"That's not the title of that song, ya fool!" Dalton's fists slammed into the wall in perfect time with the insistent clatter of drums in the man's *ta'ir*. "That one's called 'Dastyr's Folly,' an 'twas written by that bastard traitor we've been a huntin' for years now —Tegger Dan!" The big man's eyes narrowed. "Surely ya had to know that?"

"I didn't...at least not then..."

"Seriously? Ya didna know that song was written by the bard in order to embarrass the Cap'n and discredit his family?"

Mouse could only shake his head and stammer out a single word.

"No!"

No wonder the captain was so pissed!

Overwhelmed by the intensity of Dalton's *ta'ir*, Mouse slumped back against the wall. His knees threatened to give way.

The older sailor nodded, his expression softening, even though his *ta'ir* didn't.

"Yeah."

He leaned in close, whispering his words. "If'n ya want to know any more 'bout the story of that damn song, ya better ask that orc prisoner yer so fond of. I heard Haddock and Cook talkin' 'bout how that wiry ol' bastard used to be a drill sergeant in the Marines. Supposedly, he trained both the Cap'n and that bastard Dan when they was recruits. Haddock said that the orc was involved in some sort of nefarious business with the bard, too." The big man pulled back, chortling and shaking his head. "'Course, that's if'n ya can believe anythin' that animal says."

"What?" Mouse felt his cheeks turn red. "Tra'al's not an animal! He's a person!" He straightened up and pushed back against the bigger man. "And he's as brave...and wise...and honorable as anyone I know!"

Dalton took a half-step back in the face of Mouse's indignant response. His *ta'ir* warbled a bit in response as he held out his hands in mock defense from the young man.

"Easy." His eyes studied Mouse, his expression serious. "Ya don't ever see no orcs doin' nothin' but bein' Marines, mercenaries, and bullies, if'n ya know what I mean. Fightin' and dyin' is 'bout all they care about or are any damn good at, and ya certainly don't see many orcs livin' long 'nough to die of old age."

Dalton heaved his big shoulders in a shrug before his eyes narrowed, and he closed the gap again before Mouse could gather himself to reply.

The big man's voice dropped even lower as he leaned in to whisper into his ear.

"Just be careful, boy, and don't get too friendly with him 'cause there's real bad blood between the Cap'n and that bard, and the orc is on the wrong side of that feud."

The man's song intensified, developing a deep, menacing sound that hinted at violence.

"The bard isn't just some bounty for the Cap'n to claim. No, it's as personal as personal gets."

Being so close to the sounds and smells of the Mess, Mouse's stomach gurgled loud enough for Dalton to hear it. The big man chuckled and then stepped aside, shaking his head as he clapped Mouse on the shoulder.

"Ya better go eat, Mouse, afore Cook puts whatever's left away and Haddock finds ya and sets ya to work throughout the night, since ya missed all o' yer daytime duties."

As Dalton sauntered off, his *ta'ir* lingered with Mouse. For the most part, the man's song had softened as his mood had lightened, but there was...something...that was still off. Concentrating on the weakening strand of music, he searched for the elusive answer.

The pitch of his song is wrong! The realization hit him like a bolt of lightning, making the hair on the back of his neck stand on end. *How is it possible for the pitch of his own song to be off?*

Despite how hungry he was, Mouse picked at his food. Cook had found the worst possible cuts of roast to throw on his platter and served it to him with a sneering glower that matched the dark overtones of the man's brutish and brooding *ta'ir*. The man had never forgiven him — neither for being a stowaway who had survived by pilfering from the larder for weeks nor for stealing extra food for the prisoners and captive animals he was charged with tending.

Pushing the thick and gristle-laced slabs of meat aside with his fork, Mouse stared down at the chunks of gelatinous fat. They jiggled in time with the swaying and lurching of the ship in flight. His stomach gurgled in protest at the small bits he'd already managed to choke down.

He was no stranger to terrible food. Surviving on the streets of the Slant, he was lucky to scrounge up enough scraps to make one decent meal a day. There'd been many a night when he'd cried himself to sleep while his stomach gnawed on the bones of his own ribcage and spine for sustenance. His time aboard the *Ghost* had been one of comparative plenty.

Stabbing into the small mound of cold mashed potatoes with his fork, Mouse sighed. They were drenched in gravy that was so full of congealed grease that it didn't even have the decency to ooze down to cover the spot of bare white potatoes when Mouse dug into the mound. Instead, the edge wobbled with each swaying creak of the ship.

Why can't I block out anyone's ta'ir *anymore?* As that thought struck him, he sat up straighter, blinking. *Wait, why am I even using that term?*

The fork, and the hand that held it, sank down to his plate of forgotten food.

The memories of his mother and the Shining Lady were as fresh and raw as anything else he could remember.

How can I remember any of that? I was a baby!

As he cast his thoughts back to her, the Shining Lady's bright blue glittering eyes reflected back at him, and her musical, lilting voice echoed through his thoughts.

Remember this song, little Guardian. Remember it...you will need it to...

The crack of a whip slapping the table right in front of him snapped Mouse back to the moment with a startled yelp.

"Huh?"

Haddock's dark, tattooed face loomed menacingly over the table. The man's *ta'ir* slammed into his consciousness with the same force of the whip striking the table. The music was so jumbled, hectic, and off-pitch as to be indecipherable, even if Mouse hadn't been so focused on the bloodshot eyes and the angry expression of its owner.

"I don't know where you've been, boy," Haddock growled. "But I don't need a reason to beat the ever-livin' tar outta you..."

"I was...ooof!"

The bigger man's fist smashed into Mouse's jaw with enough force to snap his head back. Darkness and pain battled with each other, each of them threatening to overcome him. He would've fallen backward off of the bench, unable to keep himself upright, but a pair of strong hands snatched the front of his tunic and shook him like a rag doll.

"Don't you interrupt me, you worthless guttersnipe of a stowaway..."

His head lolling about, Mouse blinked through blurry tears. His hands felt like they were encased in stone blocks. Haddock continued yelling something but beyond the ringing in his ears, all Mouse could hear was the chaotic, pounding pulse of the First Mate's *ta'ir* and the incoherent rage that consumed it.

A distant, disjointed part of his mind focused on the strange beauty of such pure emotion as further blows rained down on his head and body. The pain flooding through his body simply became another phenomenon to study and, perhaps one day, comprehend.

He was vaguely aware of the *ta'irs* of others pressing in on him as they landed their own punches and kicks on his helpless form, but the darkness claimed him before it could fully register as to who else had joined Haddock in the assault.

CHAPTER 24

Seldy

Sinking down to the floor, Seldy set her small meal to the side and crossed her legs. She tucked the bottom hem of the tunic down to cover for her lack of underclothing.

"Would you like any of this food?" She held up the loaf of bread in one hand and the wrinkled, soft peach in the other. "I have plenty to share."

"Nay, lass. I've had enough to eat. Mouse has made sure of that."

"He doesn't seem like the kind of person who would be a jailor." Seldy tilted her head to the side, curious as to the orc's opinion. "Or am I mistaken?"

"Nay, you're not wrong on that, lass. He's a good lad."

He sank down to the floor with a groan. He sat across from her, cross-legged. The soles of his weathered feet were scored with countless scars. His toes were preternaturally long and ended in sharp and curved claws.

"He's got a good heart and a strong conscience. He certainly doesn't belong on a ship like this, that's for sure. But he may not have had any real choice in the matter."

"What?" Famished, Seldy took a bite of the crusty bread, chewed it quickly, and swallowed. "Why wouldn't he have a choice?"

"I don't know, lass." The orc shrugged. "He's a much better listener than a talker. I know that he spends more time down here caring for us than he needs to, and he has a way of getting me to talk about myself that I only appreciate afterwards. He listens to my tales about being a Marine and my time before that with relish." He paused long enough to cough and clear his throat. "All I've learned about him is that he grew up in the Slant and risked his life to escape it. I think he came aboard this ship as a stowaway. If the crew of this ship is as rough and ornery as its captain, then he is lucky to be alive." He coughed again. "He has been whipped more than once during the month that I've been locked up here."

Seldy listened attentively, but that didn't stop her from taking her first bite from the peach. Her whole body sighed at the rush of warm, sugary juice filling her mouth. The spongy flesh was so soft that she barely needed to chew it. She chewed it with relish anyway as she reflected upon the contrast between the sugary sweetness of the fruit and the bitter pain of the tale Tra'al was spinning. Remembering her manners, she finished chewing and wiped the juice from her chin before responding.

"He was whipped? Why?"

"It's happened a couple of times." The orc nodded towards the wolf. "Each time it's been after he provided us with extra meals."

"They whipped him for bringing you food? I can't believe anyone would be so cruel!"

"I don't know why they did it for sure, lass. But I've seen the way he walks afterward, and I've smelled the fresh blood on him." The old orc wrinkled his nose and wuffled, much like the dogs of the *kumpania* did when they sniffed the air. "Mouse always tries to hide it, as if he doesn't want me to know the price he's paid for his kindness."

The peach, and the hand that held it, dropped into her lap, forgotten for the moment. Seldy shook her head again.

"That's terrible! If he gets whipped for doing his job, why does he stay on a ship like this, then?"

"You'll have to ask him about that yourself, lass." Tra'al sighed. "Maybe you'll have better luck getting him to talk than I have. I can tell you, however, that there is much more to him than meets the eye." He sighed again before continuing. "He is compassionate, intelligent, and kind. And he has a rare and special kind of strength that I've only seen in one other person." The orc cast his eyes down at the floor. "But he has yet to discover that about himself. I just hope that he figures it out before his spirit is broken like the other man's was."

Her curiosity piqued by the sadness in Tra'al's voice at those last words, Seldy held off on pressing the orc about her father.

"You really care for him, don't you?"

"He reminds me an awful lot of a young Marine whom I trained when I was much younger, probably thirty-some odd years ago now — one of two young men who were best of friends, or so it seemed at the time." He looked back up at her, his eyes laden with the sadness that thickened his voice. "And their tale of friendship and trust betrayed — as tragic as it is — is relevant to our present circumstances."

"Relevant?" Seldy repeated, blinking in surprise. "How?"

"Well," he replied. "You've met both of those men...and their story explains, in part, why I was trying to protect you and how I know about your fa...ther..." His words broke off with a round of fitful coughing that had the old orc bent over his own lap, covering his mouth with his hands. "Give...me...a...few... moments."

She hadn't realized that she had been holding her breath in

anticipation until his gasping request reminded her to breathe. Helpless to aid him, Seldy turned her attention back to her own needs. When she brought the peach back up to her lips, the sweet flavor and succulence of its flesh was lost on her. Instead, her mind raced with both excitement and trepidation at hearing this strange tale that Tra'al promised.

How can I know two men he trained more than thirty years ago? No one in the kumpania *ever served in the Marines.*

"Wait," she said softly, brushing away the juice from her lips with the back of a hand. "Uncle Paandokh was a Marine! Is he one of the men you're talking about?"

"No. Though I did train him later on, as well."

He paused to take a few ragged breaths. When he regained his wind, he leaned forward, grinning widely from ear to ear.

"I'm pleased though, lass, to hear you would think of an orc fondly enough to consider him an uncle."

"Of course!" Seldy brightened. "Why wouldn't I think of Paan as family?" She flicked her hair back from her right ear. "He's Tegger's best friend, and the only other person I knew growing up who had pointy ears like me!"

Seldy couldn't help giggling at the fond memories of sitting in her normally stoic uncle's lap. She used to play with his ears and trace his fangs with probing little fingers as he made a game of ignoring her. She had taken special delight in knowing that she wasn't the only person who was so different.

"Uncle Paan used to play hide and seek with me in the forest outside of our winter camp when I was younger. I think the only time I ever heard him laugh was when I snuck up on him and surprised him when he was trying to hide from me!"

The old orc's face creased with amusement. His expression growing more serious as he studied his own clawed hands.

"It's people like you, lass — and young Mouse — who give me hope that one day the *va'areshi* will be allowed to come up into the verdant lands of the Midtere to settle down and raise families like civilized folk, instead of just bringing up the healthy warriors to fight in other men's wars." His voice grew wistful. "It would be nice to live in a place where every day isn't a battle to survive like it is in the Untere." He gazed into her eyes, his voice dropping an octave. "Promise me, lass, that you'll remember this vain hope of mine?"

Caught off guard by the strange request from her fellow prisoner, Seldy could only nod. "Um, yes?" Then she glanced around at their surroundings. "But..."

"Aye." Tra'al acknowledged. "That would require a change in scenery, wouldn't it?" Sitting up straight again, he continued. "Sorry about the distraction." He cleared his throat. "So back to my story. The two young Marines that I was speaking about were Tegger Dan and Klard Dastyr."

"What?!" Seldy choked on her last bite of the peach. "Tegger and that...monster of a man...were Marines...and...*friends*?"

"Yes, lass, they were, or at least that's the way it seemed at the time I was training them."

His thin lips pressed together for a moment, wrapping around the three fangs that extruded beyond them.

"And if you had asked me then which of the two would turn out to be the better man, I would've placed all of my coin on Dastyr and been quite confident of winning."

Before she could do anything more than stare, open-mouthed, at him, the orc continued.

"Clearly, that's a bet I would've lost."

The silence between them grew longer than she was normally comfortable with, but Seldy was still reeling.

"How could anyone ever think that...that monster...could ever be a better man than Tegger Dan?" She refused to say the name of the man who had caused so much pain. "Uncle Tegger is so brave and smart and sweet and kind..."

The old orc held up a clawed hand, causing her to halt in the midst of her praise for her beloved uncle.

"Aye lass. Tegger is all of those things — now — and much, much more. But thirty-odd years ago, none of that could've been said about him. He was a pompous, overbearing young man who had been forced into the Marines against his wishes by his equally overbearing and pompous father. Back then, Tegerion Dan was a bitter, cocky, and disrespectful scion of the most powerful noble family in the Guild Alliance — who just also happened to be one of the most skilled swordsmen in the known world. And the only person in the whole training company who saw him for the person he could be — who, in fact, idolized him — was Klard Dastyr, the eldest son of a minor nobleman from the island of Dortyn who could barely afford to get his son into that unit." He shrugged his shoulders. "It was Dastyr who was bookish and polite and considerate, the one who always strove to do the right thing at all times. Perhaps it was because he knew how much his father had to sacrifice in terms of wealth in order to get him into the special training unit normally reserved for the sons of much more prestigious families." The ancient orc's voice began to falter. "He was...however...eager to prove himself...worthy of the company...he found himself in."

Tra'al raised his hand again, signaling the start of another round of hacking coughs.

Taking the opportunity to finish her peach, Seldy stripped the last bits of tasty flesh from the stone-like pit with eager lips. When she pulled the pit back from her mouth, she found herself staring at the strangely beguiling pattern of ridges and bumps covering its surface. They reminded her of the glowing seed that she had only recently discovered deep within herself. A soothing wave of tingling energy washed gently through her body.

Letting the pit rest in the palm of her hand, Seldy felt a small, distracting tug on her consciousness. It was as if a kindred spirit within the seed was calling out to her and inviting her inside. As tempted as she was to heed that call, however, she resisted. Instead, she closed her fingers around the seed and projected her thoughts towards the entity inside, hoping that it would understand her.

::I'm so sorry! But, I must hear what my companion has to say first. I will try to understand you later, I promise!::

The only response she received was a tiny brush against her mind, one so small and slight that she might not have noticed it if she hadn't been looking for it. The brief touch resonated with an accepting and excited energy.

Seldy slipped the peach stone into one of the many pockets of the jacket she was wearing before turning her attention back to the orc. Tra'al was still bent over double, but she was glad to see that the coughing had stopped and that he was recovering.

Turning his earlier statements over in her mind, she struggled to reconcile them with the realities she had experienced. She had no doubt that the old orc believed everything he was telling her, but it was difficult to believe that Tegger could've ever been like the shallow, pompous man Tra'al described. It was even more disconcerting to think that the horrible man who had stormed in, hurt the people she loved, and kidnapped her could have ever been seen as a decent and honorable young man.

"So what happened to change things so much?"

"That tale, lass," the orc gasped out, "is going to be long and difficult for my poor lungs. So you'll have to be patient with me."

Seldy pulled off a chunk of crusty bread from her loaf and stuffed it in her mouth.

Offering her a thin-lipped grin, he continued. "They were the closest of friends during their training, or at least that's what everyone, including Dastyr, believed." He paused to take a couple of ragged breaths before continuing. "That friendship, however, ended the morning after they both graduated. Dan barely made it through training due to his lack of motivation and discipline, even though he was far and away the best fighter of the bunch. Dastyr was the shining star, in part because of the support that Dan gave him when he thought others weren't watching."

Seldy furrowed her brow. "I can't imagine Tegger being undisciplined and unmotivated. He's the most talented person I've ever met. He oozes with self-confidence and determination."

"That's true now, perhaps." Tra'al pursed his thin lips and dropped his eyes for a moment before looking back up to her. "But not then. You see, everything changed the night of their graduation. I can only speculate as to the reasons behind the events of that night, or indeed about what really happened. But by the time the sun rose the next day, Dastyr's father — a man justifiably proud of his son's accomplishments — was found naked and bleeding, tied to a stake in the middle of the parade grounds outside of Wampler's Keep." The orc paused for a few breaths before continuing. "He was permanently maimed in such a way as to make it...uh...impossible for him to have... ahem..." Tra'al's voice lowered as he shifted his legs yet again. "...any more children."

"Oh...my!" Seldy gasped, bringing a hand up to cover her lips. "But surely he didn't...he would never...?"

She didn't finish the question with her voice. Instead she sought her answers with her eyes.

"He stood mute when he was accused of it by both Dastyrs." The orc's gaze was steady and unrelenting, his dark eyes fixed on hers. "No evidence, however, beyond their testimony was ever presented. And unfortunately for them, it was well-established that all three of them had been out drinking for most of the night, and they were all seen departing from the last open tavern so pissed drunk that none of them could walk without assistance. All of their testimony was questionable, at best."

The orc shrugged. "So, when it came down to the word of a pair of minor nobles from a backwater island versus the silence of a scion from one of the most powerful noble families in the Guild Alliance, the matter was swept quickly aside. Whatever the truth of it was, or the reasons behind it, Klard Dastyr blamed his best friend for his father's maiming and the public shaming that followed. He challenged Tegger to a duel."

She tried to imagine her uncle, kind and sweet and caring as he was, facing off against the monster that was Klard Dastyr. She didn't realize she was holding her breath until her chest started to ache. Forcing herself to breathe, she managed to eke out,

"What happened?"

"It wasn't even close." The old orc chuckled. "I watched that duel with hundreds of others. Tegger beat Klard to within an inch of his life. But he didn't just beat him; he toyed with the man, like a master gladiator facing off against an untrained criminal and trying to please the crowd as he did so." Tra'al waved his hand about like he was holding a sword. "You should know that Dastyr was better than most with a sword. He had practiced with — and sparred against — Dan for the better part of six months during their training as Marines. But that was the day that many started comparing Tegger's skills with a blade to those of his legendary grandfather, Archalon Dan..."

"The Sword of Mercy!" Seldy gasped the name out, having a vague recollection of the beginning of the story that Mouse had tried to tell her before she became too sick to pay attention.

"Aye, lass. Except there was no mercy in Tegger Dan that day. He left Klard Dastyr scarred and bleeding from a dozen wounds and very lucky to be alive." The old orc's voice softened. "After he healed enough to serve out his term, Dastyr was quietly transferred to a different unit within the Marines. He was sent to join the Rangers, an expeditionary force where he was certain to be away from the capital of Ventraxis, wherever the action was hot and heavy with any enemies the Alliance had at the time. He served with distinction for many years, including leading the few surviving members of his unit during the siege of the Battle of Sendek ten years later. He became a distinguished officer and a respected leader for his courage in battle before he retired and took up bounty hunting as a second career." He waved towards the bars between them. "An otherwise honorable career, where violent and dangerous men are captured and brought to justice."

"What about Tegger?"

Her soft voice caught on the word uncle, as she wondered if she could really think of him that way again if he truly did the things that Tra'al had spoken of.

"What happened with him? And, what does any of this have to do with how you knew anything about me and...who my father is?"

"Easy, lass!" Tra'al held up his hands in mock surrender. "There's much yet to tell, but you needed that context as to why our captor hates your uncle as much as he does." He chuckled again and dropped his hands back into his lap. "As for our mutual friend, Tegger?" The orc shrugged again. "There's no getting around the fact that he was a terrible Marine. Whatever demons caused him to turn against the Dastyrs only got worse as he continued to serve. I think he set records for the number of nights he spent in the brig and for the sheer amount of arrests he accumulated for being too drunk and disorderly to perform his duties. He was doing his level best to get bounced from the military, but his father was having none of it. Lord Balderion Dan was, and still is, a hard man with little patience for the way his youngest son was acting. He hoped that Tegger would learn the discipline that a scion of House Dan would need in order to represent his family. Lord Dan — being a very powerful and wealthy man — paid for a full-time Advocate to get his son's charges reduced or dismissed as fast as they were brought up."

Seldy could only stare, open-mouthed, in disbelief at this characterization of the man she had loved and respected so much for all of her life. She wanted to ask the orc to stop his tale, to not besmirch her beloved uncle's name any further. But she wanted...no needed...to hear everything, both good and bad.

"Who knows how much longer that stalemate could've gone on until something truly dire happened where Tegger either killed someone in a drunken rage or he finally picked a fight he couldn't finish and met his own end?" The orc's voice seemed to grow stronger, his words more sure. "But I saw something in him, despite everything he'd done, and I reached out to the one person in the Grand Council who could stand up to Lord Dan and change the situation."

Blinking in surprise at the sudden change in both Tra'al's demeanor and the trajectory of the story unfolding from his words, Seldy sat back and managed to whisper a single word question.

"Who?"

"Lord Franklin Merriwether."

He said the name in a strong whisper, as if by merely stating it, that Seldy would suddenly understand. When it became evident from her blank stare that she didn't recognize the name, he continued.

"Frank, as he prefers to be called, was Lord Dan's strongest rival in the Grand Council at the time. And, as both the head of his own noble house and as the Guildmaster of the Tinkerer's Guild, he wielded enough influence to get Tegger transferred into serving him personally — you see, every Grand Council member can request a certain number of Marines to serve in their personal households or on their ships...but only someone of Frank's stature and feisty demeanor...could manage that with Lord Dan's own son..." Tra'al paused, "...if, that is, Tegger was willing and able to show that he was more than a drunken, rabble-rousing brawler with no purpose in life other than to embarrass his father."

When the old orc fell silent, Seldy found that she was leaning forward on her hands and knees again, waiting with bated breath to hear the outcome of Tegger's story, just as she had so many times before when listening to one of her uncle's enthralling tales. While Tra'al didn't possess the kind of dramatic timing or the flippant wit and smooth voice that her uncle possessed, it was all the more captivating for the fact that this tale was about him.

"What happened?"

Before Tra'al could respond, a door opened and slammed somewhere above them. The sound of heavy, booted feet treading down steps nearby captured their attention.

Her eyes darted back towards the orc. He was still sitting cross-legged in the front of his cell, but his head hung down. She whispered her question to him, afraid of what the answer would be.

"Is that...Mouse?"

"Mouse doesn't wear boots. That's Dastyr's tread." His gaze met hers and held it with a surprising intensity. "Whatever happens, lass, don't speak about anything I've been telling you; it will only provoke him. And pull the collar of that jacket up around your neck," he hissed. "You need to hide the fact that the iron collar is gone, or Mouse will be lucky to get away with just being whipped again!"

A tight, cold ball of pure dread formed in the pit of Seldy's stomach. She scrambled backwards, leaving her half-eaten loaf and her untouched cheese where they sat. By the time her back was pressed against the thick wooden wall at the rear of her cell, a line of flickering light spilled into the chamber through the gap at the bottom of the unopened door. It steadily got brighter as the steps grew louder. Her breathing grew ragged. The fear spread throughout her body, making her movements shakier than they should be. Nervous, she jerked at the collar flaps of Mouse's jacket to get them to stand up on end.

Feeling the fabric of his jacket between her trembling fingers, Seldy worried for the strange, sweet young man as much as she did for herself.

The heavy footsteps ended with a creaking pause at the door. The jingling of keys jangled her nerves further. Seldy pulled her legs into her body and wrapped herself as much as she could within the confines of Mouse's jacket, as if it alone could somehow protect her from the monstrous man who had brought so much pain and suffering into her life.

A key clattered against a lock. The door rattled in its frame. Seldy stiffened. To her left, Shadowfang growled, but that sound was quickly overwhelmed by a squealing crash at the far, dark end of the prison hold as the great boar was startled awake. The thunderous reports of his tusks smashing into the bars of his cage echoed throughout the darkness.

A flickering, yellow light flooded into the room when the door creaked open. The harsh and deep voice that she recognized from that horrible night of the storm called out into the cacophony of animal sounds.

"Mouse? Are you in here?"

She flinched. Even pressed up against the back of her cell, as far away from him as she could get, she shook like a leaf in a strong wind. Yet, despite the fear, she peered through her hair to see the man who had ruined her life.

Blinking at the harshness of so much light after being in

moon-lit darkness for so long, Seldy noted that Klard Dastyr was every bit as huge as she remembered. His massive form filled the doorway. He stepped into the small hall between her cell and Tra'al's and held the lantern high in a heavily bandaged hand, providing a stark profile of his bearded face.

That view sparked a memory of his foreboding profile il-luminated by a flash of lightning in the storm while standing in the doorway of her *vardo*, a bloody sword in hand. Seldy squeezed her eyes shut and pulled Mouse's jacket even tighter about her body.

"Mouse?" the monster called out again. "Where are you, boy?"

Shadowfang snarled. The boar continued hammering against his cage and squealing at the far end of the hall, his hooves clacking against the floor while his tusks thundered against the iron bars.

Yet, despite their noise, Seldy's ears picked up on the crunch and creak of boots stepping on the floorboards of the hall be-tween the cells. She heard the clink of a key ring as it slapped against the leather of his belt. She noted the strong and steady sound of his breathing. She felt, rather than saw, the heavy weight of his gaze settle on her. She made herself as small as she could within the jacket and fought to keep from whimpering like a scared puppy.

"What're you doing wearing Mouse's jacket, girl?"

The harsh voice slammed into her, spreading ice-cold dread throughout her veins.

"What'd you do to him, you little *Fae* witch? You better not have hurt him!"

Fae. That word slammed into her with all of the force of one of Jhana's hurled pans at a fleeing former lover. Seldy didn't dare look up. She cowered within the jacket, trembling and gasping for breath, unable to do or say anything in response.

"Answer me, girl!"

His booming voice echoed in the confined space of the hold, momentarily drowning out both Shadowfang's snarls and the boar's racket.

Something heavy crashed into the bars of her cell with a re-sounding metallic clang, momentarily silencing the animals.

"Blast you, girl, if you've hurt him, I'm gonna..."

"Leave the lass alone, Dastyr."

Hearing Tra'al speak up, Seldy found the tiniest measure of hope.

"Mouse left a while ago to attend to his other duties. Seek him elsewhere on this rat-infested ship of yours."

"Shut up, you old traitor!"

The floorboards shook at the sudden violence of the man's turn, followed quickly by an even louder clang of metal on met-al. Dastyr's voice, when he spoke again, was directed elsewhere.

"You don't give the orders anymore, remember? Or do you need another lesson on who's in charge now?"

Keys rattled.

"You're a bloody fool, Dastyr! You don't know what danger you've placed yourself — and everyone else on this ship — in by taking her captive!"

A lock clicked. Seldy's stomach churned. The terror that had paralyzed her before was subsiding and in its place a new emo-tion arose. Anger.

A door squealed open.

"You just don't know when to shut the blazes up, do you?"

"I'm telling you, Dastyr. This girl's too important to us all!" Tra'al's voice sounded strained, like a big, meaty hand was clutching at it. "It's not...too late...to turn around...yet!"

There was a meaty thud, the kind of sound that could only be the sound of flesh striking flesh, followed quickly by a raspy, "oof".

"No, stop!" Seldy squeaked. Embarrassed by the weakness of her voice, she opened her eyes and pushed to her feet. Stumbling forward, she cried out again, "Don't hurt him!"

"No one tells me..." Klard shouted. Thud. Grunt. "...what to do..."

"Stop!" Seldy screamed as loud as she could.

Her voice pierced through the cacophony created by Shadowfang and the enraged boar. Energy — fueled by her rage — flared inside of her, infusing her limbs with renewed strength.

Pressed as close to the bars as she could get without getting burned, Seldy could just make out the towering form of Klard Dastyr, his raised fist pulled back, poised to deliver another blow to the weakly struggling orc who dangled from the grasp of his other hand. Tra'al was being held up high enough that his feet didn't touch the floor.

"Stop hurting him!" she screamed again.

The big man turned his head to regard her. Her hands were balled into tight fists at her side. The image of the pulsing green seed pressed at the back of her consciousness. With each glowing pulse of the seed, the tingling inside of her grew stronger.

"Stop hurting everyone I care about!"

The massive man stared at her, his fist still pulled back.

"What's this piece of trash to you, girl?" His expression was twisted into a disdainful sneer. "He's just an old, washed-up orc who doesn't have the good sense to just die already!"

"No, he can't die!" she gasped out those words as she unclenched her right hand and reached between the bars of her cell. Sparks of green light arced between her fingers, reflecting the surge of energy that filled her body, seeking its release. "I won't let you hurt him anymore!"

Tha-throom.

"No...lass!" Tra'al hissed through battered and bloody lips.

Klard Dastyr shook the ancient orc like a rag doll.

"What has this old traitorous puke been telling you, girl? I'm sure it's all a pack of lies meant to make me look bad!"

Tha-throom.

Energy seethed inside of her, coiling about inside of her stomach, seeking its release.

Seldy wanted to lash out at this horrible man, to make him pay for the all of the suffering he had caused her and her family. The power to do...something...terrible and deadly...resided within her; she could feel it, restless and eager to respond. Teetering on the knife's edge between rage and despair, her fingers trembled. Her muscles ached both from the effort to keep herself steady and from trying to gain control of her conflicting emotions.

Tha-throom.

"Pl-pl-please, just let him go," she implored him. "Stop hurting him!"

"Or what, missy?"

The man turned, holding Tra'al's struggling form between them.

"You'll fry my arse like you did my brother?" His voice dropped even deeper. "If you do, you're gonna kill this old bastard, too."

His other hand reached for a chain around his thick neck. He pulled it out to reveal a flat circle about the size of his palm. The metal object was so dark it seemed to absorb the light around it instead of reflecting it back.

"Go on, girl. I've got the power of the Found God on my side. I'll take my chances over his."

He slammed Tra'al up against the bars of his cell.

Tha—

The circle drew Seldy's eyes like a moth to flame. She couldn't stop looking at it, even as a cold pit of dread formed in her stomach, scattering a portion of the roiling energy within her.

"Please...stop...hurting..."

Her protests came out in a hoarse whisper. The green glow around the fingers of her right hand sparked once more before fading. She took a halting step back.

—*throom.*

Dastyr tossed Tra'al aside to let him fall into a tangled heap of limbs. Stepping out of the orc's cell, he slammed the door shut without taking his eyes off of her. He continued to brandish the obsidian circle in front of him as he stepped to the door of her cell.

Tha—

Stumbling back at the feral look in the man's eyes, Seldy slipped on the wet floor and grabbed one of the bars of the side of her cell out of instinct to steady herself. Everything changed the moment her fingers came in contact with the cold iron.

—*throom!*

She screamed in agony as all of the remaining, restless energy was sucked from her body in a searing explosion that sent her spinning back as if she'd been kicked by a stallion. She slammed against the back wall of the cell with enough force to knock the wind from her lungs. Stars blinked in and out of existence, obscuring her vision.

Stunned and completely drained, Seldy struggled to remain conscious. Lacking any control over the twitching muscles in her body, she could only stare at the still smoking tips of the blackened fingers of her left hand as she crumpled bonelessly to floor. Every muscle in her body began to twitch and jerk in relentless, random patterns. Her chest constricted. Each shallow and ragged breath was a struggle.

The long silence in the immediate aftermath of the explosion ended with an eruption of howling and squealing. The noise washed over her, assaulting her ears, but Seldy was too dazed to do anything about it. She was vaguely aware of the movement in the hold, of keys jangling and the squeak of a door opening.

A presence approached.

Hands — big, strong hands — yanked her into a seated position and peeled the jacket off of her before tossing it aside.

"I'll not have a *Fae* witch wearing the uniform of my crew," his rough growl echoed in her ears.

For the first time in her life, Seldy was worried about a lack of clothing. The ill-fitting tunic showed far too much bare skin. She tried to recoil from his touch, but her hands and arms were leaden and unresponsive. Her head lolled about on her shoulders. All she could manage were small sounds of protest as he moved her twitching limbs about as if she were a doll to be dressed or stripped as he desired.

"You needn't worry about that sort of thing, girl." His eyes softened as he clucked his tongue against the back of his teeth in a sound of dismissal. "Not from me. I've no interest in the likes of you."

Her eyes were drawn to the obsidian black circle dangling from the chain around his neck.

"Now, where's that damnable collar?" he muttered, his eyes hardening again. "You shouldn't have been able to tinker with it."

He leaned forward suddenly, pushing her hair aside with thick, calloused fingers. The edge of the medallion scraped along the skin of her arm. Searing tendrils of cold, dark energy slid through the skin and coalesced into frigid tentacles that wormed their way into her spirit.

Gasping, Seldy would've screamed, but she couldn't find the breath to do so. She lacked the strength to resist them as the strange serpentine entities pushed deeper into her, slithering towards the strange seed at the core of her being. They coalesced around the seed and dissolved into a filmy covering. The warm glow of the seed was eclipsed by an impenetrable shroud of dark slime. She shivered as the cold spread from her core throughout her limbs.

"Just as I thought," the man muttered. "You can't stand the holy presence of a Seeker's Circle. You'll learn to appreciate the power of the Found God soon enough."

"W-w-why...?"

Her teeth chattered.

He stared down at her, his eyes narrowing.

"Why what, girl?"

"W-w-why do y-y-you h-h-hate me so m-m-much?"

Unable to move, she could only stare up at the shadows that obscured his face. Her insides roiled.

"It's not personal, girl," he spoke in a surprisingly soft voice as he bent down to regard her. "At least, it wasn't until I realized who your father was."

His eyes, she realized for the first time, were brown, slightly darker than Mouse's.

Seldy blinked, stunned. "M-m-my f-f-father?"

"I had some suspicions about who you were after you nearly killed us in the forest with those animals and that blasted *Fae* magick."

He reached down with warm, gentle fingers and brushed some stray strands of silver hair from her face.

"But it wasn't until I got back to the ship and checked the logs I've kept on all of the rumors and stories about Tegger Dan and the time he disappeared." His tone hardened the same way his expression did. "That's when I put it all together. You are Sarlan the Red's daughter...and that's why the High Seeker has such a high price on your head."

Tha-throom.

Seldy's spine went cold. Her breath caught in her throat. Her stomach, the muscles around it still twitching and cramping, threatened to expel her meager dinner.

Sarlan the Red.

Tha-throom.

There wasn't a living soul who hadn't heard of the notoriously ruthless *Fae* sorcerer and evil pirate captain. Between the depredations of his infamous ship, the *Bloody Sails* — and the horrors of that terrible plague he created, the Black Scourge — the man was responsible for the deaths and suffering of more innocent people than anyone else in the history of the world.

Tha-throom.

"B-b-but...th-th-that's...imp-"

"Shhhh." He pressed a thick finger against her lips and bent down until his heavy features were merely inches away from hers. "If you don't believe it, you can ask that old codger over there when I leave, if he can still talk." The man's eyes flicked towards Tra'al. "But I'm satisfied that you are his child. Sarlan's only living child."

The man's eyes bored into her, flashing with anger that was so deep, so consuming, that Seldy shivered from the sheer malevolence contained in them.

"Everyone I've ever truly cared about in this life has been taken from me or destroyed in some way by the actions of those two blasted people...Sarlan the Red and Tegerion Dan. And you are the connection between them. He was the very reason that Dan became a traitor to everything that mattered."

Tha-throom.

His expression continued to harden as he loomed over her. She couldn't see anything but his scarred face as he stared down at her with intense eyes. She felt hollow and empty inside.

"Unfortunately for you, girl," he spoke in a hoarse whisper. "You'll have to answer for the sins of your father and for those of the traitorous bastard who sold himself out to save you and your mother from the fate you should've suffered more than eighteen years ago."

Pushing himself back up to his knees, he continued to loom over her. His joints cracked as his massive hands closed into huge fists.

"I will pray to the Found God that you will find mercy and forgiveness in the justice that will have to be meted out."

Tha-throom.

Shivering and trembling from the cold that wracked her body, Seldy was too stunned and too weak to fight back or argue. Instead, she curled up on herself, clutching her cramping abdomen. She didn't know anything about the Found God or who or what the High Seeker was, nor did she want to know. Her thoughts kept racing back to the story Tra'al had been telling about the relationship between Tegger and this harsh, evil man. It barely registered in her consciousness when he bent over to collect Mouse's jacket before standing up and walking out of her cell. He took the lantern with him.

The ringing clang of steel on iron brought her out of her own thoughts, allowing her to watch as the big man sauntered down the narrow hall in the same direction Mouse had gone — towards the opposite end of the hold. He paid no attention to the snarls of the wolf or the squealing protests of the massive boar at the far end of the hall.

Darkness and silence descended upon the hold when the captain pulled the door shut behind him. The only light in the long narrow hold was the pale sliver of silver moonlight that had now shifted to illuminate the battered face of the ancient orc. He struggled to breathe, with each raspy breath forcing him into a mini-spate of coughing.

Chilled to her very core and weary to the bone, it took everything Seldy had to force her weak limbs into the agonizingly slow crawl to the front of her cell. Even that movement, however, triggered a wave of nausea and renewed cramping in her abdomen. Her head throbbed. By the time she dragged herself across the small space, she was struggling for breath much like Tra'al.

But she had to know.

"Tr-Tr-Tra'al," she gasped out his name through chattering teeth. "Is it tr-tr-true? Is S-S-Sarlan my f-f-father?"

The orc's head moved as he turned his face to regard her. In the soft, silver light of the moon, his compassion for her was clear.

"I'm...sorry...lass." His raspy words were full of sorrow. "There's so...much more to...it all..."

Tha-throom.

Even though his words hadn't answered her question, his tone had. A massive sob escaped Seldy's lips. She curled up into a tight ball, clutching her knees to her chest. It was all too much. The combination of the bone-chilling cold, the feverish ache of her muscles, and the cramping in her abdomen made her truly miserable. Beyond her physical ailments, every hope she had ever harbored for a life in the circus filled with love, family, and friends lay in ruins.

She spiraled deeper and deeper into the darkest recesses of her own mind...

Chad, Jhana-ma, Layra, and Tiagra were all either dead or badly hurt...

Tegger wasn't the man of honor and integrity that she believed him to be for all of her life. He had done such terrible things that the victim of his crime was determined to use her for his revenge...

Her whole life was a lie...she wasn't an elf or even mortal... she was *Fae*, an immortal creature who could wield dark and alien magick...worse yet, she was the daughter of the worst criminal the world had ever known...

The frigid darkness of the void closed in around her. Her thoughts continued to spiral downward. She fell further and further into the yawning chasm of hopelessness. Without the reassuring warmth and glow of the seed within her, she was cut off from everything and everyone around her.

She was adrift and alone in the utter darkness of her own despair with only the sound of her own beating heart to keep her company...

Tha-throom...

CHAPTER 25

Mouse

Kerplunk.

Nestled in Mama's arms, suckling on her breast, his eyes began to grow heavy.

"It's time, Mara." The Shining Lady's words echoed through the ethereal stillness of the cavern. "The hour when the veil is thinnest is upon us. We must begin."

"But...Anna...I don't know if I can go through with this..."

"I would not ask this of you, or him, if there was any other choice."

"I've already lost so much..." Mama's voice sounded choked. "I couldn't stand to lose Rondel as well..."

The Shining Lady pressed her lips to Mama's forehead, kissing her gently.

"You're not losing him, Mara," she whispered. "He'll always be your son. But once this is done, our children will share a bond that is truly special. It may be our only chance to restore hope to a broken and troubled world."

Kerplunk.

"Haddock! Jigger!" The captain's booming voice cut through the haze of pain and discordant *ta'irs*. "What in the Blazing Fires of the Fallen Star is going on here? Get off the boy, blast you!"

Mouse curled up on himself as more kicks and punches landed.

"But Cap'n," Haddock snarled. "This shirker's been hidin' an' screwin' off all day, avoidin' his work!"

"Yeah!" Jigger agreed, landing another sharp kick. "Wertless stower!"

Boards creaked, followed by the thud of a fist smashing into flesh. Mouse cringed in anticipation of a fresh wave of blows, but it was Jigger who yelped in pain as he crashed backward.

"Hey! What'd ya do that fer, Cap?"

"I said to get off him, you mangy cur!" Captain Dastyr's voice roared like thunder in a storm. "All of you, get the blazes outta here before I throw you all off this blasted ship!"

The chaotic mass of *ta'irs* lessened as those crowded around him backed away. One *ta'ir*, however, grew stronger. The sheer power of the captain's song pushed the others aside. He lifted Mouse as if he weighed nothing.

Cradled like a child against the captain's massive chest, Mouse slipped back towards the darkness. Before it closed around him entirely, he noted the conflicting themes within the captain's song — deep shame battling with forbidden desire, crowing triumph striving against unbridled fear. Echoes of other songs resonated as well...

Tra'al...?

Tegger Dan...?

The girl...?

"I've got you, son."

His consciousness faded as he slipped back in time once again.

"You're safe now."

Kerplunk.

Mama shuddered. Feeling her distress, he unlatched from her nipple long enough to utter a weak and milky cry. That little sound became a burbling wail of protest as warm, tingling hands pulled him away from the comfort of Mama's breast.

Despite the warmth of the hands that held him, he shivered in the cold and damp air of the cavern. The Shining Lady's bright blue eyes glittered.

"Come, Rondel, son of Randil and Mara Perth, it is time for you to become the A'lanthe ta'ir, the Guardian of the Song, for my unborn daughter, Seldirima Silversong."

Mesmerized, his cries softened and then died out.

"Do you have the pin, Mara?"

"Y-yes." Mama sounded uncertain, almost fearful. "Is this truly necessary? He's going to be inconsolable!"

"I'm afraid it is." The Shining Lady continued smiling down at him, though her words were directed to Mama. "Blood is one of the three fluids of the sacred feminine that must be shared for this to work."

"Fluids of the sacred feminine?" Mama sounded confused. "I've never heard of such a thing. What are they?"

"As women, Mara, our bodies contribute three essential fluids to the world, each one representing a crucial mystery and a particular phase of our lives." The Shining Lady's voice was filled with awe as she spoke. "As maidens, the monthly flow of our Moon's Blood signals our entry into the sorority of womanhood, giving us the potential to bring forth new life into the world. Once we become mothers, milk flows from our bodies to nourish that life. As crones, our tears anoint and cleanse the world of the pain of loss and suffering."

Kerplunk.

"There, Mara!"

The Shining Lady looked away from him to his mother, her voice excited. She waved towards the source of the dripping water.

"Those drops you hear are the tears of the Mistmother as she cries for all of the suffering in this broken world! How can I not do the same?"

There was a moment of profound silence, broken only by his soft whimpers as he sought to resume his interrupted meal.

"But how will you provide a mother's milk?" Mama's voice rose. "Or will that be me?"

"No." The Shining Lady shook her head once before looking down at him again, her magickal smile just for him. "All three fluids must come from me."

"But you haven't given birth yet! How is that going to be possible?"

"I am Fae, and I am very close to giving birth to my own daughter." She spoke in a calm, quiet voice. "He will be able to suckle from my breast, when it is time."

Kerplunk.

Silence filled the gaps between the soft echoes of the last drop of water. With the Shining Lady no longer keeping him amused with her smiles and her gaze, he looked to resume his meal, but her breast was still too far away. He grunted and squirmed, angling his lips towards the nipple that was just beyond reach.

"First, he and I must share blood." She held out the palm of her hand towards Mama. "Jab the pin into the pad at the base of my thumb. Be sure you go deep enough to draw blood, then prick the bottom of his foot in the heel."

The Shining Lady gasped in pain. There was a pause, a sharp intake of breath, and a stifled cry from his mother that was followed by a sharp stab in his foot. Lancing pain wracked his tiny body. He voiced his protest in a keening wail that reverberated through the chamber.

Kerplunk.

"Ohhhh!"

Mouse regretted it the moment his right eyelid fluttered open. Tears welled up, blurring his vision, and his headache worsened. He closed it again. His left eye was swollen shut. His tongue felt thick and dry in his mouth. Pushing the tip of it past lips that were cracked and swollen, he tasted the coppery tang of his own blood. His head throbbed in multiple locations, as did his ribs and back. Moving slowly in case something was broken, Mouse shifted his aching arms and flexed his fingers. Each movement cost him in terms of fresh waves of stomach-churning pain, but it was worth it to learn that nothing, except perhaps one or two of his ribs, was broken.

Despite the pain, he was surrounded by an unfamiliar softness. He wasn't swaying in a hammock, nor was he curled up in a coil of spare rope or lying in a pile of folded-up tarps. The fabric pressing on his skin was soft and smooth.

I'm naked...and in a bed. A real bed with covers and sheets and pillows!

His curiosity piqued, Mouse shifted first one and then the other leg. He sucked in his breath at the way the movement caused the huge knots of bruised muscle in his thighs to clench. He remembered receiving several sharp kicks to his lower body. Luckily, both legs moved, even though his bruised muscles complained. The weight of the soft and heavy covers draped over his lower body felt strange, yet comforting.

Strangest of all, however, was a small ache — a distant, phantom pain — flaring from the unlikeliest spot: the bottom of his left heel. It seemed to be coming from an old, puckered scar

— a tiny, star-shaped scar that he'd had for as long as he could remember. He had asked his mother about it once when he was seven or eight, but her only reply had been a tearful shake of her head and a quick change of the subject.

Now I know why — she gave it to me!

The ship shuddered and creaked with a sharp gust of wind, causing the lamp overhead to rattle as it swayed from its hook. Curious as to where he was, Mouse cracked his right eye open again. He kept it open long enough to adjust to the light. Blinking, he looked around.

What am I doing in the captain's cabin and in his bed? He's going to kill me!

That small amount of movement, however, was too much. The room began to spin. The disconcerting movement continued even as his head dropped back down onto the pillows. The darkness opened its gaping maw and swallowed him whole, sending Mouse spiraling back down into the depths of that far away cavern...

Kerplunk.

As the haze of pain lessened, a warm, soothing tingling spread outward from the place where he had been pricked. His cries faded into soft sobs of remembered pain that soon subsided further into an entranced silence as he became ensnared by the ethereal beauty of the Shining Lady's song.

She rocked him back and forth, smiling down at him through the tears in her eyes. His sobs ceased the moment she rocked his head close enough to her breast for him to latch on to her nipple. He was surprised by how...different...she was from Mama. The Shining Lady's breast was warmer and softer than Mama's, and the taste of her skin was slightly sweeter. Yet, unlike with Mama, milk didn't gush into his mouth with each pulling draw of his cheeks. At first, nothing came, but that only caused him to suckle harder.

The Shining Lady's song faltered as he latched on even tighter. It ended in a surprised gasp.

"Oh, my! I've...never..."

Mama was there. Her hand brushed the soft hair on his head as she spoke.

"Are you sure you have milk for him?" Her voice dropped to whisper. "He'll get frustrated if something doesn't come soon."

"I feel it coming." The Shining Lady gave a small cry of triumph as the first drops of warm milk flowed into his mouth. Her eyes lifted to meet the curious gaze of his mother. "This is so amazing!"

"It is magickal, isn't it?"

"Thank you for this, Mara!" Her voice was choked with emotion. "For everything. I may not have the chance to know this joy with my own daughter."

Kerplunk.

He suckled greedily for every drop of her sweet milk.

"He's so hungry!"

"Yes," Mama agreed. "Don't be surprised if you're a little sore before he's done, especially since this is your first time."

"Mara, I'm going to have to be undisturbed for this next part." She spoke in a low, hushed voice. "I need to take him out into the water to finish the ritual, and what I say to him must remain just between the two of us."

"He's just a baby, Anna." Mama frowned. "He's not going to remember any of this."

He continued to suckle.

"Part of the magick of this ritual is that he will remember everything that happens here tonight. When the last of the conditions I have set are met, he will remember everything and be given a choice as to whether he wishes to become her Guardian."

"A choice?" His mother regarded the other woman with a confused look. "How can he have a choice in any of this?"

Kerplunk.

"There must always be a choice, Mara, or the magick becomes dark and twisted. That is how Fae magick works."

The Shining Lady turned her glittering eyes down to stare at him in wonder as he suckled from her breast.

"Growing up, he's going to be different. He'll be sensitive to the world in ways that others are not. He will hear things that no one else around him can. He will experience the world in ways that you won't be able to understand or explain to him."

She stroked his cheek with her soft fingers, leaving a trail of tingling warmth where she had touched him.

"He may not like being so different. But when the time comes for him to step into the role of becoming a true Guardian, for him to come into the fullness of who he will have the potential to be, he will have an impossible choice to make."

Mama gulped. "How can I help him, Anna?"

"He's going to need your unconditional love and support because it will not be easy for him to be so very different."

"Of course! He'll always have that!"

"I know. Love is so critically important. Even the smallest act of love can give him strength and reassurance that will last a lifetime." The Shining Lady smiled at her, reaching out to touch Mama's cheek. "Another thing you can do is to teach him how to play the f'leyn that your beloved husband gave to you."

"But it was taken from me..."

"It will be returned." The Shining Lady's eyes burned brighter than ever. "That instrument is special. It was crafted by the Aelfani at the height of their knowledge and power before the world was broken. With my gift to him, he will gain a special affinity for music and being able to play a musical instrument will help him to understand and process what he hears better."

The Shining Lady paused. "But the most important thing you can do, Mara, is to make sure that when you leave here, you take him someplace where he will grow up knowing what it is to struggle and suffer. If you return to your family, his life will be one of privilege and ease, and this sacred gift could become very dangerous when he reaches his full potential."

"Dangerous!? How? Why?"

Kerplunk.

Her smile faded, and the Shining Lady's voice lowered to a whisper. "If he chooses to accept his gift, Mara, Rondel will not only be able to hear the ta'irs of others, he will have the ability to influence them in profound and powerful ways."

"What? I don't understand!"

"I can't say that I understand completely, either. I have been given this opportunity by the Mistmother to help our children, to give them a chance against an unbelievably powerful and evil enemy, so I am doing everything I can to plant the seeds that they will need to harvest. I just know that Rondel's gift will be all too easy to subvert and use for personal gain if he doesn't develop empathy for others. If he succumbs to those temptations...well, there is only darkness and despair down that road."

"Why don't we go together, Anna? My brother will come for us, I just know it. He's in command of the Guild Alliance forces hunting for us. And he's the best musician I know! He hates the rest of my family as much as I do." Emotion choked Mama's words. "With Randil dead, Rondel's going to need a father figure in his life..."

"I would love nothing more..." the Shining Lady's voice broke, "than to have you at my side when Seldirima is born, to have you be...a mother to her..." She sobbed and pressed her forehead against his mother's before continuing. "But...it is not to be...after this ritual is finished...these two children cannot be together again until...they are ready to make their choices

and face the Enemy...it is just too dangerous...for them and for
everyone else..."

Kerplunk.

Music — strong and powerful — pressed against his consciousness. It was a duet of conflicting songs. The first, and closest, of the *ta'irs* was the captain's. It had a strident, purposeful
tone that no longer seemed in conflict with itself. It was calmer
and slower than normal, almost as if he was deep in thought.

The second *ta'ir* — if it could even be considered a song —
was a chaotic and discordant mess. The source of the song,
whoever it was, wasn't in the room, but it wasn't far away.
What sense he could make of the discombobulated notes told
him that there was some sort of struggle going on; a struggle
that the source of the few remaining semi-coherent notes was
clearly losing. It was almost as if the person's *ta'ir* was reflecting a descent into a deep madness filled with despair.

The clash of the two powerful songs made the pounding of
his head worse than it already was.

Sitting up with a jolt, Mouse pushed his blankets aside.

"What? Where am I?"

He regretted the sudden movement, slumping back down to
the pillows with a groan. He tried, without success, to erect
some sort of defense against the hammering of the *ta'irs* against
his already pounding skull.

"Easy, Mouse." The captain's voice cut through the clashing
music. "You're safe now."

Opening the one eye that was willing to cooperate, Mouse
shifted his head to look towards the sound of the captain's
voice. The room was darker than it was before, illuminated
now simply by the soft light of the Ugly Sister — the smallest
and most misshapen of the three moons that appeared in the

last few days of each month. Its meager light shone through the port hole.

Despite the gloom, it was easy to make out Captain Dastyr's massive form in the armchair just below the circular window. The big man straightened up. His dark eyes fixated on Mouse.

"I'm sorry, sir. I didn't mean to..." Mouse struggled to form words with his wooly tongue. He paused as the memory of the captain saving him forced its way to the front of his mind. "I mean, thank you for saving me, sir."

"Hmmm." Captain Dastyr cleared his throat. "Yes, well about that now." The big man leaned forward, his eyes focused intently on Mouse. The notes of his song slowed and sharpened with what seemed like genuine concern. "So why don't you tell me why you were in need of being rescued?"

"Sir, I don't know why they hate me so much!"

The captain grunted, his *ta'ir* subsiding slightly at Mouse's answer. There was a shift in the other song as well, a rallying of the coherent notes into the semblance of a real *ta'ir*. It still wasn't complete, but there was definite improvement.

Mouse's tongue was so dry it felt like it was wearing a woolen sock. He pushed himself up, first onto his elbows and then into a seated position. He grunted from the effort required for each movement.

Surging to his feet, Captain Dastyr closed the distance between them in one great stride. Mouse flinched when he brought his hands up, but the big man simply reached for something on a shelf above the bed. He pulled down a pair of extra pillows in clean white linen cases and pushed them behind Mouse's back.

"Thank you," Mouse muttered as he leaned back into the soft, but supportive, pillows with a pained sigh. He fidgeted with his fingers, pulling the covers more fully over his naked torso. Despite being in the most comfortable bed he'd ever experienced, it felt like his brain was trying to hammer its way out of his skull. His ribs ached, and each tiny movement caused him to wince with renewed pain. The long muscles in each limb throbbed where knots had formed from each blow.

Silently, the captain turned and opened a cabinet behind him. He pulled out a silver flask and opened it with one twist of his thick fingers before handing it to Mouse.

"Here, take a few swigs of this," he grunted. "It'll put some hair on your chest, but it will also dull the pain."

Tentatively taking the full flask in both hands to make sure he didn't spill anything, Mouse gave the open mouth a quick sniff. The sharp, acrid odor curdled his nose hairs.

"What is it, sir?" Mouse focused his internal attention on the captain's song, trying to pick out any elements of true or falsity in whatever answer the man provided.

"It's called *chag'rak*, son. It's an orc brew, made from stuff you don't even want to think about. But it's the best booze money can buy to ease aches and pains." The captain chuckled as he nodded towards the flask. "Go on, take a drink or two. It'll help, I promise you that. It's the one redeeming thing that orcs make."

The captain's words were matched by subtle changes and shifts in the underlying music of his song that made it easy to know he was telling the truth. Mouse noted a level of concern that the captain had for his well-being, a sentiment that was as surprising as it was welcome.

Mouse brought the flask up to his lips and tipped it up. The fiery liquid filled his mouth, instantly setting all of the nerve endings in his mouth aflame. The burning heat traveled down his throat when he choked it down with a gasp. The noxious stuff hit his already gurgling gut with the heat and force of an exploding cannonball.

Captain Dastyr was there, catching the flask before it fell into the covers. He pressed the flask to Mouse's lips for a second big swig before he could protest.

"That's alright, son. The first shot is the worst. The second will go down much smoother."

True to his words, the second mouthful was intensely warm but not unpleasantly so. The pounding in Mouse's head was already fading to a dull roar by the time it hit his stomach. The aches and pains throughout his body lessened. The two pounding *ta'irs* faded into mere background noise.

Mouse blinked as the muscles in his body relaxed. He was so warm that it felt like his whole body was glowing. He pushed the covers back from his torso, enjoying the feel of the cooler air on his bare skin too much to care about such a silly thing as modesty. Staring down at his hands, he flexed his fingers, noting how the world had slowed down, how everything was becoming more fluid and just...smoother.

"Wow." His voice sounded thick. "I do feel better."

"Good."

The captain screwed the cap back on the flask and set it on a shelf. Reaching over, he picked up a pile of clothing and set it at the foot of the bed. Mouse was surprised to see the jacket he had left with the Wilderling.

"Because we have some things to talk about, son, and I don't want you distracted by pain."

"Oh?" Mouse was surprised by the flippant tone in his voice. "There was something...important...I was supposed to tell you, too!"

Captain Dastyr's bushy eyebrow arched up as he turned back around with three curious things in his big hands — the collar, Mouse's lock picks, and the folded parchment.

"I'll be curious to hear if what you have to tell me has anything to do with this."

He brought the blood-encrusted collar that had been around the young woman's neck up to just under Mouse's nose.

Recoiling from the smell of burnt flesh, Mouse didn't miss

the hard look in the captain's eyes. His gaze kept shifting between the collar in the man's hand and Captain Dastyr's face.

Mouse's brow creased as he tried to listen to his *ta'ir*, but the *chag'rak* was clouding his ability to hear it. All he heard was a distant buzzing sound as both local *ta'irs* blended into an incomprehensible mix of pain, disappointment, and fear.

"Well, boy?" Captain Dastyr's voice took an impatient edge. "Don't just stare at the blazing thing. Why was the *Fae* girl's collar in your bag?"

Blinking, Mouse straightened up. The scared voice inside his head was trying to come up with some sort of convincing lie, but his lips and tongue moved on their own accord.

"Because I took it off of her."

"You what?" The captain's voice raised several decibels and at least an octave in those two words. He raised the collar towards Mouse and loomed in closer, asking his next question before he could respond to the first. "Why?"

Mouse should've quailed at the captain's fury, but some other part of him, emboldened by the alcohol, urged him to sit up straighter.

"The collar was killing her, so I took it off." His shoulders elevated into a haphazard shrug. "I didn't want her to die, and I don't think you did either."

"How did you open it, son?" The man's eyes narrowed dangerously. "I didn't give you a key."

"I picked the lock." Mouse shrugged again before nodding toward his other hand. *Why can't I shut up? He's going to kill me!*

"With these?" The captain held up the small leather toolkit.
Mouse nodded.

The big man's expression became unreadable as he looked down at the tools. Letting the kit fall to the bed, the captain turned to pick up something else off of his desk. He held out the crumpled parchment and unfolded it.

"Where did you get this poster?"

"At the customs booth in Nashae." The words tumbled from his lips before his rational mind could stop them. *Please don't ask me anything else about that!*

"And why did you take it?"

"Because I recognized the men on it. I bumped into them in town, when I was getting the ale for Dalton." *Stop talking! Stop talking!*

Captain Dastyr's eyes were focused on the images on the poster. The parchment trembled in his fingers for several tense moments.

He couldn't help studying the fascinating array of emotions play across the captain's face. Rage and anger dominated, but there were brief flashes of wistful longing mixed with bitter disappointment. Each spike of emotion was accompanied by just enough clarity within his *ta'ir* for Mouse to correlate the expressions with the notes of his song.

The moment of reflection ended with the poster being crumpled into a tight ball and tossed aside. Before Mouse understood what was happening, the captain moved in closer and sat down on the bed right next to him. The solid frame of the bed creaked as his bulk settled down. The captain made no secret of sweeping his gaze across Mouse's naked form before bringing his eyes up to meet Mouse's.

Mouse blushed all over, and he would've pulled the covers up, but the captain's bulk prevented it. Instead, he merely flinched when the big man placed a heavy hand on his shoulder and forced him to meet his gaze.

"I know why the crew hates you so much, Mouse."

His voice was low and thick. His *ta'ir* was pressing its way insistently into Mouse's consciousness, pushing aside the alcohol-induced haze and forcing him to hear the...desire...in the man's song. Just what kind of desire, however, was unclear.

"It's because you're a dreamer, an idealist who thinks that the world would be a just and fair place if only you did the right things; if only you tried harder and were a better person." He gave a half-hearted chuckle. "And they are a bunch of bitter and hard-hearted men who lost their ability to dream long ago. I can tell you from personal experience how disturbing that is."

"I..."

"Shhh." The captain pressed a calloused finger to Mouse's lips. "I can forgive you for all of your mistakes because I was the same kind of person at your age and so was Valk before he fell sick." The big man fell silent for a moment, the knot in his throat working hard before he spoke again. "It was the kind of person my mother wanted each of us to be."

The big man cleared his throat. "And the Found God knows how hard I've tried to stay that way. But that belief in fate? That idealism and hope that I could somehow make the world a better place simply by being a good and decent person who tried his best?" He paused for a moment, seemingly lost in thought. "No. That was snatched away from me bit by bit. First, it was losing my mother — such a sweet and gentle soul she was — to the Scourge when I was young and Valk was a toddler. Then it was my father — a cruel and demanding man — who wasn't content to leave me to my books and dreams of becoming a scholar. He didn't want some pansy of a son who was content to read and study; he needed his eldest son to be a real man, someone who he could be proud of — a warrior, a Marine."

Mouse could hear the need for the captain to share in his *ta'ir*. He bit his bottom lip to keep from interrupting.

"I'm not going to bore you with my story of woe, son. You'll just have to trust me when I say that the world is not a nice place. It doesn't reward hope, and the only peace or justice you'll ever find in this world is that which you bring about through your own efforts." The captain leaned closer. "Don't fall into the trap that Valk and I did, Mouse. The sooner you accept the world for the hard and cruel place that it is — and learn how to impose your will upon those who oppose you — the better off you will be."

His hand tightened on Mouse's shoulder, hard enough to be painful. "I understand that you look at that little *Fae* girl in the prison hold and you feel sorry for her. She looks sweet and innocent, but let me tell you: she's tougher, and far deadlier, than she seems. She can make animals do her bidding. She has magick — Mouse — magick that nearly killed Valk." He leaned in closer. "The only thing that saved us that night, son, was my faith in the Found God and the undeniable power of good, solid iron."

The captain's other hand found its way to his neck, where he pulled on the chain until his Seeker's Circle tumbled free from his tunic.

Something large and heavy crashed against the wall behind them, quickly followed by howls of rage and pain that was only slightly muffled by the solid wood between them. The chaos of the other *ta'ir* slammed into his consciousness with all of the force of those limbs thrashing against the wall, overpowering, at least for the moment, the captain's song.

Without any warning, the images from the tapestry of his vision forced their way into the front of his consciousness. Reminded of the urgency of the need to warn the captain of the danger that the whole ship was in, Mouse opened his mouth to speak.

Captain Dastyr shifted his grip to the back of Mouse's neck and squeezed. "That girl is Sarlan's daughter, Mouse. She escaped the fate she deserved with the help of that bastard who once called himself my friend. Any sympathy you have for her is wasted because she is doomed to pay for her father's sins." He nodded towards the wall, where the sounds of thrashing continued. "Get dressed, son, and join me in Valk's room. There, you'll see the damage that *Fae* magick can wreak on a man. Then we'll see how much sympathy you have left for her."

The big man released his grip and stood up. He nodded towards the flask still standing on the bedside table.

"Take another drink if you need it."

Without waiting for Mouse, he moved to the one door leading out of the room, opened it, and stepped out.

"I'm coming, Valk!"

Mouse sat there, too stunned to immediately obey. Pieces of a puzzle that he didn't know existed snapped into place. Unbidden snatches of his mother's voice slammed into him — *How can you love that monster? He killed my husband!*

The memory of his mother crying and yelling at the Shining Lady as she cradled him to her chest hit him with stunning power.

The Shining Lady was carrying Sarlan's child! She was there with us in captivity! Why hadn't I seen it before? How could Mama have agreed to work with someone who loved the monster that killed Papa?

A tiny portion of the pent-up rage and sorrow he'd been carrying all of his life was released in a sudden, violent sob and a torrent of hot tears.

"Why Mama?" he cried out in a voice every bit as wretched and broken as he felt. "Why?!?"

Kerplunk.

CHAPTER 26

Seldy

The ship lurched, jarring her awake.

Seldy didn't bother to open her eyes because it didn't really matter where she was or what she saw, it could only be bad. The constant creaks and groans told her that nothing had changed — she was still a prisoner on the ship of that horrible man.

All of her muscles still ached. The fingers of her left hand still tingled as if they had been stung. And she was shivering again, unable to get warm in any position. Her stomach churned, and her head was throbbing, but it was the familiar cramps in her abdomen that added another level to her misery.

Seriously? On top of everything else, now my moon comes?

Still curled up on herself, Seldy pulled her arms in tighter and hugged herself, trying to tamp down the cramps wracking her shivering body. The rough fabric of the loose woolen tunic was scratchy against her bare skin, but she was beyond caring.

Pressing her thighs together, Seldy dreaded the thought of having to clean up the sticky blood that was sure to flow in the next day or two. After seeing the look of disgust and hatred in her captor's eyes, she doubted that she would be given the supplies she needed to avoid creating an embarrassing and disgusting mess.

A hazy memory bubbled to the forefront of her consciousness, a fragment of a strange conversation on the night of her first Moon's Blood...

Clutching her covers, all Seldy wanted was for the vardo *to stop spinning. With the windows open, snatches of laughter and music filtered through the chilly air, drifting in from the bonfire. The rest of the* kumpania *was celebrating the monthly passing of Lahanya — the Crone's Shard — from the night sky. Her passing from the sky marked the end of Narock and the coming re-birth of Fortunya — the Maiden's Shard — that would take place on the first evening of Dorrin.*

She longed to be back out there, dancing and singing and laughing with all of the others — especially with Uncle Tegger performing many of his newest songs and telling all of her favorite stories — but her first Moon's Blood had decided to show up. Only an hour earlier, she'd been doing fine, but the sweet berry wine she guzzled to help stem the pain of her cramps had quickly gotten the best of her. Jhana had ordered her to bed.

As the alcohol continued its work, her eyes began to grow heavy again. She shifted gingerly to her side so that her face could be bathed in the cool air streaming down from the open window above her. Her thoughts began to drift as the haze of sleep settled on her.

"Jhana." Tegger's voice cut through the night air and her sleep-fogged brain as footsteps crunched in the gravel outside. "We need to talk."

"I don't know what for, Teg," Jhana snapped back in a harsh whisper. "I've already told you she's not going anywhere."

Seldy fought free of the grasping clutches of sleep but kept her eyes closed as she listened to them.

"I need to know if you've seen any changes in her since my last visit." Seldy marveled at how even his whisper sounded melodic. "Have you seen her do anything strange? Has anyone else seen anything?"

The footsteps stopped. Seldy could imagine the look on her Ma's face when she whirled around.

"Why? So you can justify taking her away from me just twelve years after you brought her for me to raise as my own?"

Seldy sucked in her breath.

"You know why." His volume dropped even lower. She strained to hear the next sentence. "You know the danger she's in if she's discovered. You've let her have too prominent a role in the circus!"

"Now you listen here, Tegerion Dan!" Her mother's agitation was clear. "I'll not have you telling me how to raise my daughter, MY DAUGHTER..." She hissed those two words loudly before lowering her voice. "Or telling me how to run a circus. She's a blazing good performer, and she's the only one who can do those tricks with the animals as safely as she does them." Ma dropped her tone even lower. "Besides, she's doing what she loves, and I'm not going to let you or anyone else take that away from her."

"But Jhana..."

"But nothing. You're not taking her anywhere, and I'll raise her the way I choose to." There was another crunching footstep. "Remember, Teg. You brought her to me because you wanted her to have a chance to grow up with a normal life. Well, I'm giving that to her. She's not going to have that if she goes off with a pair of wanted criminals to go who-knows-where and do Goddess-knows-what! She's still a child!"

"Look," Uncle Tegger sighed. "I get why you're upset. But

you have to understand the dangers to her and the kumpania! Frank says that there's a potential that puberty can unlock certain things about her and publicly reveal her for..."

"To the Blazing Fires with Frank! He doesn't have a say about anything to do with her," Jhana's voice cut him off. "She's Istimiel Seldirima, my daughter. Besides, look where listening to that crotchety old fool has gotten you in all of this!" She snorted. "You went from being a blasted hero in the Alliance to becoming a traitor and a wanted criminal."

There was a sharp intake of breath and a pregnant pause before Uncle Tegger spoke again, this time in a much colder tone. "Be careful, Jhana. If I hadn't listened to him, we'd've never met, and you wouldn't have a daughter to begin with. I owe that man everything. He saved me and, more importantly, it was his order that saved Seldy. Don't forget that."

"You don't know any of that for sure..."

"But I do, Jhana."

A wave of fatigue washed over her, making it hard for Seldy to concentrate, especially as their voices lowered further. Laughter and music continued to drift in from the bonfire, further obscuring what was being said.

"...forbid you to say anything to her about her heritage..." Jhana's insistent whisper picked up and then faded away just as quickly.

"...find more men to watch each stop next year..."

Sleep claimed her in the middle of her uncle's reply.

"She knew..." Seldy couldn't stop her teeth from chattering. "Ma knew that I was Fae..." A sob escaped her lips. "But she still wanted me...still loved me..."

A wave of fond memories flooded her mind. She recalled how her adoptive mother spent the first few minutes of every *morning of her childhood cuddling with her. They traded silly jokes and funny stories from the day before in order to start out each new day with a few smiles and a bit of laughter. And no matter how busy she was in her duties, Jhana always stopped what she was doing to answer Seldy's questions, bandage up a cut, or kiss a bruise to help her feel better. There were countless small moments where Jhana demonstrated her love for Seldy with kind words and knowing looks that could only be shared between a mother and daughter.*

The tiniest of smiles touched her lips as she remembered it all.

When Seldy had blossomed into a young woman and started to fall for Chad, Jhana didn't try to get in the way or discourage it. Instead, she had given them the time and space they needed to discover that their love for each other was different and more powerful than either of them realized.

Thinking of her consyrtu, *however, caused the small, fragile smile on her lips to crumple into a stifled sob.*

I hate the Fae! *Chad's words came rushing back, hitting her with even more force than they had when she first heard them.* I'll sure be glad when the last of those creatures are all dead and gone!

A lump formed in Seldy's throat.

...the Fae really aren't people, are they? They're monsters!

Remembering the spite in his voice when he said those things, Seldy erupted in sobs again.

"Oh, Chad!" She collapsed further in on herself, drawing her knees in towards her chest in an attempt to ease her cramps. "I'm sorry! I didn't know that I was born a monster!"

::Leafsister.:: *Shadowfang's mental voice pushed up against her consciousness.* ::Our time to reach the Land of Dreams grows short, a great darkness comes.::

Lost in a morass of hopelessness and despair, Seldy struggled to find the strength to reply to the wolf.

::What does it matter, Shadowfang? What does any of this matter?::

::The Elder Spirits are calling out for you, Leafsister. Can't you hear them?::

::No! I can't hear anything but the creaks and groans of the ship!:: *Despite the pain she was in, her curiosity was piqued.* ::What are the Elder Spirits?::

::They are the ancestors of all of us. The beasts and creatures of the fields, forests, skies, and seas, Leafsister. They walked the earth, flew through the skies, and swam the waters when the world was fresh and whole. They brought life, in all of its wondrous variety, to the world that the great and mighty Treemothers and their children prepared for us.::

The wolf's thoughts grew stronger and clearer with each sentence. A powerful image blossomed in her mind of a pair of great wolves standing proudly on a rocky outcropping on a moonlit night, their profiles unmistakable as they lifted their heads to sing into the wind.

::The Elder Spirits remember, Leafsister, and keep their vigil.::

As he continued, more images flashed through her mind. She raced through a forest at night, streaking through the trees and ferns and brush on four paws as she strove to keep up with the rest of her pack.

She swam in a great body of water so vast that she couldn't see the shore in any direction. She wasn't afraid because she slid through the water at tremendous speed, leaping out of the waves with her sleek, strong body. She belonged in the water.

She flew, her great wings pushing downward as she rose from the surface of the great sea and soared high into the air. From her new vantage point, she saw a distant shore backed by mountains and trees.

::Watching from the Dreamlands and waiting, the Elder Spirits preserve the memory of the world that once was in the hope that someday, a Leafsister like you will return and find a way to heal the broken lands, to restore the lost seas, and to calm the angry skies.::

Between the solemn dignity of his words and the incomprehensible beauty of the images he transmitted with them, Seldy was left stunned and breathless. Compared to the grand visions that the wolf had showed her, she was tiny and insignificant. It took several moments before she was able to collect her wits enough to reply.

::But I don't understand, Shadowfang! How can I do anything like that? I'm just a...::

She paused, unsure of what it truly meant to be Fae, *to be the daughter of Sarlan the Red, and to command the magick that she had found in both the battle with the captain and his men, and in her failed attempt earlier.*

::I...I don't know anything about being a Leafsister! And I don't hear any songs or anyone calling out to me.::

Curled into a tight ball, Seldy clutched at her abdomen and shivered. She hadn't dared to move yet.

::Look at me, Leafsister.::

Reluctantly, Seldy straightened her legs and torso. Wincing in pain, she rolled over and focused her eyes on the wolf, expecting him to be curled up in the back of his cage as he usually was. Instead, the great wolf was standing up and staring down at her. The moment his eyes met hers, she was transfixed, captured by the sheer intensity of his yellow, lupine gaze.

::You must answer their call. You must seek out the Elder Spirits before the Enemy returns to prevent you from being able to make that journey.::

Tha-throom.

Unable to look away or even blink, she struggled to form a coherent reply.

::Answer...what call? The Enemy?::

It was all she could do to project the half-formed questions.

::Find your answers in the Land of Dreams, Leafsister.:: *There was more than a little hint of impatience in the wolf's mental voice.* ::He grows stronger, and your path becomes more dangerous, with every passing moment.::

Tha-throom.

"B-b-but...I don't know how!" She couldn't stop her teeth from chattering.

::I know, Leafsister. You have been poisoned again by Firestone. I can see that your own path is befouled, so I will serve both as your guide and your path. I will be your bridge to the Land of Dreams.:: *The wolf's response was calmer than his previous words. His mental voice changed with his next projection, becoming even deeper and stronger.* ::Keep staring into my eyes. Go deeper. Seek the forest within.::

Tha-throom.

There was an undeniable power in the wolf's mental command. Fascinated by his gaze and unable to resist, Seldy obeyed. She stared deeper into his eyes, searching...

::Good,:: *he reassured her in a calm, soothing voice that vibrated to the core of her being.* ::Go deeper. The pack leaves no one behind.::

His presence all around her soothed her aches and pains.

::Go deeper!:: *The tone of the wolf's voice changed, becoming more insistent, more urgent.* ::The path will soon become dark and dangerous! But you must press on and go deeper yet!::

Seldy's breathing deepened. She began to lose awareness of her body. The urgency in the wolf's voice spurred her on as she pushed her consciousness deeper into his eyes. Something shifted... She was no longer laying on the wooden deck of a ship, surrounded by darkness and iron. Instead, she was walking in a long tunnel composed of soft, shimmering, silver light. She felt the wolf's presence all around her, but he was particularly strong just to the right and behind her. She paused, wanting to turn her head to see if she could see him.

Tha-throom.

::Don't stop, Leafsister! Hurry! The Enemy comes! Keep going! You must reach the forest, no matter the cost!::

Seldy stumbled forward, her toes digging into the spongy surface as she pushed herself deeper into the strange tunnel of light.

::But I don't see a forest! It just goes on forever!::

::The forest is ahead. Don't stop!:: *The worry and urgency in the wolf's mental voice was unmistakable.* ::No matter what happens, Leafsister, you must press on until you reach the forest! Worry not for me!::

Tha-throom.

The whole tunnel shook, as if something large and angry was coming from behind. The soft, silver light surrounding them dimmed slightly.

::Shadowfang! What's happening?!::

::Run, Leafsister! Run like the wind!::

Tha-throom.

"STOP!!!!" The deep-throated and primal howl of rage shook the walls of the tunnel, dimming the light even further with its spine-tingling power. "YOU CANNOT ESCAPE ME, MY BRIDE!!!"

Seldy needed no further urging from Shadowfang to redouble her efforts. She didn't need to understand where she was or how she got there to know that she couldn't let the monster catch her. The scratchy, loose-fitting tunic flapped wildly about her body as she raced forward using every bit of her strength, every ounce of her resolve, to escape.

She stumbled to her hands and knees. Shadowfang stopped behind her, turned, and faced their pursuer.

::Get up and keep moving! Don't stop, Leafsister! No matter what! Get to the forest, and the Elder Spirits will find you!::

Tha-throom.

Too frightened of that dreaded voice to even consider anything else, Seldy pushed back to her feet and raced ahead. Behind her, Shadowfang growled his defiance.

"A MERE WOLF?!?!" *the voice raged.* "YOU THINK A SINGLE MORTAL BEAST WILL KEEP ME FROM CLAIMING YOU?!"

There!

Far ahead, Seldy saw the end of the tunnel: a circle of darkness that seemed too small, too distant to reach, but it grew larger with each staggering step. She clamped her hands over her ears at the terrible sounds of struggle behind her, too afraid to look back to see what was happening.

Tha-throom.

I have to reach the forest! I can't let him die in vain!

Her lungs burned, her legs ached, and her heart thudded wildly against her ribs. She gasped when the last of the light in the tunnel faded, leaving her in near total darkness.

"HAHA! YOU ARE MINE NOW!"

Tha-throom!

The entire tunnel shook as something massive thundered after her. Seldy concentrated all of her dwindling strength on running. The only light remaining came from the opening ahead. Closer now, she could see the merest sliver of silver moonlight bathing what appeared to be a forest clearing at night. Each faltering step made the view clearer, gave her the tiniest bit of hope.

Only a few more steps!

Tha-throom!

The tunnel walls began to constrict, as if the tunnel itself was shrinking. Pushing up with both hands to keep the elastic walls from collapsing on her, Seldy stumbled and fell. She squirmed and pushed and wriggled her way forward, fighting both against the rising panic in her chest and the strangely malleable walls of the tunnel collapsing on her.

Behind her, the walls were being forced apart by something unimaginably powerful. His rasping breath sounded closer every time he drew another.

Tha-throom!

Seldy's fingers brushed against something different than the spongy walls of the tunnel with her right hand. It was rough to the touch, flexible in her grasp, and it vibrated with life and energy and strength.

A branch!

She grabbed it with her left hand and yanked for all she was worth, pulling herself free from the collapsing tunnel. Something bitterly cold and scaly grabbed her ankle. She screamed and kicked wildly, snatching her foot out of its frigid grasp but not before sharp talons scored her skin, leaving several trails of blood on her pale skin.

Tha-throom!

Scrambling with every ounce of her skill and strength she had acquired in a lifetime of practice as an acrobat and as a dancer, Seldy pulled and yanked and kicked until she was free of the dwindling, suffocating tunnel and the creature's cruel, searching talons.

Tumbling forward, she fell...

Tha-throom!

"AARRGHH!" the dreaded voice called out in pain and shock as the clawed hand reached after her. A loud snap of wood cracking against wood cut off his shout.

Seldy crashed to the ground, landing on her side in the soft leaf-litter of a forest floor. Gasping for breath, she shivered. The memory of the frigid grip of the creature's talons on her skin filled her with terror. She clenched her eyes shut, afraid of what she would see.

"Help!" she cried out, breathless. "Help me!"

Her cries faded into the background noises of a quiet forest at night. Crickets chirped. Bugs buzzed. An owl hooted. And the wind sighed through the leaves of countless trees swaying in unison.

Cracking an eye open, Seldy stared up in wonder at the whispering canopy of leaves above. Peeking through the lush foliage was a big, round, full moon that dwarfed the three Shards that she'd known for all of her life. The cool silver light felt refreshing on her skin, bathing her in its soft, loving luminescence.

Turning back towards the tunnel, Seldy saw a blackened knot only a few feet above her on the trunk of one of the largest oak trees she'd ever seen. The ebony tip of a talon protruded from the middle of it. The tree shuddered. Another loud snap and the remnants of the claw — about as long as a tiger's top fang — fell to the forest floor to land directly in front of her nose. Tendrils of smoke curled upwards from the blunt end.

"Hoo hoo!"

The owl's call was the loudest sound of the night, overcoming even the thunderous beat of her own pulse pounding against her eardrums.

"Hoo hoo!"

CHAPTER 27

Mouse

*Y*ou *know the truth now, my little A'lanthe ta'ir."*
The Shining Lady stared down at him with sparkling blue eyes and a bittersweet smile that spoke of both unimaginable loss and deep-seated hope.

"In order for you to be hearing these words, the last conditions of this ritual must have been met."

Kerplunk.

He couldn't see anything beyond her face. His eyes felt heavy, like they wanted to close, but he couldn't stop looking at her. He felt warm and tingly all over. His tummy was full, the taste of her sweet milk still on his lips. He couldn't see Mama, but he was too content to miss her.

The Shining Lady's eyes were filled with a deep sadness.

"The father of my daughter was the same man who killed your father. I cannot excuse the actions of my beloved nor do I have the right to ask for forgiveness on his behalf. Despite how it may seem at the moment, I cannot know what else you have been told about Sarlan or what Mara has taught you of what happened between him and your father. But I do want to say

that much of what you have likely heard from others is either blatantly untrue or, at best, a twisted version of the truth."

Kerplunk.

"There is likely, however..." She paused for a moment staring down at him. "...also a great deal of truth in much of what is said about him as well. To most people, he is a monster — a powerful Fae sorcerer and dreaded pirate who has been responsible for the deaths of far too many innocents. To others, he is a freedom fighter defending the helpless against the depredations of the heartless men who would destroy them and their way of life. Like many who take up arms and use them to protect others, he has done terrible things, some of which are simply unforgivable." She paused, swallowing hard. "To me, he has been both a hard-hearted captor and a cherished lover. He is both the father of my daughter and the principle reason that I have to take this drastic action."

Kerplunk.

The Shining Lady closed her eyes and took several deep breaths.

His eyes grew heavy again, but the sound of her melodious voice stirred him back awake.

"I would be surprised if your heart didn't ache and you weren't upset to learn that the person whose ta'ir I have entrusted to you is the daughter of the man who slew your father."

Tears formed in the corners of the Shining Lady's eyes. A stray drop slid down her cheek to land with a warm, wet splash on his nose.

"There is no avoiding that awful truth or the terrible pain that you must surely feel at learning it. For that pain — and for all of the losses you have had to suffer so far in your life — I am forever sorry, my little Guardian."

More tears streamed down her face, each of them landing on him. But he was transfixed by her eyes, unable to look away, even if he had wanted to.

"This is the last of the dreams of this place, of this moment, that you will receive from me. This is my last chance to speak directly to you, Rondel."

She bent closer, her sad face growing larger in his blurry vision, until her lips met his in a soft, tingling kiss. Pulling back again, her lips formed a gentle smile, even as the tears continued to flow from her eyes, bathing his small body in their salty warmth with every falling drop.

"Please know that what has been done this night has been done out of the love I have for my daughter — a love so fierce, so strong, that I will do anything I must in order to give her a chance to grow into the woman that she has the potential to become — and for that, I cannot apologize."

Kerplunk.

"Your mother loves you every bit as fiercely as I love my Seldirima."

The Shining Lady's smile deepened, and her eyes softened even further as she looked up, away from him for a brief moment, before turning her eyes back on him.

"Mara is an amazing woman, and the best friend I could ever ask for. If anyone can raise a child alone, in the most trying circumstances imaginable, it is her."

Her tears continued to flow and fall on him even as she smiled down at him.

"You're a very lucky young man, Rondel. I hope that you treasure every moment you get to spend with her."

Kerplunk.

The Shining Lady's eyes widened. Her bottom lip began to quiver until she bit down on it with her teeth. She drew in a long, slow breath before continuing.

"Our time grows short, my little Guardian, so let me explain,

as best I can, about what has happened here tonight. I must also give you a choice to make."

The tears slowed as her face grew solemn.

"Through my gift to you of the three fluids of the sacred feminine — the blood of my body, the milk of my breast, and the tears of my love and sorrow — I have planted a special seed within you. As it grows and matures, this seed will allow you to not only hear and understand the hidden songs that form the spirits of each and every living thing in this world but also to heal those songs when they are broken."

Kerplunk.

The last tear from her cheek splashed onto his cheek.

"These songs, or ta'irs as they are known in the ancient tongue of the Fae, are incredibly important. They reflect the overall health, strength, and the deepest unconscious thoughts and emotions of each living being. They also reflect the larger events and themes with which each individual is engaged. Every ta'ir is unique and distinct to each individual, though you will find that there are common themes, especially amongst relatives or close companions.

"If you grow into the young man I think you will — and you listen close enough to the ta'irs of those around you with compassion and humility — you will be able to discern the truth of things in a way that no else alive can, whether they are mortal or Fae. This is a gift that is beyond precious.

"With the Mistmother's blessing, I have planted this seed within you, my little Guardian, because..." The Shining Lady took a deep breath and swallowed before continuing. "...because I must do something to my own daughter that is beyond horrible. The moment she is born, I will lock up her song in such a way as to leave her blind and deaf to the true nature of her own heritage. She will not be able to truly appreciate the full wonder of the world around her as she should. I could *never have imagined doing to my own daughter what my own parents tried to do to me." She shook her head, clearly trying to fight back the tears that threatened to overcome her. "But it is the only hope I have to save my daughter — and all of the* Fae *— from a fate that is so terrible that I cannot bear to describe it."*

Kerplunk.

"Just as I have planted a seed that will give you access to the power of your own ta'ir..." The Shining Lady's voice faltered again. She paused, sucking in her bottom lip and chewing it a bit before she continued. "I...I...I must...silence and imprison... the ta'ir of my own daughter in order to save her."

She drew in a long, ragged breath before bending down and kissing him on the forehead. Pulling back, she began again in a halting, shuddering voice.

"You must remember her song, little Guardian, because she will not have access to it until it is unlocked by someone who can help to heal her from what I must do to her."

For the first time, he felt cold in the Shining Lady's arms. He squirmed and uttered a small cry of protest.

Kerplunk.

"I know, Little One," she said in a sad, tired voice. "We are almost done."

She pulled his shivering body even closer to hers and cupped the top of his head with her free hand, bringing him a small measure of warmth.

"But this is critical. I must tell you...that you have a choice in all of this...a choice that only you can make." She stared down at him with her intense, glittering blue eyes. "First, you must know that while I have entrusted you with the key to healing my daughter, there is another who holds this power as well. He will not seek to heal her, however. Rather, he will try to claim her inheritance, to steal her very essence, for his own. He will

seek to claim her power for himself and, if he succeeds, he will finish what he started long, long ago...he will destroy the Fae, and all that we once stood for, forever.

"I cannot name him, other than to call him the Enemy, for names have power and to utter his name is to draw his attention. You, my little Guardian, are my hidden hero; the hero that the Enemy doesn't know exists. The gift I have given you will allow you to see the truth. If your heart stays strong and pure, you will be able to resist the terrible power of the Enemy's ta'ir when no one else can.

"He is a master of deceit who controls and manipulates others with powerful lies and the power of his disruptive song. Be wary, for he can be in multiple places — and wear many guises — at the same time. He feasts on a harvest of fear, anger, and hatred grown from the seeds of discord he is constantly sowing. If he gets to Seldirima before she has been healed, she may not be able to resist his strength for very long."

Kerplunk.

"Your choice, Rondel, is whether to heal her or not. I cannot compel you. You will have to judge for yourself whether or not my daughter is worthy of this boon. And you will have to decide whether or not you can forgive all that has been done to you in order to save her. I cannot see the future, Rondel, so I don't know what choice you will make. Your gift will grow stronger the closer you are to her, and..." She paused, looking at a loss for words. "...it will fade in time if you choose not to help her, or..." Her voice caught in her throat. "...if she dies...or worse yet..." She closed her eyes against the tears that threatened to flow. "...if the Enemy captures her and manages to break her."

The Shining Lady opened her eyes again and bent down, kissing his forehead once again.

"I have placed all of my trust...everything I love...my only hope...in the truth and goodness of your heart and in the *strength of your spirit. Only by working together, as Treemaiden and Guardian, will the two of you be able to defeat him for good."*

She smiled down at him, *"Please...please help her..."*

Kerplunk.

"YOU CANNOT ESCAPE ME, MY BRIDE!!!"

"What're you talking about Valk? You've never been married!"

Confused by the muffled shouts filtering through the cabin wall, Mouse blinked through the tears. Still reeling from the vibrant dream and the orcish liquor, he swayed in place. Blinking again, he realized that he was sitting on the edge of the bed, still naked, with his legs dangling over the hard wooden rail.

"Hold still, damn you!" The captain sounded strained after the first of several loud thumps shook the wall between the cabins. "Or you're going to hurt yourself even worse!"

Every time he blinked, Mouse saw an afterimage of the Shining Lady's beautiful face and bright, glittering eyes burned into the inside of his eyelids. Her last words echoed softly in his memory.

Please...please help her.

"Mouse, blast you! Hurry up and get in here!"

The captain's thundering commands cut through the haze of the alcohol and half-remembered dreams. His knees buckled under the impact of his full weight when he slipped off of the bed. The room started spinning. Mouse caught the railing with a desperate grab, steadying himself.

Pushing aside the tangled mess of conflicted thoughts and feelings, he started to get dressed. The trousers, drawers, and tunic laid out for him were all new and clean.

"A MERE WOLF?!?!" A harsh voice raged from behind the

wall, coinciding with a surge of the chaotic, incoherent *ta'ir* that was struggling against the weaker, softer song of a much gentler soul. "YOU THINK A SINGLE MORTAL BEAST WILL KEEP ME FROM CLAIMING YOU?"

"What are you babbling about, Valk?"

The captain's song strengthened as the sounds of struggle grew louder behind him, but it paled in comparison to the chaotic noise making the hair on the back of Mouse's neck stand up.

"There's no wolf here!"

Wolf?

Mouse slipped first one leg and then the other into the set of silk drawers laid out for him. The fabric was cool and luxurious against his skin.

Shadow?

As if in answer to his questions, something heavy crashed against the wall, followed almost immediately by the captain's guttural cry,

"Mouse! Blast you! Get in here!"

Mouse scrambled to pull his clothes on, fumbling with the new belt and brass buckle.

"HAHA! YOU ARE MINE NOW AND FOREVER, MY BRIDE!"

The foreign voice was so deep and so powerful that it was almost as if there wasn't a wall separating the two rooms.

Hearing the desperation in the captain's *ta'ir*, Mouse slipped his lock picks into his trousers' pocket. After a moment of reflection, he tossed the new pair of boots at the bottom of the pile of clothing and the silver flask of orcish liquor into his bag.

"I'm coming, Captain!"

Mouse stepped into the small dark corridor that ran between the captain's office and his personal quarters. The door to Valk's quarters was cracked open.

The sounds of both a physical struggle and the clashing *ta'irs* grew stronger with each halting step he took towards the partially open door.

"ARRGGH!!!"

The scream was accompanied by a sharp increase in the volume of the chaotic *ta'ir*, staggering Mouse with its intensity.

A single, swaying lantern cast its flickering yellow light on a room that was in as much disarray as the *ta'ir* of its inhabitant. The layout of the small room was a mirror image of the captain's room but where the captain's cabin was neat and clean, Valk's was a study in chaos and disorder.

Before he could sort out the scene before his eyes, his other senses were assaulted. He crinkled his nose at the overpowering stench of blood, feces, pus, and urine. The acrid odors settled on his tongue when he stopped breathing through his nose. His gut lurched in an attempt to empty its meager contents. It took all of his willpower to fight that urge and swallow his bile back down.

Valk thrashed about in his bed, fighting against his brother. The thinner man howled at the top of his lung in a wordless rage. The captain struggled to hold him still, using all of his larger bulk. His face purpled from the effort.

But it wasn't Valk's howls or the captain's angry shouts that captured Mouse's attention. It was the struggle taking place within the captain's brother. The maelstrom of discordant and chaotic noise that he had always associated with the man sought to overwhelm the strains of a mournful, yet beautiful, *ta'ir* of someone who desperately wanted to be free from an overlong captivity. Compared to that struggle, even the captain's normally vibrant and powerful song had no more chance of being heard than a single musician playing in the midst of a storm.

Mouse stood rooted in place as the image from the tapestry of *ta'irs* returned to him full force. With every twist and turn in

Valk's internal conflict, the tentacles of the giant tree slithered and snaked about, each one trying to take hold of the mortal *ta'ir* within the wounded man. Somehow, the captain's brother continued to resist, fighting back against the overwhelming swarm of tentacles. But it was clear that there could only be one victor.

"Don't just stand there, boy!" the captain cried out breathlessly. "Come help me!"

He heard the captain, but it was the Shining Lady's voice that caught and held his attention.

If he chooses to accept his gift, Mara, Rondel will not only be able to hear the ta'irs *of others, he will have the ability to influence them in profound and powerful ways.*

"Boy! Get over here!"

Mouse closed his eyes and took a halting step backwards, his mind focused on a small portion of an image from the tapestry — the image that had troubled him the most. The realization struck like a thunderbolt from the sky.

Kerplunk.

When his back hit the wall in the narrow corridor, Mouse turned and dashed for the closed door that led into the captain's plush office. Between the rough winds buffeting the ship to and fro and the lingering effects of the alcohol, he stumbled about as he yanked the door open and staggered behind the captain's desk.

"Where in the thrice-blasted shards are you going?!" Captain Dastyr called out, desperation tinging his voice. "Help me, blast you!"

The clash between Valk's personal *ta'ir* and the discordant mass of noise that was seeking to claim him continued to pound against Mouse's mind. The horrifying image only served to blur the tenuous distinction between reality and fantasy as he knelt down, digging around in his pocket for his picks.

"Get back here, you blazing coward, or I'll have Haddock flay the skin off of more than your back!"

The captain's words, muffled by distance, managed to slip into his consciousness enough to make handling the tiny picks all the more challenging. His back muscles twitched at the unnecessary reminder of the damage that Haddock would be only too happy to inflict on him yet again.

Pushing the distractions aside, Mouse slid the ends of both picks into the keyhole in the drawer. The captain continued yelling, sending an endless stream of imprecations his way. Valk's *ta'ir* continued to struggle, fading further and further into the background. The chaotic music — of the Enemy, Mouse now recognized — continued to grow stronger, getting closer and closer to taking full control of Valk's body with each passing moment.

Once the lock clicked into place, Mouse turned the tumblers and yanked the drawer open. He only paused long enough to collect and stow his tools before staggering to his feet, instrument in hand. He stumbled back the way he came.

Kerplunk.

"I'm coming, Captain!"

Please don't let me be too late!

Valk's *ta'ir* faltered. The discordance surged, triumphant. Someone crashed into a nearby wall with a grunt and a muffled curse.

Mouse pushed into the putrid-smelling room. The captain had been thrown from the bed to crash against the desk, his face a mask of stunned surprise. Valk sat up in the bed, his restraints falling away in tatters from his naked limbs. Mouse sensed that it wasn't truly Valk who was in charge of his own body.

The man's eyes were glowing with a reddish hue as he turned his terrible gaze upon Mouse, freezing him in place before he could even bring his flute up to his lips. Staring into those eyes, all Mouse could see was the image of that monstrous tree reaching out to him now with all of those deadly tentacles. All of the warmth left his body as a wall of chaotic sound smashed into him, driving him back with all of the crushing force of Bulger's hoof slamming into his chest. The noise enveloped him, grabbed at him, and sought to worm its way through his pitiful defenses and into his consciousness.

"SUBMIT TO ME, MORTAL!"

Stunned by the force of the attack, and the undeniable power of that command, Mouse slumped back against the wall. It took every bit of strength he had to keep the flute from dropping from his numb, nerveless fingers.

"N-n-no!" Fighting for breath, he could only whisper his defiance. "Never!"

Unable to move, Mouse stared at Valk's battered and naked body as the man stood up. It didn't seem possible that someone as badly damaged could stand, let alone throw a much larger man across a room. Yet, despite the mass of unhealed claw wounds scoring his naked body in more than a dozen places, the blackened star of a scorch mark on his chest, and the way one shoulder hung lower than the other, he stood up.

There was no doubt that the creature, whatever it was, was going to consume him just like it was doing to Valk.

"What in the name of the Found God are you doing, Valk?" The captain's voice was strained; yet, he stood up. "You're too wounded to get out of bed yet!"

When the Enemy's gaze shifted from him to the captain, the relentless assault on Mouse's mind eased up just enough for him to shift his focus deeper into the core of Valk's being. He searched for any remaining vestiges of the man's *ta'ir*.

"YOU SHOULD BOW BEFORE ME, MORTAL FOOL! I AM YOUR MASTER!"

"I don't know wh...!"

The captain was cut off as Valk took a single step and grabbed him around the throat. The thinner man lifted Captain Dastyr off of the floor and slammed him into the bulkhead in one single, shockingly powerful, movement.

Captain Dastyr flailed about as he tried to pry the hand from around his neck. His feet convulsed, kicking out weakly as his face began to purple up.

"I AM THAT WHICH YOU SEEK!"

Desperate, Mouse pushed deeper into the maelstrom of sound emanating from the man's body. He heard a tiny, mournful echo of what had once been a powerful song.

There! He's still in there!

Kerplunk.

Without giving it a second thought, Mouse pushed off from the wall behind him and raised the flute to his lips. The captain flailed helplessly in his brother's deadly grip. Mouse did the only thing that felt right...

He began to play.

CHAPTER 28

Seldy

*H*oo hoo!"

Seldy sat up. Her eyes darted about the clearing, searching for the owl amidst the towering, moonlit trees. Before she could find it, however, a fresh round of searing cramps doubled her over.

Biting down to keep from crying out in pain and frustration, Seldy couldn't stop the tears leaking from her eyes. She rocked back and forth, trying to ease the cramps.

"Why?" she wailed into the night air. "Why is all of this happening to me?"

Lost in her grief, Seldy surrendered to the sobs wracking her body.

A twig snapped. A presence loomed behind her.

She stiffened but didn't otherwise move. There was nowhere else to run, no one who could help her.

"It is finally time, rehla," a familiar, but impossible voice whispered in her ear. "Time for you to discover the answer to that question and perhaps to some others that you must have."

Seldy bolted upright and whipped her head around.

"Tia!"

She scrambled to her knees even as the naked woman knelt down with her arms thrown wide.

"But how?! I saw you die!"

She buried her face in the ancient woman's wispy grey hair and wrapped her arms around her frail shoulders in a fierce hug.

"My dear sweet *rehla*," Tia sighed into their mutual embrace. "How I wish things could have been different."

Seldy clutched at her mentor as if the old woman might disappear the moment she released her. Tears streamed down her cheeks in a relentless torrent. Keeping her eyes closed, she breathed in the distinctive and soothing scent of the unique blend of herbs and incense that always accompanied the old seer. She basked in the softness and warmth of her wrinkled skin.

The old woman took hold of Seldy's cheeks and pushed the two of them apart.

"Open your eyes."

Seldy couldn't resist the soft command for long. When she complied, all she could see were those mesmerizing grey eyes and the wrinkled and blotched skin that surrounded them.

"The deceptions of the Enemy are beyond counting, so it is good to doubt whatever he shows you. But..." Tia's voice wavered for a moment before she could continue. "But what you saw happen to me was the truth."

"But...I don't understand! How are you here, if you're... dead?"

"Remember what I taught you of this place, *rehla*. We are in the Dreamlands."

Tia pushed her hands gently into Seldy's wild hair, working her way back until she was able to start rubbing the length of Seldy's ears with well-practiced motions. The soft, familiar strokes melted the tension from her body.

"Oh! So this is...a dream...and not real?" She couldn't keep the panic from her voice.

"Who is to say that dreams are not real? Does this not feel real to you?" Tia continued, smiling. "Should I stop, then?"

Knowing how much she would regret it, Seldy brought her hands up to Tia's and took the ancient woman's fingers into her own. There was an immediate pang of loss once the contact with her ears was broken.

"Yes, Tia. Stop." She swallowed the lump that formed in her throat. "I'm not a child anymore." She sat up straighter as she studied the ancient seer's face. "If this is a dream, I'm still a captive on that ship, right?"

Tia nodded, her expression solemn.

"Then I need information that I can trust right now more than I need comfort."

"Good." Seldy could hear both satisfaction and relief in Tia's tone. "It has been so difficult waiting for this moment."

"How long have you known that I was Fae, Tia?" Seldy squeezed the old seer's fingers.

Tia closed her eyes and took a long, deep breath. Released from the piercing gaze, Seldy glanced down at the woman's wrinkled, withered body in wonder. There was an austere dignity and an elegant and untouchable beauty in how she carried herself even though she was completely naked. It was easy to believe the stories about how when she was much younger, Tiagra had been considered one of the most beautiful women on all of Timos.

When the seer's eyes opened again, she captured Seldy's gaze.

"I've known that you were Fae from the moment I first held you in my arms."

Seldy's mouth dropped open. Before she could collect herself, the old woman continued.

"I was drawn to Jhana's *vardo* that first night you were brought to us, when you were no more than two weeks old. Until that night, she had been avoiding me like the Scourge, even though she'd been back with the *kumpania* for several years by then."

A wry smile found its way to Tia's lips. "Jhana had her reasons for avoiding me, troubled as she was by her personal demons." The ancient woman's frail shoulders rose in a brief shrug. "But with a babe in her arms who was a newcomer to the *kumpania*, she couldn't avoid me any longer. As Seer, I had a duty to perform."

"A *shavaryn?* You performed a *shavaryn* on me?" she gasped. "I thought those were only done right after a baby was born?"

Tia cackled. "Ah, my bright little *rehla!* Yes, well that is when they are normally done, but you were an adopted child. Thus, I took you in my arms and called on my gift to show me what it would of your potential futures."

The old woman's eyes closed again as she drew back from Seldy, shuddering at the memory.

"What's wrong, Tia?" Seldy leaned forward, still holding the woman's hands in her own. "What did you see?"

Shaking her head from side to side, the ancient woman muttered, "Terrible and wonderful...amazing and horrifying... saddening and triumphant." When she finally looked up, there was a haunted look in those tear-filled grey eyes. "Do you want to see what I saw? To hear what I heard? To feel what I felt?"

Taken aback by her questions, Seldy pulled back. "Should I?"

"Only you can answer that, Seldy," Tia whispered her reply. "But those visions are your birthright, just as access to this place is. It begins with a message from your birth mother."

"How can I see what you saw back then?"

"Here, in this place, much is possible." Pulling her hands

free from Seldy's, the ancient seer held them up, trembling. The old woman's voice had a sharp edge to it. "Are you ready, reh-la, to experience your shavaryn?"

Tha-throom.

A hush descended. The peaceful sounds of the forest fell silent. Insects no longer buzzed. Nocturnal creatures had stopped rustling about in the leaf litter. Even the breeze calmed, allowing the trees to end their whispering conversations for a time.

Seldy shivered. Swallowing her fear, she nodded.

Without a moment's hesitation, the ancient woman leaned forward, placed her hands on each side of Seldy's head, and pulled her into an open-mouthed kiss. The moment their lips met, the older woman exhaled strongly, filling Seldy's mouth and lungs with pungent dreamvine smoke.

Tha-throom.

The powerful effects of the drug spread through her like wildfire. Every muscle in her body loosened and relaxed. She would have collapsed if Tia hadn't wrapped her arms around her and pulled into a full-bodied hug, gently stroking Seldy's hair as she cradled her lolling head against her body.

Tha-throom.

Rocking back and forth, Tia began to hum a slow and haunting tune...

A pair of brilliant blue eyes opened. They illuminated the darkness as if they were lit from within. Seldy recognized those eyes and wanted to cry out to her birth mother, but nothing happened when she tried.

Helpless to do anything but watch and listen, the view shifted, pulling back from those magickal eyes until a pale, delicate, and very feminine face coalesced around them. Curly golden hair framed the breathtakingly beautiful face, but those glittering eyes continued to dominate. She ached to reach out, to touch her and feel her warmth.

Her mother began to speak in a soft, lilting tone, a haunting voice that echoed in the darkness.

"Greetings, Spiritsister. My name is Chirianna Silversong, and you hold in your arms my one and only daughter, Seldirima Silversong. That you are seeing this means that everything I have sacrificed to make this moment possible has been worth it.

"I apologize that I do not know your name, for I do not have the gift of the Sight."

The woman closed her mesmerizing eyes for the briefest of moments and paused before continuing.

"That gift was passed from my ancestor to yours many, many generations before I was born." A tear trickled down the woman's face. "But I do know that only a Freeborn woman, blessed with that rarest of gifts from my ancestor, Loradanyelle the Lost, can access this vision."

Her mother's eyes grew brighter as her face drew nearer.

"More than six centuries ago, my ancestor came to the gates of Lisandria — the great walled city of your ancestors — seeking refuge in a time of great danger."

As she spoke, the woman's sparkling eyes grew larger until the entire field of vision was taken up by a single brilliant iris surrounding a fathomless pit of the deepest black. At the mention of Lisandria — the fabled homeland of all those who called themselves Freeborn — an impressive city wall built from massive stones loomed up out of the darkness, dwarfing the viewer. Beyond the top of the wall, gleaming spires covered in shining silver and gold and lofty towers reached high into the sky. The city behind the wall was clearly both prosperous and mighty.

The air was cold. Loose flakes of snow swirled down from the laden skies to further deepen the fresh, untrodden snow that covered the path towards the closed gates of the city.

"My ancestor was afraid, alone, and heavy with child," her mother's voice continued. "She was carrying the future of her folk both within her womb and in a small, covered basket dangling from her arm."

The wall seemed to grow larger and more ominous with each staggering step taken by the viewer.

"When Loradanyelle reached the gate, she called upon the guards to honor the ancient covenant between the Lisandrians and her folk. They refused."

The fading light of the setting winter sun glinted off of the metal helmets of the guards.

"Weak and tired from her long journey, her heart heavy with the slaughter that had been visited upon her friends and family by the Enemy and his minions, Loradanyelle pleaded with the heartless, jeering men. 'Please, in the name of all that you hold sacred,' she cried out to them, 'grant me sanctuary within your stout walls! My daughter will be born soon, and she needs the warmth and safety that only you can provide!'"

Above, arms appeared just beyond the parapets. They hurled things down at her. Seldy could only watch in horror as bits of rotting food and small stones came hurtling towards her. She wanted to duck, to run from the coming barrage. Instead, the person whose vantage point she was watching from dropped the basket to the ground and simply hunched over, covering her bulging belly with her arms even as she turned her face towards her tormentors. She felt the sting of a partially eaten apple strike one shoulder and a hunk of rotting meat smash into the other. But the worst impact was the small, sharp stone that sliced her cheek open, sending waves of pain throughout her body. She dropped to her knees.

"Wounded in body and spirit by their shameful response, my ancestor was still unwilling to let her pride prevent her from making every possible effort to save her daughter. Loradanyelle stood back up and called out once more, 'People of Lisandria, I beseech thee, please honor the ancient laws of hospitality! I beg of you! The Enemy is immortal, and his hunger is insatiable! He will not stop with the Fae! He will come for you and your fair city next! My daughter is your only hope! I have Seen this!'"

Another round of hurled debris was followed by a single, bellowing answer in a deep masculine voice that echoed through the vision.

"'Some magick you have, witch! Did you not See your own fate?'" The voice laughed. "'Our walls are impregnable! Our blades are sharp and our archers are keen! Our soldiers have never known defeat! Lisandria shall stand tall and strong against any foe, mortal or not! We don't fear Drak'nuul or his Reavers!'"

"Despite the terror that gripped her and threatened to overcome her," her mother's voice continued softly, "Loradanyelle rose up to her full height and called out in a voice that she enhanced with her magick so that all within the city would hear her. 'Fair Lisandria, you were once known throughout Sundatha as the Jewel of Davyos. Hear me now! In your prosperity and security, your hearts have hardened. You turn away from the plight of others, thinking yourself secure behind strong walls and sharp swords! But I, Loradanyelle, the last Treemaiden of Davyos, declare that you have forsaken your ancient vows of friendship and alliance with the Fae! You have broken the covenant between our peoples. I withdraw the blessings and protections that were granted to this fair city at its foundation when your ancestors came begging to mine, ragged and forlorn, seeking shelter from the chaos and destruction of the Great Sundering, lo those many, long centuries ago!'"

The touch of her ancestor's fingers upon her torn and bloodied face felt as real as if Seldy had touched it herself. She experienced Loradanyelle smearing blood upon her hand and holding it up for the ogling crowd of guards and dignitaries gathered above to see as if she had done it herself.

When her mother continued reciting the words of her long-deceased ancestor, her voice changed ever-so-slightly, becoming deeper and darker, filled with a terrible vengeance, until Seldy was certain that the voice that was speaking was that of Loradanyelle and not her birth mother.

"'By the power of this blood that you have shed from one who only sought a moment of succor and safety behind your walls.'"

She moved forward, placing her hand upon the closed gate and smearing her blood across it.

"'I curse this city, and all of its folk, to suffer as my people have! Until this wrong is righted and these sins are atoned for, neither you nor any of your descendants will find safety behind any wall. Those few of you that survive the coming storm of fire and blood shall be left forever homeless, doomed to wander the Sundered Lands as gypsies and vagrants — welcomed by none, suspected by all!'"

An incredible rush of power surged through their shared body as the last words of the curse flowed from their lips and landed upon the city and all of its inhabitants. Her ancestor dropped to her knees. Seldy experienced every bit of the sheer exhaustion that Loradanyelle exhibited. This, in addition to the waves of anger, frustration, and sorrow, was nearly too much to bear. It would have been so much easier to simply collapse and fall asleep in the snow.

"My ancestor," her mother's voice returned to her normal tones. "Had one overriding thought, one single motivation that gave her the strength to rise to her feet despite the increased size and intensity of the things being thrown from the walls above: her daughter."

The narration paused for a moment as the image focused on

the bruised and battered hands of the long-dead ancestor as she protected her bulging abdomen covered only by the sheer fabric of a silken summer dress.

"She couldn't give up because she had Seen that her daughter — or one of the daughters or granddaughters that would follow — would someday, somehow, find the strength and courage to stand against the Enemy and end his reign of terror."

The narration fell silent as Loradanyelle gathered her fallen basket and struggled to her feet despite the increased rain of objects landing on and around her. More rocks and bones thudded into the snow, often only after bouncing painfully off of her back or head. Bucketfuls of refuse splashed against her cloaked back and onto her bare feet, staining the snow with the city's shame.

The broken and battered woman stumbled to the low stone wall of an abandoned well. There, with one final glance back at the people jeering her from the wall, she let the basket fall into it. Turning back to the well, the woman closed her eyes, and uttered a word that Seldy couldn't hear.

Energy sizzled. The ground shook. The stone walls of the well crumbled, collapsing in on themselves. Behind the woman, the folk at the top of the wall cried out, but those walls stood firm.

"Beyond exhausted and bleeding from a number of deep wounds, Loradanyelle limped back in the direction she had come through sheer determination and willpower alone," Seldy's mother resumed her narration in a voice tinged with fresh depths of sorrow even though it seemed to be one she had long ago memorized. "She did not have the strength to get far. She collapsed less than a mile later, stumbling into a ditch and falling unconscious."

The vision went dark at the moment of her ancestor's collapse and stayed dark and silent until those bright blue eyes opened and illuminated the darkness once again.

"Loradanyelle was discovered later that night by a young woman — the eldest daughter of a poor peasant farmer. She was taken in by that family and even though they didn't have enough to feed or clothe themselves properly, they gave her shelter and care until her daughter was born and she was well enough to travel once again."

There was awe in those blue eyes and a tenderness in her voice that hadn't been there earlier in the vision.

"Before she left, my ancestor pulled the oldest daughter of the household aside and spoke to her. 'Mistress, a rain of fire and blood is about to strike your people, something that I no longer have the strength to forestall, even if I so desired. The people of Lisandria have, in their arrogance and cruelty, earned the fate that is about to befall them. I have but one precious gift to repay your kindness.'

"She stared deep into the woman's eyes. 'I offer you the gift of the Fae Sight. This gift is beyond precious.'

"'What is this Sight, and how can it help save my people?'

"'The Sight cannot save your people from the fate they have earned. It will, however, give you the ability to see dreams and visions of possible future events. If you are brave enough to accept this gift, these visions can bring you wisdom that can help you, and those female descendants of yours who inherit it, to guide the survivors of the coming tragedies in their wandering. The Sight will mark you in ways that you cannot yet understand, just as it will for all those who follow in your path. And perhaps one day, it will provide your descendants with a path to redemption and salvation.'"

Silence descended upon the darkness as Seldy's birth mother stopped speaking for several long moments. She continued to stare unblinking directly at Seldy. When she started again, her voice was broken.

"Know this, Spiritsister — the Enemy who hunted down and

slew my ancestors is the same foul creature that later brought down the walls of Lisandria and scattered your ancestors to the four winds. He is the same powerful foe who brought about the Great Riving that plunged the world into chaos and warfare for more than two hundred years. If he hadn't been defeated in the Founder's War by a most unlikely coalition of allies, the Enemy and his servants would have enslaved all of the free peoples of the Sundered Lands.

"But the Enemy was never fully defeated. Instead, he simply hid until he found ways to turn allies into bitter foes. He has secretly placed legions of minions loyal to him within the ranks of his former foes, co-opting them and setting the stage for another great war — a war that few even suspect is coming.

"The Enemy, who once hunted my ancestors, now seeks my daughter." Her words stopped in a choked sob. "He knows that she is also the daughter of Sarlan the Red, that she is the descendant of two different Treemothers and has the potential to become a Treemother herself."

Tears streamed down her cheeks as she paused to swallow down another sob.

"He would have found her already, if I hadn't been forced to do...something beyond horrible...to my own child..."

Her eyes closed again and paused for many long moments before resuming.

"I have imprisoned her song to keep the Enemy from coming for her before she is ready to face him."

The plea in her eyes was as clear as the one she voiced.

"Spiritsister, I come to you now — through the very gift my ancestor bestowed to yours — begging refuge for my daughter, Seldirima. Please, keep her safe until she is old enough to fend for herself. Teach her of her heritage without revealing to her who she really is. Love her. Protect her. And help her grow into the person she must become." She paused again. "There is another who will help her when he is able — my hidden hero. If he survives, he will have the key to restoring her song.

"Keep my daughter safe, Spiritsister, for as long as you can, and perhaps the dark deeds and betrayal that led my ancestor to lay her curse upon yours all of those centuries ago shall be cleansed."

Tha-throom.

"*No!*"

Seldy awoke with a gasp. She flailed her arms and kicked her feet, thrashing against her captor. Her heart hammered. Her pulse throbbed.

"*Easy now, rehla.*" *Thin arms, stronger than they appeared, held her in a tight embrace.* "*I am here for you,*" *a raspy voice whispered into her ear.* "*The dreamvine still has you in its grip. It intensifies things.*"

Tha-throom.

"*So...many...people...*" *she gasped again, her limbs twitching.* "*So...horrible...*"

"*I know,*" *the husky voice sympathized even as its arms continued to clutch her close.* "*I was there as well.*"

Afterimages of the towering walls of Lisandria, and the cruel and heartless people standing atop them as they pelted her with rotting food, stones, and other detritus, were burned into her memory. Her skin felt hot and flushed, even though her teeth were chattering. Her limbs were heavy and unresponsive. Her body ached. Every time she tried to open her eyes, the forest spun in a new direction. Her tongue felt thick and woolly in her mouth and rasped against swollen and cracked lips. The muscles of her abdomen churned, twisting and clenching with each labored breath. Heavy fabric pressed down on her shoulders from above and chafed against her skin, making her itch everywhere the rough fibers touched.

It weighed her down...confined her...limited her...

Tha-throom.

"Itchy....off..." She snatched at the hem of the garment with desperate, clumsy fingers. "...needs to come...off..."

The arms holding her loosened just enough.

Seldy yanked upwards peeling the offending cloth over her head and tossed it aside. Relief flooded throughout her body the moment she was free. Her skin — kissed by the cool, gentle breezes of the night air and warmed by the soft skin of her companion — could finally breathe.

Two withered arms wrapped around her shoulders and pulled her back into a full-on embrace. Familiar, calming energy flowed into Seldy from each point of skin-on-skin contact.

"Easy now, rehla. I've got you."

Tha-throom.

Those tender, whispered words unleashed a torrent of pent up emotion. Seldy stopped struggling and collapsed into the embrace. She sobbed uncontrollably. Hot tears fell like rain down her cheeks. Tia rocked her back and forth, stroking her back, ears, and hair with a gentle and loving touch.

Each shoulder-wracking sob eased a small bit of the heartache with it. Every tear carried away a tiny portion of the pain from both body and mind. Each shuddering gasp expelled some of the darkness that had been weighing down her spirit.

Tia held and rocked her through all of it, not seeming to care how long it took for her to recover. She whispered soft words into her ear, planted soft kisses on her cheek, and stroked the tips of one of Seldy's ears with her well-practiced and soothing touch. But mostly, she was just there — loving and present — as Seldy healed herself in the only way she knew how.

Gradually, piece by piece, Seldy assimilated everything that her shavaryn revealed to her and came to terms with it.

"How did you do it, Tia?" She pulled back from their

embrace to look the ancient woman in the eyes. "How did you find the strength to keep all of that to yourself?"

"A seer learns early on, *rehla*, to keep those secrets that must be kept because failure to do so often leads to disaster." The old seer's expression softened. "But this secret was harder to keep than all of the others combined, by far."

"But what if the *shavaryn* was wrong? How do you know if any of it is true?"

"Good." Tia's eyes lit up. She flashed Seldy a grin as she tapped her own forehead with a finger. "You should question everything, child, because the truth of such things is not easy to discern." Reaching out a wrinkled hand, Tia pressed her palm to Seldy's chest, right above her heart, and held it there as she continued. "But the truth is here, if you have the strength to hear it. Listen to your heart and follow your truth."

As she absorbed Tia's words, Seldy noted the contrast between the wizened, leathery skin of the ancient woman's hand pressed against her own unblemished, youthful flesh.

Tha-throom.

In that loving gesture, the various connections between them became complete — between teacher and student, crone and maiden, mortal and immortal, dream and reality, and between the dead and the living. Realization dawned that this timeless moment was a farewell.

Goosebumps prickled up all over her body.

Seldy brought Tia's fingers, bent with age, to her lips and kissed each of them.

"How can I ever thank you, Tia, for all you've done? For all that you've given me over the years?"

"Find your song, *rehla*," Tia sighed. "And find a way to defeat the Enemy. Remember our lessons together and how you were raised. There was purpose and love behind every lesson."

Her words were so quiet that they could've easily been lost

amidst the background noise of the forest at night, but Seldy's ears were as keen as her heart was full.

"Become that which you were born to be, and remember all of the sacrifices that made it possible."

Unable to contain herself, Seldy leaned forward and kissed Tia on the lips. She blinked through the tears blurring her vision.

"If I get through all of this, it will be because of...the lessons..." she sniffed, "and love...that you and Jhana-ma gave me."

For the first time that she could recall, the ancient woman seemed to be at a loss for words. She simply nodded as Seldy disentangled herself and sat back on her heels.

"Tia!" Seldy gasped, pointing towards the woman's lap. "You're bleeding! Are you okay?"

"That isn't my blood, rehla." She offered Seldy a disconcerting smile. "I am long past the time of my monthly moons."

"Oh, no!" Seldy gasped. "I...I...I'm so sorry, Tia!"

Her stomach lurched. Her inner thighs were even messier than Tia's. She dropped her hands down to cover herself without touching the disgusting blood.

"I didn't know I was flowing, yet. Honest!"

The seer chortled. "Just wait until you have children, rehla. You will see that there is no point in being embarrassed by any fluid our bodies produce."

"But why is there so much?" Seldy reached for her tunic. "I shouldn't be bleeding this much! What's wrong with me?"

"There is nothing wrong, rehla." Tia hadn't moved to wipe herself off in any way. "This is a moment of powerful magick. A sign we must heed."

Unconsoled, Seldy swiveled her head around in a panic. "I'm so sorry, Tia! Let me clean you up!"

When she saw tunic crumpled atop a nearby fern, she started to stand.

"No."

Tia's stern command froze Seldy in place.

"Your Moon's Blood is sacred and holds great power. We will not waste it."

She swiped her fingers through the blood smeared on her and held them up. The dark red fluid glistened in the soft moonlight.

"Come closer, rehla."

"Wha—?"

A single snap of the fingers of Tia's other hand silenced Seldy. Her expression hardened.

"Come."

Chastened, Seldy inched closer. She grimaced at the feel of the fluid seeping out and oozing down her thighs.

"I have one more task now that your Moon's Blood is here." Tia's tone brooked no questioning of her authority. "You have much to learn about yourself, and you have more allies in this fight against the Enemy than you know of, especially here, in this place."

She grabbed Seldy's elbow with her clean hand and held on tight. "You must also know, however, that the war that looms in the world below is already being fought here. The Enemy cannot come to this place directly. Not yet, anyway." She nodded towards the still smoking remnant of the claw near the base of the tree. "But he sends forth his Reavers to hunt for you and your allies. They will be relentless and merciless in their search. Without access to your song, you are helpless against such dangers. But we are about to change that."

A lifetime in the Istimiel kumpania had taught Seldy to listen whenever the Seer spoke in her Maestra-voice. She merely nodded, attentive to every word.

"I am not alone in waiting for you to come to the Dreamlands. The Elder Spirits have been calling for you. You must answer their call."

"*Shadowfang spoke about the Elder Spirits! But who are they? And how do I find them?*"

"*Yes, well, I am getting to that child. I want you to name three animal species that resonate with you, that you most admire.*"

"*Well, that's easy! Tigers, elephants, and horses!*"

"*Tigers, yes, that'll do for one.*" Tia nodded. "*They are powerful creatures who possess great strength and stealth.*" She waved off the other answers with blood-smeared fingers. "*But elephants and horses will not do, though they are noble beasts and can be very useful. Not given what you must face in the coming war.*" Tia leaned forward, her eyes gleaming. "*Think of predators who are deadly and have skills or talents you admire or desire.*"

Seldy blinked a couple of times before responding. She wanted to argue that point, because Bessie was the strongest and bravest creature she knew of even if she wasn't a predator, but something in Tia's demeanor dissuaded her from arguing.

"*Umm...what about wolves, then? They are strong and fast and brave!*"

Tia said nothing as she waited.

"*Owls!*" she exclaimed. "*They can fly and hunt at night, and they are super quiet when they want to be. And because, Tia, they remind me of you!*"

The ancient seer remained quiet, her expression unreadable. Without warning, her eyes turned milky white.

"*Do not move and remain silent until I finish, no matter how strange my actions seem or how uncomfortable they make you.*" The seer's tone had an even harder edge than before. "*Do you understand, rehla?*"

The air between them crackled with restless energy, causing goosebumps to prickle up all over her body.

"*Yes, Maestra.*"

Tia released her elbow and dipped that hand in the blood that remained on her own thigh. A moment later, she held up both of her glistening-wet hands until they were illuminated by a silvery beam of light shining down from above. She began to speak in a low, gravelly voice.

"By my rights as a Crone, by the sweet light of Mother Luna, by the transformational power of the menstrual blood of this Maiden — I hereby summon the essences of Wolf, Tiger, and Owl from amongst the Elder Spirits."

The energy crackling around them was so thick it made Seldy's skin tingle. It was all she could do to sit still amidst the swirling vortex of energy, but she didn't move. When it seemed that the energy couldn't grow any stronger, Tia pulled her hands down and began swiping her fingers across Seldy's abdomen.

Each swipe of the ancient seer's fingers left trails of freshly smeared blood mixed with tendrils of that same restless energy. Her skin tingled everywhere that Tia touched. Profound feelings of disgust and wonder warred within her. It took all of the self-discipline she had to remain still and not scurry away.

"For the Maiden," Tia sang out in a low howl. "The Wolf. She is wild and free. She is a huntress in the night. In her fertility, she carries the future of the Pack. Bold, courageous, ever-curious and joyfully social — she is steadfast and loyal to those who have earned her love."

Falling silent, the ancient woman leaned back to survey her work. Satisfied, she nodded before bending down to gather more blood from Seldy's right thigh.

Biting back a surprised yelp at the rough and determined way that Tia went about collecting the blood, Seldy sucked in her lower lip and bit down on it.

Tia straightened up and began drawing again, this time concentrating on her breasts and upper torso. The power flowing *around them grew stronger, even more vibrant. If the seer felt it, she didn't react in any visible way. Her fingers were a blur of activity, swiping right and left and up and down in broad and rough strokes leaving thick stripes of smeared blood wherever they went.*

"For the Mother," Tia growled in a low voice that reminded her of a tiger's rumbling purr. "The tigress. Her strength is unyielding. She is fierce and deadly, protective of both her young and her territory. She is comfortable with solitude and wary of strangers. She is never one to be trifled with or dismissed."

When the seer stopped speaking, she leaned back to study her handicraft through milky-white eyes.

Glancing down, Seldy gasped. Each dark line of blood stood in stark contrast to the paleness of her skin. In the pale light of the full moon, the fresh lines of blood felt hot against her otherwise cool skin. Her head swayed as the forest spun around her. Despite her dizziness, Seldy saw the rough details of a tiger's face drawn across her chest, the areola of each breast served as a pupil for the great cat's eyes. Beneath that striking image, there was a rougher outline of a wolf's head in profile turned upwards to howl into the night. The wolf covered the entirety of her stomach and abdomen, stretching from just above her pubic hair to the bottom of her breastbone.

Seldy was so distracted by the power and beauty of each of those images that she didn't realize until it was too late that the ancient woman had gathered yet more blood from her left thigh and was reaching for her face.

Wrinkling her nose at the sharp, coppery aroma of her own blood being brought so close to her nose, Seldy renewed her fight against the urge to pull back. She made no attempt, however, to hide her disgust at the prospect of having her face painted with her own Moon's Blood.

But the seer, locked into her task, seemed oblivious. Bent and withered, her fingers were still strong and sure as one hand held her chin in place while the other hand applied the newest blood in quick, yet determined, strokes across Seldy's forehead, nose, and cheeks.

"For the Crone," Tia hooted. "The owl. She is swift and silent, a deadly hunter in the night. She can fly where and when others dare not. She has the wisdom to know when it is best to observe and the patience to wait for the proper time to act."

With the last stroke in place, Tia released Seldy's chin and lifted both blood-smeared hands high into the moonlight.

"Maiden, Mother, and Crone — I call upon the Sacred Trinity! Bless this child of light and those allies who will serve as her guides and guardians in the coming conflict! Please accept this sacrifice of her monthly Moon's Blood and grant her the courage, strength, and wisdom she will need to survive all of the challenges ahead! Let the balance between Life and Death be restored and, by her actions, let the Sundered Lands be healed!"

Tia dropped her head to stare into Seldy's eyes. Her eyes had returned to their normal grey hue, but they were somehow shining from within. There was an unspoken farewell in the look Tia gave her. The seer's lips formed into a blown kiss before she turned her head skyward again and called out in a voice that trembled with power.

"To seal this prayer, oh Elder Spirits, I offer my eternal spirit into your everlasting service!"

All of the energy swirling around them and within Seldy surged at the exact moment of Tia's last spoken syllable. Faster than thought or sight or feeling, it coalesced around the ancient woman in a searing, crackling flash of explosive energy that was so bright Seldy had to snap her eyes shut. Even then, the afterimage of Tia's outlined form was burned into her eyelids.

The force of the explosion sent Seldy sprawling backwards.

When she collected her wits enough to push herself up onto her elbows, she opened her eyes again.

She was alone.

The forest was eerily silent. Even the trees had stopped their ceaseless whispering.

Where Tia had been kneeling, only a single, brown feather remained.

CHAPTER 29

Mouse

Mouse closed his eyes as soon as he began playing. Instead of the comforting darkness that normally welcomed him, a chaotic world of vibrant, wildly shifting colors opened up to him. Each note emerged from his flute into this strange new soundscape as colorful and tangible shapes that fluttered about his head in a swirling menagerie of dancing figures.

That display, however, was dwarfed by the maelstrom of sound and fury raging around Valk. The vast array of warped and twisted notes circling the captain's brother was in the process of engulfing the captain's dimmer and smaller song. Each time one of the darker notes of the creature inhabiting Valk struck one of the captain's, they both shattered in a sonic explosion that diminished the captain's song while adding to the overwhelming mass of broken and dissonant sounds of the other song.

Unsure of what he was doing, Mouse hurled the first few notes of his song at the Enemy with reckless abandon. He might as well've been trying to tickle a dragon with a feather. His warbling notes were quickly absorbed into the vortex of sound spinning around Valk.

Frustrated, Mouse pulled away from the flute and opened his eyes to study the physical struggle taking place in front of him. The world of sonic fury faded into the background of his mind as he focused his eyes on the tangible world.

Valk's left hand tightened around Captain Dastyr's neck while his right grabbed the obsidian Seeker's Circle and held it up to the bulging eyes of its bearer.

"IN THE NAME OF THAT WHICH YOU SEEK, MORTAL, SURRENDER THIS SHIP TO MY COMMAND, AND YOU SHALL BE SPARED!"

"V-v-valk...don't...be...delusional...," the captain strained to respond. "The...crew...would...never...follow...awk!"

Closing his eyes again, Mouse focused his efforts on finding Valk's *ta'ir*. All he could perceive, however, was the overwhelming and incoherent wall of sound that had expanded to surround both Valk and the captain. Distracted by the chaos of the soundscape, Mouse didn't hear the creature's reply to the captain's protestations.

The Enemy is consuming Valk's ta'ir *and if I don't do something he's going to do the same to the captain!* Mouse shuddered. *But what can I do about it? He's so strong!*

The Enemy's colossal song kept hammering the captain's shrinking defenses. A deep dread settled over Mouse. His limbs became heavy and unresponsive. Every hair on his body stood up on end. His throat closed up, threatening to cut off his breathing. His toes curled up against the wood beneath them, as if trying to force him into moving.

I need to get out of here! I can't beat this creature! If I don't run for it, I'm going to be next!

Fingers of cold dread wrapped around his heart and squeezed. His breath came in short, ragged gasps. His fingers trembled around the flute.

But if I run, what happens to the Shining Lady's daughter?

His thoughts raced at a faster pace than his pounding pulse. Memories of all of the times he ran from confrontation or curled up in the face of conflict flooded his consciousness. In every instance, the choice to flee or surrender to a beating had only impacted him. The last image was of the Shining Lady's sparkling blue eyes looking down at him. Her voice echoed in his mind.

Please...please help her...

Her eyes were red with tears; yet, they brimmed with hope that he would be strong enough and brave enough to help her only child. Even across the twin gulfs of distance and time that separated them, her smile warmed his heart.

His cheeks flushed red. He took a deep breath and rocked forward onto the balls of his feet. Pressing his fingers tighter against the sound holes of the flute, Mouse set his shoulders.

I will not run from this moment! There has to be a way to fight this monster!

As soon as those words formed in his head, a distant, high-pitched buzzing sound echoed in his memory, taking him back to the tiny little garden that his mother had created back in the Slant. Mouse had spent countless hours tending to the multitude of plants and herbs that his mother had somehow found a way to grow within the stacks of makeshift planters and pots. Their secret garden — used to grow the herbs and medicinal plants that his mother depended on to help tend to her patients — was an oasis of color amidst the otherwise dull browns and grays of the Slant. He spent more time practicing there with his *f'leyn* than anywhere else. It was there, in that garden, that he had watched with wonder as honey bees worked their own special magick.

The bees lived in a small hive that had formed in a special box his mother had cobbled together for them in the top corner of the hidden garden. The tiny creatures explored the garden on wings that moved too fast for the eye to see. They never bothered him as they went about their tasks of pollinating the blooms and collecting the nectar and extra pollen they used to make their precious honey, but they were quick to swarm to the defense of the hive against any perceived threat, no matter how much larger or more powerful that threat was than the bees themselves. Individually, the bees were tiny compared to the other insects and creatures that sought to steal the fruits of their labor, but that didn't stop them from banding together and using their collective strength to harass and deter any would be invaders.

The bees liked his music. Occasionally, one of them would land on the end of the *f'leyn* and dance to whatever song he was playing. Once or twice a year, his mother would ask him to play a special song that he had invented for them so that she could collect a small portion of their golden treasure without getting stung. She was always careful to leave most of the honey in place, taking only what they needed. She used it in her practice and for a rare treat on special holidays or whenever Mouse had been especially helpful.

Hope sparked by the nostalgic memory, Mouse began to play again with a speed and frenzy that he hadn't known was possible. The notes that swarmed out of his flute were loud, high-pitched, and frenetic like a hive full of agitated bees that were having their hard-earned honey stolen from them. The individual notes buzzed about him in the air like the living, breathing creatures they represented.

Time slowed even as Mouse's fingers and breathing sped up. The swarm of notes grew in size and strength. Just like the honey bees of his youth drew together in tight clumps each winter in order to protect the queen of the hive, his bee-notes circled around him, forming a protective barrier against the chaos of the Enemy's *ta'ir*.

Bolstered by his new defenses, Mouse crossed the threshold into the cramped cabin, closing the distance between them.

Mouse kept his eyes closed, trusting both in his memory of the physical space and the accuracy of the strange new soundscape that had opened up to him. His mental map of the cabin grew clearer as the sonic struggle became louder and yet more chaotic.

The pulsating, energetic form of the Enemy towered over the shielding wall of sound between them, standing much taller and stronger than any creature Mouse had ever seen. Massive wings sprouted from his back that would've scraped the ceiling of the room had they been flesh and bone. Instead, the sharp, hooked talons that topped each wing appeared and disappeared with each jerky movement, slipping through the wood of the ceiling as if it didn't exist. One powerful arm easily held the captain up, while the other drew back as if to deliver a powerful blow with the gleaming talons.

Mouse redoubled his efforts, adding to the furious swarm of notes. He had to find a way to help Valk.

"WHAT IS THIS FOOLISHNESS?!"

The booming words thundered throughout his very being, pushing him back a step with their power. Mouse struggled mightily but lost the clash of wills that left him staring into the baleful glare of those glowing red eyes.

"WHO ARE YOU?"

Mouse's fingers faltered. The last few notes warbled and slipped away. His throat tightened, and his mouth became dry. Every hair on his neck and arms stood on end, and all of the warmth left his body. The power of the creature's command shook him to his very core.

"I'm nobody important." Shaking like a leaf being blown about in a strong wind, Mouse was more than a little surprised by the strength of his voice. "But I'm not going to let you hurt these men anymore!"

As casually as he might've cast aside a dirty tunic, the Enemy tossed the captain towards the far wall. The big man cursed as he was flung, but his objections were silenced by the loud crash into the wall. He slumped limp and unconscious to floor. The monster swung around to face Mouse. He spread his wings, swelling to fill the small chamber with his presence.

"FOOLISH MORTAL! YOU HAVE NO IDEA OF THE DANGER YOU ARE IN! I WILL CONSUME YOU!"

The sheer menace in the creature's voice washed over Mouse with unstoppable force. He'd never been more afraid in his entire life. But the flute was solid and real in his fingers. The notes were buzzing all around him, ready to defend him.

"I know who you are and what you seek!" Mouse shouted back at the creature. "And she's not your property!"

The creature straightened up to its full height and loomed closer.

"IF YOU TRULY KNOW WHO I AM, WORM, YOU WOULD BE GROVELING BEFORE ME, BEGGING FOR YOUR PATHETIC SOUL!"

His voice boomed in the small cabin, grating against every fiber of Mouse's body with malice.

The creature reached towards him. As the talon-tipped hand emerged from the swarm of sonic chaos surrounding him, Mouse noted that the tip of one of the wicked talons had been sheared off, leaving a blunt stub in its place.

Pinned in place by the being's piercing glare, Mouse could only watch helplessly as that deadly hand reached for him. Before it grabbed him, a sizable portion of his swarm coalesced into a tight ball around the Enemy's arm, stinging him for all they were worth.

"AAARRGH!!! WHAT IS THIS!?" The creature jerked its hand back, scattering the surviving notes as it drew back. "WHAT FOUL MAGICK IS THIS?!?"

"It's not magick," Mouse gasped. "It's music!"

The creature roared in anger and thrust both hands forward as if it was pushing something massive towards Mouse.

"I WILL CONSUME YOU!" The words thundered off of the walls. "IT WILL BE AS IF YOU HAD NEVER EXISTED!"

Mouse's eyes widened as the entire cyclone of dissonance surrounding the Enemy gathered into a giant orb. The orb smashed into him with all the violence of a ship crashing to earth.

Mouse lost all sense of bearing. He couldn't tell up from down, left from right, or reality from nightmare. The remaining notes of his defensive swarm were swept away by the cacophony that overwhelmed him.

Images flooded into Mouse's consciousness — the broken and battered faces of countless people, so many of them with the pointed ears and glittering eyes of the *Fae*; their eyes filled with terror. Sound hammered at him from every direction, alternating from screams of terror to urgent, whispered prayers in languages he didn't understand. Every voice was different; yet, they all sounded desperate and frightened. The sharp coppery tang of blood, hot and fresh, filled his mouth. The unmistakable scent of putrefied flesh filled his nostrils. Every inch of his skin was aflame with the pain of a thousand different needle pricks, each one jabbing again and again.

The assault was too much. His mind began to break. Memories, both happy and sad, fell away like layers of an onion being peeled back. It wasn't long before he couldn't remember his own name or where he was.

...running through the streets, afraid for his life, the members of his own gang hunting him like they had hunted so many others before...

He couldn't understand why he was suffering so much.

...his mother, her skin blackened by the Scourge, lay still. Her

chest no longer rose or fell. The gurgling and rattling sounds of her breathing had stopped. The all-too-familiar sickly sweet smell of putrefied flesh filled his nostrils. He was hollow and empty inside...

His cries of pain joined with all of the others, lost in the multitude of those who had been broken before him.

...the gentle hum of the bees as they went about their work soothed him. Rondel sat for a moment with the f'leyn in his hands, enjoying the quiet music of the bees before he began to play...

The bees! Their buzzing penetrated the haze of pain and the noise, reminding him of something, someone very important...

Kerplunk.

...a soft feminine voice spoke softly in his ear:

The gift I have given you will allow you to see the truth. If your heart stays strong and pure, you will be able to resist the terrible power of the Enemy's ta'ir when no one else can....

The Shining Lady! Her voice echoed through what remained of his consciousness, giving him a newfound strength. He became aware of his body again, pressed against a solid surface by a heavy, unmovable force. Pain flooded through his limbs, but it was a good pain, the kind of ache that told him he was somehow still alive and whole. The Shining Lady's voice continued to speak, her words bolstered by the gentle hum of bees.

I have placed all of my trust...everything I love...my only hope...in the truth and goodness of your heart and in the strength of your spirit. Only by working together, as Treemaiden and Guardian, will you be able to defeat him for good.

Kerplunk.

The buzzing grew louder as the Shining Lady's last words faded. Memories and awareness came filtering back to him as, note by note, the swarm reassembled around him. Each returning note brought back a tiny snippet of his consciousness that had been peeled away, like worker bees collecting pollen before returning to their hive.

"THIS IS IMPOSSIBLE! I AM DRAK'NUUL, THE SOUL REAVER! I SHATTER WORLDS AND HARVEST THE SOULS OF THE *FAE*! NO MERE MORTAL CAN WITHSTAND ME!"

Mouse blinked the haze out of his eyes just long enough to see Valk, naked and bleeding, approaching him with his hands extended. Desperate, he searched blindly for his fallen flute.

His left hand came across a small, hard object lying next to him. The moment his fingers came in contact with the ridges of the peach stone, a gentle, life-sustaining music flooded into his being, adding its strength to his own. His fingers closed around the stone as he continued searching for the flute with his other hand.

"WHO ARE YOU? WHAT ARE YOU?" the Enemy's voice boomed, echoing in the tight space. "I DEMAND TO KNOW!"

There!

Mouse snatched the flute with his right hand and pushed back up to his feet.

The angry buzz of his swarm grew stronger and more threatening as the Enemy drew nearer, reaching the threshold of the cabin. The creature's eyes blazed with fierce red energy as it staggered into the cramped hallway towards him.

Ducking the first clumsy lunge, Mouse slipped sideways and then back when the creature reached for him again. When his back hit the closed door behind him, Mouse dropped the seed into a pocket and opened the door into the captain's luxurious office. He tried to slam the door shut on the Enemy, but the creature was too fast and too strong. Valk's battered hand and arm emerged through the diminishing space between the door and jam and stopped it cold.

In the back of his mind, Mouse heard the agitation in his

swarm as the remaining notes stung at the hand. The creature roared, slamming into the door. He was knocked back, bit-by-bit as the door was forced open.

Realizing he couldn't win in a battle of brute strength, Mouse jumped clear and darted into the middle of the carpeted space. Bringing the flute back up to his lips, he took a deep breath and forced his awareness once again into the surreal soundscape.

My only chance to survive has to come from my music. But what song? There aren't enough notes left from the swarm to protect me for much longer.

The Enemy stepped into the office and spread his wings. Easily topping eight feet tall and as broad as two full-sized men across the chest, the monstrous form was an ebon nightmare. No longer surrounded by the obscuring wall of dissonance, however, Mouse noticed a hazy glimmer of soft light around the bottom of the creature's image, as if something small and desperate was somehow still resisting being extinguished.

Focusing all of his concentration on that frail flicker of hope, Mouse listened with his entire being.

Mouse heard the distant wail of an infant crying out for its mother.

That's it!

Steadying himself, Mouse began to play. The notes were longer and softer than the ones he'd used before. Remembering how his mother used to sing this soft lullaby to him nearly every night, he infused every note with all of the aching loss he felt for her. Somehow, that longing came out as sweet and pure as his mother's love for him. He translated the beauty of her voice into the notes he was playing. Her undying and unconditional love resonated through every note...

Sweet little baby, crying out for me...

His heart swelled. He poured every bit of focus and power into the song. Another familiar voice joined in. The sing-song melodic voice of the Shining Lady doubled the amount of love and joy flowing through his heart, into his lungs, and out through his lips.

Hush now, tiny star. 'Tis time to sleep...

The song took up so much of his attention that it barely registered when the creature roared in frustration, shouting something that Mouse couldn't hear. Instead, he continued playing. A third voice joined the female chorus that fueled him. He didn't recognize this voice, but he felt she was somehow connected to the baby whose cries could still be heard.

Sweet little angel, cute as can be...

The power of the song reverberated through Mouse's spirit. He no longer cared what the creature was going to do when it got to him because he was in his mother's loving arms, safe and warm and happy, with not a care in the world. The fierce power of that comforting love couldn't be — wouldn't be — denied.

Mama's gonna sing, until you dream...

Something shifted in the room around Mouse. His spine tingled with energy as a fourth voice — utterly haunting in its otherworldly tone — chimed in. It magnified the strength and power of the song. He caught a brief glimpse of an unknown woman whose face and features were obscured by the darkness just beyond a pale beam of moonlight that fell, instead, upon the babe in her covered arms. She sang, adding her voice to the chorus as she rocked the tiny infant back and forth. The child had rounded ears, bright brown eyes, and a delighted smile.

Sweet little baby, smiling up at me...

As the image began to fade, the strange woman stepped into the light, one glove-covered hand moving up to push the hood of her cloak back, but the image faded before any part of her face was revealed.

Mouse ended the song when the image faded away. Opening his bleary eyes, it took a moment for them to adjust so that he could make out the strange scene in front of him.

Captain Dastyr knelt on the floor cradling his younger brother — naked, battered, and bleeding — to his chest like a mother holding her child. The bigger man sobbed uncontrollably as he rocked Valk back and forth..

"What've I done to you, brother?" The captain threw his head back and howled like a beast in pain. "I'm sorry, Mama! I tried to save him!"

Mouse took a deep breath, closed his eyes, and listened to the *ta'irs* of each man. The captain's song was slow and quiet, echoing the notes of the lullaby that Mouse had been playing with a profound sense of loss and sadness. He had to strain to hear the soft *ta'ir* of the captain's brother. But it was there — an innocent, playful, and teasing song without any of the dissonance that Mouse normally associated with Valk.

Taking another calming breath, Mouse pushed himself deeper into the soundscape, seeking any signs of the Enemy. The office still vibrated with the loving energy of the lullaby, but tiny patches of darkness clung to the edges of the room, pooling beneath the desk and slipping behind the drapes that covered the massive window.

When he turned back to the two men, Mouse gasped. Both of them appeared to be much younger versions of themselves. The captain had the clean-shaven and fresh-faced appearance of a young Marine. But it was the changes to Valk that were the most profound. Instead of a fully grown man in his forties, the captain's brother appeared to be a young boy, perhaps ten- or eleven-years-old. There was no sign of the haggard, sunken features or the deep-set and feral eyes Mouse associated with the man. Unlike the captain, however, there was a slight tinge that still darkened the boy's form.

Mouse shuddered. A deep, spine-tingling chill settled over him. A cold, grating voice wormed its way inside of him, penetrating his consciousness with the deliberate and unstoppable force of a tree taking root. The Enemy spoke directly to his mind in a way he'd never experienced before.

::YOU THINK YOU'VE WON, MORTAL.::

His limbs went ice cold.

::BUT KNOW THIS, FOOL — YOU'VE ONLY DELAYED THE INEVITABLE, AND NOT FOR LONG.::

Mouse tried to push the voice from his mind, but it was as effective as pushing against the trunk of a healthy tree.

::FOR THIS INSULT, YOU AND EVERYONE ELSE ON THAT SHIP WILL PAY THE ULTIMATE PRICE. I WILL HAVE MY BRIDE, AND YOUR BLOODY HEART WILL BE MY WEDDING GIFT TO HER!::

An image blossomed in his mind: a vision of more than a dozen winged creatures flying in a formation in the night sky. Some were larger than the others, but they all possessed the wicked claws, massive fangs, and glowing eyes of the demonic beasts from his worst nightmares.

::EVEN NOW, MY MINIONS APPROACH. READY TO CLAIM WHAT IS RIGHTFULLY MINE!::

The Enemy withdrew from his mind.

Mouse's knees buckled. He collapsed to the carpeted floor, gasping for breath. The flute slipped from his fingers, rolling to a stop a few inches from his face. He couldn't stop shivering even though his arms were clutched tight against his body.

CHAPTER 30

Seldy

"T*ia!*"

Seldy *scrambled on hands and knees to the bare patch of ground where the seer had been only moments before.*

"*Tia! No!*"

She picked up the feather and cradled it to her chest.

"*You can't leave me like this, Tia!*"

The edge of the feather fluttered in the cool evening breeze.

Seldy gripped the shaft tightly in her right hand and closed her eyes.

All of the fear and pain and sadness of the last couple of days overwhelmed her. She felt brittle and hollow. Biting back the tears that threatened to flow yet again, she gritted her teeth.

"*No! I'm done with crying!*"

She balled her empty hand into a fist and shook it skyward.

"*I'm not going to run away again, you bastard! I'm going to find a way to fight you!*"

The dark energy continued to churn inside of her, growing more and more restless. Unable to contain it, Seldy threw back her head and let loose a howl. Her voice cracked. Her limbs trembled from the effort, and her lungs ached, but it felt too good to stop. She howled again.

Some of that restless energy was released into the night with each subsequent howl but even more of it settled into her quivering muscles. The lines of the image painted on her abdomen tingled. Strength flooded into her limbs.

The tiny hairs all over her body stood on end giving her itchy goosebumps, but it felt so good to release all of her pent up emotions. Seldy kept howling. Dropping to all fours, she dug her fingers and toes into the rich, earthy loam. The tingling became a burning sensation. All of her long muscles twitched.

Feeling stronger than she'd ever felt before, Seldy arched her back and tossed her head high into the air. She let loose the longest and loudest howl yet and was surprised by the deepening pitch of her voice. As the last note faded into the background sounds of the forest, the ball of energy in her belly exploded. Every muscle spasmed at the same time. She cried out in shock as wave after wave of muscle-stretching and bone-lengthening pain wracked her entire body, leaving her breathless and shuddering.

When she finally mustered the strength to look up, everything was different. Her vision was sharper. Her eyes were drawn to movement — the restless twitch of a small creature scurrying in the underbrush, the swirl of a fallen leaf being pushed around by the breeze. Her mind assessed the potential dangers posed by each movement in a way that she'd never thought to do before, discounting them as harmless before she was even consciously aware that she had noticed them. Her nostrils were assaulted by a flood of scents that were both intensely familiar and wholly new at the same time. She smelled the fear of the mouse as it scurried away to safety. She tasted the scents of others of her kind in the air.

Looking down at what should have been her hands planted

in the dirt, Seldy discovered a pair of large white paws. She yelped in surprise, dancing backwards. She stopped short, however, when she noticed how her body was moving. Swinging her head around, she was greeted by the view of a fur-covered flank and a long, bushy tail dangling between her hind legs.

A chorus of howls filled the night air. Her ears swiveled without any conscious thought on her part to better catch the sounds.

"We hear you, Sister! Join us! We hunt this night!"

The Pack! My Pack! They're calling for me!

Her heart hammered against her ribcage, sending a rush of blood coursing through her veins. Her paws danced in the dirt. Her powerful muscles twitched. She ached to be moving with every fiber of her being; to join the hunt; to answer the call of the Pack.

Throwing back her head yet again, Seldy let loose a full-throated howl in reply.

"I come, Brothers and Sisters! I come!"

Without further thought, Seldy set into motion, effortlessly adopting the ground-eating lope the Pack used on the hunt. She glided through the thick underbrush with ease and darted fearlessly across clearings. The wind ruffled her fur as she raced ahead, clearing the trunks of fallen trees and the banks of tiny streams with perfectly placed bounding leaps. Her keen ears swiveled as she ran, alert to any danger, while her sharp eyes easily spotted the best hidden pathways through the concealing forest to join her pack.

Seldy was reminded of the first time she ever rode on Layra's back. Her powerful body was moving naturally, instinctively, like the tigress had, while her consciousness felt like a child-like passenger clutching to its back. She marveled at the strength and stamina coursing through her veins. And with *each passing moment, she grew more accustomed to how her muscles bunched and rippled as she loped; how her sharp claws dug unconsciously into the earth, propelling her forward and upward with each purposeful step; how her tongue lolled between the massive fangs in her jaws, dissipating the heat created from her efforts. It didn't take long before the confused, scared, and angry young woman of a few minutes ago receded into the background. Instead, she became a lupine huntress — a calm, collected, and confident predator that could rip through the muscles and tendons and crush the strongest bones of her prey with a single snap of her powerful jaws.*

The excited cries of the Pack spurred her to even greater speeds. Their musky scents filled her nostrils, adding to her joy of joining the hunt. The joy dissipated, however, when she got the first whiff of their prey. It was a harsh and twisted scent that reeked of wrongness. She crinkled her muzzle in distaste.

A deep bellow tore through the night air. The playful howls and yips of the chase shifted into the fierce snarls, growls, and yelps of a fight in progress. The tangy scent of fresh blood infused the air.

The battle was hidden from her sight by a thick ring of bushes and ferns. The huntress crashed through the underbrush with reckless abandon, eager to join the fray. She emerged into a large clearing occupied by the Pack circling a massive black form several times her size.

The reality of the fight, however, gave even the huntress pause. Seldy stood blinking as she surveyed the scene in front of her. The strangeness of it all struck her dumbfounded. Her body trembled from the desire to join the fight. Her senses were fully engaged, keen and hyper-alert. Her mouth watered at the possibility of sinking her fangs into the hide of that creature — the enemy of the Pack.

At her core, the idea of eating meat sickened her, as it always had. There was no doubt, however, about how much this body craved meat.

Pushing aside her doubts, Seldy focused on the foul and twisted creature. The monstrous beast roughly resembled the bears she had seen shambling through the woods of Timos throughout her childhood, but it was far larger than any bear she'd ever seen or even heard of. The creature reared back on its hindquarters and swiped at a darting grey and black wolf with its own razor-sharp claws. It snarled in defiance as the wolf danced, just in time, back out of reach.

The bear's eyes glowed with a pulsing red energy that sent a chill down her spine and caused her hackles to rise. The creature's black fur was matted and blotchy, revealing patches of skin that were grey and festering with open sores. It reeked of filth and disease; yet, it seemed to be animated by an unflappable strength and vitality.

Her lips curled back from her fangs. She snarled at the pervasive wrongness of the creature.

Another pair of wolves, sensing their opportunities, leaped towards the creature's unprotected back with snapping jaws. The bear reacted with impossible speed and agility, whirling around and swatting aside one of the attackers with ease before pouncing on the other with massive jaws and curved, ebon claws.

Both wolves yelped: the first one in surprise as it was sent spinning away and the other in both pain and surprise at being enveloped by the much larger creature. The second wolf thrashed wildly against the overwhelming strength and size of its captor. When it chomped down on the huge foreleg of its attacker, the bear merely responded by rearing back to open its own maw wide enough to envelop the wolf's neck and spine with its outrageously large mouth.

Seeing the imminent danger to one of her Pack, the eager

huntress within pushed aside Seldy's self-doubt and hesitation. She gave a low growl and raced towards the tangle of struggling forms. She launched from the ground the moment she passed through the outer edges of the circle formed by the other wolves.

Throwing all of her weight into the attack, the huntress knocked both the bear and the captured wolf sideways with her momentum and tumbled away to land splay-legged on the ground. Bouncing back to her feet in one smooth, instinctual move, she darted in on the still prone and surprised bear and clamped down on its exposed throat with her jaws, prepared to end its life.

What she saw, however, gave her pause. There was a moment when the glow had faded from the creature's eyes. They widened in surprise and confusion.

Just as she was about to release her grip, the creature stiffened. A sense of menace returned to its glowing eyes, and it snarled at her in defiance. All sense of reason and mercy abandoned her. Seldy snapped her powerful jaws closed for the killing blow and ripped at the soft, spongy flesh with all of the ferocity and anger she felt towards the Enemy for everything he'd done to her and her family.

Hot blood surged into her mouth, befouling her tongue with its sharp tang. But that didn't stop her from tearing a huge swath of the creature's flesh from its neck. With a piece of its hide still dangling from her fangs, Seldy was jostled backwards as the rest of the pack rushed in to finish the kill.

::That was reckless, Shapesister.:: A powerful feminine voice echoed in her mind. ::You could have easily been slain by this Reaver and sent back to the waking world too soon.::

Seldy swung her head around to see who had spoken to her and came eye-to-eye with a tall, broad-shouldered she-wolf with bright yellow eyes. Her coat was predominantly grey but

364

with patches of black interspersed. She had been the first at-tacker when Seldy first entered the clearing.

Realizing that the creature's flesh still dangled from her mouth, Seldy shook her head to free herself from it.

::I'm sorry Fangsister, but I couldn't stand seeing a Pack-member in danger!::

::The hunt is always dangerous, Shapesister.:: *There was admonition in the she-wolf's mind-voice and an air of unquestioned authority. The older and taller wolf nodded her head towards the dead creature.* ::But you are too valuable to us to risk yourself so soon and so recklessly against one such as this. You have much to learn about this place and about the Gifts you have been given::

Taken aback by the sharp tone of the mental rebuke, Seldy ignored the strong lupine urge to submit to the higher ranking wolf and instead stood as tall and straight as she could. Her bloody lips curled back defiantly from her fangs.

::In this body, I'm strong and fierce! And I'm tired of running away!:: *Seldy didn't try to keep the vehemence of her anger out of her projected thoughts. She nodded towards the dead creature that was still being torn apart by the rest of the pack.* ::Whatever that creature was, it scented of the Enemy, and I hate him! I won't let him hurt anyone else I care about! Not as long as I have the strength to stop it!::

Something about her words and the forceful and defiant way she had projected them brought an eerie silence and a strange stillness to the clearing. All of the other wolves, Seldy realized, were staring at her. Their thoughts, however, were guarded and silent as if they were waiting to see the reaction of the larger grey and black female to her challenge.

The powerful she-wolf stalked forward until she stood muzzle to muzzle with Seldy, her strength and anger held in check. She met Seldy's defiant stare with a look of patience.

::The Pack endures because not one of us is as strong as the whole. We are an ancient folk, Seldirima Silversong. Our ancestors sang when Luna was whole, back when the world was young and fresh and the Enemy did not yet exist.::

Unable to resist the power of the she-wolf's gaze, Seldy became lost in the amber depths of those pupils. She felt a sense of connection to this wolf and the pack she led.

::The value of the gift bestowed upon you, the Gift of the Pack, lies not in the strength of your muscles, the speed of your legs, or the power of your jaws in this form. No! These are the least valuable aspects of our Gift to you!::

The she-wolf rubbed her muzzle against Seldy's, somehow keeping their gazes locked as she did so.

Caught up in the wolf's powerful gaze, a rush of memories flooded into Seldy's mind. She was inundated with images of thousands upon thousands of successful hunts, of countless gatherings of many packs under the bright light of the Luna before the world was broken as they howled and celebrated their freedom. She felt the burning desire course through her body that came with each mating season and the unbridled passion that accompanied the joining of mates. She experienced the pain of giving birth and the soft, loving joy of nursing young wolf pups. She felt the sorrow of loss each time a member of the Pack passed from the world, either from the dangers of the hunt or simply from being too old and tired to keep up.

Seldy watched from the shadows as groups of men and women and children danced in the silver light of the moon. They all resembled her normal form with their pointed ears and slender limbs. They had bright eyes that glittered like jewels. They were a mysterious folk that sang and played naked in the moonlight-dappled glades of the past. Their wondrous singing and joyful laughter filled the air as they brought the wolves and other beasts of forest and glen into their peaceful circles and celebrated with them as equals.

::The true value of our Gift, Seldirima,:: *the wolf leader continued,* ::is the strength, knowledge, support, and connection you gain by becoming a member of our sacred Pack. So long as even one lone wolf hunts in the waking world, the Pack endures and our memories of the world that once was do not fade. Now you, too, will carry forth these collective memories of the Pack so that you will be able to sing our sacred songs long into the night so that all who hear them will truly remember what it is to be wild and free.::

With those words, the elder wolf finally broke eye contact. She raised her head and howled. Her voice was soon joined by the rest of the pack as each of the others added their voice to the joyous chorus. Listening to the haunting melody, Seldy somehow understood the words of their song.

"We are many, we are one,
Our voices fill the night.

We hunt, we fight, we sing,
The Reaver falls tonight.

We are wild, we are free,
By Luna's sacred light.

We remember, we celebrate, we join,
Shapesister's deadly fight."

Stunned by the collective power of their song, Seldy tilted her head and blinked.

When the elder wolf dropped her head, she locked gazes with Seldy once again.

::Your fight against the Enemy, Shapesister, is our own. But you must understand and remember that the Enemy draws his power from anger, fear, and hate. So even though you may win a battle when you draw upon one of those emotions in order to prevail, you bring yourself ever closer to losing the war. Those emotions are the lures that he uses to snare such poor souls as that one.:: *She nodded towards the mutilated carcass.* ::If you do not learn to control those feelings, all of the sacrifices that others have made on your behalf will have been in vain. And that will doom us all.::

Recognizing the wolf for what she was, Seldy surrendered to her lupine instincts. She dropped her head and tucked her tail submissively between her hind legs, then lowered herself to the ground. She whimpered in apology.

::I'm sorry, Packmother.:: *She rolled over onto her back, offering her belly in a final act of contrition.* ::There's so much to learn! Will you teach me?::

Before the Packmother could reply, however, Seldy was mobbed by the other wolves in a jostling flurry of enthusiastic body rubbing, tail wagging, mouth-licking, whining, and scent-marking that accompanied the welcoming of a returning member back into the Pack. The press of happy, wriggling bodies was so tight, that she struggled for a moment to scramble back to her feet. Their thought-greetings bombarded her mind with as much fervor and energy as their bodies.

::Welcome, Shapesister! I am Leafdancer::

::Well done, honored Shapesister!::

::I look forward to many more hunts with you, Sister!::

::Your scent reminds me of Starfire, Sister!::

Overwhelmed, Seldy struggled to associate the projected voices with their owners. She couldn't ever remember being around so many active mental voices all at once. She responded instead with the body language and noises that came naturally to her in this form. She wagged her tail, rubbed muzzles, and made happy whimpers and whines to show her joy at being accepted by the Pack.

It didn't take long before she'd been greeted and welcomed by all dozen members. When the last two stepped back — the smallest and youngest pair, litter-mates it seemed — the Pack-mother stepped between her and the others. Her thoughts came across loud and clear to the whole pack.

::My Hunters, together we have slain this Reaver and you have shown your love for our Packsister. Now it is time for you to resume the hunt for, as you know, there is never just one. Crookfang shall lead until I return.::

An older male wolf raised his head higher at being named. The jagged lower fang sticking out sideways from his muzzle made it clear as to how he came by his name. One of the youngest wolves, however, spoke up.

::Why won't you lead us, Mother? And where is Father?::

The Packmother shot Seldy a sideways glance before responding.

::Our new Shapesister is summoned to the Bloodstones.::

All of the wolves except the Packmother dropped their heads and whined in submission at hearing that name, only looking up again when she continued.

::And Shadowfang has answered the call of the Elders, sending Seldirima here in his stead. He will not be hunting with us this night.::

Seldy blinked in surprise, feeling guilty.

::Shadowfang? Do you know him? Is he okay? It sounded like he was hurt!::

The Packmother turned her unblinking amber gaze back on Seldy.

::He is my mate and the Packfather. We miss him dearly.::

There was more than a tinge of sadness in those projected

words. ::But we will honor his choice to aid you in your journey to see the Elder Spirits.::

At that, the larger wolf started walking towards the edge of the clearing, glancing back at Seldy.

::Come, Shapesister. We have far to travel. The Bloodstones are not so close as to be an easy journey.::

CHAPTER 31

Mouse

Are you hurt, son?"

Fuzzy blobs waggled in front of his bleary eyes. The captain's words bounced around inside of his head, adding to the rhythmic pounding in his already throbbing skull.

"Huh?" Just uttering that single syllable caused Mouse to groan. "Ugh."

"Are you hurt?" Concern colored both the captain's voice and his *ta'ir*. "Did my brother hurt you?"

Mouse couldn't muster the energy to answer him. Instead, he clutched his trembling arms around his chest in a vain attempt to find warmth.

Strong hands pulled his arms away from his chest and prodded his ribs.

"Easy now, son. I'm just seeing if you're bleeding or if anything is broken."

Unable to resist, Mouse merely grunted. The captain's restored *ta'ir* washed over him. The music and the rough contact from the man's calloused hands warmed both his body and spirit, easing the lingering hold the Enemy had over his mind.

"I'm not seeing any fresh wounds on you." Captain Dastyr's deep brown eyes narrowed. His song shifted from concern back to the insistent urge for constant action. "Can you get up?"

Swallowing the bile that burned the back of his throat, Mouse nodded, then pushed himself up into a seated position on the soft rug. His eyes were drawn back to Valk. The man's bloody and battered form was sprawled out not five feet away on the edge of the carpet.

"How is he?"

"Lucky to be alive with all of those wounds." The shaggy man shook his head. "I don't know how Valk found the strength to break loose and throw me around like that, let alone chase after you like he did!"

"Valk didn't."

"Of course he did!" The captain's head snapped around. "You were there! You saw him rip free from those straps and attack me! What's wrong with you, boy?"

"That wasn't Valk doing any of that..." Mouse knew he should shut up, but he continued over the objections of the little voice in the back of his mind. "That was someone else, *something* else."

The captain's *ta'ir* took on an ominous tone.

"What in the name of the Found God are you talking about?" The big man swept his hand towards his fallen brother. "He's right there, blast you!"

Pushing himself up straighter, Mouse noticed the flute lying on the floor between him and the captain. It took every bit of his will to not reach for the instrument. He looked directly at the captain.

"That attack wasn't any of Valk's doing."

The big man's beard bristled as he loomed closer. The captain's boots narrowly missed crushing his flute.

"Just what are you trying to say, boy?"

More worried about his flute than the captain's question, Mouse ignored him and ducked down low. Desperate, he darted between the captain's polished boots and snatched the instrument.

"What the...?"

The big man caught the collar of Mouse's jacket before he could get back and stood up, jerking him up to his feet as he did so.

Squirming, Mouse clutched the instrument to his chest.

"I can't explain it! You wouldn't understand!"

"You'd blazing well better try, boy!"

The captain held Mouse in place with one hand. The angry man's roiling *ta'ir* hammered at his senses, overpowering his defenses.

Closing his eyes, Mouse slipped into the soundscape, looking for clues as to what was driving the man's sudden anger. The sheer volume of angry red notes swirling about the man made it seem like a miniature version of the maelstrom that surrounded the Enemy.

But there was something deeper and darker than the anger.

Hate.

The black stain of hatred tinged almost everything within the captain's surging ta'ir. It was a deep and baleful emotion that twisted everything he saw and felt. It fed the spiraling storm of rage that drove him incessantly towards violence and action.

Shocked at the depths of the captain's pain, Mouse struggled to make sense of the barrage of painful images and memories slamming into his consciousness...

...young Klard flinching as a book slammed against the wall next to his beautiful, brown-haired mother. She used her

body to shield him as a loud male voice thundered in the shadow-drenched background.

"Blast it woman! I don't want a sissy for a son! If you're going to teach him to read, make it something to help him grow into a real man like tactics! Not this pansy-arsed shite about flowers and worthless plants..."

...a young boy's hand reaching towards the haggard face of a once beautiful woman as she lay dying. Another child...Valk, his younger brother...was being held back from clambering into bed with her. She reached out to touch his face.

"Promise me...Klard...take care of him...love him for me..."

...Valk, a doe-eyed and frightened adolescent boy with curly brown hair, stood facing him with tears streaming down his face. He looked up with fear in his eyes at the heavyset, bearded man with a stern expression, dark hair and even darker eyes who held his hand...

...the heavy-set man, again. He was older as well but now stripped naked and shaved of both beard and hair. Blood dripped from the mangled and burned stump of his otherwise bare crotch. He hung, limp and unconscious, from a practice dummy while his bloody and limp manhood lay on the ground, just below his dangling feet...

...he was looking up from his knees, feeling helpless and weak as a tall, lithe figure with familiar blue eyes and a derisive sneer on his face advanced, a pair of already bloody blades in his hands...

...of standing beside a bed, looking down at Valk's sunken face and Scourge-darkened complexion, barely recognizable as that doe-eyed young boy. He was clearly dying...

"Well, boy?" The captain's voice broke through the *ta'ir* induced reverie. "You better answer me!"

Despite the rage boiling over into the captain's voice, a profound sense of calm washed over Mouse. Opening his eyes, he swallowed the last of his nervousness and stared back at the captain, not in defiance or anger but with compassion. He didn't flinch when the big man jerked his fist back as if to strike him.

"Hit me if you must." Mouse kept his voice calm. "But it won't help your brother or change what was done to you or your father. And striking me won't bring your mother back."

The captain's body stiffened, but the furor in his *ta'ir* lessened. "Wha—"

"You miss her terribly, Captain. And it hurts so much to see Valk in such danger." He nodded towards the unconscious man behind the captain. "It enrages you to feel so helpless." He kept his voice quiet and soothing. "But lashing out and causing pain to others is not the answer to your pain. It never has been." He added in a soft whisper, "You're a better man than that."

The grip on his jacket weakened, and the drawn-back hand lowered. The confusion swirling through the captain's *ta'ir* showed in his eyes. But then the anger in his song spiked from a fresh infusion of fear.

"What can you possibly know about how I feel, boy? Or about what kind of man I am?"

Mouse didn't shrink back. Instead, he stood up straighter and took a deep breath. At the exact moment his lungs reached their capacity, a church bell sounded in the captain's *ta'ir*.

Dong!

His eyes were drawn to the large obsidian Seeker's Circle dangling from the captain's neck. His eyes narrowed. He focused on the smooth and featureless ebony depths of that circle. His stomach churned.

Dong!

The world around him came to a full stop. The captain stood

stock-still, unmoving, as if he were caught between breaths. Mouse's eyes narrowed. All sounds, except for the resounding vibrations leftover from the clapper striking the brass housing of the bell, ceased. There was no wind, no creaking of the ship, none of the ever-present rocking of the ship in flight.

Dong!

The Church of the Found! The thought struck Mouse like a thunderbolt. *There's a connection here. But what is it?*

Closing his eyes, Mouse focused his attention on the resonating vibrations of the church bell. He opened up fully — allowing himself to become as vulnerable as the captain was — to the deepest truths of the man whom he had both feared and revered.

Dong!

Mouse sank deeper into his trance, pushing his awareness in as deep as he could go and still remain conscious.

When the last vibrations of the latest clapper-strike died out, he found himself deep inside the captain's personal soundscape. The same younger, thinner, and less hirsute version of the captain he had seen before stood motionless in the center of a small plateau surrounded by a deep and shadow-filled chasm. Looking down into the ring of darkness surrounding the plateau, Mouse shuddered. It had shape and substance. It exuded a cold and anxious hunger, constantly turning over on itself in its restless churn.

Disconcerted, he shifted his focus to the scenery beyond the shadows. In every direction beyond the circular chasm, there were colorful hillsides dotted with buildings and structures of various sizes. Images from important and meaningful events from throughout the captain's life flickered in the windows and doorways of each of the buildings.

DONG!

The bell echoed like thunder throughout the soundscape, shaking Mouse to his very core. The vision shimmered and faltered. He struggled to maintain his focus. Unwilling to leave without the answers he sought, he redoubled his concentration.

The edge of the plateau was lined with broken posts or rotting stumps — the ruins of what must have once been bridges that crossed the chasm without dipping into the darkness below. The hillsides opposite each set of ruins exhibited similar decay, as if the failure of each bridge led to the ruin and decay of the accompanying memory sequences.

One bridge, however, remained. It was weathered and beaten but intact. The badly frayed rope bridge extended from the plateau to a small but crowded hillside filled with landmarks of happy memories that included Valk. Mouse was struck by how much he resembled the younger version of Valk that he had glimpsed in those memories. It was almost like looking in a mirror.

DONG!

The mindscape shook from the violence and power of the bell's desperate sounding, as if the bell itself was trying to drive him from the captain's mind. The vision rippled.

Focusing, Mouse narrowed his attention towards that one accessible hillside.

Valk is the key.

Each structure and every flickering image showed serious signs of decay, except one. Soaring closer, Mouse recognized the structure that housed the bright, clear image.

That's the Grand Cathedral of the Church of the Found God back in Vandermal!

He remembered the building from the one time they'd docked there on the captain's home island of Dortyn.

But why is Valk there?

Stretched between two intricately carved towers of the cathedral was an image of Valk being carried in the captain's arms.

Time was slipping by. Gritting his teeth, Mouse propelled himself with reckless abandon towards that image. High above, in the tallest tower of the cathedral, a massive brass bell swung on its hinges, the great clapper within drew ever-so-close to striking the inside with more power and more force than any previous sounding.

DO—

The cold, wet shock of a bucket of icy cold water hit him full force as he plunged into the image at the same moment as the clapper and bell collided.

—NG!!!!

"Blast it! I demand to see the High Seeker!"

Klard stormed into the candlelit inner sanctum of the Seeker's Hall of the Church of the Found. His chest heaved. His dying brother was clutched in his arms. With a glare, Klard dared any of the mewling men gathered in the center of the chamber to challenge his right to call for their leader.

He stomped down the central aisle of the chamber, brushing aside anyone who didn't move fast enough. Most of the figures scrambled to get out of his way, but a pair of robed, hooded figures remained still, standing near the large central altar. They continued with their whispered conversation as if he wasn't there.

Klard bellowed again as he approached them from behind.

"Which of you pukes is the High Seeker?"

The taller of the two figures turned ever-so-slowly towards him, reaching up with two pudgy, pale hands to pull back the hood from his head. He was a middle-aged man with a fresh-ly-shaved bald head. He had a bulbous red nose and a heavy-set, elongated face with thick jowls and fleshy neck. His brown eyes were puffy and ringed with dark circles that stood out starkly from his otherwise pale skin.

"I am the High Seeker of Vandermal, Sir." The haughty man took in Klard and his brother in a sleepy-eyed glance before add-ing in a patronizing voice, "How may I assist you this evening?"

The other figure's hood remained up as it retreated a few steps into the shadows formed by a set of tall, heavy pillars not far from the heavy stone altar.

Klard turned to the priest, ignoring the retreating figure and those that had scattered from his approach. He had no interest in those lesser men or in examining the opulent furnishings of the Seeker's Hall.

His target now acquired, Klard's eyes narrowed. He was less than five feet from the man, but he yelled as if he were on the far end of the deck of his ship.

"I've heard it said that you churchy bastards have a cure for the Black Scourge. Is that true?"

He couldn't help but glance down at his beloved younger brother's Scourge-darkened face, framed as it was by the oily, lanky locks of brown hair.

The priest didn't flinch. "Are you a man of faith, sir?"

The man's quiet demeanor threw Klard off balance for a mo-ment. He blinked as if he had been punched in the nose. He threw back his shoulders and responded with even more force.

"What in the Blazing Fires of the Fallen Star does that have to do with anything?"

"With faith," the man said softly, "all things are possible."

"Yeah, well the only blasted faith I have is in the strength of my two hands, the quality of my weapons, and that all men are — at their core — greedy and heartless bastards!" Klard took a step closer, looming over the shorter man in a way that made it clear that violence was definitely an option. "Now answer my question. Do you have a blasted cure for the Scourge or not?"

The priest brought his two hands together, joining his arched fingers at chest level, with the thumbs below to form what looked like a circle. He dipped his head briefly to look at Valk. When he looked back up at Klard, his face didn't exhibit any of the wide-eyed fear or panic that most people had when they came this close to a victim of the Black Scourge.

"The Found God has provided his faithful Seekers with a cure for the plague that the vile Fae have brought down upon us mortal folk." The priest looked up into Klard's eyes, his face serene. "But the cure is not cheap, and it is only available to the faithful."

"Look here, arsehole." Klard loomed over the priest, lifting Valk back into the priest's view. "My little brother's got it. He's going to die from it today if you don't do something about it. Our mother died from this blasted plague, and I'm not going to let the same thing happen to him." He was now within a foot of the priest. "If you've got a cure, you're going to give it to him. I'll pay for it, blast you, whatever the price."

"Is your brother a Seeker, sir?"

"He'll be a corpse if you don't help him!" He loomed in closer to the man. "And I can tell you right now that if you can help him and don't — he won't be the only person dying here this night."

The priest didn't back down or flinch, neither from the threats being hurled at him nor from the spittle that was landing all over his face. Instead, he smiled.

"No Seeker fears death." His fingers were still touching in front of his chest. "The Circle always leads us back to the Source. Threats to my person do not concern me."

Klard stepped back, blinking. He turned and laid Valk down

on one of the long wooden pews beside him. He swung around and took a step forward, coming face-to-face with the priest again.

"I was a Ranger in the Marines, you little self-righteous prig. A lot of men say they don't fear death just before battle, priest." Klard spat that last word out as he drew forth one of his pistols. "But in my experience, most of those men become blubbering fools when the dying actually starts."

He cocked the pistol and held it to the priest's forehead.

Gasps echoed throughout the cavernous chamber. The sound of booted feet running on tile signaled that armed men were coming to the priest's rescue. The other hooded figure — the one who had retreated to the shadows nearby — took a menacing step forward, one gloved hand on the hilt of a newly revealed dueling sword.

But the High Seeker stood still. His eyes were open and calm; he was unperturbed by the barrel of the pistol pressed to his forehead. He offered Klard a smile.

"Sir, if you slay me now — something which I have no doubt that you are capable of — you will be arrested or slain yourself and your brother will be beyond any help in this mortal world. I will simply return to the Source and serve the Found God in whatever new way he calls for me to do. But if you and your brother die without seeking Him, truly seeking Him, you risk your immortal souls."

The priest raised his left hand slowly, as some kind of signal to those armed men now gathered behind Klard. No one moved to interfere.

"May I ask your name, sir?"

"Klard Dastyr."

More gasps behind him.

The priest smiled. "My Lord Dastyr, it is not too late for you or your brother."

Klard's eyes narrowed, the barrel of the pistol was still poised to shoot.

"What do you mean? You'll cure him?"

The priest's hand returned to join with the other hand in front of his chest. Otherwise, he remained still, looking into Klard's eyes.

"If a man of your obvious means and influence were to join the Church and become a Seeker, much good can be done."

"Be clear, man. Are you saying that if I join your blasted church, you'll cure my brother?"

"If you join the Church, we will try to cure him, but you must know that it is no sure thing. It is a long and difficult process to counter the cursed Fae magick that fuels the Black Scourge. There is also a small matter of the cost, in terms of both coin and service. You must have faith in the Found God, my Lord, for that is who has guided you here today."

"Why would I join your blasted church if it doesn't work?" Klard's voice was hard. He could feel the eyes of many men on him. The itch in the center of his back told him that a number of weapons were aimed at him right now.

"My Lord," the priest spoke in a soft voice. "What choice do you have? Are you really ready to allow your brother to die while you are slain or rot in jail? The dye is cast. The circle will be complete. If you but open your mind you, too, can seek the truth."

Klard's shoulders slumped as he lowered the pistol and uncocked it.

"Do it, then," he sighed, glancing down at his younger brother, remembering the promise he had made to his mother years ago on her death bed. "I don't care about the cost; I'll pay whatever it is."

The priest smiled as he placed a consoling hand on his shoulder.

"A man of your skills, resources, and determination is sorely needed in the Quest against the Fae, My Lord. A year of your armed service against the Wilderlings in Aerhythia will bring us that much closer to ultimate victory and show you the truth of our cause..."

DONG!

Mouse staggered backwards from the unexpected impact of a blow to his face. Fresh pain exploded from his cheek. Stars and tears blurred his vision but not so much that he couldn't see the captain looming over him.

Two huge hands grabbed his shoulders and yanked him upright.

"By the Sacred Circle, boy!" The captain's voice was choked, as if he were trying to hold something back. "What in the blazes is wrong with you?! Can't you see that I don't want to hurt you?"

Disoriented by the sudden and violent end of his visions, Mouse shook his head.

"It'll sting for a bit." The captain's voice softened. "I'm sorry, Mouse."

"I'll be okay, Captain." Straightening up, Mouse noted that the flute was still in his hands. He slipped it into the interior pocket of his jacket. "I know you mean well."

The big man stepped back and studied Mouse from head to toe.

"Where in the Blazing Fires does your mind go, boy?"

"It's hard to explain, sir. I've always been a bit of a dreamer."

"There's more to it than that, Mouse." The captain glanced behind him towards his brother. "Valk was always getting into trouble because of his daydreams, too. You remind me of him in so many ways." Turning back to Mouse, he sighed, heaving his heavy shoulders. "Come, we need to get him back into bed and dress his wounds. He needs a treatment."

Dong!

The whispering sound of the bell sounded right after the captain's last word.

"Treatment, sir? What kind of treatment?"

"The potions I bought from the High Seeker with my own blood and more coin than I care to remember in order to cure him of the Scourge. They're beyond expensive, but they're the only thing that helps him regain his strength."

As the captain bent down to slide his arms under his brother, his Seeker's Circle swung into view, absorbing the flickering light of the oil lamp illuminating the office.

The ring of shadows! Mouse fought back the gasp that came from his realization. *The Church of the Found belongs to the Enemy!*

A frigid wave washed over Mouse. His stomach churned, and the hair on the back of his neck stood on end. Fighting a growing sense of unease, Mouse watched the captain lift Valk — naked and bleeding — with an unabashed tenderness. He followed the captain back towards the chaotic cabin where his struggle with the Enemy had begun.

How can I tell him that he's following a false god? Or that the creature who is pretending to be his god is actually consuming his brother's spirit instead of saving his life?

CHAPTER 32

Seldy

*C*rouching low behind a fallen log, Seldy fought to keep her tail from twitching.

::What is it? Why are we hiding?::

The Packmother bared her fangs.

::Still yourself and silence your mind.::

She blinked at the sharpness of the rebuke. Before she could decide how to respond, hooves clomped against stone and a malodorous scent assaulted her nose. They were downwind from something that smelled disgusting and wrong.

Peering through the gaps in the undergrowth, Seldy tried to see as far down the path as possible. The hoof beats grew louder while the scent sharpened from an obnoxious odor to a caustic assault on her nostrils. They burned as if they were on fire. She opened her mouth hoping to relieve the discomfort, but that just led to a foul taste settling on her tongue.

Curling her paws against the dirt, Seldy flicked her ears. She tucked her tail down between her hind legs. Her muscles bunched, loaded springs on the edge of being released.

Clack! Thud! Clump!

She jerked. Seldy might have leapt right through their cover if not for the Packmother. The larger wolf clamped her jaws down on the loose skin and fur at the back of her neck, pinning her in place.

::Do. Not. Move.::

The words were barely audible to Seldy's mind as the wolf whispered her thoughts to her.

More surprised than hurt, Seldy fought the urge to whimper in submission. She forced her muscles to relax. The Packmother's grip loosened and then released.

The first flickers of movement down the path focused her mind on the approaching danger. She was expecting a horse and rider but, while the figure was tall enough, the shape was all wrong. There were only two legs, not four, and only one head.

Her eyes widened at the sight of the nightmarish creature. It was a hulking brute, easily standing over eight feet tall. It had a massive, barrel-sized chest and heavily-muscled arms. In one meaty hand, he held a strung bow with a barbed arrow knocked in place. The other hand dangled down past its oddly bent knees. The creature's head was a strange mixture of boar and man, with massive tusks curving upward from behind its lower lip and a short, pug nose with rounded nostrils. Small, beady eyes glared out from behind heavy brows. Its ears stood up from the side of its block-like head, each one coming to a sharp point just above the crown of its bald head.

The boar-man's lower torso was more porcine than man, naked except for the coarse dark fur that covered his legs and lower abdomen. His semi-flaccid sex flopped about, easily visible through the matted fur of his uncovered crotch. Cloven hooves thudded against the ground with each ponderous step. The only articles the creature wore were a pair of crisscrossed belts across his chest; one held a pair of sheathed blades with *dark handles, and the other belt held a quiver of dark-fletched arrows.*

His stench was overpowering. He reeked of unwashed skin, hatred, and the Enemy.

Seldy's lips curled away from her fangs. She wanted nothing more than to leap out and slash this monster's throat with her fangs and to taste his blood on her tongue. Her mind raced, trying to calculate the best approach to the creature so that he wouldn't have a chance to loose his arrows at her. But the distance was too great, and the space between them too open.

The creature paused in its advance, snorting and grunting as he scanned the undergrowth for his prey. His hands were poised to raise the bow and shoot in an instant.

Next to her, the Packmother remained still and silent. Seldy followed the elder wolf's lead and remained still.

Snorting, the creature pawed the dirt before shuffling forward again. It was several moments before they saw the back of his head through the foliage as it ambled further down the path.

::Run now, Shapesister! Run like the wind!::

Startled by the strength and urgency of the wolf's command, Seldy couldn't help yipping. The Packmother dashed straight through the covering brush and raced silently towards the cover of the trees on the other side of the path.

It didn't take Seldy long to recover. She leapt after the larger wolf, catching up a little bit with each racing stride.

It felt good to be moving again, to be exercising her powerful muscles as they were meant to be used. She was so excited, she forgot all about the strange creature until a bellow of rage tore through the air. He hadn't forgotten about them.

Seldy yipped again when a dark shape whizzed past her ears and thudded into a nearby tree. She redoubled her speed, catching up to the Packmother and then matching her stride-for-stride *as they skittered up a slick hillside studded with stunted pine trees.*

Hooves thundered against the ground as the creature bellowed in frustration, loosing arrow after arrow at them.

The ground became rockier and slicker, causing them to scrabble for purchase. The creature's bellows grew more distant and his arrows less frequent. By the time they reached the crest of a wind-swept ridge, he was far below and, finally, out of sight.

Standing silhouetted against the full moon, the Packmother's sides heaved.

::We can rest for a moment; he will not be able to climb this ridge or reach us with his weapons.::

::What was that?::

Unable to contain her excitement or her questions any longer, Seldy projected her thoughts even as she fought to regain her breath.

::He looked like he was half-boar and half-man! I've never even heard of such monsters before!::

::That creature is also a Reaver.:: *The Packmother shook her head.* ::Like the monster you slew earlier. Reavers are formed from the twisted spirits of mortals ensnared by the Enemy's lies. Their inhuman strength is fueled by the fear and hatred he instills in them for both the Fae and the Elder Spirits.::

::But this one was different than the other. Why is that?::

The elder wolf leveled her gaze at Seldy.

::Each of them is different, often taking on the warped image of some long-dead Fae creature to try and trick us into believing that they have turned against us. But the Pack remembers, and the Elder Spirits remind those who don't have the benefit of our long memories. Some look to be more beast than man, and others walk on two legs and carry weapons such as that one.:: *She cast a glance in the direction from which they came.*

Her sides heaved in a sigh that was audible in her thoughts as well. ::We do what we can against them; however, each time they return, they come back stronger and filled with even more hate than before.::

::They come back, even if you kill them?::

The Packmother moved in close and brushed her muzzle against Seldy's.

::There is so much for you to learn about this place, Shapesister, and so little time to teach you.:: *She pulled back and locked gazes with her again.* ::Each Reaver is the spirit-body of a living mortal, much like you, except that they are held in thrall by those that serve the Enemy. Their bodies here in this place are temporary; thus, when they are slain, they merely wake up in the world of the living.:: *The elder wolf shrugged her shoulders.* ::Perhaps frightened and scared, but otherwise unharmed.::

::So this really is all a dream then?::

::For the living, yes.:: *The Packmother cast her eyes down, shifting her body so that she was gazing in the direction they had been heading.* ::But for those of us who have passed from that world and are waiting for our loved ones to join us, being slain here means the continuation of our journey to the Great Beyond.::

Stunned by the implications of her words, Seldy remained silent for a moment before she asked the obvious question.

::So you...and the Pack...are all...?::

::Yes, Shapesister. We have passed from the world of the living. We await my mate — and their father — Shadowfang to join us.::

The wind played and tugged with their fur as it caressed them.

::We are with him each time he dreams. He hunts the Reavers with us, knowing that if he falls in battle, he will wake up and be able to return again until his time finally comes. Then we will choose whether to remain together and fight on behalf of the Elder Spirits for as long as we can or simply cross the Gloaming Sea to see what awaits us in the Great Beyond.::

::I've heard that name before!:: *It hit her in a flash.* ::My birth mother! She said I could find her on the shores of the Gloaming Sea!::

The wolf's sides heaved as she wuffled. She nodded towards the other side of the ridge.

::Look there, far to the west.::

Seldy followed her gaze. The land on the other side of the ridge was shrouded by countless trees, with rippling hills and tiny, glittering ribbons of water cutting through the landscape. On the far edge of her vision, the entire horizon sparkled with tiny, sparkling lights that alternated between brighter and dimmer modes in a rhythmic fashion.

::That is the Gloaming Sea,:: *the wolf continued.* ::The land itself may be different each time you dream. But know that the shore of that sea lays ever to the west and is always within reach of one's night journey, should you choose to go there.::

::You mean I can find her?:: *A bud of hope blossomed inside of her chest.* ::I could reach her tonight and talk to her?::

::Yes, if a Reaver didn't catch you first.::

The Packmother turned to regard her with an intense look.

::But be wary. The call of the Great Beyond grows stronger the closer you get to the shores of that sea. It takes great strength to resist the promise of that journey once you reach those shores.::

The Packmother shifted her body, brushing Seldy back from the edge and nudging her to look back to the right. There, much closer than the shores of the distant sea, was a wooded hill topped by a formation of reddish stones ringing the top like a crown. Inside that jagged crown, the top of the hill was dominated by a single massive tree growing amidst a field of bright green grass at the exact center of the hill.

::Our destination this night, Shapesister, is there. The Elder Spirits wait for you there.::

Staring at the distant hill top, an electric tingle ran up and down Seldy's spine. Her stomach lurched, and her heart started to race. Even from this distance, the dark opening at the base of that tree called to her: a small, quiet whisper that promised answers...

::Come, Seldirima,:: *the older wolf projected to her in a calm voice.* ::Our time grows short. There is much for you to see and learn yet before you awaken.::

By the time they reached the base of that distant hill, Seldy struggled to put one paw in front of the others. Her tongue lolled out of the side of her mouth, her sides heaved with each labored breath, and her legs trembled with each staggering step.

Three times during the relatively short journey they had been saved by the keen hearing, sharp nose, and wily instincts of the Packmother. Each time, she had sensed the approach of a Reaver or a group of them and led them to safety with a combination of stealth, speed, and elusiveness. Every escape, however, had taken its toll. Even the Packmother showed uncharacteristic signs of weariness, letting her head hang low as the tops of her paws brushed the ground with each weary step.

The sound of water burbling and splashing perked Seldy's ears. She found the strength to move forward. Slipping around a tall oak tree and through the wispy branches of a pair of willows, the two wolves came to the banks of a small, rapidly flowing stream. Sinking to her belly, Seldy dipped her head into the refreshing water before pulling up far enough to simply lap the water with her parched tongue. The Packmother drank just as noisily beside her.

Once she drank her fill, Seldy rolled over on her side next to the brook and let her eyes close, hoping to rest. The moment she did so, something within her snapped. Her muscles began to twitch and tighten.

She arched her back and let out a howl of pain and surprise. Bones cracked, tendons snapped, and muscles contracted and twisted. Fur receded, slipping back inside of her skin, as claws melted away and fangs dwindled back into mere teeth.

Seldy shuddered as the last of the transformation took place, leaving her naked and exhausted. She curled up into a tight ball of trembling limbs on the bank of a small stream and uttered a whimper of relief when the last of her muscles stopped twitching.

::Rise, Shapesister, for you must continue.::

Even with her eyes closed, Seldy could feel the presence of the elder wolf looming over her.

::Give me a moment,:: *she grunted as she replied.* ::I just need to rest.::

::There is no time, Seldirima. Danger approaches once again in the waking the world. There is much for you to learn about yourself and the gifts you have been given. This is the last opportunity to do so before the machinations of the Enemy come to fruition and it is too late.::

Opening her eyes, Seldy gazed up into the yellow eyes of her guide. She reached up with tentative fingers to touch the wolf to see if any of this was really happening.

"What just happened?"

::The Gift of the Pack has receded.:: *The wolf gave her fingers a lick.* ::You are safe for now. Neither the Enemy nor his Reavers can reach you here in this place, at least not yet.::

"Why is he coming for me? What does he really want with me?" *Seldy sat up.*

The Packmother's eyes softened. She wuffled in Seldy's ear then rubbed her long muzzle along Seldy's shoulder and neck.

::I do not have the answers to your questions, Shapesister. But know that the Pack hunts with you. Call for us, and we will come if we can.::

When the wolf pulled back, Seldy regarded her.

::Why does it sound like you are saying goodbye?::

::Because I am.::

The elder wolf turned her head to look up the slope of the base of the hill, following the stream in reverse.

::I have guided you as far as I can this night. You must climb the hill and seek the answers you crave from those who are wiser than I.::

::But...but...::

Seldy blinked at the yawning chasm opening between them.

::When will I see you again?::

::Seek us in your dreams, Shapesister, and I will be glad to hunt with you again.:: *The elder wolf paused and dipped her head.* ::Please tell Shadowfang that Meadowrunner misses him. I will wait for him before deciding when to seek the shores of the Gloaming Sea.::

::I...will.::

She pushed herself to her knees and wrapped her arms around the great wolf's thick neck. She squeezed the wolf hard.

"Thank you so much, Meadowrunner," *her voice cracked.* "I'm honored you welcomed me into your Pack!"

As she approached the line of stones crowning the hill, Seldy paused and took a deep breath. Her stomach was churning as if a host of butterflies were trying to find their way out. Her legs quivered with fatigue. Sweat ran down her forehead and cheeks, plastering her bangs in place. Brushing the stray

strands behind her ears, she turned her face into the breeze, grateful for the relief.

Closing her eyes, Seldy took a deep, slow breath and just listened.

A strong breeze kicked up. Trees whispered their indecipherable secrets to one another. Crickets chirped, and leaves rustled. Small creatures scurried through the leaf litter blanketing the slope. The cool light of the full moon filtered through the swaying leaves above.

The sound of the forest at night calmed her as it always did. Digging her toes into the layer of leaves and pine needles, Seldy relished the small crinkling sounds created by her movements and the feel of the earth squishing between her toes. Warm and soothing energy flowed through the soles of her bare feet.

The breeze picked up again. She heard something in the answering whispers of the forest...

Seldirima...sweet Seedling...

Swaying in the breeze, Seldy allowed herself to be guided by the wind until she drifted close to a nearby tree. Her eyes still closed, she leaned against the trunk of the tall oak. The rough texture of the bark pressed delightfully against the bare skin of her back, forming connections between her and the ancient tree in a thousand different places. She raised her arms and pushed them back against the trunk as well.

Soon...Seldirima...our sweet little Seedling...

She dug her toes deeper into the soil at the base of the tree, letting them take root deep into the earth...her limbs lengthened, reaching towards the sky. Her skin thickened as the bark of the tree enveloped her. The wind caressed them, moving their leaves, allowing the thoughts of her neighbors to be understood.

Soon, Seldirima, our sweet little Seedling. First, you must find your song...we yearn to hear it...the "Maiden's Song"...

Deep inside, the last remnants of the inky darkness that had obscured the green, glowing seed disappeared. The great seed pulsed once again, flooding her with a warm and living energy. Finally clear of the heavy shroud over her heart, she took another slow breath.

The wind died down, and the forest fell silent. Coming back to herself, Seldy opened her eyes and blinked. She lowered her arms and stepped away from the tree, hugging her arms about her torso. Overcome with relief at finally being free of the oily touch of that foul iron, she collapsed to her knees and looked up at the bright moon.

"But how?" she cried out. "How do I find my song?"

The only answer was the sighing, indecipherable whispers of the trees and soft sounds of the forest at night.

"Why is all of this happening to me?" Taking her cue from the trees, Seldy's voice dropped to whisper. "And how can this all feel so real? Why does it feel like a wondrous dream and a terrible nightmare all at the same time?"

After a few moments of waiting for answers that didn't come, Seldy glanced down at her abdomen and traced the faded silver lines of the wolf howling up at the moon. The image had already changed when she had thought to examine her own reflection in a placid pool after Meadowrunner had left her near the creek. The thick and heavy lines of the tiger, and of the owl on her face, remained untouched — dark red stains standing out in stark contrast to her pale complexion. Try as she might, however, the images of tiger and owl remained unscathed, seemingly immune to any amount of scrubbing, even as the other blood — likely from the Reaver she had slain — washed off easily.

Seldy traced the lines of the tigress' face drawn on the side of her breast, marveling at the skill Tia displayed.

"I wonder if these, too, will fade when I learn what gifts they bring?"

With no one available to answer, Seldy shrugged and gathered her strength for the final ascent to the crown of the hill.

"At least the cramping and bleeding have stopped." She took another deep breath and let it out slowly, relishing the freedom from the pain and discomfort she had experienced earlier. "I sure don't miss that!"

Not far above her, huge slabs of worked stone stuck out from the edge of the hill like the dulled fangs of some great earth dragon. In the pale light, the stones were the same dark hue of aged blood as the still visible lines on her chest and face. Seldy clambered up the last thirty feet to the nearest pillar. Her hair whipped about in the stronger, stiffer breezes at the top of the hill.

The stone pillar just ahead towered over her, easily fifteen feet tall. It was both thicker and wider at the base than she was tall. Once, long ago, the pillars had all been of a similar size and shape. But over time, some of them had become worn. Some now leaned at odd angles and yet others had been toppled onto their sides or had been broken by forces too terrible to comprehend. The remnants were evenly spaced every thirty feet or so for as far as she could see in either direction. The constant wind passing through and among them created a haunting, low-pitched whistle that changed in pitch and volume with the shifting of winds, reminding her of the howling of the Pack.

Ancient carvings peeked out beneath thick patches of red and green moss, but the markings were so worn and faded that she couldn't tell whether they were supposed to be words or pictographs.

The moss-covered stone was cool and slick to the touch. The moment Seldy's fingers found a patch of bare stone, she both heard and felt a deep, earthy hum emanating from within. A warm tingling spread up through her fingers and into her arm. The sensation was strangely soothing.

::Be welcome, Seldirima Silversong.:: *A chorus of voices brushed up against her mind, speaking in unison.* ::We've waited so very long for this moment.::

Seldy fought the urge to yank her fingers back. Instead, she took a deep, steadying breath and pressed her palm against the bare stone to strengthen the connection.

::Are you the Elder Spirits?::

::We are.:: *The collective voices hummed, their words resonating throughout her entire being.* ::Be welcome within our circle, Seedling. Seek us within the Hearth Tree.::

The humming and the tingling sensation stopped, leaving an ache in her heart at the sudden loss of their presence.

Tentatively, Seldy pulled her hand back from the surface of the stone and stepped around it. The swirling winds snatched at her hair, whipping it around like a playful child to cover her eyes. Laughing, she brushed aside her long, silver tresses to see a familiar figure advancing towards her.

::It is good to see you, Cubling.::

"Layra!"

Seldy stumbled forward, sobbing. She threw her arms around the great tigress' neck and buried her face in her luxurious orange- and black-striped fur.

"I've missed you so much!"

CHAPTER 33

Mouse

*T*he light, it burns!"
"*He hears us!*"
"*Help us, Songbreaker!*"

Standing at the threshold of Valk's room, Mouse tried to ignore the insistent whispers trying to push their way into his consciousness. Instead, he focused on watching the captain settle his brother back into the nest of tangled covers, soiled sheets, and shattered restraints of his bunk.

Shadows danced and stretched in the flickering light of the single lantern swaying from its hook in the ceiling of the small chamber. Dark pools of sonic energy gathered in the corners, feeding on the shadows created by the lantern. Stray chords of discordant music writhed from shadow to shadow, unwilling to surrender their disruptive and distracting existence for mere lack of a host.

Harsher, louder sounds hammered against the edges of Mouse's consciousness as well.

Words, Mouse realized. *The Captain is speaking to me again.*

But the words, whatever they had been meant to convey, were too muffled, warbled, and distorted for him to make out.

Gasping, Mouse turned his attention back to the man instead of the distracting remnants of the Enemy's presence.

"—ards, boy!" The captain's hissed whisper was almost as insistent as his swirling *ta'ir.* "I need your help!"

"I'm sorry, sir." Mouse bobbed his head and stepped across the threshold of the cabin. His stomach lurched but he ignored it. "What do you need me to do?"

"Get his treatments." The captain nodded towards the tall cabinet at the foot of Valk's bunk.

"They're in the black wooden box on the top shelf."

Easing around the captain, Mouse ignored the shadowy figments that darted away to join the darker clumps of writhing shadows in the corners of the room. Each frigid, ghostly brush of one of those figments made his skin crawl and the short hairs on the back of his neck to stand on end. Faint, indecipherable whispers came from every direction.

"Are you sure this is a good idea, Captain?" Mouse swallowed. "I don't think the Church is what you think it is, sir."

He shuddered at the sight of the ebon circle emblazoned on the wooden box resting near the front of the top shelf. It stood out in its darkness for the way it drew the surrounding shadows in, consuming them as it stared, unblinking down at him. The whispering grew louder.

"What do you know about anything, boy?" the captain growled at him through clenched teeth. "The Church saved my brother when no one else could!"

It took every bit of strength Mouse had just to touch the box. Glass clinked against glass as the box shifted. The moment his fingers touched the wood, the ship dipped and tilted so that the box practically leapt into his arms. It was far heavier than he expected it to be. It knocked him back. He hit the wall behind him with unexpected force. The impact drove the air from his lungs. Mouse strained to lift it but, instead, slipped further down the wall.

The captain shouted, but his words were muffled. Mouse sank to the floor, cradling the crushing weight of the box to his abdomen. He gasped for air as a horde of hungry shadows gathered to swallow him whole...

Clank. Clank.

Chain links scraped against the stone floor of the dark corridor, sending echoes in every direction.

My chains, she thought to herself, fighting the urge to cry out in pain. *No! I will not give them the satisfaction of seeing my pain! I will be strong, no matter what comes!*

Clank. Clank.

She stared instead at the back of the tall, cloaked form ahead of her.

How can they do this? Don't they remember what our peoples once meant to each other? She shook her head. *I must think of the forest; I must remember what it is to be* Fae.

She fought to recall happier moments...the verdant greens and vibrant blossoms of the forest in the full bloom of spring... the smiles and loving caresses of her mates and their children... the fragrant aromas of bread baking in clay ovens...but it was so difficult after being captive for so long, with cold iron shackles binding her ankles and wrists; when everyone and everything that she had ever loved had been taken from her.

Clank. Clank.

She knew that each staggering, shuffling step took her closer to the end of her life. Her gait slowed as the reality of her situation slammed home.

"Keep moving, bitch!" A gloved hand pushed at her bare back from behind, the voice of the cloaked figure behind her hissing through the darkness. "The Master waits for no one!"

Clank. Clank.

Determined to remember the joys of her life rather than her present sorrow, she closed her eyes, no longer caring about the chafing of the iron shackles or what the guards said or did to her. Peals of childish laughter echoed throughout the glades of her memory, bringing a smile to her lips. Other cherished moments came rushing forward — the gentle pitter patter of rain falling and trickling through the canopy of the forest, the fragrant scents of spring blossoms, dancing and singing through the night with her brothers and sisters in the soft light of Luna's Shards, the sparkling eyes and the feral grins of each of her various lovers through the many seasons of her long life, the tiny mewling cries of each of her newborn children, and the sacred mixture of utter exhaustion, throbbing pain, sheer joy, satisfaction, and accomplishment as she cradled each of her babes to her breast for the first time...

Clank. Clank.

She opened her eyes when the echoes of her chains softened and disappeared, swallowed in a vast space. The corridor expanded and widened into a great, vaulted chamber illuminated by the harsh red glow emanating from a sight she could never have imagined.

"No!"

She yanked against the chain that was attached to her iron collar, feeling its sharp bite digging into her already raw skin. She closed her eyes again, squeezing them tight against the view.

"It isn't possible!"

"Open your eyes, bitch." Strong hands grabbed her from behind, turning her head back towards the horrible sight. A voice gloated in her ear, "Take in your fate."

Clank. Clank.

"NOOO!"

She continued to struggle, but it was a hopeless battle that had been lost long ago.

"Please! No!"

More hands grabbed at her. She was lifted into the air and carried forward, each step bringing her closer to the perversion of everything that she held sacred and dear, to a doom that was far worse than any death she could have imagined.

She kicked and screamed. She lashed out with her chains and bit at the gloved hands with her teeth, but they were too many and they were too strong. She was slammed onto a hard, flat surface.

Clank. Clank.

The chains binding her arms and legs clattered against stone as she thrashed about.

"Cut her eyelids," a harsh, female voice grunted. "The Master demands to see her eyes!"

"Be quick about it!" a male voice shouted over her screams. "Before he takes us too!"

Pain erupted from the top of her eyelids. The useless flaps of skin were torn away. Bright, red light, forced its way into her consciousness, tinged even deeper red by the blood that spurted around her blurry vision. She couldn't help but stare up in unblinking horror at the perverse monstrosity that loomed over her.

The massive canopy was larger than anything she'd ever seen before. The profane, heart-shaped leaves were blood-red on one side and bone-white underneath. With each heartbeat-like pulse of the tree, however, unique runes became briefly illuminated on the white side of each leaf. Branches with strange, translucent bark creaked with each swaying motion of the hideous tree.

Craning her head as much as the chains binding her would allow, she cast her eyes to the side, hoping to avoid staring at the tree. But the tree was so massive that it filled the chamber, from the branches overhead that reached from sloping wall to sloping wall to the towering trunk that was easily thicker and stronger than that of any other tree she'd ever seen. There was

402

no escape. Even straining to stare at the ground only brought her new horrors as the floor of the chamber was littered with the bleached white bones of the thousands upon thousands of victims who had preceded her.

Clack. Clack.

Her blood-smeared and tear-stained eyes widened as bones shifted and moved. Something skittered beneath the carpet of skeletal remains. She could only watch in uncomprehending horror as dozens of white-furred and pink-eyed rats scurried about, squeaking in excitement and fear as they scrambled to avoid the serpentine forms snaking their way towards her.

The first tendrils slithered against her bare limbs, sliding up to her torso. She screamed, but there was no stopping their advance as first one and then a second and third tentacle latched onto her. They began to drain both her blood and her spirit.

She tried to resist, but the hunger of the tree was insatiable.

::FIGHT ME IF YOU WISH, MY SWEET. BUT YOUR ESSENCE, AND THAT OF YOUR SISTERS BEFORE AND AFTER YOU, SHALL SUSTAIN ME UNTIL I HAVE THE BRIDE THAT WAS PROMISED TO ME!:: The voice, undeniably masculine and impossible to resist, resonated throughout her being. *::I WILL NOT BE DENIED WHAT IS MY DUE!::*

Her screams of terror melded with the voices of the countless others who had been sacrificed before her. Her voice added to the terrible and dissonant song of agony and suffering that gave the presence within the tree its unmatched strength.

Even as her vision was beginning to fade, her eyes focused on a branch far above where a new leaf sprouted from a bare branch, growing fuller and richer as she weakened. On the underside of that leaf, new runes formed, different from those on every other leaf. She didn't have to read those runes to know that her name was being inscribed, binding her to this perversion of a Hearth Tree.

As her struggles ceased, the chains binding her limbs clattered against the stone slab one last time.

Clank. Clank.

Distant voices cried out in terror.

Crushing weight pinned him down.

Cold! I'm so cold!

Darkness enshrouded him.

I can't breathe!

::*I'M COMING FOR YOU, IMPUDENT MORTAL!*:: The voice was all too familiar. ::*YOUR INTERMINABLE MEDDLING IS ABOUT TO COME TO AN END!*::

Clink. Clink.

A massive presence loomed over him, bristling with rage.

"Blast you, boy! If any of these vials are damaged, I'll let Haddock have his way with you!" The captain's voice cut through the fog clouding his mind. Big hands snatched the unbearable weight from his chest as if it were light as a feather. "Give me that!"

Clink. Clink.

Gasping for breath, Mouse watched as tendrils of shadow dangled from the box and tangles of others coalesced into serpentine forms to slither after the captain. The power of the box drew them like moths to flame. Voices whispered from the shadows, barely loud enough to be heard.

"Yes!"

"Give us the blessed blood!"

"Feed us!"

"We will be strong again!"

Clink. Clink.

The captain placed the box next to Valk's head and opened it, his dark eyes intense and glowing with a fervor that Mouse had never seen before. Wispy shadows circled about the captain's head, whispering in his ear before being drawn into the vortex of darkness that dangled from his neck. The ebon circle was painful to look at but, at the same time, impossible to avoid once his eyes settled upon it.

"Ah, Valk. My poor little brother." The captain's voice was slurred as he held up a vial of thick, dark liquid and removed the cork. "The Blessed Blood of the Found God will make you strong again! It will bring you back to me better and stronger than before!"

Clink. Clink.

The pressure in the cabin doubled. Mouse's ear's popped.

The temperature dropped. He shivered.

The swirling shadows darkened, becoming more and more substantial. Voices — countless voices — cried out in agony and fear, hammering into his consciousness.

Clink. Clink.

Mouse struggled to his feet. Time slowed.

The air grew thick and cold. His skin was clammy, and every one of his muscles protested, but he ignored it all. The captain raised an uncorked vial to Valk's lips.

Clink. Clink.

Straining against the bitter cold that tried to lock his muscles in place, Mouse dove forward and knocked the vial from the captain's hand. It spun free of the captain's grasp and hung in the air for one tantalizingly long moment before shattering against the headboard.

Clink!

Crack!

A glob of reddish-black goo hit the wooden wall with an audible plop that was the only sound to be heard for several interminably slow heartbeats.

An explosion of sound and pain ripped through the fabric

of the world. A fraction of the pain came from the impact of a massive fist hammering at his back and shoulders. The rest of it arose from the eruption of ethereal screams slamming into him from every direction as the goo began to sizzle, burning into the wood beneath. A thousand different voices shrieked out in undying horror from amidst the tendrils of shadow-drenched smoke curling up into the air.

"You traitorous gutter snipe!" the captain roared through the cacophony of other voices. "I'm going to kill you!"

Clink. Clink.

Lashing out with a desperate foot, Mouse kicked the captain in the gut, earning him enough of a respite from the beating to twist around and knock the box of vials aside with a sweep of his arm. It careened from the bed.

The captain's eyes widened. He lunged towards the box, trying to catch it before crashed.

Time slowed again. The voices fell silent in tortured anticipation.

Clink. Clink.

The only sound in the tiny chamber was that of glass vials jostling against each other as the partially open box tumbled over the side of the bed. As the captain dove to catch it, Mouse reached for something else — the true source of the man's pain.

The fingers of his left hand wrapped around the outside edges of the obsidian-black circle dangling from the captain's neck at the same moment the big man's hands intercepted the wooden box just inches from the floor.

Cold! He gasped at the searing pain lancing through his fingers. *So cold!*

Clink. Clink.

Frozen in place, Mouse gazed into the captain's eyes but found nothing but abject hatred.

Twisting his body, Mouse jerked the chain hard enough to

snap it. In a move that only a Slant Rat would try, he leapt up, crashed onto, and then rolled over, the captain's hunched back before spinning again to land on nimble feet. He didn't waste any time, darting back out into the hallway as the captain roared and staggered after him.

Clink. Clink.

His hammering heart obscured every other possible sound as Mouse skidded to a halt in front of the massive windows in the captain's office. He threw back the curtain to reveal the sliver of rosy-hued light dawning on the eastern horizon.

His entire left arm hung limp at his side, burning from the frigid cold of the amulet still clenched in his agonizingly twisted and unmoving fingers. Freezing cold numbed the entire arm, working up to his shoulder and needling towards his neck and heart. Desperate, Mouse reached down with his right hand and grabbed the broken ends of the chain dangling below the Seeker's Circle. Then, before he could even consider the consequences, he yanked at the chains with all of his strength. There was a flash of searing agony as patches of frozen skin ripped free with the circle.

"NOOO!!!!" the captain roared like a beast behind him. "Stop!"

But the captain was too far away to stop him. Blinking through blinding tears, Mouse spun and hurled the cursed object with all of his might through the plate glass window.

Clink.

CRACK!

Glass shattered into thousands of shards, both great and small. The wind roared.

Cold air blasted into the room.

And a circle of ebon darkness tumbled into the dying night sky, falling towards the Untere, far below.

"What in the blazes have you done!" The captain's voice

thundered above the swirling wind. "You're going to die, you traitorous little bastard!"

Click.

Breathless, shivering, and struggling to deal with the searing pain in his left hand, Mouse turned to face the captain.

The man was aiming a cocked pistol at his head. He settled back on his heels and stared up into the captain's eyes. Composing himself as best he could, he waited for the bullet that was sure to come.

"I'm sorry, Anna." His whispered words were mostly to himself. "I wish I could've been the Guardian your daughter needed."

CHAPTER 34

Tra'al, Klard

Stirring at the sound of soft humming near his ear, Tra'al groaned. He sucked in his breath when something — no, someone — touched his shoulders. Insistent fingers worked their way beneath his tunic. They were unfamiliar but warm and tingling. They moved with a surprising gentleness as they probed both sides of his sore ribcage. He winced as they found every tender spot from his most recent pummeling.

Whoever it was seemed to know what they were doing. They were gauging the seriousness of his wounds without doing any further damage. Tra'al had survived enough battles to know better than to disturb someone who was trying to help him. Besides, after the shockwaves from each initial contact subsided, all that remained was soothing warmth that relaxed his muscles and brought much needed relief to his aches and pains.

The throbbing in his head felt like a blacksmith had taken up residence inside of his skull and was trying to pound his way out of it. The bitter tang of his own blood lingered around the gaping hole in his lower jaw.

The soft humming continued unabated as those skilled

fingers slid up his neck, leaving a lingering trail of tingling energy behind. The person tending him shifted their bodyweight as they did so, swinging a leg over his abdomen to straddle him without putting any weight on his torso.

Tra'al sighed as the fingertips found the bruises and cuts on his face and eased the fiery pain from each of them with gentle caresses. He was afraid to open his eyes, worried that doing so would reveal this to be just a dream and banish the magickal fingers that were somehow healing him. The pounding in his skull faded entirely as they slid from point to point, soothing the soreness from each with their deft touch.

When the last of his pain subsided, however, his curiosity won out.

"Mouse, where did you learn that?"

The humming ended with a soft and feminine giggle. That surprising sound was followed by the feathery light touch of what felt like long hair pooling against the weathered skin of his cheeks. Before he could react to either sound or sensation, he experienced something even more unexpected — a set of soft lips pressing against his in what could only be a kiss.

The female exhaled into his mouth through parted lips. The energy in her breath spread like wildfire throughout his body, infusing his old, tired muscles with a strength that he hadn't felt in years. He felt as fresh and vibrant as a newly budded oak leaf in spring.

As the kiss continued, Tra'al's ingrained disgust at the broken taboo melted away. It was such a strange and wonderful feeling that he no longer cared if this was a dream or not. He just didn't want it to end.

All-too-soon, however, the lips pulled back, leaving him aching for their return. The person shifted, swinging her leg off of him before shifting to sit back and off to the side.

He groaned.

"Oh," she gasped in a breathy voice. "That felt really good to me. I hope that means it worked for you as well!" The voice of his benefactor was as familiar as it was impossible. "Are you feeling better, Tra'al?"

He opened his eyes. In the near darkness of the prison hold, Seldy's delicate features were illuminated by the soft green light emanating from her eyes. The long strands of her untamed hair framed her face.

He tried to respond but couldn't. Those magickal eyes captivated him. Staring up into the glittering radiance of her gaze, he remembered a chilly, mist-shrouded night more than eighteen years ago when he should have — and would have — died, if not for the most unlikely of saviors...

Bleeding from half a dozen wounds and close to utter exhaustion, Tra'al stumbled through the roiling wall of mist. Just when it began to feel endless, he emerged into a rare open clearing in the vast and untamed forest of the Aerhythian hinterland. Near the center of the clearing, the pale light of the Crone — the smallest and dimmest of the three Shards of ancient Luna — reflected off of a small pool of water. Licking his parched lips with a swollen, dry tongue, he staggered towards what he hoped would be a welcome relief for at least some of his suffering.

Uncaring about whether or not his pursuers found him so long as his thirst was slaked, Tra'al dropped to his hands and knees at the edge of the shallow pool and plunged his face into the crystal clear water. The shock of the cold water was invigorating, so he kept his face in it for as long as he could stand before pushing up and throwing his head back. Sopping wet hair swung back, slapping the back of his neck and sending rivulets of cold water running down his back.

::You defile this place with your presence, mortal.:: *The frigid, feminine voice sounded inside of his head, completely bypassing all of his physical senses.* ::And you have also brought corrupted metals — foul steel and cold iron — into a place where such things are forbidden.::

He scrambled back from the edge of the pool.

A hooded and cloaked ethereal figure emerged from a column of mist. It drifted towards him, floating above the surface of the water. A cold chill ran down his spine. He reached for a blade.

A pale hand, gnarled and bent with age, emerged from the robes of mist and fog, pointing towards him.

::Bestill yourself, mortal. I am far beyond the reach of such crude weapons, even as unpleasant as it yet remains to be in their presence.::

Tra'al froze, unable to move. His eyes widened. The figure drifted closer, surrounded by thicker mists. Even though her face was obscured by a massive hood, he had the distinct impression that the figure was a woman of incalculable age. As she approached, her hood billowed back, as if blown by an invisible and unfelt gust of wind. He glimpsed a pair of glittering green eyes, glowing as if lit from within.

His blood ran cold. Tra'al had no doubt who she was — the legendary and dreaded Wraith of Aerhythia. He had scoffed at the tales of her existence. She was whispered about in fear by both the superstitious settlers and the Quaestidors *of the Found God.*

It was rumored that she was both revered and feared by the Fae. *Their wild stories spoke of how she once ruled a mighty nation-state of* Fae *and* Aelfani *before the Sundering and that in protecting her realm during that great catastrophe, she had sacrificed much of herself, eventually fading away into the famous mists that covered Aerhythia night and day, no matter the season.*

Those glowing eyes locked onto his and wouldn't let him go.

"What do you want with me?"

His teeth chattered. The temperature dropped further as she drew closer.

::Your wounds are fatal, mortal, though you recognize it not. Your death is certain and by far nearer than you wish for it to be.::

The intensity of those eyes burned into his very soul, preventing him from fleeing, or even responding.

::But your death here, in this place, will serve no more purpose than to perpetuate a war that should never have been fought between foes who were once allies. The Enemy seeks to finish the destruction he started. If he succeeds, then Love shall wither, Truth will fail, and the seeds of Hope may never be sown. I have need of you, mortal warrior.::

The mists enveloped him. He no longer felt the ground beneath his knees or heard any of the sounds of the forest. Suspended in a cloud of churning white mists, he was frozen in place, unable to speak or move. A pair of claw-like hands touched his chest. Her touch was so cold that it burned.

::Seek out the former protégé of yours, mortal, the Traitor Who is Not.

::Serve as his eyes and ears, for there will come a time when your worst failure may become your greatest triumph. Befriend the friendless. Find and draw out the Hidden Hero from the unlikeliest of places. Show the Hunted Maiden that all is not as it seems.

::For as long as you work towards these purposes, the poisons that steal your strength shall lie dormant within you and your life will have the meaning it lacks now. It is your choice, mortal, whether you live or die. Choose well, and Love may bloom, Truth can prevail, and Hope has a fighting chance. Choose poorly, and the poisons shall attend to their unfinished work with all due haste.::

"*Maestro* Tra'al?" His name floated in the air, wavering with uncertainty and concern. "Are you okay? Can you speak to me?"

"Seldy?" he croaked out her name. "How did you...? Did Mouse come...?"

She nodded at her name but pressed a finger to his lips, silencing his follow-up questions.

"First things first," she spoke in a quiet, but serious tone. "Are you feeling better? They said that you would." She removed her finger from his lips, leaving them tingling and aching with the loss of her touch.

"They?" he sputtered. "What fool told you to kiss an orc?" He wiped at his lips with the back of his hand. "We don't kiss! Ever!"

Her expression broke out in a big grin. "You sound just like Uncle Paan!"

"You kissed Paandokh Tahl? And lived to tell about it?"

Her laughter rang like a small silver bell through the hold. "Well, only a few times because he was always so serious and so hard to catch by surprise!" The reminiscent glow had faded, but her eyes still sparkled in the near darkness of the hold as she leaned in a little closer. "It started when I was little. It became a game of whether I could catch him off guard or not."

"But why did you kiss me, lass?" He tried to look indignant, unsure of how successful he was. "And why, by the Ancestors, on the lips?"

"What can I say?" She shrugged. "Gypsy girls love to give out kisses, even to grumpy old orcs." Her mischievous grin faded. Her eyes became unfocused. "The Elder Spirits said that even without my song, that my touch can still heal, and that the more intimate the touch was, the stronger the connection would become." Focusing on him again, she asked, "So, did it help?"

"Aye, it helped, lass." he replied. "I feel better than I have in... years."

His eyes trailed down from her face to note with some small measure of relief that she was at least wearing the sleeveless tunic. It didn't do much to conceal the soft curves of her bare backside, however, leaving little to his imagination with the way she was sitting. His cheeks grew flush at the sight.

"I see that Paandokh was just telling stories when he said that orcs can't blush!"

Apparently noticing his discomfort, Seldy adjusted the hem of her loose tunic, covering her backside. She tucked both of her pale bare legs beneath her body, sitting back on her heels as she waited for him to get up.

"I'm so glad you're feeling better, *Maestro*."

"No more than I am, lass."

Sitting up with surprising ease, Tra'al took and held a deeper breath than he had in years. His muscles were loose and relaxed. His joints weren't cracking and popping with each movement like they normally did. His only remaining ailment was the familiar tightness in his lungs, but even that felt better for the moment. Glancing around, he noted that the doors to both of their cells remained closed and locked, and there was no obvious sign of anyone else in the prison hold. He arched an eyebrow as he turned back to face her.

"Tell me something, lass. How did you get from over there to here?" He waited for her answer.

Her eyes grew bright and wide. "Magick!" She gasped the word out, leaning forward in obvious excitement.

"Magick?" A cold tingle shot down his spine. "What kind of magick?"

"*Fae* magick!" She reached out to touch his knees with her fingertips.

He blinked as the return of her warm, tingling touch gave him renewed strength and banished the sudden chill.

"So, you're acknowledging that you're *Fae*, then?"

415

Tra'al tried to keep his emotions even. Until that night when the Wraith of Aerhythia had changed everything, he'd been a lifelong skeptic on the existence of magick.

"And that you have magick? Real magick?"

Seldy's expression brightened. Words began tumbling out of her mouth in a breathless rush. "Yes! You were right, *Maestro*! I am *Fae*, and I do have magick, powerful magick! And it's not evil like everyone believes!" The wonder and awe in her words matched the expression on her face. Her voice grew hushed and more serious as she continued. "But something is still blocking most of it. I can feel it deep down, trapped inside of something that looks like a giant glowing seed, but I don't know how to open it or how to control the little bit of it that leaks out when I get really angry."

Seldy paused to take a breath before continuing. "Tia came to me in the form of an owl in the Dreamlands before turning back into herself and performing a ritual on me with my own Moon's Blood. She called upon the Elder Spirits to give me some gifts before she disappeared in a big explosion! All that was left of her was a feather!" Without stopping the narrative, Seldy pulled a dark feather from her hair with her free hand, gesticulating with it as she kept speaking. "I was so sad and upset that I turned into a wolf right there on the spot. Then I heard the Pack calling for me and went rushing to find them, which is when I helped them to kill a nasty creature called a Reaver. The Packmother chastised me, though, saying that I needed to be careful before she led me to where I could meet the Elder Spirits. They were inside of the biggest tree I've ever seen — it's called a Hearth Tree! — and there, they taught me how to use the gifts they gave me to protect myself from the Enemy until I can find the Guardian who will help me find my song and become the Treemaiden I'm supposed to be!"

Tra'al sat in stunned silence, unable to make any sense out of the strange-sounding names and references.

"Oh!" Seldy exclaimed, cupping her palms together and pushing them towards him so that he could see the feather she held. "And as strange as it all sounds, I know it all really happened because when I woke up, my cramps and bleeding were all gone just like they said they would be, and this feather was sitting on the floor waiting for me!"

Not sure what else to do in the face of her excitement, Tra'al picked the feather up by the stem and examined it.

"It looks like an owl feather." He glanced towards the high ceiling. "But it might have just fallen from an old nest in the rafters."

Grinning, Seldy gave him a wink as she took the feather back and carefully wove it back into the hair above her right ear.

"It was a gift from Tia; I just know it!" She spoke in a giddy voice. "It looks exactly like the feather that was left after she disappeared. It was meant to show me that my dreams were all real!"

"Dreaming of strange rituals and people who turn into beasts is one thing, lass." He tried to bring the conversation back around to the reality of their situation. "But nothing you've said so far explains how you got out of your cell and into mine unless you've got some keys hidden on you. Or just maybe you and Mouse are trying to play a trick on a gullible old orc." He raised his voice and glanced around, hoping to catch sight of the young man trying to hide. "But if this is a joke, you two need to cut it out and get on with whatever plan you have to escape from this shitehole of a ship."

"Oh, Tra'al." All of the giddiness left Seldy's expression. She bit down on her bottom lip. "This isn't a joke." Moisture glistened in the corners of her eyes. "I...I...I'm sorry. But I don't know how to explain it all in a way that will help you understand it." She turned her head in the direction the wolf's cage, staring off into the darkness before speaking again in a quiet voice. "I used one of my new gifts to escape my cell and come in here." Her chin began to quiver. "I can escape now...from this cell...from this ship, even...whenever I want to...but I...just can't bring myself to do it...not yet, anyway."

"What? Why by the Shards of Luna wouldn't you, lass?"

She flinched as if his words had bitten her.

"If you can escape, you need to get off this blasted ship right now!"

"No!" She looked at him with red-rimmed eyes swollen with unshed tears. "I won't do it without helping you and Shadowfang! But I don't know how to get either of you out of these cages!" She sobbed and grabbed at the hem of her tunic, her small, pale hands balling into fists of frustration. "I don't care what happens to me if I can't help the two of you as well!"

Seeing the tears leaking out of the corner of her eyes and the way her shoulders shook with barely contained sobs, Tra'al's heart melted. He leaned forward and wrapped his arms around her thin shoulders, drawing her into an embrace.

"I...don't...want...to cry...any...more!" She buried her face in the crook of his neck. "But...what...use...is...having...magick," she sniffled, "if...I...can't help...those I...care about?"

"I don't know, lass." Tra'al soothed her by holding her tight and running a hand up and down her back. "But I do know that there's no shame in your tears."

Seldy collapsed against him, sobbing so hard that anything she was trying to say was lost. Her tears were hot and wet against his neck, soaking the shoulder of his tunic. He kept holding her, rocking back and forth. His thoughts turned towards the one person on this ship who had the potential to be the hero that Seldy needed.

Where in the Blazing Fires of the Fallen Star is Mouse? And how did I misjudge him so badly?

His shoulders heaved in a disappointed sigh. *Maybe he's not the hero I hoped he could be...*

The brisk morning wind howled through the shattered window, snapping the curtains inward and scattering the papers from his desk to swirl about the chamber. Klard stomped forward, pistol in hand, cocked and aimed squarely at the forehead of the young man kneeling in front of him.

Mouse clutched his bleeding left hand to his chest, but his right hand was open and held up as if to show that he offered no threat.

The young man stared up at him with wide, brown eyes that reminded him so much of Valk when he was younger, before the Scourge. Curly, unkempt brown hair framed a tanned, innocent-looking face marred by a massive purplish bruise over one eye and a number of smaller nicks and bruises. Unlike most other foes that had faced death at his hands, however, the former stowaway's eyes were not filled with terror. He didn't tremble in fear nor did he beg for mercy. There was a strange aura of peace, an acceptance of his fate that brought Klard to a stunned halt, three paces away.

Blinking away the tears of yet another betrayal from the corners of his eyes, Klard fought to keep his pistol steady.

"Why, boy?" His voice was thick with phlegm. "Why — despite all I've done for you — have you turned against me?"

"I haven't, Captain. I'm trying to help you keep your promise."

"Lies! All lies!"

"Kill the traitor!"

The strange, whispering voices clouded his ability to think. Klard took another step closer to the traitor.

"What are you talking about, boy? What promise?"

The young man's throat worked like he was swallowing before he answered but, otherwise, he didn't move.

"The promise you made to your mother as she lay dying."

The boy's voice was quiet; yet, somehow Klard heard every syllable.

"You promised to take care of him, to love him like she would."

Those words, and the calm demeanor with which they were delivered, staggered him like he'd been hit with a club.

"How do you know about that?" Klard stumbled backwards, the gun shaking in his hand. "I've never told anyone about that!"

"Magick! Foul magick!"

"Slay him!"

"You're hearing voices, aren't you?" Seemingly unconcerned about the trembling gun leveled at him, Mouse stood up and took a step forward, his brown eyes pulsing with an unnatural inner light. "They're urging you to kill me."

"Wha—?" Incredulous, and more than a little scared, Klard took another halting step backward. "How do y—?"

"Because I can hear them, too, despite how they try to hide from me."

The rays of the rising sun cast a dim, rosy hue throughout the disheveled office. Pieces of paper and parchment fluttered around the room, caught up in the swirling winds. Klard nearly jumped out of his skin when the heavy fabric of a blowing curtain snapped against his back. Mouse, however, didn't flinch.

"What are they?" Klard called out, his voice hoarse. "Who are they?"

"They are the remnants of broken spirits, Captain; leftover shards of the great darkness that was consuming Valk." The young man took another step forward as he continued to speak. "They're flocking to you now because their source of strength is gone, at least for the moment. They feed off of your fear and anger. They want you to kill me because I can see them for what they are."

"*Liar!*"

"*He's bewitching you!*"

"*End his lies! Slay him!*"

The voices screeched. His trigger finger twitched with each overwhelming command. An image flashed into his mind — of the pistol bucking and roaring in his hand, of a flash of powder and blood splattering as Mouse crumpled to the floor, his limbs flailing; of those brown eyes staring up at him in shock and betrayal. Squeezing his eyes shut, Klard fought the urge that would make that image a reality.

"Weapons can't stop them, Captain. You have to fight them in a different way."

Mouse was beside him. He placed his right hand on the extended barrel of the flintlock pistol and pushed it gently down towards the floor. The young man whispered, his words somehow finding their way to him even over the howling winds and the screeching of the hidden voices.

"Think back to a time when you were loved unconditionally, just for being you."

Against his will, an image flashed into Klard's mind of his mother holding him close, rocking him back and forth as she sang to him. He was safe and warm and loved.

"Yes!" Mouse whispered as soon as that image formed. "Your mother is a great choice. Think of how much she loved you. Think of her voice, and the way it sounded when she called your name. Remember the softness and warmth of her arms when she held you close, protecting you from the cares of the world!"

"*NOOOO!!*"

"*Witchcraft! Foul* Fae *witchcraft!*"

The gun slipped from his fingers and tumbled to the carpeted floor, forgotten. Despite the strident, panic-stricken efforts of the hidden voices, more memories flooded into his mind, stirred by Mouse's words. Klard sank to his knees. His heart hammered against his ribcage; his blood pounded in his ears. The wind shrieked and howled its fury, but it paled in comparison to the building chorus of voices screeching at him.

"Get up! You'll be helpless!"

"Fight! Kill the threat! It's the only way to be safe!"

"You're going to regret this!"

But even as the voices grew louder and more dissonant, Klard sank into his own little world. All that mattered was the way his mother once held him, the sound of her voice as she sang her soft lullabies, and the merriment in her laugh whenever he made a funny face or uttered a silly sound at her.

Warm arms wrapped around his heaving shoulders and pulled him in close. A soft voice continued whispering in his ear.

"Her love for you and Valk was unconditional, unyielding, and undying! It's still there, deep inside of you. I've seen it, and I can hear it in your *ta'ir*! Make it your anchor in this storm, Captain, and no darkness, no matter how strong it is, can unmoor you!"

Klard sobbed in relief as he pressed his face into the welcoming warmth. For the first time in decades, he experienced the unconditional love of a hug from someone who accepted him for who he was, despite the unbearable weight of the countless unforgivable sins that burdened his spirit. As more and more memories of his mother — and his time with her and his baby brother — came flooding back to him, the tension melted from Klard's shoulders and back. Held in those arms, supported by the kind of quiet strength he once possessed, the voices finally fell silent.

It took several long and quiet moments before his sobs subsided and a sense of normalcy returned to his thoughts.

"What the bl—?"

Klard's words were muffled by the fabric pressing against his face. Realizing where he was, and who was holding him, Klard pushed Mouse back and staggered roughly to his feet. Swaying unsteadily, he tried to clear the fog from his thoughts.

"What in the Blazing Fires just happened?"

Before Mouse could reply, a word that the young man had used echoed in his memory — a special, secret word that he'd only ever heard one other person utter in his entire life.

"Who taught you that word—*ta'ir*? And how in creation can you hear mine?"

Clang! Clang! Clang!

The alarm bell of the ship, mixed with the thumping noises of boots and feet running in response on the deck above, competed with the shouts of surprised and scared men. Against every instinct he had, Klard fought the urge to respond to it. Instead, he advanced on Mouse.

"I need to know, boy. Where did you learn about that word?"

His arms wrapped around her slight frame, Tra'al marveled at how much her scent reminded him of the forests of Aerhythia. Memories of his time on that dangerous and wondrous island came racing back.

Ironic, he thought. *I was there to hunt down and kill her father, and now I am here, a captive myself, charged with protecting her. Is this the failure that the Wraith spoke about?* He sighed. *I certainly failed at both missions.*

His keen ears pricked up at the high-pitched cries of a flock of birds, barely audible through the heavy hull of the ship. Yet, those indistinct cries reminded him of the hauntingly beautiful cries of the countless unfamiliar creatures hiding in the lush foliage of the untouched forests of Aerhythia. The muffled shouts of the crew brought back memories of the men and orcs of his unit calling out to one another while on the march in the mist-shrouded night in order to keep from getting lost or separated. The squealing grunts of the newly restive Gretch were all too similar to the screams of his Marines and their Wilderling foes during that wild battle. Everyone in his unit had perished, except him.

Too many good Marines — Wilderlings, too — died because of that futile hunt for Sarlan. He sighed again. *Why did she pick an old, washed-up failure like me? There were others who were stronger and better than I will ever be.*

As his thoughts continued to race, Seldy burrowed her face even deeper into his neck. She slipped her bare arms around his chest and locked her hands together, clutching to him as if he was a tree and she was in danger of being blown away in a storm of sorrow.

But, Ancestors-be-burned, if she stays a captive or dies on this ship because she cares for the likes of me or that blasted wolf, all that we have sacrificed will have been for nothing. No! I have to find a way to get her to use her magick to escape this ship and go find Tegger.

Her face was pressed hard against his neck, and her arms clutched his upper torso. Her tingling warmth continued to spread throughout his body, easing the constant ache of his joints and the stiffness of his tired muscles. She seemed to be oblivious to the fact that her chest was pressed tight against his and how it reminded him of how long it had been since he had enjoyed the company of a female.

Clang! Clang! Clang!

Tra'al stiffened at the sounding of the ship's bells. Decades of military training and ingrained warrior instincts kicked in.

There's no time to waste now!

"What's that sound?" Seldy's mumbled words were thick

424

from her recent tears as she stirred from his neck. "What's wrong?"

"Lass. Don't worry about the bells; they're probably doing some sort of drills." Placing his hands on her shoulders, he pushed away from her. Suppressing a shudder, he kept his expression blank. "Perhaps if you told me or showed me how you got in here, I can help to think of ways for you to get us both out of here."

Seldy's expression brightened.

"Really?"

"Really."

She glanced towards the wolf's cage before turning her gaze back on him. She nodded, her mouth set in determination.

"But only if we can help Shadowfang, too!"

"Uh..." He coughed. "He's a wild animal...a wolf...I don't know how that would..."

"I can talk to him." Her voice was insistent as she cut him off. "He will help us fight our way free."

Tossing his hands up in surrender, Tra'al nodded, not wanting to argue. The sounds of activity above had increased. A voice called out muffled orders to man the cannons.

Could it be Tegger and Paandokh in the Sword of Mercy?

He tried to picture a small private yacht like the *Sword* daring to take on a large, fully-armed galleon like the *Hunter's Ghost*. As much as that idea gave him a flash of hope, however, he brushed it aside.

They'd be too badly outgunned! It would be sheer madness!

"Very well." He noted the wolf's bright yellow eyes staring at them from across the small hall. "I'll try to think how we might free the wolf, too. But first, how did you get out of your cell and into mine?"

"It's probably better if I show you." The cheer had returned to her voice. "That way, you'll see for yourself!"

At his grunt of agreement, Seldy scooted backwards and reached for the hem of her tunic with both hands, as if she was going to remove it.

"Wait!" He held out a hand in her direction but not before she had the hem up past her navel. "What're you doing, lass?"

Seldy giggled. "I have to be naked for the magick to work, silly."

Before he could object further, she shucked her garment in one movement and tossed it to him, her eyes sparkling with amusement.

"Of course you do." Tra'al caught the balled up tunic with one hand.

A sliver of rosy-hued light provided the only illumination in the otherwise dark hold. The slim shaft of dust-filtered light created a small, luminous pillar, right where Seldy was now kneeling. Her eyes glittered bright green, both absorbing and reflecting the morning sunlight simultaneously. It was probably just a trick of the light, but it seemed as if she was glowing.

"Please watch carefully, *Maestro*." She flashed a bright smile his way. "I'm curious as to how this process looks to someone else."

Tra'al grunted in agreement, not trusting himself to speak. It was easier than he expected to ignore the frantic sounds of the crew above preparing for battle.

"And don't worry about any expressions of pain you might see on my face," she added in a quieter tone. "It doesn't hurt nearly as much as it might seem."

"Wait, this hurts y—?"

Before he could finish his question, Seldy gave him a playful wink and closed her eyes. As she did so, the glowing outlines of a stylized owl appeared on her face and forehead. In one smooth motion, she rose to her feet and extended her arms out to either side, palms facing out.

Tra'al sat utterly still as her body began to shift and change in front of his eyes. He was transfixed by the transformation that was taking place. She shrank, her body folding in on itself even as the tiny hairs all over her body sprouted thick and full before thickening into feathers.

A chill ran down his spine, making all of the hair on his own body stand on end. His nostrils widened, capturing the host of strange scents flooding the stale air of the hold. His keen ears picked up the painful sounds of bones and cartilage popping and cracking.

Her arms expanded downward and outward, extending into wings. Her breasts flattened and became covered in feathers before expanding with the muscles and sinew needed to power those wings. Her feet lengthened and then shriveled into bird-like proportions while her toenails erupted into the deadly talons an owl needed to capture its prey. But it was Seldy's face that captured Tra'al's full attention.

Her expression changed a dozen times in less than a second, flashing a look of dogged determination followed in quick succession by grimaces of pain before her last recognizable expression, that of pure, ecstatic joy, was erased by the formation of a sharp, hooked beak where her soft lips had been.

Before he could process the impossible feat he'd just witnessed, he was staring at a small, silver-feathered owl that blinked at him with enormous green eyes. It cocked its head and hooted at him before folding its wings and taking a couple of short hops towards him.

"Hoo! Hoo!"

Tra'al fought the desperate urge to jump back. Every fiber of his being screamed out that what he'd just seen was impossible. He remained rooted in place, however, as he tried to make sense of it all.

"Seldy?" He extended a tentative hand towards the creature. "Is that you? Can you understand me?"

The owl took two more hops, hooting each time. When she was close enough, she pressed the top of her tufted head against his outstretched palm.

The same kind of tingling energy flowed from the owl into his hand. Tra'al arched an eyebrow, studying her new form. He leaned down to look into her eyes, hoping to cover the movement of his free hand.

"Now I can see how you slipped out of your cell and into mine." He nodded towards the bars. "You shifted into this form and used the tunic to keep the iron from burning you, didn't you?"

"Hoo! Hoo!" she cooed at him excitedly, dancing from one talon to the other.

Tra'al found the balled up tunic with his free hand just as a massive shadow passed over the shaft of light, momentarily throwing the hold into utter darkness.

Taking advantage of the owl's surprise, Tra'al swept the tunic over her head, quickly wrapping her in the fabric before she could gather the wit or the strength to fight her way free.

"Listen, lass," Tra'al hissed at the struggling form of the owl. "This ship is under attack! Do you understand me?"

The owl stopped struggling. A single, muffled sound emerged from beneath the tunic.

"Hoo."

"Good, then I need you to do exactly as I say." He had to raise his voice to be heard over the cacophony created by the squealing of the crazed boar and the growling of the wolf. "I'm going to push you back through the bars of this cell. You need to fly up into the rafters and hide in the shadows until one of those damn doors open! Then you need to fly through it and get off of this damn ship and go find Tegger Dan as fast as your wings can carry you!"

Without waiting for Seldy to respond, he crawled over and

pushed the bundled owl through the bars of his cell. It took more than a little effort, especially since she started to struggle. His greater strength, however, won at the cost of a few minor scratches on his hand. Once she popped through, he twisted the tunic open and dumped her fluttering and rumpled form onto the floor of the narrow hall. Before she could do more than right herself, he pulled the tunic back through the bars. He held it up for her to see.

"I figure that you can't stand the touch of iron long enough to try coming back through those bars without this." He gave her a hard look before nodding towards the rafters. "So get up there and hide, lass!"

Tra'al couldn't be certain, but the set of the owl's shoulders showed defiance.

BOOM!

Seldy jumped at the loud explosion, hooting in surprise before launching into the air on silent flapping wings.

Mouse stared up at him, his soft brown eyes wide.

"Well?" Klard demanded, his patience wearing thin as the sounds of alarm wore on his nerves. "Where did you learn of that word?"

"My dreams!"

The young man tried to slip backwards, but Klard cut him off by grabbing the front of his tunic and pinning him in place against the front of his desk.

"Don't you try to bamboozle me, boy!" He shook the boy roughly. "No one learns a long-forgotten and foreign word like that in their dreams!"

Boots hammered against the deck above their heads. Haddock shouted for men to arm the cannons as yet others called out words that sent chills down his spine.

"Oh shite! It's a murder of Gargoyles!"

"Shards! There's Harpies, too!"

But Klard couldn't let go of that word, not when it was so tied up with his most cherished memories. His mother had often cuddled him close as she read stories to him of that time long ago when the world was whole and full of wonderful, mysterious music. Her tales of the ancient doings of the people of that long dead world were so full of rich detail that it had been like he was there, witnessing history. When she described to him how every person had a *ta'ir* — a special and private song that reflected all of their deepest truths and inner emotions — she had been driving home a powerful lesson of how important it was to be true to himself and to align his words and actions with his heart because there had once been a few truly special individuals who could hear the *ta'irs* of other people. She used to place her warm hands over his little ears and press her lips to his forehead.

Rehlo, *I just know that your* ta'ir *is sweet and pure. I love you so very much.*

"Captain, I'm telling you the truth!" Mouse's eyes darted towards the broken window and the billowing curtains. "I can... try...to tell you more later, but we're in terrible danger! The Enemy — the same foe that was killing your brother — is coming for her right now!"

Furrowing his brow, Klard snapped, "Who is coming for who?"

"It's Drak'nuul! He's coming for the *Fae* captive!"

Blinking, Klard stared at the boy in disbelief.

"Don't you try to scare me with the name of some long-dead boogey-man!" Spittle flew from his lips. He pushed a finger into Mouse's scrawny chest. "Drak'nuul was defeated and slain in the Founder's War between the Guild Alliance and those bastard *Myrkuul* over three hundred and fifty some blazing years ago!"

Overhead, Haddock's voice cut through everything.

"Fire!"

BOOM!

The ship rocked from the blast of the cannon, snapping Klard back to his senses.

"Blazing Fires, boy!" He pushed Mouse back, releasing his jacket as he did so. "I'll settle up with you later. I've got a battle to fight." He waved a hand towards his brother's room. "You stay here and watch over Valk. Make sure that nothing happens to him, blast you!"

Swinging around without even bothering to see if the boy had acknowledged his orders, Klard stalked over towards his fallen pistol and bent down to pick it up.

"Captain! Watch out!"

Something slammed into him from behind with enough force to knock Klard off-balance and send him sprawling. He caught a glimpse of Mouse's bare feet on the way down.

But before he could roll over, a massive shadow darkened the entire frame of the shattered window. Wood splintered and glass crunched as a monstrous form burst through the frame and landed with a jarring thud where Klard had been standing. The beast — the biggest, nastiest looking gargoyle he'd ever seen — stared down at him with red, glowing eyes before turning its gaze on Mouse.

"Son of a bitch!" Snarling his words, Klard scrambled for his fallen pistol. Once his fingers wrapped around the familiar weapon, he rolled over and raised it up. "Die, you bastard!"

The creature's misshapen head swung around, and those baleful eyes flashed. Its mouth opened, and the most horrendous screech Klard had ever heard erupted from it.

The horrible sound washed over him, opening the floodgates in his mind...

THUNK!

He watched in horror as his father smashed his fist into his mother's face, sending her crashing to the floor.

"Blast you, bitch!" His father's voice reverberated off the walls of the nursery. "How many times do I have to tell you to stop sissifying my boys!"

"No, Daddy!" Klard, just seven-years-old, cried out as he rushed forward to get in the way of his father's onrushing boot.

"Get away, boy!" He was swept aside by a meaty hand. "I'm teaching your whore of a mother her lessons!"

THUD!

His mother exhaled a whimpering grunt as she collapsed around the boot that landed in her gut.

From the crib nearby, baby Valk's tremulous cries cut through every other sound...

He was small and weak and helpless, no more able to stop what was going on than the seven-year-old boy who was brushed aside by his monstrous father.

Movement crossed in front of Klard's eyes, but he couldn't make out who or what it was.

Something crashed, hard and loud, beyond his clouded vision.

Mouse called out to him. "Remember her love for you, Captain, not her pain!"

Another crash and roar interrupted his words.

"...fight the fear with love!"

"FOOLISH BOY!" A thunderous voice filled the room with rage. "THAT WEAKLING CANNOT STAND AGAINST MY POWER! I HAVE GROOMED HIM FOR YEARS!"

Klard struggled to blink, to move even a single muscle. His

arms shook, growing weaker by the moment. Another memory crashed into him...

His mother stared in his direction with unseeing, vacant eyes. Her normal, rosy complexion now blotched with mottled spots of dark grey. Her hair — once brown and lustrous — hung limp and grey against her forehead. Every rattling breath was labored.

"Mama," Klard whispered as he brushed her hair back. "I'm here." He swallowed the lump that formed in his throat. "Can I get you anything?"

Drawing a shallow breath between bouts of coughing, his mother stirred at his voice.

"Is th-...is th-...is that my...dear...sweet...Klard?"

"Yes, Mama."

"Come...closer...rehlo..."

He leaned in even closer, pressing his forehead to her limp hand, ignoring the strict orders of the herbalist to avoid touching her at all costs.

"I'm here, Mama."

"I...need...you...to...promise...me..." She licked her dry, cracked lips with a swollen tongue. "Promise...me...that...you'll love...Valk...take...care...of...him..."

Klard's throat closed up. His younger brother was scrambling up into the bed, crying for her.

"Mama!"

He had to be strong. He had to be. For her. For Valk.

"I prom—"

The door behind him crashed open. Klard flinched back, knowing what was coming.

"By the Shards of Luna, you stupid boys!" There was no mistaking his father's voice. "Get your blasted arses away from her before you get the rest of us sick!"

"*But, Fa—*"
SMACK!

Shadows swirled, barely seen.
Winds howled, protesting their confinement.
A voice thundered; it's words unheeded.
Wood splintered; glass shattered.
And hungry flames danced.

The hungry flames danced, licking their way up the pyre towards the shrouded form of Mama laying still and silent just above them.

Valk cried out, struggling to free himself from the strong hand that gripped his shoulder.

"*No burn, Mama!*"

Klard's eyes burned, not from fire but from the forbidden tears that leaked from them. Father's other hand clutched hard at his shoulder, but he made no move towards the growing flames. He choked back a sob, knowing that Father was watching...and judging.

Father knelt down, turning his hard gaze from Valk to Klard, taking their measure.

"*Remember this day, son.*" *His deep voice was low and hushed. "Remember this pain, and how it unmans you.*"

"*But, Father...*" *His protest was silenced by the tightening grip on his shoulder.*

"*Love is for fools and women.*" *Father spat out the last word like it was a curse. "Dry those tears and listen to me. As your father, boy, I don't need or want your love. I demand your respect, your loyalty and, most important of all, your obedience.*"

Father was staring into his eyes, holding his own gaze from watching his mother's body burn.

"Show me those things. Become the man I need you to be. And help me take House Dastyr to the heights of power and influence that we deserve."

Klard could only nod before turning back to helplessly watch the hungry flames dance ever closer to the one person in the whole world who loved him unconditionally.

"AARRGGHH!"

The cry of pain was punctuated by the crashing of a heavy form against wood. Flames danced, fed by the blistering wind. A flailing shadow blocked both the light and the wind.

"Remember her love for you, Captain," the soft, warm voice whispered breathlessly in his ear as arms wrapped around him from behind. Sure hands steadied his tiring arms, the pistol still held within his weakening grasp. "I can hear her in your *ta'ir*. She's always been there. Let her love for you be the anchor you need in this storm, Captain. Let it be your strength. Listen for her."

Klard strained to hear anything above the whipping winds and the restless thrashing about of a large, heavy form.

"I...can't...hear...her."

"Shhh." Mouse shifted behind him, bringing his bloody and blistered hands over Klard's eyes. "Ignore what's going on and look and listen within. She's calling out to you. Listen with your heart."

A strange calm descended over Klard, as if Mouse's fingers could block out the troubles of the world. Somehow, despite everything that was going on around him, he felt safe, if only for the briefest of moments. The wind stopped howling. The sounds of battle, both above and within this room, died down. The world fell quiet and still. All he heard was Mouse's heavy breathing and his own heartbeat pounding in his ears.

Deep inside, something stirred — a soft, feminine laugh; a gentle, cooing whisper; the quiet notes of a familiar lullaby.

I will love you forever, my little rehlo.

The sweet, pure sound of his mother's voice reverberated throughout his being, filling him with renewed strength. Her love enveloped him like a warm blanket on a cold night.

You will always be close to my heart, no matter the time and distance that may come to separate us.

His heart swelled. The realization hit him of just how broken and incomplete he had been. How empty he had felt inside. A tremendous weight lifted from his shoulders. Klard felt his spirit begin to expand, filling his body near to bursting with renewed strength.

Shifting behind him, Mouse dropped his hands from Klard's blurry eyes.

"Look now!"

At first, he could just make out the indistinct struggling form of the gargoyle as it fought to extinguish the last of the oil-fed flames that had been burning its head and chest.

"Use both your eyes and your heart, Captain, and you'll see this monster for who and what he truly is." Speaking just loud enough to be heard over the roar of wind and beast, the strange boy's words spilled out in a breathless rush. "The physical form is only a shell, inhabited now by Drak'nuul, the same creature who has been stealing your brother away from you. He's been using both of you to get to the *Fae* woman you have imprisoned, and he's not going to stop until he has her."

The last of the veiling shadows over his vision dropped away, allowing the scene before him to come into sharp focus. The gargoyle struggled to remove the remnants of the smoldering curtains from its head. It crouched near the shattered frame of the window and tore at the offending fabric with tooth, horn, and claw.

As the last tattered shreds of cloth were blown free by the

unrelenting wind, Klard got a good a look at the gargoyle. The mottled, charcoal grey skin, corded muscles, and massive, bat-like wings were all typical of other gargoyles he had seen. The iron collar around its neck, and the thick shackles on each wrist and ankle, were not. Ebon horns sprouted from its forehead, curling back around dog-like ears to end in wicked, forward-angled points. But it wasn't the horns or the fangs that captured Klard's attention. It was the glowing red eyes and the waves of malevolent dread rolling off of the creature.

"YOU WILL NOT STAND BETWEEN ME AND MY BRIDE ANY LONGER, MORTAL FOOLS!"

As the gargoyle focused its rage back on them, Mouse remained calm, pushing them both to their feet, his breath hot against Klard's ear.

"Hold on, sir, and remember her love for you!"

The creature opened its maw, letting forth the same kind of screeching cry that had paralyzed Klard before. The wall of sound smashed into him, pushing him back a step. But Mouse was there, arms still wrapped around him from behind, somehow both supporting and shielding him from the full power of the creature's attack. This time, instead of memories of helpless fear, he only saw his mother's soft brown eyes and gentle smile.

"IMPOSSIBLE! YOU CANNOT BE THIS STRONG!"

"You were too small to stop the monster who beat your mother," Mouse said, his voice strong and firm. "But right here, right now, you can stop this one."

Klard's hands were still wrapped around the handle of his pistol. Squinting, he aimed and squeezed the trigger just as the creature gathered itself to leap forward. The pistol flashed and bucked in his hand, its roar muffled by the myriad of conflicting sounds already swirling around the once tidy chamber.

The creature stiffened and spun to the side, staggering as its head snapped around with the impact of the bullet.

"Die, you bastard!" Klard roared. "Die!"

He dropped the pistol and tore free from Mouse. He crashed into the beast shoulder first. The creature staggered back, clutching at the shattered sides of the windows with desperate claws.

Hammering away, Klard pounded at those clawed hands with balled fists and booted feet until the creature's grasp weakened, and the wind snatched the dying beast from the threshold to send it tumbling into the void below.

Breathless, Klard collapsed to his knees, completely drained. He would've tumbled after the creature if Mouse hadn't pulled him back to safety.

CHAPTER 35

Mouse

*B*OOM!

The cannon blast reverberated through the wind-tossed room, slamming into Mouse's consciousness. The whole ship rocked. The captain jerked in his trembling arms. Every muscle in his body ached. He was bone-weary. His stomach grumbled. Blood trickled down his back, leaking from the reopened scabs from the whipping that seemed so long ago. The burning in the fingers and palm of his left hand grew worse every time he tried to flex it, but he knew that if he didn't keep moving it, scabs would form, and he would lose the ability to use it without tearing them open. The somewhat pleasant buzz from the *va'areshi* liquor had long since worn off. His head throbbed.

The captain stirred again in his arms, mumbling something, but even if Mouse could've heard him over the rushing wind and the horrific din of the battle taking place around them, he was lost to the chaos of the soundscape. The screams and screeches of men and beasts fighting and dying on deck were nothing more than tinny notes in a concert that only he and the Enemy seemed to perceive. Buffeted by waves of thunderous and discordant notes of the *ta'irs* of the combatants above and around him, Mouse experienced the conflict in ways that he would've thought impossible before freeing Seldy from that collar.

The piercing agony of a bullet tearing through a gargoyle felt as fresh and raw to him as his own reopened wounds. The sudden, eerie silencing of each *ta'ir* — both familiar and otherwise — snuffed out by tooth and claw or blade and bullet stung like a fresh slap across the face.

Yet, through all of it — the pain, the exhaustion, the sheer chaos of the battle — Mouse's attention was focused on understanding the moment when the Enemy's host body had stood dying in the shattered frame of the window, just before the captain had thrown himself recklessly at the beast.

His ta'ir *changed in that moment...but why?* He lingered on that moment and the strange shift he felt in the song of the Enemy. *All of his defenses opened up, and his* ta'ir *became coherent for a moment. I wonder if I can use that?*

Before he could ponder that thought any further, the captain pushed away and staggered to his feet. He grabbed Mouse by the shoulders and shook him.

"Mouse!" he shouted loud enough to be heard over the wind. "Answer me, blast it! Did that gargoyle cut you with its claws?"

"No, I don't think so. Why?"

"Those things have poison in their claws, stuff that'll kill you right quick! Even a single scratch can leave you dead within a day unless it's caught soon and cleaned out properly."

The captain's eyes scanned Mouse from battered and bruised head to bloody toes. When he seemed satisfied that Mouse hadn't been scratched, he looked at him with a new respect.

"I'd like nothing more than to talk about what just happened, Mouse, but my ship and crew are in danger. I need to get out there and lead that fight."

Mouse took a deep breath and swallowed down his own questions.

"Wait in there." He waved towards his brother's room again. "Watch over Valk until we cleanse the ship of these blasted vermin. I can't risk losing you, Mouse. When you heal up, we'll sit down and talk about…well, everything." The captain's voice softened with those last words.

"No." Mouse didn't shout his reply. He simply spoke his truth.

The captain stood up to his full height, blinking. All hints of any softness gone as his reply came out in a low, dangerous voice that was echoed in his *ta'ir*.

"What did you just say?"

BOOM!

"Aaaiieee!"

Mouse swayed on unsteady feet as the ship rocked again, but he stood his ground even as the captain loomed closer.

"No. I'm sorry, Captain, but I can't."

"You can't?" The big man bristled with outrage. "What do you mean 'you can't?' You can't what?"

"I can't stay here, sir. There's something more important that I have to do."

Without waiting for the captain's reaction to his response, Mouse stepped around the big man and darted through the doorway leading to the private quarters of the captain and his brother. Once inside the small hallway, he picked up the burlap sack containing his supplies. When he turned around, the captain was standing there, blocking the way to the rest of the ship with his massive frame. His curved swords were drawn, one held in each fist.

"Where do you think you're going, boy?"

The growled question stopped Mouse in his tracks as much as the big man's armed, intimidating bulk did.

Mouse stood up as straight as his aching body would allow.

"I have to get her off of this ship!"

"Who? The *Fae* girl? Off of this ship?" Each rapid fire question came out harsher than the last. "How in the blazes...?" The big man's song spiked.

Ignoring the man's outburst, Mouse moved to slip past the captain but a quickly raised sword stopped him cold.

"I don't know how yet!" Swinging his bag, Mouse slapped the exposed blade aside, shouting his reply. "All I know is that I have to get her off of this ship, or we're all going to die!" He pressed himself into the bulk of the captain's frame, backing the bigger man up through sheer determination and outrage. "Every! Last! One! Of! Us!"

"Who the in the name of the Found God do you think you are...?"

Pressed back against the door frame leading into his ruined office, the captain roared and punched Mouse in the chest with a double-fisted jab and with the basket-hilts of both swords. The captain's turbulent *ta'ir* flared outward in indignation, hitting him with even more force than his fists did.

"You owe me your life, blast you!"

Staggered by the blow, Mouse stumbled backwards and sank to one knee. The unrelenting sounds of the raging battle hammered away at his senses. Pain radiated from every one of his various bruises and wounds, both new and old. Exhaustion pulled at each of his limbs, making them heavy and unresponsive. Doubt gnawed at his mind, and guilt tugged at his pounding heart. He dropped his head and closed his eyes.

It would be so easy, he thought, *to surrender and wait here.*

A single tear leaked from his unbruised eye. It trickled down his cheek and fell to the floor.

Kerplunk.

The tiny sound of the teardrop splashing on the wood reverberated.

Time slowed.

The sound washed over him, evoking a series of images that blocked everything else out.

...of two blonde-haired women cooing over him long ago in a faraway cavern...of the Shining Lady's crystalline eyes beseeching him to help her daughter...of the desperation in the green eyes of a collared, nearly naked silver-haired young woman locked in a cell...of that same woman, standing tall and defiant in the face of impossible odds, surrounded only by the animals who were defending her...

The sounds of battle dissipated. The wind died down. There was no pain. Even the captain's *ta'ir* became still, freezing in place within the soundscape. Strands of the man's song lit up, glowing softly in the background. Opening all of his senses up, Mouse recognized them as bits of the captain's psyche that had only just been repaired. They stood out like loose threads that could be yanked out to unravel an otherwise solid and strong piece of fabric.

If I just reach out and pull those, I can get him out of my way!

The realization sent a cold chill down Mouse's spine.

I can make him do what I want him to do! What I NEED him to do!

The temptation was so strong that it was palpable. It would be so easy...

::YES!::

::Bend him to your will!::

::He is weak, and you are strong! The weak must always serve the strong!::

Mouse didn't need to look around to know that the hallway had grown darker. Shadows gathered, filling in the tight space and feeding on the raw anger, fear, and frustration thrumming through his body.

"NO!" His defiant shout shattered the moment, blasting shards of sound outward in a manifestation of all of the emotional and physical pain he had suffered in the last few days. Shredded by the eruption, the shadows fled, their pleading cries silenced.

The captain staggered back, blinking, as if he'd been punched between the eyes. Rushing forward, Mouse reached out and steadied the bigger man, capturing his eyes with his gaze.

"Captain, there's no more time to explain any more than this — that *Fae* prisoner is the reason that all of this is happening! I know you thought you were capturing her to get back at Tegger Dan, but you were being deceived! I've heard your song! I know that you're a good man, not some slaver who would sell an innocent person for profit! But none of that matters now! She's the reason I can hear your *ta'ir* and could give your mother's love back to you! She's got some kind of special magick that needs to be unlocked so that she can make things right in the world again, and I have to help her do that." Mouse had never felt more sure of anything before in his life. "Except Drak'nuul is coming for her, and nothing will stop him from trying to enslave or kill anyone who stands in his way! I have to get her off of this ship, somehow, someway!"

Seeing the captain's confusion, Mouse pressed in closer.

"You've got a battle to fight and a ship to save, but you won't be able to succeed in that as long as she's on it."

He loosened his fingers from the captain's jacket, blinking in surprise at the strength of his passion and the conviction in his words.

"You've grown, Mouse." The captain stared back at him, his demeanor softening. "You're not that scared little stowaway boy who runs from every fight any more, are you?"

"No. I'm not." Stepping back, Mouse squared his shoulders. "I'm a Guardian — her Guardian — whatever that means." He cleared his throat. "And I need to help her to find a way to beat the Enemy."

The big man stood staring at him, visibly torn. He sucked in a deep breath and exhaled it slowly. Mouse sensed the shift in his *ta'ir* as all of the chaos and turmoil of the moment fell away and the previously scattered notes of his song fell into a calm, deliberate pattern reflective of an earlier time in his life. It wasn't the bristly captain and jaded bounty hunter who stood before him now, but the essence of a young, clean-shaven Marine recruit, brimming with purpose and a clear conscience.

The captain stepped back out of the hallway and pointed towards his desk.

"In the same drawer you found your flute, there's a ring of keys and a heavy bundle wrapped in black cloth." He paused, his gruff manner battling to reassert itself, yet failing. "The bundle is Tra'al's. The rescue skiff is just outside the stable hold. It's big enough for the three of you. He will know how to operate it."

In the blink of an eye, the rough-hewn, hard-edged man returned. His eyes narrowed as the sounds of the nearly forgotten battle raging overhead returned with a renewed violence.

"Go on now, Guardian, before I come to my senses and change my mind."

The captain turned toward the exit, swords in hand. He glanced back at Mouse just before reaching the door to the outer hall. He raised his swords and crossed them in a solemn salute.

"My crew and I will buy you as much time as we can!"

CHAPTER 36

Seldy, Mouse

*B*OOM!
"Watch out!"

"Reload!"

"There's too many!"

"Hold on!"

"Aaaiiieee!"

"Alrighty, boys!" A dreaded and familiar voice boomed above her. "Let's get these vermin off of my ship!"

Bang!

"To the Captain! Rally to the Captain!"

Tucked into the darkest, smallest corner of the rafters that her owl form could fit into, Seldy flinched with each scream, shouted curse, and ear-splitting battle cry. The whole ship rocked with each deafening blast of the cannon. Wood groaned. Metal screeched. Bodies thumped to the deck above. Unable to shut off the horrible sounds of the raging battle, she dug into the rotting wood of the rafters with sharp talons and opened her wings as far as she could in the tight space.

Retreating within, Seldy's thoughts drifted back to her time with the Elder Spirits, reflecting on what she had learned of her new gifts...

Mouse crept down the darkened hallway with all of the skill and stealth of his namesake. The battle between the crew — now led by Captain Dastyr — and the Enemy's minions raged on above him. The cannons had fallen silent, but the occasional sharp crack of a pistol still cut through both the rallying cries of the men and the screams of the wounded.

Despite his best efforts to shut it out, the ebb and flow of the struggle for the ship continued to press against his consciousness. Before the captain arrived on deck, the crew had been on the edge of defeat, overwhelmed both by the number and ferocity of their foes. The momentum of the fight, however, swung back in their favor when the captain announced his presence with a bellow punctuated by the sharp report of his pistol.

Something heavy crashed onto the deck just above and ahead of him. Mouse flinched. Wood cracked and splintered. A muffled, gurgling scream slipped through the gaps in the wood. The cry ended at the same moment that Jigger's song faded from the soundscape. Swallowing the lump in his throat, Mouse shifted his attention towards the ceiling.

They're dying up there! Am I just running away again?

Blood dripped down onto the floor ahead of him through a fresh crack in the thick slats of the deck above. Through the soundscape, Mouse felt the struggle of a strange creature overhead, trying to extricate its sharp claws from the decking beneath Jigger's body. The wood groaned in protest. That struggle, however, ended with an angry bark of a nearby pistol. Yet another *ta'ir* fell silent.

Sucking in his bottom lip, Mouse bit down on it in order to keep himself from crying out at the suffering above him.

"I'm not running away, blast it! I'm running to *her!*" He clenched his fingers into tight fists and hissed, "Their sacrifices have to mean something!"

Readjusting the bag of pilfered supplies slung over his left shoulder, Mouse winced at the shooting pain in his raw, bleeding hand and the way the weight of the bag rubbed against the reopened scabs on his back. He stepped around the growing pool of blood and continued down the hall.

As he approached the open archway leading into the Mess, a heavy thud splintered wood somewhere ahead of him. A primal, high-pitched screech tore through the darkness, followed by Cook's booming voice.

"Get out of here, you blasted flying rodent!"

He couldn't see the struggle that was taking place, but the burning hunger of the creature hunting Cook was overwhelming. Mouse dropped to his knees, clutching his gut as wave after wave of stomach-churning pangs washed over him. The rage and anger of Cook's song fueled the big man as he turned and stood his ground against the ravenous beast.

Thunk! Screech!

The sound of a cleaver striking flesh followed by the creature's cry of pain paled in comparison to the blast of agonized notes that dominated its *ta'ir*. The pain, however, only drove the beast inexorably forward.

Rip! Grunt! Crash!

Through the curse of his gift, Mouse both felt and heard the wet slurping sound of razor sharp claws slicing through the copious layers of gelatinous fat wrapped around Cook's body. The big man staggered back, crashing into the wooden wall between them, and slumped to the floor.

"Blast you!" Cook's words burbled out in a thick, wet tone that ended in a gasp.

The creature trumpeted out its victory, banishing the haze of its own pain as it prepared to feast on its prey.

Mouse's gut churned. Bile burned the back of his throat. Lowering his bag to the floor, he reached for his flute — the only weapon he had. Wincing at the stiffness and pain in the fingers of his left hand, he stretched the hand as he concentrated on separating the sonic signatures of man and beast, looking for some clue for how to scare the creature away.

Cook's fading *ta'ir* was nearly as dark as Valk's, colored by his constant suspicions and outright hatred of nearly everyone around him. While the creature's song was alien, the raw and primal nature of its drives, motivations, and feelings made it easy to locate and mimic if he found something he could use.

Despite how dark and confusing the predator's song was, Mouse plunged his consciousness into it. The first wave of the creature's most recent memories were as shocking as they were vivid. It had endured an unending stream of torturous confinement, unrelenting hunger, and painful beatings administered by the same hooded figures with harsh voices, tattooed faces, and cruel, glittering eyes that he had seen before. Despite the fact that it was looking to eat Cook, Mouse shuddered in sympathy for the gargoyle.

Steeling himself, Mouse pushed deeper. He sifted through the flood of gory memories of it feasting on the carcasses of past kills and slipped past the recollections of the battles for dominance and the frenzied mating sessions that often followed those feasts. Something else, something more important, echoed in the furthest depths of the gargoyle's consciousness. Digging deep into the roots of its earliest memories Mouse found it — a sound that no young gargoyle survived without learning to heed and flee from.

There! That's what I need!

Pulling back within himself, Mouse immediately set to re-creating that sound. Pursing his lips against the sound hole of the instrument, he began to blow a rapid series of high-pitched notes.

The notes were almost too short and clipped to be recognizable as music. They were barely audible and sounded more like unintelligible clicking than notes of a song played on a flute. Nevertheless, the gargoyle reacted immediately, pulling back from his victim and taking up a defensive position. It hissed, cowering behind an overturned table.

Increasing the volume and varying the pattern of the strange, clipped notes so that some of them were longer than others, Mouse stood up and moved closer to the edge of the archway.

Howling in fear, the gargoyle burst from the mess hall, crashing into the wall in front of him. In its haste to escape the perceived threat, the gargoyle didn't look in Mouse's direction. Instead, it skittered away from him in a mad scramble of flailing limbs and flapping wings. Its claws gouging furrows in the wood of the hallway with each panicked step.

Once he was certain the creature had fled, Mouse slipped the flute back into his jacket, scooped up his bag, and braced himself for what he was about to see. He took a hesitant step forward, rounding the corner to the Mess.

"Hold on, Cook! I'm coming!"

Cook had ruled the galley of the *Hunter's Ghost* with an iron fist longer than Mouse had been alive but now he leaned against the far wall with his throat torn open. Blood soaked the front of the man's apron as it often did, but this time it was his own rather than the splatter created from butchering the carcass of some other poor beast. The huge man's vacant eyes stared back at him, his mouth moving as he tried to say something.

Dodging around the scattered benches and overturned tables, Mouse rushed over to kneel in front of the wounded man. He was greeted, however, with a look of spite.

Doing his best to ignore the man's hate, Mouse studied the thick gashes in his throat. He was horrified to see flashes of white bone and moving strands of red sinew amidst the carnage. Blood seeped out in places and spurted weakly from one side. He'd never seen anyone survive a wound like that before, but that didn't stop him from reaching for the bottom of Cook's apron, hoping to use it to staunch the flow of blood.

"I'm so sorry, Cook..." He swallowed hard as his throat tried to close up in sympathy. "I don't know if I can..."

His words were cut off as the bigger man's hands came up and grabbed the front of his jacket, yanking him close enough for Mouse to smell his fetid breath. Cook's *ta'ir* spiked, growing as strong and turbulent as his grip. It was full of dark and angry notes that slammed into Mouse's consciousness with vitriol and contempt.

"...it's...all...your...fault...stower..."

Blood gurgled up through his mouth, spattering on Mouse's face as he tried to pull free, but the big man's grip was too strong.

"...you...doomed...us...all...when...the...Cap'n...let...you...live..."

Hate fueled Cook's gaze and his grip as he pulled Mouse even closer. Stunned at the unyielding strength of the dying man's anger towards him, Mouse kept struggling.

"...knew...you were...nothing...but a...blasted thief...and a...traitor..."

Cook's *ta'ir* fell silent at the same moment his strength gave out. Mouse fell hard on his backside, then scrambled back. The combination of the man's palpable hatred, the sight of his gory wound, and the jarring impact was just too much. His stomach lurched. It was all Mouse could do to turn his head to the side and retch up the burning bile that was all that remained of the orcish liquor.

Pushing up with quivering arms, Mouse forced himself to unsteady feet. He staggered over to collect his fallen sack, picked it up, and turned to face his former nemesis one last time.

"After all of the times you turned me in to get whipped by Haddock," Mouse said in a low whisper. "I don't know why I feel like I should be apologizing to you." He shook his head. "But, for what it's worth..." He swallowed the leftover bile still tickling the back of his throat. "I'm sorry you never discovered what it is to love or be loved."

KA-RUMP!

The first shuddering impact on the door at the far end of the room startled Seldy into ruffling her feathers and dancing from talon to talon.

"Watch for your chance, lass!" Tra'al whispered just loud enough for her keen ears to hear him. "Remember what I told you!"

KA-RUMP!

The door bowed inward under the force of the impact. Wood splintered and groaned in protest. The boar snorted and squealed, gnashing his tusks against the bars of his cage. Shadowfang crouched in the back of his cage, his teeth bared as he turned to stared up at her between growls.

::Flee when you can, Shapesister! You cannot face what comes on your own!::

The battle continued to rage overhead. The wooden beam beneath her talons vibrated from the ruckus above her. Feet stamped. Guns fired. Bodies thudded to the deck.

CRASH!

The door exploded inward in a shower of broken boards, splinters, and a tangle of snarling limbs and bony, flapping wings. Despite the darkness, Seldy noted the razor-sharp claws and teeth, feral eyes, and brooding hunger of what was clearly an apex predator of some kind. Even as she recognized the creature as something similar to the flying beasts that the Enemy had sent after Uncle Tegger, her owl instincts took over. She hooded her bright eyes down to mere slits and slipped further back into the little crevice she'd found between the ceiling and the rafter.

Rising to its feet, the creature shook itself like a dog coming out of the rain, sending bits of metal and splinters of wood flying in all directions. It opened its wings and rose to its full, man-sized height, bellowing out its rage in a horrible shriek that resonated throughout the entire chamber.

Raising its head, the beast sniffed the air and turned its attention towards the nearest occupied cage. The boar squealed and snorted, backing up as far as he could. Crying out, the creature slashed at the bars between itself and the boar. Sparks flew as the creature's talons struck iron. While the bars rattled and the boar squealed in fear, the battered cage withstood the assault.

::*What kind of monster is that?*:: she projected her question to the wolf.

::*Still your mind and be silent!*:: Shadowfang's harsh rebuke was accompanied by a low growl as he crept forward in a low crouch, his eyes focused on the creature.

"You want some of this nasty old orc-meat, you stinking gargoyle?" Tra'al called out in a defiant voice as he came to the front of his cell and rattled a tin cup along the bars. "Once it's past you, lass," he added in a quieter tone, "flee, just like I said! Go and find that uncle of yours!"

The gargoyle swung around, spread its wings, and leapt at the wolf's cage in a gliding lunge. The beast moved with surprising quickness, crashing into the top and side of the cage and plunging its razor-sharp claws between the bars.

As quick and wily as the beast was, however, Shadowfang was quicker and smarter. The wolf whirled around, dodging each attack, yet somehow finding the time to snap with his own snarling jaws. He ripped a patch of tough hide from the back of one of the beast's claw-tipped hands.

The gargoyle roared, jerking its damaged hand back even as it lashed out again with its other set of claws. Shadowfang slipped away from that attack, slamming his body against the back of his cage in the process. The bars of the wolf's cage rattled and protested with each renewed attack from the creature and each snarling and snapping response from Shadowfang.

"Flee now, lass!" Tra'al shouted. "While it's distracted!"

Tra'al's yell snapped Seldy out of watching the mesmerizing struggle between the two deadly predators.

Flee? she wanted to cry out, but the instincts of her owl form kept any sound from escaping her hooked beak. *I can't flee! I need to help fight!* Seldy wriggled forward, desperately looking for a way to help Shadowfang. *I can't watch another friend die!*

Sinking her talons into the wood of the rafter, Seldy fought against the white hot anger that burned inside of her. She wanted nothing more than to shift into her wolf or tiger form and attack the creature who was threatening her pack. As she prepared to do so, however, her last exchange with Layra in the grove of the Elder Spirits came bubbling up to the surface of her thoughts...

::*Each of your forms, Cubling, offers unique skills and abilities. The owl will be your wisest form, the one where you must exercise patience and careful thought. The wolf is strong and can be used to run or perhaps fight as part of a larger group. The tigress, my form, will be your strongest and most dangerous form, but it will not be easy to harness the strength, speed, and instincts of a fully grown tigress. It will be all-too-easy to lose yourself when those instincts take over. Tigers are territorial and solitary hunters. We slay without mercy using tooth, claw, and overpowering strength. Draw upon the strength and ferocity of the tigress when you must. But remember this — even in*

the fiercest battle you must always keep love in your heart and remember who you truly are or you will risk bringing harm to those you care for. If you fall prey to the temptations of the Enemy, you will doom everything and everyone you hold dear. Do not surrender to fear. Do not fight out of anger.::

"But how..." she whispered. "...How do I keep love in my heart when the people I love are being hurt? How can I fight against someone — and kill them when I must — without feeling fear or anger?"

::When there is no choice in the matter, fight for something or someone — fight to protect your own life or to save someone else's. Fight to defend others who are threatened and cannot protect themselves.:: Layra's rusty, rumbling purr filled Seldy's ears. *::Look within yourself, Cubling. If you cannot find a noble and loving reason in your heart to fight for, then you should flee or avoid conflict altogether.::*

Would attacking that creature be out of love or anger? I love Tra'al and Shadowfang, and I don't want to see them in danger. But I'm afraid for them, too! She wrestled with the conflicting emotions. *Oh, Layra? How do I know what to do?*

"Blast it, lass! Get ou—!"

Tra'al broke down in a hacking cough after yelling at the top of his lungs. He dropped his tin cup and fell to his knees. Clutching at the bars in the front of his cell, he was bent over, seemingly unable to catch his breath.

The gargoyle paused in its fruitless efforts against Shadowfang and looked up. It hunched over, bunching corded muscles to prepare for another leap. Seldy tried to shout a warning but all that emerged from her hooked beak was a fierce,

"HOO!!"

Somehow it was enough.

The ancient Marine pushed off of the bars and rolled away at the last possible moment before the gargoyle crashed into them — a fierce whirlwind of slashing talons, flapping wings, and snapping teeth that cried out in frustrated fury.

::It senses you now, Shapesister! Flee before it is too late!::

Reacting with the speed and instincts of a natural killer, however, the gargoyle was up onto its feet and flapping its wings. It tilted its head up and locked its feral gaze onto her. Using its arms, legs, and wings, the creature propelled itself into the air. The desperate hunger in those eyes was unmistakable.

Her instincts told her to flee just as Tra'al and Shadowfang wanted her to, but she wanted to stay and fight. Torn between those two equally compelling urges, Seldy couldn't move.

The ship shuddered, pitching to the side as a massive gust of wind slammed into it. Men and beasts continued their vicious battle above her, shouting and screaming — some in triumph, others in agony. Blood and other less savory fluids dripped down in multiple places, adding to the overarching reek of fear and death that already permeated the prison hold.

Shadowfang growled as he continued projecting his demands for her to flee.

The gargoyle shrieked as it ascended towards her, its great wings swirling up dust and detritus in their wake.

The boar grunted and squealed and slammed into the front of his cage, thrashing his tusks against the metal bars.

Even Tra'al added his weak, choked voice to the cacophony of sound and self-doubt that kept Seldy frozen in place.

A single, mournful note of music rang out, stripping away all of the other noise in the same way that the first rays of the dawning sun banished the deepest darkness of the night. Long and low, the note echoed, reverberating through — and amplified by — the thick walls and vibrating iron bars of the hold.

Seldy gasped. Every being in the chamber stopped what they were doing and listened, each of them caught up in the same wonder that something could be so evocative...so ethereal...so beautiful...that it transcended the madness and carnage engulfing the ship.

The gargoyle slumped back to the floor, turning to stare in the direction of the shattered doorway. A shadow fell across the threshold. The source of the strange, unending note — a musician — stood there, just beyond sight, playing some sort of small wind instrument. The person's movements could only be discerned by the projection of his flickering shadow onto the floor of the hold.

Seemingly without effort, the drawn-out note shifted in tone and tenor, turning into a flourish of distinctive and beautiful notes — it became a song. Yet, Seldy had never heard anything like it before. The sheer beauty of it snatched the air from her lungs and left her aching to hear the last note that was played, yet yearning to hear the next one even more.

Each new chord brought up snippets of her favorite childhood memories — of snuggling between Layra's paws; the fresh, buttery scent of Jhana's special rolls fresh out of the oven; the feel of the wind blowing through her hair as she launched herself from her trapeze bar towards Chad's strong arms; the roar of applause from the crowds; the glowing smile on Tegger's face as he returned for yet another celebration of her birthday bearing those special cacao treats he knew she loved so much... that image brought her up short.

She blinked.

Could it be Tegger?

She blinked again.

Who else could it be? I've never heard anyone else play music even close to this!

Her heart soared at that possibility.

But why would he be doing something so silly as playing music in the middle of a battle?

The shadowy figure of the musician moved, stepping through the doorway. Focusing her eyes, Seldy hooted in surprise at the same time that Tra'al gasped out the figure's name.

"Mouse?"

The gargoyle reacted as well, snorting before rising to its full height and stalking towards its newest prey...

CHAPTER 37

Mouse, Seldy

Mouse's muscles — already strained far beyond the point of exhaustion — screamed in protest. Blood seeped from the open scabs on his back. His lips were dry and cracked, his tongue felt thick and woolly, and the back of his throat was as raw as it had ever been. Swaying on his feet more out of fatigue and dizziness than in trying to keep time with the music, Mouse wondered how much longer he could keep it up. It was only through the sheer force of will that his fingers continued to work, flying fast and sure to cover the proper holes on the flute as he reached for even greater depth and complexity in the most powerful and important song he had ever played.

Stepping into the hold, the soundscape pulsed with the vibrant energy of all of his cherished memories from his all-too-brief childhood. Weaving his mother's boundless love for him into the fabric of his song — note by note, memory by memory — was the only way he could dispel the overwhelming pall of fear and desperation that pervaded the prison hold. He didn't bother to fight against the stream of tears flowing out of the corners of his eyes.

The darkness had been pushed back from the hold and even from the deck above. But like the quiet calm that almost always precedes a terrible storm, the peace would not — could not — last for much longer. His song was holding back the massive storm through the sheer force of his will but not without taking a corresponding toll on his body, mind, and spirit.

It became harder to sustain with each passing moment.

The roiling clouds of chaos and carnage loomed large, pressing heavily against the edges of his consciousness. Largely concealed within the darkness of the storm, the countless tentacles of his foe seethed, probing for any weakness in his will, searching for any flaw in the continuing spell of love and peace that he cast with each note he played. Sensing that even a single discordant note in the song could create an opportunity for the Enemy, Mouse redoubled his efforts.

The terror instilled in the gargoyle by his earlier song was gone, but persistent shadows clung to the creature at the wrists, ankles and neck — where heavy shackles and a familiar-looking thick iron collar served as constant reminders of its status as a slave to the whims of the Enemy and his cruel minions.

Aware that the gargoyle was stalking towards him, Mouse closed his eyes and narrowed the focus of his song even further. He couldn't possibly outrun or outfight the creature. Instead, he dug deeper and spun out even more loving notes.

Beneath the layers of pain, suffering, and insatiable hunger forced upon the gargoyle by its cruel masters was a yearning for the freedom it once enjoyed. Focusing on that unfulfilled desire, Mouse wove new chords into his song, passages that evoked the creature's long-suppressed memories of how it felt to be the master of its own fate.

Desperate and angry shadows clung to the iron bindings, cloaking the gargoyle in their frigid darkness, reminding it of its servitude. Dark coils of mist formed around the creature's throat, weaving back and forth like deadly cobras poised to strike. It raised its head, trying to screech out in defiance, but the cry was choked off.

Stumbling towards him, the gargoyle stopped within easy reach, its hands curling and uncurling as it loomed up over him. Then, it stiffened; its face twisting in agony.

A burst of discordant notes pushed their way through the thin envelope of peace that Mouse had created around the hold, knocking both him and the gargoyle back a step. The beast's *ta'ir* receded, as if shrinking back in fear. Shadows coalesced around the creature's neck — growing darker and stronger by the moment. They danced skyward, reaching up towards something, no...someone. The first discordant notes of a terrifying but familiar song rang out.

The Enemy! He's trying to take over this creature!

A blast of frigid air washed over him. Mouse shivered.

No! I won't let him!

Recovering his balance, Mouse rooted himself to the floor, refusing to give another inch. He continued to play, undaunted and unmoving except for his flowing fingers, blowing lips, and heaving chest. He kept his eyes closed, intent upon studying the soundscape and the impact his music was having against the swirling mass of the Enemy's *ta'ir*.

The music flew fast and furious from his flute. He honed each note into a weapon that he could fling at the Enemy in order to disrupt his attempt to take over the gargoyle. Three times, his foe's *ta'ir* formed into a wispy cloud — the shadow-snakes reaching towards it from the gargoyle's neck — and three times Mouse disrupted the connection before it could be made, scattering the Enemy's unformed essence with an all-out assault of furiously hurled notes.

But each towering crescendo, each manic assault, drew on his already nearly empty reserves of strength, bringing him closer and closer to the end of his wick. Wobbling, Mouse's arms trembled. His lips, tongue, and throat were beyond parched. Every muscle screamed in agony. He couldn't feel anything beyond the pain and cramps in his fingers. He couldn't keep fighting against the impossible for much longer.

After his third victory, Mouse paused to collect both his breath and his scattered thoughts. He continued to play, but it was a slower, simpler song that he could play without much thought and even less effort. The stately song wouldn't do much to keep the Enemy at bay, but it fueled the yearning for freedom at the core of every being in the befouled hold.

As the shadowy coils fell limp and the gargoyle's *ta'ir* expanded again, a single, previously repressed, memory from early in its captivity burst into view...

...of hooded, tattooed figures looming to shackle it at the wrists and ankles...of the collar being fitted into place and locked...of dark, unknown words being spoken over it, infusing it with terrible power...of staring up at strangely glowing red and white leaves...of feeling helpless as a terrifying, frigid presence entered his body, seizing total control...

Mouse's eyes snapped open. Blinking, he stared at the black iron collar around the beast's neck. The hair on the back of his neck stood on end. The more he stared at it, the more...wrong...it felt.

That's it! The thought hit him like a thunderbolt, causing him to stumble over a few notes. *It looks just like Seldirima's! And the dark magick in it is what is drawing the Enemy to it!*

Sensing that he only had moments before the Enemy returned even stronger and harder to stop than ever, Mouse pulled the flute from his lips and slipped it inside his jacket. Fumbling around in his pocket for a different set of tools, he stepped closer to the paralyzed beast. Somehow, his tired, aching fingers drew out the tiny picks he needed.

The fetid smell of the old blood and rotting flesh rolled over him with every huffing breath the gargoyle took. Mouse tried not to think about how easy it would be for the beast to tear him to pieces...

As the last notes faded into memory, silence settled on the prison hold like a blanket of fresh-fallen snow. For a blissful moment, there was no fighting above her, no chaos swirling around her, and no pall of doom and death pervading the air itself. There was only a profound silence — delicate and peaceful in its stillness.

Awash in the warm memories evoked by the beautiful music, Seldy would have been crying like a baby if her owl form had been capable of shedding tears. She had spent her entire life amongst talented singers and musicians of all kinds, and no one, not even Uncle Tegger — the best musician she'd ever heard perform — had moved her like Mouse just had. It seemed as if the whole world had stopped to listen to him.

How did he do that?

The rhythmic creak and groan of the ship and the raspy, labored breathing of the strangely still monster that loomed over the young musician were the only answers provided to her unspoken question.

Is it all over?

Her keen eyes took in the incomprehensible scene unfolding in the hold below.

The creature stood tall and imposing, its wings and forearms spread wide as if it were about to strike someone or something; yet, the monster was rooted in place. Its corded muscles trembled, as if it were trying to move but was — for some unknown reason — unable to do so. The only part of the young musician that was visible was the top of his head — and that was uncomfortably close to the creature's open maw.

::*Shadowfang!*:: Seldy projected her thoughts towards the wolf. ::*What's happening? I can't see Mouse!*::

::*STILL YOUR MIND!*::

The wolf's rebuke slammed into her consciousness with palpable force.

::*This battle is still being fought! The Enemy draws near again and may yet win! You are hidden, and he cannot sense you unless you make yourself known to him! So be SILENT!*::

Seldy shuddered at the wolf's stern warning. Recognizing the wisdom of it, however, she quieted her thoughts, folded her wings in close to her body, and hunkered down to watch with keen eyes and open ears.

"Lad!" Tra'al's croaking voice shattered the silence. "What are you doing? What's wrong with that thing?"

"Gotta...free...it..." Mouse's voice sounded even hoarser than Tra'al's. He sounded as if he was on the brink of exhaustion.

"What?" The incredulity in the orc's voice matched Seldy's own thoughts. "Why would you do that? It's a gargoyle! Kill the damn thing or come over here and let me out so I can kill it!"

Mouse's head snapped up at Tra'al's last words.

"NO!"

His face was battered and bloody, but his brown eyes flashed, and his voice cracked as he shouted his reply. The young man swayed, clearly on the edge of collapse, but there was a fierce strength to his refusal.

"This creature is even more of a prisoner than you are!"

The gargoyle jerked, staggering back a step before stiffening again, its muscles twitching and its chest heaving. The boar thrashed against his cage, squealing in fear.

"That thing'll kill you, lad!" the orc cried out, clearly exasperated. "Gargoyles kill! That's all they do!"

"If I don't free it...we're all going to die!" Mouse's voice cracked again. Then, shaking his head, he leaned in even closer to the creature. "Can't talk...not much time..."

Seldy blinked. She couldn't wrap her mind around the idea that such a fearsome monster was a prisoner.

Before the orc could reply, the ship shuddered to a sudden halt, as if it was caught in the grip of a great hand. The sole sliver of bright sunlight streaming in from the tiny window above faded into a dull band of diffuse light. It became harder to see in the near darkness of the hold. The air became bitter and cold.

Despite her thick covering of warm, insulating feathers, Seldy shivered. The guard feathers all over her body stood on end, quivering. The ice cold ball of fear forming in the pit of her stomach told her that something about this chill was unnatural...and all too familiar.

The Enemy!

"Ready yourselves, boys!"

Seldy jerked within the tight confines of her crevice at hearing the booming voice of that evil captain just above her. It was dull and muted by the wood between them, but she cringed nonetheless.

"Here they come again!"

The boar gave a frightful squeal and pressed itself as far back within its cage as it could. Shadowfang growled. The ship shuddered again, the wood groaning in protest.

Yet, through it all, Mouse continued what he was doing, leaning in far too close beneath the looming monster's slavering jaws. The bulging muscles visible beneath the gargoyle's stone-like charcoal grey skin twitched and jerked, even as the beast remained otherwise still.

"S-s-so c-c-cold." Mouse's teeth chattered as he worked.

A crushing pressure pushed against Seldy's consciousness. It felt as if something terrible was about to happen.

"I don't know what you're doing, lad, but you better hurry up!"

"I...almost...have..."

A soft metallic click echoed throughout the hold, followed by Mouse's mixed cry of pain and triumph.

"...IT...ARRRGGHHH!"

Metal screeched on metal followed by a loud snap as two half-circles of heavy, black iron sprang open from their position around the gargoyle's neck. Everything slowed down — the two pieces of the collar tumbled towards the floor; Mouse stumbled and fell backwards, his blackened hands held out in front of him in disbelief; the gargoyle staggered back as well, flapping its wings in slow motion to try and steady itself.

Clank. Clank.

The collar clattered to the floor, the two halves of it splitting away from each other at the hinge, each piece skittering away in opposite directions.

::NOOOO!::

The Enemy's booming voice echoed against Seldy's already battered mental shields, driving her further back into her crevice with a frightened squawk.

The ship shook with the violence of a frustrated toddler refusing to relinquish his favorite toy while in the midst of a tantrum. Seldy dug her talons into the wood of the rafters and wedged herself in as tight as she could. None of those below, however, were as fortunate.

The boar slammed from side to side in his cage, squealing in rage and surprise. Shadowfang yipped and snarled as he, too, was thrown back and forth, although he somehow managed to catch himself enough to avoid slamming into the bars each time. Tra'al uttered a curse as he was pitched sideways to land in a heap on the floor of his cell.

The gargoyle was thrown backwards in the small hall

between the cages and cells, the violence of the shaking drove it down to its hands and knees. Mouse landed on his backside but didn't stop there. He crashed into the debris of the shattered door behind him. His head smacked into the wall, causing his eyes to roll up into his head, leaving just the whites of his eyes visible as he lay dazed and groaning amidst the debris.

"Mouse!" Tra'al yelled. "Get up, lad!"

It wasn't Mouse, however, who got up first. Seldy could only hold her breath in trepidation as the creature rose up, shook itself off, and stalked towards Mouse on all fours. When it reached his prone form, it sniffed him from the toes up to his head, until it was fully straddling him, looking down its muzzle at the young man's face.

"You leave him alone, damn you!"

Tra'al's outraged cry didn't distract the beast. Instead, it snorted, dousing the young man in snot and spit before opening its maw and licking him on the face with its thick tongue.

Sputtering, Mouse opened his eyes. He sounded as surprised as Seldy felt when he spoke.

"Okay, I get it!" Turning his head, he squirmed as he pushed against the creature's snout. "You're welcome...but you...you better get out of here!"

Pulling its head back, the monstrous creature tilted its head and regarded the young man.

CRACK!

"Aaiiyeee!"

"Hold steady, men!"

Jerking at the sounds of the resumed battle overhead, the gargoyle snarled and bounded off in the direction from which it had originally entered the prison hold.

It wasn't until she remembered to breathe that Seldy realized that the temperature of the hold had returned to normal.

"Well, that's a first, lad!" The relief in Tra'al's voice was palpable. "I never thought I'd live to see a gargoyle give up a free meal!"

Mouse sat up, looking even worse than before. His cheeks were bruised, sunken, and gaunt. The dark circles under his eyes only added to the image of someone who was beyond the point of exhaustion. Somehow, though, he pulled himself to his knees and then managed to stand up. He didn't seem to have any energy to respond to the orc.

"Now, how about letting me out of this damn cell?"

The young man stumbled to the doorway, picking up a sack, before turning and staggering towards Tra'al's cell.

"Where's the *Fae* woman?" Mouse managed to squeak out in a dry, cracking voice as he stared at her former cell, now empty.

"Seldy's safe!"

"Good," Mouse replied in a soft voice, dropping his gaze. "Don't tell me anything else about her, just in case."

"Blazing Fires, lad, just in case of what?" Tra'al's voice took on a tone of someone who expected to be obeyed. "Get me out of here so we can all escape!"

"No, Tra'al. Not yet."

He thrust the sack through the bars of the cell and into the surprised orc's hands.

"You need to get back into the corner and play dead."

"What?" The orc's voice rose an octave. "Why the blazes would I do that?"

Something massive smashed into the deck above Seldy, just as a familiar, booming voice cried out in rage, sending tendrils of black terror piercing through her body.

"KILL ALL OF THESE VERMIN!"

Shuddering, Seldy was surprised that she could hear Mouse's quiet reply to the former Marine through the resurgent din of battle and the cries of the dying men and beasts above her.

"You need to stay alive so that you can help her."

Another crash rocked the ship, coming from the stairwell behind and above her, the one leading down to the steps into the prison hold. Mouse shook his head in defeat.

"I won't be able beat him again."

His brown eyes flashed a hint of defiance as he stared at the door that the Enemy was forcing his way down to.

"But I might be able to trick him into thinking I have."

CHAPTER 38

Seldy, Mouse

Crack. Thump. Hiss.

Icy fingers of dread wrapped around Seldy's fluttering heart and tightened their grip. She couldn't stop from shivering, despite the thick feathers and fluffy down covering her tiny body. Each breath escaping through her hooked beak emerged as a tiny puff of mist before dispersing.

Crack. Thump. Hiss.

The beam beneath her talons creaked. The sturdy door between the stairwell and the prison hold rattled a little louder with each approaching step. Blood pounded against her eardrums.

Tra'al continued to plead for Mouse to open his cell, but the young man stood steadfast and silent in the middle of the small hall, his eyes fixed on the door that the Enemy would soon be coming through.

Crack. Thump. Hiss.

The battle raging above — and Tra'al's frantic shouting below — both faded from her consciousness, but the struggle within Seldy only intensified. Despite the growing pit of fear deep inside her gut, she wanted nothing more than to leap down to the floor to face the Enemy in one of her more deadly forms. She yearned to lash out at him with tooth and claw, to taste his vile blood, and to let him feel even a fraction of the pain that he had inflicted upon her and her family. She had been gifted — at far too great a cost — with the strength to finally be able to fight back against this monster, but something held her back, keeping her rooted in place.

Crack! Thump! Hiss!

Her heart hammered against her ribs. She clutched and released her talons a half-dozen times during the interminable pause that came after the creature's most recent step — the one that placed it just outside of that door. She opened her wings, uncurled her talons, and swiveled her gaze from the door that shuddered in anticipation to the exhausted and battered young man who was barely able to stand on his own.

Why should he face certain death while I hide? She quivered from barely contained rage. *I can fight!*

Do not act out of anger or draw upon the tempting, but false, strength of hate... The memory of Tia's mind-voice echoed softly in the depths of her consciousness, followed shortly by Layra's deep, rumbling warnings. *...remember this...keep love in your heart and remember who you truly are...Do not surrender to fear. Do not fight out of anger...*

Those words froze Seldy in place. Torn between the urge to act and the desire to honor the words of those who had sacrificed so much for her, she remained still and silent.

How? How can I keep love in my heart when I hate him SO much? And what's left to love in this world?

"AN-ASH-TAHL-SCREE-TU'UL!"

The deep voice grated against her eardrums. The unpronounceable words wormed their way into her consciousness. They burned everything they touched even as all warmth was sucked from her body.

"AN-ASH-TAHL-SCREE-TU'UL!"

The boar collapsed to his belly, uttering a high-pitched squeal unlike anything she'd heard before. Shadowfang yowled and backed into the farthest corner of his cage, whimpering and whining. Tra'al staggered back from the front of his cell, clutching his ears and crying out in agony...

"AN-ASH-TAHL-SCREE-TU'UL!"

The very air inside of her lungs burned. Wooden boards warped and popped. Metal screeched against metal. The door — the only barrier remaining between those in the hold and the owner of that voice — darkened and shrank in on itself, taking on a brittle and icy sheen. Billowing waves of dark mist leaked through the growing cracks between the door and the warping frame.

The mist coalesced into slithering tentacles of darkness that probed the room beyond the door before gathering at the back of the door. Mist continued to flow through the few remaining gaps, forming into yet more tendrils until the door disappeared beneath a writhing mass of inky black horror.

One figure remained still and seemingly untouched by the pervasive sense of impending doom.

Mouse.

He stood facing the door with bloody fingers wrapped around a simple wooden flute that he raised to cracked and bleeding lips.

Seeing him standing tall in the face of such utter darkness, his face a mask of calm determination, a tiny bud of hope formed inside of her heart. Seldy stopped shivering.

How can he be so strong?

As the door groaned and cracked under the assault, the crystal clear notes of a simple, yet achingly familiar, lullaby rang through air. The lyrics of the cherished song came bubbling up to the front of her consciousness, each line being sung by a different voice that took her farther and deeper into her past than the one before it...

Sweet little baby, crying out for me,

Tia's reedy voice burbled from withered lips as she rocked Seldy back and forth — even though she was long past the need for lullabies — stroking her ears in that comforting way that only she knew how to do.

Hush now, tiny star, 'tis time to sleep.

Jhana's smoky voice was warm and comforting; the voice that was always there in the dark of night whenever Seldy awoke from one of her nightmares as a toddler, crying and shaking. Her arms were strong and sure, her eyes full of love and fierce concern for her only child.

Sweet little angel, cute as can be,

Tegger's voice was clear and strong as he cradled her close enough for her to reach out with tiny hands to stroke the warm, soft fuzz that surrounded his mouth and extended out to his cheeks. She didn't know his name then but, even as an infant, Seldy sensed that when the Fuzzy One held her, no harm could come to her.

Mama's gonna sing, until you dream...

The last voice was blurry and distant at first, just like the image that accompanied it. But as the voice grew stronger, the view sharpened into that of an exhausted, but beautiful, woman with a heart-shaped face framed in curly, golden hair. Her blue eyes sparkled with a fire from within. They were bright and clear as she gazed down at her wrinkled and red newborn child. Her expression brimmed with love and hope, yet was somehow also tinged with a deep and poignant sadness.

Fear not, my Little Seedling, she whispered in a gentle but tired voice. *For the Guardian's light will shine when the night grows darkest, when all Hope seems lost. He sees Truth where others cannot and draws strength from Love. His music will guide the way, though he knows it not.*

CRACK!

The memory faded with the last notes of the lullaby, mere moments before the door shattered in a shower of icy shards. One by one, the writhing black tentacles released the tidbits of ruined wood and mangled iron before slipping back into the wall of utter darkness. A looming presence stood just out of view...the Enemy. Waves of fear and dread rolled off of the creature just beyond the open doorway. But those icy waves crashed against, and were dispersed by, the invisible and unassailable shores of an impossible island of light and love just a few feet inside the prison hold.

Blinking in surprise, Seldy swiveled her gaze from the blasted door back to the center of the hold. In a moment of dramatic flair that would have impressed even the most cynical old circus performer, Mouse stood, defiant and proud, in the center of the solitary ray of brilliant sunshine that had found its way into the hold from the tiny window above.

A horrible thought struck her as she watched Mouse calmly slip his flute back inside the pocket of his jacket.

He's going to be killed!

But before that thought was even finished, he straightened up, and she caught a glimpse of his brown eyes. In that one determined look, she saw a flash of the strong, confident, and secure man that resided within the battered, broken, and exhausted shell of a teen-aged boy.

Her breath caught in her throat.

He's the Guardian! Mouse is my Guardian!

The tiny bud of hope that had emerged when she watched him prepare to play had been nurtured by his music into a full-blown bulb. Something in the calm way he stood, in how he prepared himself to face whatever new and horrible form the Enemy was in now, triggered that bulb to burst forth into a majestic blossom of love and hope. Her heart swelled, shattering the icy grip of despair that had settled over her.

Releasing her talons from the death-grip that they had had on the wooden beam beneath her, Seldy shifted her posture and filled her lungs with a deep breath. Calling upon the depths of Tia's ancient wisdom, Layra's fierce strength, and Starfire's uncanny cunning, she knew now what must be done...

The sunlight felt good on his skin, providing the only warmth Mouse had felt in what seemed like days. The respite, however, didn't last long. The beam of light faded as a cloud passed between the ship and the cool winter sun.

Barely able to summon the strength to remain standing, Mouse stared up into the impenetrable abyss beyond the doorway as the notes of his lullaby faded into silence. Feeling empty and hollow inside, he lacked the energy or strength to extend the protection his music offered against the dreadful might of the Enemy's presence beyond the small circle that encompassed Tra'al, Shadow, and Gretch. Even that meager protection, however, wouldn't last much longer than a few more blissful moments.

Something is different this time. Mouse set his jaw at that thought. *He's stronger, more purposeful and deliberate. He's not rushing in like he has before. Is he afraid of me?*

His arms hung at his side. His bloody fingers wouldn't stop twitching. The muscles in his forearms cramped. The raw wounds on his back had finally stopped bleeding but every time he moved, the newest scabs caught on the rough fibers of his tunic, sending stinging reminders of the whippings he had endured only a few days ago.

His fear of facing me is all I have left. I might as well use it if I can.

Despite how utterly exhausted and spiritually drained he felt, Mouse stood tall, straight, and defiant. He had beaten this foe twice already and kept him from taking over the gargoyle before he freed the creature from slavery. Somehow, during that time, the *Fae* prisoner had escaped her cell and was now safe.

Yet, licking his cracked lips, the crusty bits of coppery blood clinging to them tasted more like defeat than victory.

I'm glad she's safe, but I wish we could've gotten to know each other a bit more. There's so much I wanted to tell her: about our mothers...about the cavern...about her song...her song! He gasped as a pang of regret shot through his aching heart. *How is she going to find it now? I was supposed to help her remember it!*

A few tiny notes of beautiful music echoed in the back of his consciousness. Reminded of its presence, he slipped a hand briefly into his pocket and felt for the rough texture of the peach pit. It was warm and tingly beneath his fingertips. Soft pulses of gentle energy flowed up into his arm and spread throughout his body. The welcomed warmth was accompanied by the hauntingly sweet and soft music that seemed simultaneously familiar and new at the same time.

Does this seed hold part of her song?

Tired of looking at the featureless wall of darkness in front of him and hoping to find out more about the strange music, Mouse closed his eyes. Taking a deep, calming breath, he opened himself up once again to the soundscape.

The song stopped in mid-note and faded from his consciousness like it had never existed. The wooden husk of the seed felt dull and lifeless beneath his fingers.

Huh. That's strange.

But it wasn't just the peach pit that had gone quiet. For the first time since he'd discovered the ability to access it, the greater soundscape — except for his immediate surroundings — had fallen deathly still.

Struck by how quiet and barren it was, Mouse pushed his senses outward, but it was to no avail. An impenetrable blanket of tightly woven notes had been draped over the hold, shielding the rest of the ship from his unique abilities. The only other *ta'irs* he could sense were in the prison hold with him. Behind him, Gretch's normally chaotic song was quiet, calmed perhaps by the remnants of the lullaby he had played earlier. Shadow was backed into the far corner of his cage, crouching and watching both him and the wall of darkness expectantly. His song was tightly contained within his body, reflecting his customary alertness and caution.

Tra'al, huddled in the back of his cell, was finally digging into the bag that he had passed to him. Mouse could tell from the notes of surprise and confusion in the old Marine's normally steadfast song that he'd already found the items that he'd collected from the captain's desk and the ring of the keys that he'd slipped into it right before handing it to the orc.

Good, he thought to himself. *He'll know what to do with that stuff.* His smile deepened. *I wonder how long that flask of* chag'rak *will last? He better not get too drunk; he's going to need to help her after I'm gone.*

Shaking off that morbid thought, Mouse turned his attention back to the seamless barrier surrounding the hold.

The Enemy doesn't want me to know what's going on beyond this room.

Shifting back to normal vision, he opened his eyes. The welcomed, hopeful music of the seed resonated once again throughout his being. Glad to hear that it still sang to him, he released the peach pit and brought his hand out of the pocket. This time, the music faded softly into the background of his mind.

Just like Seldirima, that seed's song can't be heard in the soundscape where the Enemy's senses and powers are much stronger than mine. That can't be a coincidence...

His thoughts were interrupted by a bone-chilling screech of rage tearing through the silence.

Gretch squealed like a tiny piglet and grunted as he pressed himself even further against the back of his own cage. Shadow gave a low growl.

"That's a harpy's cry!"

Tra'al's head snapped up, his eyes wide with fear. The old Marine's hands were trembling as he clutched at the wrapped package that Captain Dastyr had said was his.

"Get out of here, lad! Run for your life!"

"It's much worse than a harpy, I'm afraid." Mouse swallowed down the lump of fear that had fought its way out of his gut, seeking to paralyze him. "There's nowhere to run, Tra'al. I need to give Seldirima time to get as far away as she can."

"Don't be a fool, lad!" the orc hissed his words in a desperate, hoarse voice. "You'll be killed for nothing!"

"I'm her Guardian," Mouse replied in a soft whisper. "I have to do what's needed."

Setting his shoulders in a defiant pose, Mouse turned towards the wall of shadows that stood in place of the destroyed door.

The still air of the prison hold crackled with anticipation.

The darkness shimmered and shifted. Two sets of wicked talons poked through the barrier together before pushing in opposite directions, as if parting a set of curtains. Waves of dread rolled into the hold, washing over and erasing all memories of that brief moment in time when there had been an aura of peace, love, and hope in that dreary place. The figure that stepped through the void between the ebony curtains towered over him, so tall and gaunt and full of spite that it seemed impossible for it to be a living creature.

Yet, its raspy breath was timed to the expansion and contraction of its sunken chest and hollowed-out belly. It had impossibly long and thin limbs. Every movement of its corded, rope-like muscles showed beneath the rippling, hairless skin that was drawn so tight against the bones and muscles beneath it as to give the creature a starving, skeletal appearance. Massive, folded wings sprouted from its back, each of them tipped with a barbed, bony hook. The creature was naked except for a chain-link belt wrapped around its waist and the thick iron bands that loosely adorned its neck, wrists, and ankles. Two sets of empty shackles dangled from a metal clip on the belt.

A forked tongue darted out of its mouth, moving amongst the dagger-like fangs lining both jaws. Goat-like horns sprouted from the creature's wolf-shaped head, curling around its ears before coming to glistening, deadly tips that pointed towards whatever it was looking at with its blazing red eyes. And it was looking squarely and solely at him.

Those glowing eyes paused on Mouse the moment they became visible, freezing him in place with the unrelenting power of that feral gaze.

Mouse's breath caught in his throat. His heart bucked and hammered against his ribs, like an unbroken colt trying to kick its way free from the confines of its stall. His knees buckled.

There was no doubt as to who was in control of this creature. The Enemy had come for his prize, and he would not be denied again.

CLANK!

Dangling metal slapped against bone and metal as the creature took a slow, but otherwise silent, step forward.

Mouse's teeth chattered as all warmth fled his body. His empty gut danced and twisted itself around the cold pit of despair deep inside. The hair on the back of his neck and his arms stood on end.

CLANK!

Boards creaked and wood splintered beneath each deliberate step.

The glowing eyes of the creature bore down on him, their hateful red glare draining away more and more of Mouse's remaining strength with each passing moment. Staggering back a step, he flailed about with twitching hands, looking for something, anything, to give him some support.

But there was nothing but empty space and silence behind him.

CLANK!

The Enemy didn't say anything. He didn't glance to either side or waiver for even a second as his pounding, relentless *ta'ir* peeled its way through every fragile mental defense Mouse could throw up between his implacable foe and his innermost thoughts and beliefs. Every cherished memory became twisted and blemished with doubt and blame. Each loving touch and warm kiss his mother had given to him faded as if they had never happened. All of the kind words and tiniest bits of encouragement or praise that had ever been given to him crumbled to dust and were blown away by the cyclonic storm of anger, terror, and fear that tore away at the very foundations of his being.

CLANK!

The heel of his foot banged into something hard, heavy, and metallic. He lost his balance and stumbled. Beyond exhausted and completely overwhelmed by the Enemy's evil glare, he was unable to adjust. He pitched backwards and landed hard on his tailbone. The jarring impact sent fresh waves of pain radiating throughout his body, but it also broke the control Drak'nuul had over his eyes.

A tiny flash of movement in the rafters far above the Enemy caught Mouse's eye.

What's that moving around up there? An owl? When did that—?

CLANK!

Before he could finish that thought or get a clearer view of the bird, a massive shadow loomed over him, blotting out all light and hope. The Enemy stared down at him, a taloned hand reaching towards one of the pair of shackles at his belt.

THWUNK!

"ARRRGGHHH!"

The towering form arched its back, dropped the shackles at its feet, and uttered an ear-splitting screech of pain. As the irons clattered to the floor, the creature grabbed at the dark hilt of a large blade buried in its back.

"Take that you blasted harpy!" Tra'al's cracking voice was barely audible over the horrible screech of the Enemy. He was shouting at Mouse from the front of his cell, holding what appeared to be an empty sheath in his left hand.

Roaring in anger, the Enemy swung around and pointed a single talon at the old Marine.

"Run, lad! Run for your li—ERK!"

The orc's eyes bulged as he clutched at his throat, seemingly unable to breathe or speak. He staggered backwards, away from the bars and the approaching harpy.

Finding reserves of strength and determination he hadn't known he possessed, Mouse reached for his flute. He scrambled back to his feet, filling the hold with the light and hope of his music before he was fully upright.

Mouse was so focused on helping Tra'al that he didn't notice the Enemy turning back around and lashing out at him until it was too late.

The first blow smashed into the side of his head with all the force of a tree falling on him. Blinding pain flashed from multiple fresh wounds in the side of his head as massive, razor-sharp claws did what they were designed to do. Too stunned and staggered by the first blow, Mouse was unable to stop the flute from being snatched from his grasp by a second strike that left even more cuts on his hands.

"No...!" Mouse gasped, even as his legs crumpled beneath him. The whole room began to spin. "Not the flu—!"

His protests, however, went unheeded. Drak'nuul held the flute out in front of Mouse with a taunting look in his blazing eyes.

"FOOLISH MORTAL! SO LONG AS YOU NEED A CRUTCH LIKE THIS, YOU CAN NEVER HOPE TO STAND AGAINST ME!"

CRACK!

"NNOOOOO!"

The shards of his precious flute fell from the brute's bloodied talons in a slow-motion shower of shattered dreams and crushed hope.

Collapsing against the door of Shadow's cage, Mouse slumped to the floor. He reached out towards the broken pieces of his flute scattered near the creature's feet. He wrapped unfeeling fingers around the largest surviving piece and snatched it back. He brought his other hand up to cradle the piece — less than a third of the original flute — to his chest.

Deep in the back of his fading consciousness, the gentle, hopeful song of the peach pit blared out a few reassuring notes. A smile found its way to Mouse's lips even as he looked up into the face of his own doom. The Enemy loomed over him.

His blurry eyes, however, were drawn instead to the shimmering, pale, and completely naked form of the *Fae* woman crouched high above the Enemy in one of the more open rafters. Her emerald green eyes flashed brighter than any light he'd ever seen, illuminating the fierce expression on her face as she leapt from the rafters towards the unsuspecting back of the Enemy. Her pale hands were extended in front of her while her mouth was wide open as if she were going to attack him with tooth and nail.

The lines of her body began to blur as she descended towards the Enemy. However, before he could make sense of any of it, Mouse's vision faded. The darkness that had been clouding the edges of his vision closed in on him before she completed her doomed leap...

The instant before she landed on her unsuspecting prey's exposed shoulders, the tigress let loose with a rumbling and bone-shaking roar of defiance. The force of her all-out attack drove the foul-smelling creature to all fours and knocked the air from its lungs.

It was a killing blow, although her prey likely did not yet realize it.

Her claws ripped through the creature's tough, leathery hide as if it were paper, sinking down into the muscle and sinew below. Bones crunched and snapped beneath her powerful jaws as she clamped down at the base of its neck, just beneath the nasty iron collar that protected the weaker flesh and bones of the neck itself. Foul blood fountained into her mouth, eyes, and nostrils, but she ignored it.

She raked her rear claws downward, tearing into the creature's back and wings while sinking her fore claws even deeper into the front of its shoulders. Determined not to be thrown off when the doomed creature tried to buck her off its back, she pressed down with the considerable weight of her upper chest. The tigress clamped down even harder with powerful jaws, sheering through blood vessels, bone, cartilage, and muscles with equal ease.

The creature bellowed and shrieked in agony beneath her. It thrashed about, barely missing the unconscious young human male slumped against the door of a cage nearby. Blood spurted and seeped everywhere. There was none of the welcome, coppery warmth in its surprisingly cold flesh. Instead, the prey reeked of dirty iron, rancid meat, and disease. But the tigress was undeterred.

Her prey's thrashing weakened, its protesting cries softening until the creature became still and silent. Wary, the tigress kept ripping and tearing until she was drenched in its blood and pieces of its flesh hung, tattered and bleeding, from exposed bones. The final confirmation of the creature's death came with the rank odors created by the release of bowel and bladder.

Only then did the tigress feel the strange, yet familiar, tickle against her mind and looked up blinking in the direction of a dark-furred wolf staring back at her through the bars of his cage.

::*Seldy...Shapesister...you must remember who you are!*:: The wolf's thoughts forced their way into her mind. ::*The Enemy is gone.*::

The tigress exposed her bloody fangs and snarled in the wolf's direction, her eyes flashing with warning.

::*Stay back, wolf! I do not tolerate intrusions into my territory!*::

Metal clanked on metal and then screeched, startling her. She was up and turning to face this new potential threat, curling her lips back at she faced the two-legged predator staring at her with wide eyes and an outstretched paw.

"Easy, lass. I'm not a threat to you; I'm here to help."

The sounds he uttered burbled in her ears at first, until they settled into recognizable words.

"Seldy, come back now."

Her low, rumbling growl of warning caught in her chest.

Seldy? Why does that word sound familiar?

::*Because it is your name, Seldirima.*:: The wolf's thought-voice barged into her mind again, daring far more familiarity than any wolf should. ::*You are Seldy, a Leafsister who has been blessed by the Elder Spirits with the ability to take up this form when needed. You must control this form, however, and force the tigress back within or risk losing yourself to her.*::

"Come on now, lass." In his other paw, the two-legged creature was dangling something like a loose flap of skin or hide. "Come back to me..."

She could smell his fear of her, but she also caught other scents emanating from the waving object in his hand. The scents — of a female with two-legs...and the young male now behind her — triggered something...flashing memories...

...of watching a bold young man stand brave and tall against a dark and fearsome foe...

...of hearing music that was as beautiful as it was haunting and powerful...

...of seeing how he was willing to sacrifice himself for someone...no...her...

...of how he helped her to find a way to fight from a place of love instead of hate or fear...

...of hearing the anguish in his voice when his instrument was destroyed...

Blinking, the tigress stared down at the mess beneath her...at the blood drenching each of her paws. She felt how sticky her face was with the blood of that creature...

She backed away from the carcass, struggling with a foreign, and quite sudden, revulsion at seeing the carnage. She glanced back towards the wolf, but her eyes settled instead upon the unconscious form of the young man. His face was covered in blood, his body slumped awkwardly against the door to the wolf's cage. His hands were pulled in tight to his chest, clutching a piece of broken wood to himself as if it were the most precious thing in the world.

Mouse...my Guardian...his flute is...broken...

She staggered back even further, feeling weak and wobbly despite having the strength of a tigress coursing through her limbs and having four paws on which to stand.

Seldy. My name is...Seldy.

Everything began to shimmer and shake, her body contorted inwards. Bones shifted, shortening and lightening. Muscles contracted and softened. Fangs, claws, and fur all retracted into jaws, fingers, toes, and soft, pale skin respectively. Searing pain battled with indescribable ecstasy until Seldy was left on hands and knees, breathless and quivering as she stared down at the dark blood and gore that stained her wrists and hands. Sticky strands of blood-stained silver hair dangled in front of her face.

Seldy looked up through the tangled mass of her bloody hair to see what she'd done. She stared at the shredded and lifeless carcass of her...kill. The foul taste of the Enemy's flesh was heavy on her tongue. Her stomach heaved. The contents of her gut spewed forth, erupting like a fountain from her lips. Blackened blood and bits of partially chewed flesh splattered onto the floor, forming yet another pool of bodily fluids in the already rank and putrid hold.

Seldy collapsed to the floor, sobbing, and curled up into a tight ball.

"Wh-wh-what have I d-d-done?"

CHAPTER 39

Tra'al, Seldy

A quiet settled over the prison hold, disturbed only by the steady creaks and groans of the drifting ship and the shoulder-wracking sobs of the blood-drenched *Fae* lass. Her tunic still clutched in his trembling hand, Tra'al tried to take enough air into his lungs to calm his frayed nerves but the all-too-familiar ache deep inside his chest left him gasping.

"What's happened to this world?" His muttered question was uttered in the guttural tongue of his ancestors. He wasn't expecting anyone else to answer. "Talking harpies? A shape-changing lass? A young man taming a gargoyle and performing some kind of weird magick, all with a blasted flute. It's enough to drive a sober orc to drink!"

He shuddered, fighting off the urge to return to his cell and open the flask that Mouse had left in the bundle.

If Tegger had ever tried to tell a tale this strange, he would've been laughed off the stage. By the Ancestors, I don't even think Frank would try to pass off this level of craziness, and he can't ever stop talking about those Wilderlings and their strange ways.

A distant screech tore through the air. It was silenced by the muffled crack of a pistol.

Spurred into action by that reminder of the ongoing battle above, Tra'al squared his shoulders, stepped over the carcass in front of him, and yanked his blade free of the body. He stuck it through his belt to be cleaned later. Careful to avoid the puddles of blood and gore, the former Marine took another step before kneeling next to Mouse.

A quick check for a pulse and breathing showed the young man was still alive.

There's more blood than I would like, he thought as he studied the wounds on the young man's face. *But he's not in any danger of bleeding out. That poison though...*

Tra'al stopped his morbid thoughts cold, refusing to accept the likelihood of the boy's impending death.

"Hold on, lad." His hoarse voice cracked. "Looks like I'll be the one getting you off of this blasted ship instead of the other way around."

Mouse's only response was a nearly inaudible groan as he shifted his head against the bars. Standing up, Tra'al stepped over the carcass once again. He dropped Seldy's tunic next to her head on his way to the far end of the hall.

Gretch was still pressed as far back into his cage as a massive, six hundred pound boar could be in such a tight space.

"Alright you wretched bastard." Tra'al wrinkled his nose at the fouler-than-usual stench wafting from the boar's cage. He bent down to manipulate the locks on the cage door. "I'm thinking you don't want to die in this blasted crate any more than I did in mine."

Snorting, the boar stared at him through beady and distrustful eyes. He pawed the bottom of his cage with a filth-caked fore hoof.

Tra'al slipped the blade of his razor-sharp Marine dagger between the bars.

"Don't try anything stupid, you great oaf, or I'll take away the freedom to choose your own death."

A look passed between them, the kind of knowing look that only two old, battle-scarred and world-weary warriors can share. When the boar bobbed his head, Tra'al withdrew the dagger and finished with the latch. With a final yank, he pulled the door open and stepped back, giving the beast a hearty Marine send-off.

"Huuu-raah!"

Squealing, Gretch darted through the opening and crashed through the debris of the door. He thundered down the wooden hallway that ran the length of the ship.

"Woe be to any dumb bastards who get in your way." Tra'al chuckled, imagining the chaos that the deranged and enraged boar of his size would likely create. "That should buy us a little time."

Wiping his Marine-issued blade clean on a burlap sack hanging next to Mouse's rack of tools, he sheathed the blade and turned back to the work at hand. He grabbed some fresh rags and one of the empty buckets, dipping it into the barrel of stale water next to the door.

He stomped back down the narrow hall, stopping just behind Seldy's curled up form.

"Seldy?" He tried to keep the urgency from his voice.

Her shoulders continued to heave, shaking her whole body. She didn't respond.

Drawing in a deeper breath, Tra'al infused his next attempt with the sharp tones he used to reserve for fresh recruits.

"Seldy! Get up, lass!"

The wolf glared at him from the front of his cage, his lips curling back from his yellowed fangs. Seldy, however, only flinched at the bite in his tone.

"There'll be time enough to cry later, lass."

Sighing, Tra'al set the bucket and rags down. He lifted the catatonic girl with ease. Cradling her pale and gore-covered form to his chest, he ignored the wolf's bared fangs and baleful glare. He ignored the stench of death that covered Seldy from head-to-toe as he shuffled back towards the half-full water barrel across from the boar's empty cage.

He couldn't help staring down at the delicate features of her face, marveling at how recently this same lass had been wearing the form of a creature so ferocious as to be able to single-handedly slay a harpy.

And before that, she had been an owl and could have flown for her freedom. He snorted. *If only she'd've listened to me!*

Her bloody fingers curled and uncurled reflexively. Bits of torn flesh and strands of sinew still clung to her relatively short and utilitarian fingernails. He shuddered.

Her emerald eyes were half-open, but they had the kind of vacant stare he'd seen in all-too-many young Marines who'd survived their first deadly battles. Most of them snapped out of the shock through the calculated application of techniques that called upon their years of training as warriors and their pride and determination as young men. Some of them, however, never recovered and had to be discharged from service to be cared for by their families until they could function again.

"I believe, Seldy..." he spoke to her in the Trade tongue she was familiar with in a soft, caring voice. "That while you're neither a warrior nor a lad, you are far stronger than anyone I've ever met." The old orc paused to swallow the lump of unexpected and unfamiliar emotion that got stuck his throat. "I just wish I didn't have to ask you to draw on that strength so much right now."

Carefully positioning his arms over the mouth of the barrel, Tra'al released her...

"No, Layra!" Seldy cried out, "Don't leave me again!"

In a single, graceful leap, the tigress landed on the lip of the massive stone bowl in the chamber beneath the Hearth Tree of the Elder Spirits. She swung her head around and stared into Seldy's eyes.

::It is the appointed time, Cubling.:: *Her mind-voice brushed soothingly against Seldy's consciousness.* ::To delay further brings too many risks.:: *Those great feline eyes blinked once.* ::This way, Cubling, we shall always be together, and you may call upon my strength whenever it is needed.::

"Layra, please don't go! I love you!"

::I love you too, Cubling. I always have, and I always will.:: *With a final nod, the great beast turned her head and leapt towards the flickering fire at the center of the stone bowl. An eruption of yellow and orange flames engulfed the tigress.*

"NOOO!"

Seldy lunged forward, seeking to follow her beloved tiger-ma into the flames but another large, fur-covered body blocked her way. She slapped her palms against Starfire's flank before burying her face in the wolf's luxurious white fur, sobbing.

"Why?!?" *she wailed.* "Why does everyone I love leave me?"

::They leave because they must. But their love for you does not cease when they do.:: *The wolf's mind-voice sounded far older than she appeared.* ::The love you have shared, and the memories you have made together, remain behind.::

Something in the wolf's words brought Seldy up short. She released her hands from the wolf's fur and pushed back, blinking away the few unshed tears left in her eyes. Instead of trusting her failing voice, she replied to the wolf using her mind.

::I know Tia and Layra loved me, and I understand why they would sacrifice for me, but we've never met before, Starfire. Why are you doing this?:: *Seldy paused, looking around at the vast and strange chamber. When she turned her gaze back to the wolf, her eyes narrowed.* ::And why do the Elder Spirits want to help me against the Enemy?::

The wolf dropped her head down low and turned her body, brushing up against Seldy's torso, pushing her a step or two back from the edge of the gently lapping water.

::Those are excellent questions, Seldirima Silversong.:: *The wolf circled again before laying down in the cool sand.* ::Come sit with me, and I will give the best answers I can before I, too, must leave.::

Eager for both answers and comfort, Seldy joined the wolf, leaning into her solid warmth. She began stroking the soft, thick fur as the two of them stared up at the flickering flames in the center of the bowl.

::I learned of you through my sire, Shadowfang. He recognized you as a Leafsister the moment he saw you...::

::But how?:: *Seldy interrupted.* ::I didn't even know that I was *Fae* when we met!::

::I do not know, Seldy, except that my sire knows all of the ancient songs better than any other in the Pack. When I was a pup, he sang them to us every night to ensure that we would know them ourselves, but we were young and often grew bored.:: *There was a wistful quality to the wolf's mental voice and a couple of images of young wolf pups tussling with each other as a younger, even darker Shadowfang looked upon them.* ::Those songs tell of a time before the lands and the moon were broken, when Leafsisters and Branchbrothers danced and sang in the moonlit nights, living in harmony with all of the animals of the forest. Their leaders — the wise and powerful Treemothers — kept the magick of the living world in balance.::

Images accompanied Starfire's story: breathtaking views of vast, endless forests filled with wondrous and magickal beings,

492

and she heard the echoes of many packs singing out to the bright, full moon.

::Here in the Dreamlands, the beauty of the living world is but a pale reflection of what it once was; yet, it is all that remains to us. The Pack fights to defend the Elder Spirits for as long as possible by hunting down the Reavers that the Enemy sends to destroy them.:: *The wolf swung her head around so that she could stare into Seldy's eyes.* ::But as my sire would surely tell you, I have always been a restless and curious spirit. I know that the battle we fight here, in this place, is one that cannot truly be won. Individually, the Reavers may fall beneath our fangs, but each battle brings the risk that one or more of us will fall, never to rise again. They return — essentially unharmed — to battle again the next night, just as all of those who yet live can.

::So to remain here,:: *the wolf continued,* ::means to fight an endless and losing war. Yet to move on beyond, to cross the Gloaming Sea, is to give up hope for this world.:: *The wolf turned her gaze back towards the flickering flame.* ::When my sire spoke of you and how the Elder Spirits had called out to him to aid you in your journey here, we both knew that I would answer that call.::

The wolf's calm strength brought more comfort and relief to her than Seldy could ever express with mere words, so she sent those feelings, instead, with her next question.

::But what does that really mean for you, Starfire, to answer the call of the Elder Spirits? And does it mean the same thing for Tia and Layra as well?::

::It means that some portion of who we are will live on inside of you in the forms that have been bestowed upon you. I do not know whether you will have access to our memories or whether we will be able to speak to you as individuals again, but perhaps our love, unconditionally given, will sustain you during those times when your journey feels impossible, when the night becomes darkest.:: *Shifting her body, the wolf leaned her weight into Seldy.* ::And the rest of who we are will join with the Elder Spirits. We will add what strength remains in us towards keeping this sacred space open and accessible to both the spirits of the departed and those of the living world who yet dare to dream.::

Seldy laid her head on Starfire's flank, enjoying the closeness of a kindred soul. She continued to stare up at the hungry flames, the fire that would soon claim her newfound friend.

::Is there really a threat to the Elder Spirits? How can they be threatened?::

::Oh yes.:: *The wolf regarded her.* ::The Enemy has been working to destroy them ever since he discovered how to access the Fearscape, not that long after the world was broken.::

Seldy sat up with a start, her heart racing.

::The Fearscape?::

Starfire nodded, then dropped her head onto her crossed forepaws.

::The Fearscape is a dark place that is home to nightmares fueled by anger, despair, and fear. It is there that the Enemy marshals his power, growing ever stronger by feeding on the fears and sorrows of those who are trapped there.::

::I think I've seen that place!:: *She shuddered, remembering how it felt to be held captive there.* ::It was cold and dark and devoid of hope!::

The wolf rolled onto her back, staring up at Seldy through the gap between her bent forelegs.

::Yes, it is certainly a dark and twisted place now, but it was not always so terrible.::

Seldy rubbed the soft fur of the young wolf's exposed belly.

::How could a place called the Fearscape not be terrible?::

The wolf's lips curled back slightly as Seldy continued to rub her belly, revealing the tips of her fangs in a gap-toothed smile that seemed oddly reassuring.

::The Dreamlands and Fearscape have co-existed together, linked to each other in innumerable ways since the world of the living was formed in the great void. Together they envelop the world in a permeable barrier that protects it from the swirling chaos and utter darkness of the Great Beyond. They are, however, as two sides of the same leaf, with each side being necessary for the leaf to exist at all. The Dreamlands, like the light side of a leaf, connects each of us to our higher Source, drawing in and utilizing the sacred light from the Source above in order to create life and give it meaning through boundless and unconditional love, hope, and inspiration.

::The Fearscape, like the underside or dark side of the leaf, gives shape and structure to life, motivating us to reach higher, dig deeper, and try harder. Fear itself is as necessary for life as love and hope are. In measured and reasonable amounts, it teaches us what to avoid in order to live and gives us the strength to fight or flee when necessary. The Fearscape, back when it was healthy and normal, was a safe place for us to face and overcome our fears as we slept and to see them for what they truly are: simply fears. But once the Enemy discovered it and found a way to access its power, he twisted it towards his dark purposes. And, once he conquered the Fearscape, he turned his attention towards expanding his realm and destroying the Dreamlands and the Elder Spirits who preserve them.::

Seldy tried to absorb everything.

::But why? Why would he want to destroy this beautiful place?::

Shaking her head from side-to-side, the wolf responded, ::That is beyond me, Seldy. I have no way of knowing what motivates someone such as the Enemy.:: *The wolf righted herself, rolling back onto her stomach. She turned and gave Seldy a warm, wet lick on her hands.* ::I just know that the Elder Spirits have been able to keep him from intruding into it, so far. But with each passing season, more and more Reavers roam the Dreamlands, and the Elder Spirits grow weaker. I don't know how much longer they can hold the Enemy back or for how much longer those of us that remain can keep the Reavers at bay. That is why the Elder Spirits have bestowed these gifts to you, and why they have called for you to come here.::

Sitting back on her heels, Seldy felt the weight of the world settle onto her small shoulders.

::But how...?:: *She tried to form coherent thoughts to transmit.* ::How can I do anything about any of this? I'm just one person, and I don't know anything about being a Leafsister, let alone a Treemother!::

The wolf's eyes were solemn and sympathetic. She stood up and rubbed her head against Seldy's cheek.

::I do not know these answers, Seldirima Silversong. Perhaps when you speak to them, the Elder Spirits may be able to answer such questions. I am unable to do so. But I, and my sire, both believe that you represent our only hope of defeating the Enemy. When there were Treemothers and their children tending to the forests of the waking world and singing their sacred songs, the world was whole. Let us hope that once you find your song, you will be able to defeat the Enemy and heal this broken world because no one else, the Elder Spirits included, have been able to do so.::

Starfire backed up and swiveled her head towards the flickering flames.

::It is time, Seldy, for me to complete this ritual. Once the fire returns to this state, you must follow but not before.::

A lump formed in Seldy's throat, threatening to cut off her breathing. A cold chill travelled down her spine.

::You mean...I have to...jump into the fire, too?::

The wolf nodded.

::Yes.::

::But...won't I die?::

::Yes.::

Seldy blinked at the blunt answer.

::What if...what if I...can't?::

::Then,:: *the wolf's words were accompanied by the inde-scribable ache of sadness,* ::the Enemy has already won.::

SPLASH!

She awoke with a start, engulfed in darkness and water.

She was cold. So very cold.

She thrashed about in the water, smashing her knuckles into something solid. Fetid, blood-tinged water rushed into her mouth. Kicking downward, her heels smacked into wood beneath her. Her eyes snapped open, but the churning water was too dark to see anything.

Her feet planted, she pushed up. She burst through the surface of the water, coughing and gasping for breath. Weak-kneed, she grabbed the wooden frame in front of her. She sensed the presence of the other figure before she saw him. He had a worn, familiar feel about him, but she couldn't quite remember his name.

"What happened?" She managed to gasp out her question between hurried breaths.

"I've got no idea, lass." The owner of the gravelly voice chuckled. "I was going to ask you the same blasted thing." The voice continued. "First, we've got to get the blazes off of this ship, and I'm going to need your help to do that."

Wiping away the water that was dripping down her face, she looked up into the scarred face of an old orc.

"Tra'al?"

"Aye, Seldy?"

"Seldy?"

"Blazes! Did you get your head smacked, too?"

He began probing the sides and back of her head before she could object, but his fingers were deft and his touch gentle.

"I'm not feeling any lumps."

::*Leafsister.*:: Another familiar feeling brushed up against her consciousness. ::*Are you hurt? Has that two-legs hurt you?*::

"Leafsister?" she couldn't help whispering the strange, yet compelling, word. "No, I don't feel hurt."

Glancing down at her hands, she noticed that she was gripping the rounded rim of a wooden barrel, and that she was standing, naked, inside of it, chest deep in scummy water that smelled of blood and filth.

"What am I doing in this barrel?"

The orc blinked, pulling his hands back.

"Leafsister? What's that now? I've never heard those two words put together in quite that way before. Maybe all of that magick you've been doing isn't all that good for you, lass."

"Magick?" Her eyes widened. "Me?"

Tra'al arched a thin eyebrow before glancing over his shoulder down the darkened hall. Her eyes followed his. The moment she saw the shredded carcass sprawled out beside the unconscious form of the young musician, everything came rushing back to her, including the sick feeling in her gut and the terrible taste of foul blood in her mouth.

Her stomach heaved again, doubling her over as she attempted to retch the deep sense of disgust out of her body. Horrible, gagging sounds erupted from her throat. Pressing her forehead against the cool support of the lip of the barrel, she watched helplessly as thick strings of bloody bile and phlegm — all that remained in her stomach — dangled stubbornly from her trembling lips.

She felt Shadowfang's worried inquiries brush up against her mind and heard Tra'al's attempts to comfort her, but Seldy was too caught up in remembering the twisted feeling of satisfaction she felt at sinking her claws and fangs into that horrible monster, at ripping the life right out of it.

*It felt so good...*She shuddered at that thought...*to kill.*

A pair of strong hands cupped her cheeks as they gently pulled her gaze back up towards their owner. Tra'al stared down at her with concern in his eyes but when he spoke, there was steel in his voice.

"Now you listen to me, lass. The battle for this ship might be almost over, but it is still being fought. We need to get out of here and get to the rescue skiff. There are likely more of those damn creatures crawling about. We don't have time for you to deal with whatever this is that you're going through right now. Mouse is hurt bad enough that he's going to need my help to get off or be left behind." His voice sharpened, becoming even more insistent. "And I'll be thrown into the Blazing Fires of the Fallen Star before I leave him. I don't know how he did it, but he brought the captain's keys, the very keys we need to escape this ship. We'll never get another chance like this to escape." His eyes bored deep into hers. "So, I'm going to go collect Mouse and our supplies and let that blasted wolf you're so fond of loose from his cage. You've got however long that takes to clean yourself off, collect your wits, and get dressed before we have to move out of here. Do you understand me?"

"Yes, *Maestro.*"

When Seldy clambered out of the barrel, her thoughts were still churning as fast as her stomach. Water sluiced off of her naked body, forming small puddles around her feet. Shivering, she reached for the tunic that Tra'al had brought for her.

::There will be no need for the man-fur, Shapesister.:: Shadowfang's mind-voice pressed itself into her mind as he padded towards her, head hanging low and eyes shining. *::Join me in your wolf-form.::*

The idea of shifting again scared her.

::But what if I lose myself again?::

She clutched at the tunic, feeling the woolen fabric strain beneath her grip.

::What if I have to...kill again?::

Following right behind the wolf, Tra'al clutched Mouse to his chest like he was a small boy instead of a nearly full-grown adult.

"What're you waiting for, lass?" he snapped at her between huffing breaths. "Put that blasted thing on so we can get out of here!"

Surprised at the snap in the orc's voice, Seldy glanced from wolf to tunic to orc before her eyes settled on the battered and bloody form of the unconscious musician.

"Can you fight if you need to, Tra'al?"

"No, not if I'm carrying him." The orc looked defeated. "But you're too small to do it, and he can't walk on his own."

::I am here for you, Shapesister.:: The wolf's mental voice was gentle yet firm. *::The Pack only fights when it must. Join me in that form, and neither I nor my daughter will let you forget yourself. And if we must fight our way free, we will do so together, as a Pack should.::*

"We'll have to be a little lucky, I suppose," Tra'al snapped at her, glaring down at the wolf who stood between them. "Well, are you going to put that on?"

Biting her bottom lip, Seldy let the tunic fall to the floor.

"I won't be needing that," she spoke in a quiet voice. "Shadowfang and I will protect you both."

She was already shifting into Starfire's form before Tra'al could object.

CHAPTER 40

Klard, Mouse

"Take that you worthless bastard!"

The blade of Klard's sword bowed before the tip finally punctured the stone-like hide of the still squirming gargoyle with an audible pop. Its vile heart pierced, the creature fell still and silent.

Thump. Thump.

His blood pounding against his eardrums, Klard released the blade and threw his head back to let loose a wordless cry of triumph from amidst the carcasses of his fallen foes.

"We'll rid our ship of these vermin yet, boys!" His voice cracked, but his will was undaunted. Stepping forward, Klard reached for the hilt of his sword.

The sudden movement, however, was too much. A wave of nausea and fatigue washed over his body. The blood-spattered deck spun and tilted. Klard's knees buckled. Overcome by the combination of blood loss, fatigue, and gargoyle's poison coursing through his body, he leaned forward and pressed his forehead against the cool pommel of his sword. Bleeding from more than a dozen wounds across his torso, limbs, and face, he knew it would only be a matter of time now before he surrendered to the inevitable.

Thump. Thump.

"No!" Roaring in defiance, he pushed himself up. "I'm not done yet, blast it!" Sucking in a great chestful of air, he bellowed, "To me, my hearty crew! Rally to me!"

Staggering to unsteady feet, Klard blinked against the morning glare. A break in the clouds allowed the winter sun to drench the scene in unrelenting bright light. It glinted off of countless bits of polished brass adorning the lower deck and reflected off of those few unbloodied steel blades scattered around him. He kept blinking until his pupils adjusted. When they did, he noted with surprise the lack of movement and the ringing silence that greeted his rallying cry.

Nothing alive was moving. Tattered bits of bloody clothing and torn sailcloth flapped in the stiff breeze. Random bits of tackle hung from shredded lines, knocking against wood in a solemn rhythm...

Thump. Thump.

His crew — his hand-picked crew of rough and tumble men who had entrusted their lives and the future of their families to him — were nothing more than bodies and pieces of bodies littering the blood- and gore-stained deck of his beloved ship.

"Wait! By the Circle, what hap-"

The words died in his throat as numbness, followed by a deep, bone-weary fatigue washed over him. Stumbling and nearly blind with grief, Klard moved between the piled-up corpses of beasts and men. His eyes darted from body to body looking for someone, anyone, who might still be alive.

Thump. Thump.

"Jigger!" the thin man's name slipped through his chapped lips when he recognized the back of the trouble-maker's head. He'd bailed the young man out of more jails than he cared to remember, but there was no better rigger in the entire Mariner's Guild.

Kneeling down, Klard ignored the pop in his knee and the flash of pain that accompanied it.

"Get up, Jigger!"

He flinched at the desperation that leaked through in his voice but needn't have worried. The gaping wounds in Jigger's throat made it clear that the man would never be able to tease him about the unusual show of emotion.

Thump. Thump.

Numb, Klard straightened up. His eyes glazed over. Seeing so many of his men scattered about the deck brought the weight of an island crashing down on his shoulders.

"Haddock?"

His eyes darted from man to man, but he couldn't see the bald head or distinctive tattoos that marked his long-time First Mate. He turned to scan the upper aft-deck, the place he'd last seen Haddock leading a defense of Bennet, the hapless Chief Navigator, and his young assistant, Trevend.

Bennet, however, was splayed across the rear half-wall of the Navigator's Station, his torso ripped open from groin to neck, exposing his ribs and leaving his entrails spilled out all over his normally pristine white uniform. Neither Trevend nor Haddock were anywhere to be seen.

Thump. Thump.

"How is this poss-...?" The question stalled on his tongue, unfinished. He began to count the carcasses of their attackers.

Ten...fifteen...twenty...This just doesn't happen in the Mid-tere. Gargoyles and harpies don't attack fully armed and crewed ships in broad daylight! Or blazes, even at night!

Drak'nuul is coming for her... Mouse's voice echoed in his memory, his intense brown eyes flashing as he spoke with a power conviction that Klard had never heard from the meek young man before. *...and nothing will stop him from trying to enslave or kill anyone who stands in his way!*

Drak'nuul. The Reaver Lord.

Thump. Thump.

He shuddered. It had been burned into his consciousness as a youth by his mother. While other kids his age were reading chap books of sappy children's tales, she had him reading dusty old books about the centuries-long period of chaos and strife known as the Great Riving in which the Reaver Lord and his *Myrkuul* slavers had reigned in terror over the frightened and unorganized folk of the Midtere from their fabled city of Glamdaaryn in the Untere. The Great Riving only ended with the forming of the Guild Alliance, which finally gathered enough men and allies to defeat the *Myrkuul* in the long and bloody Founder's War over three hundred and fifty years ago.

YOU WILL NOT STAND BETWEEN ME AND MY BRIDE ANY LONGER, MORTAL FOOLS!

Recalling the bizarre glow in the first gargoyle's eyes, Klard staggered back, its shouted words bouncing around in his mind.

Gargoyles are nothing more than dumb beasts!

He blinked, surprised that he hadn't found it strange in the moment.

They can't talk! They don't have brides, either!

Thump. Thump.

"But how?" the question sounded weak and unsure to his own ears. "How is any of this possible?"

A playful breeze feathered its way through his bushy beard and tangled mane of sweat-soaked hair, its soft caresses bringing him back out of his own twisted and tangled thoughts. Beyond his own ragged breathing, the only sounds to be heard were the creaking of the nearby mainmast, the unhurried snap and pop of canvas sails responding to the wind, and the gentle, rhythmic tapping of a piece of unsecured tackle bumping into an iron socket.

Thump. Thump.

Those mundane noises — sounds that were as familiar to him as his own heartbeat — brought him back to an awareness of the moment. But it was the missing sounds — the hue and cry of Haddock's orders being relayed to the crew as they worked the rigging, the ribald banter between rough and rowdy men, the creative and bawdy curses shouted whenever someone pinched a finger or slipped and banged an elbow, and the good-natured taunts and retorts that accompanied each eruption — that tore at his raw and aching heart.

He took in the carnage anew. Everywhere he looked, the bloodied and torn faces of old friends gazed back at him with vacant, accusing stares. Dalton, the gruff and blunt elder statesmen amongst the crew, sat with his back against a bulkhead beside the gaping doorway into the officer's quarters, his hands frozen in the act of trying to hold back the red and grey mass of innards from spooling out around his splayed fingers.

Thump. Thump.

Reaching for the Seeker's Circle that was always close to his heart — the only thing that brought him any comfort since Valk's illness — Klard's fingers found only cloth and his own flesh. He gasped, his breath catching in his chest.

That's right! It's gone! He shuddered at the memory that came rushing back. *Mouse threw it out the blasted window! But why? What am I missing?*

"Dada?"

A shrill cry pierced his heart; the cry of a small child calling out in fear.

"Dada!"

"Valk?"

Worried that he was hallucinating, Klard stood still and listened with his entire being, his aching muscles taut with tension.

Thump. Thump.

"No want more, Dada!" the tiny voice choked and coughed before crying out even louder. "Want, Mama!"

Hearing the terror in Valk's voice, Klard sprang into action. Ignoring the searing pain and the unrelenting waves of nausea, he snatched a fallen sword from the deck and thundered towards his brother's voice. Splashing through the pool of Dalton's blood, he plunged into the gaping maw of darkness, heedless of anything but trying to help the only family he had left in this world...

"I'm coming, brother!"

Thump. Thump.

Thump. Wheeze. Thump.
Ouch!

Floating in darkness, Mouse flinched from the agony lancing throughout his body but even that small movement sent fresh prickles lancing up and down his back. It didn't take long, however, for the heady mix of odors flooding into his nostrils to overcome the shock of the pain. The strongest scent matched the coppery taste in his own mouth — blood — while the acrid odor of days old sweat was unmistakable. But there was a hint of something else — of something green and fresh — that distracted him from dwelling too long on the less pleasant smells.

Where am I? And why does everything hurt so much?
Thump. Wheeze. Thump.

Unable to see anything, Mouse took a deep, shuddering breath and tried to open himself up to the soundscape.

Nothing.

Just silence, darkness, and a pounding headache that blossomed into a pain so sharp and terrible that it seemed as if his head would explode. Whimpering, he stopped searching and curled in on himself.

He felt empty and hollow inside, as if a vital piece of his being was missing.

The music that he'd heard for his entire conscious life — from the subtle shifts in tone or pace in the sounds around him that so often warned him of danger to the sharp changes in the *ta'irs* of the people nearby that so often distracted him from what they were actually saying — was gone.

He couldn't hear anything. He couldn't see anything. It was as if the soundscape and all of the strange and bizarre colors and sensations had never existed.

Why can't I hear any ta'irs? *Is this what it's like to be dead?*

Thump. Wheeze. Thump.

The pressure around his body, particularly at his knees and shoulders, increased with each thump, accompanied by a jarring sensation and a fresh wave of sparkling agony along his back, neck, and head. The wheezes in between varied in length and depth but sounded as if someone was expending a great deal of effort. His left ear was mashed up against something warm and hard, allowing him to hear a deep, gurgling rattle at the end of each wheezing breath.

Maybe I'm a prisoner?

"Down!" Tra'al's raspy voice sounded far more strained than it normally did as it erupted next to his ear. "Go...down... the...blasted...steps!"

It's Tra'al! Relief flooded through him. *And he's carrying me!*

Thump. Wheeze. Thump.

A heavy weight pressed down on his chest, forearms, and hands. He opened his eyes, but something was covering his face. His fingers were stiff and sore yet still clutched around something small and round. The surface was smooth, except for one jagged end. Rubbing a finger along the broken end, he gasped from the sharp jab of a small sliver imbedding itself.

My flute! That realization sent his thoughts spinning. *It's broken!* His heart started to race in panic. *How am I going to...the music...her song...the Enemy!*

His last memory of the *Fae* girl sprang up, unbidden. She had been leaping towards the Enemy — sparkling green eyes flashing, her pale hands extended like claws, her mouth open in a feral grin.

Tra'al jerked to a halt.

Claws clicked against wood. There was a low whine followed by several loud wuffling snorts.

"Go on...blast it!" the old orc snarled. "We...have...to...go...down!"

More wuffling, more scrabbling. Then the clicking grew softer and less distinct with distance.

Thump.

"Shite..."

Wheeze.

"How...in..."

"Screeeee!!!!"

Mouse recognized Gretch's squealing cry, but it was far behind them, and it was soon swallowed by another blood-curdling cry of rage. Hooves thundered and wood splintered as the boar crashed into something before everything grew too chaotic to sort out by sound alone.

Thump.

Wheeze.

"Ah...screw...it."

Thump! Thump! Thump! Thump!

Searing pain jolted throughout his body with each jarring impact as they descended a stairwell, pushing deeper into the bowels of the ship. But from the deep rattle mixed in with the wheezing and the groans of pain coming from the ancient orc, it was clear that he was suffering nearly as much as Mouse was.

"Unh!" Mouse groaned. "Ow!"

"M-m-mouse?"

The movement stopped, sending one last jolt through his aching back.

"Thank..."

Wheeze.

"The..."

Wheeze.

"...Ancestors!"

His world tilted as his feet were lowered to the deck. The weight on his chest shifted and tumbled to the floor, crashing with a heavy, clattering thump.

"I...need...you...to..."

Wheeze.

"Walk...lad..."

Wheeze.

The cloth that had been covering his eyes slipped off as he was stood up, leaving a lingering scent of freshness as it slipped down to his chest. The dim, flickering light of a lantern swaying from its hook in the ceiling provided the only light. Shadows danced and twisted as the lantern swung from side to side.

Mouse blinked, trying to make sense of the two figures ahead of him.

Two large, four-legged, lupine forms, one nearly all black and the other almost completely white, moved slowly away from them. They had the long, bushy tails of wolves. Their claws clicked on the wood with each step, and their noses wrinkled, exposing long, sharp fangs, as they explored each crevice, doorway, and object on their respective sides of the hallway.

He blinked again and would have shaken his head to clear the double vision if he'd been capable of it.

Mouse tried to stand, but a wave of vertigo washed over him. His knees buckled. He would've fallen, but Tra'al supported his shoulders.

"Easy, lad." Tra'al wheezed out his words, even as he shifted his arm to provide more support. "I'm gonna...lean you...against the wall...for a moment...okay?"

Mouse gave an unsteady nod to the orc, not trusting his voice. The hallway continued to sway and spin, making him feel woozy. If he'd had anything left in his gut, it would've been fighting to get out. Instead, his stomach twisted up on itself and gurgled angrily. His head felt stuffy and swollen. Even the smallest movement made the whole ship spin. He let his chin drop slowly down to his chest. Tra'al bent down to gather whatever had fallen.

Blinking the wetness out of his eyes, Mouse tried to focus on the stubby shaft of the shattered flute still clutched in his stiff, unfeeling fingers.

You look like how I feel. A deep, dark sadness welled up inside of him, made all the deeper for the forlorn silence inside of his own head. *I don't see how either of us will ever make music again.*

He transferred the shard of the beloved flute into his right hand and carefully slipped it into his jacket pocket. His fingertips brushed against the rough texture of the peach pit. His breath caught. His heart swelled with hope as he wrapped his fingers around the large seed.

Please let me hear your song again!

Nothing. Hope shriveled in the face of resounding silence.

Fighting back tears, Mouse swallowed the bitter bile fighting its way up his throat. When Tra'al straightened up — with a familiar sack in one hand and one of his old tunics in the other — he found the strength to croak out a single word.

"Seldirima?"

"Seldirima?" The old orc raised an eyebrow. "Oh, you mean Seldy!" He chuckled, nodding towards the blurry wolves in the distance. "She's ahead." He shook his head at Mouse's confused look. "C'mon lad...it'll take...too long...to explain."

Before he could find the strength to object, Tra'al slipped his arm back around Mouse's shoulders and began ushering him down the hall, following the wolves towards the stable hold in the bottom rear of the ship...

"No, Dada!"

Valk's plaintive tone urged Klard on despite the nausea and pain that threatened to drop him to his knees. He stepped over the pieces of Telly's dismembered body and crunched through the debris of his office door. Books, scrolls, and maps lay scattered about the office, pages and pieces of loose paper idly shifting in the light breeze coming in through the shattered window.

He knew better than most how limited his time was. The gargoyle venom coursing through his veins was a death sentence. If the Dastyr family name was to survive — and its honor be restored — Valk had to live. He was the last chance for future generations of the family.

Unless...No.

He clamped down on the unbidden images that came to mind, pushing them aside before they could fully form.

He's the one. He has to be.

He pushed himself to get moving again.

It's for the best that way.

Heedless of any lurking danger, Klard staggered past the shattered window and through the debris of the broken door into the small hallway.

"DRINK, SWEET CHILD, AND WE SHALL BE WHOLE AGAIN, REUNITED IN OUR SHARED RA—!"

"NOOO!" he roared at the familiar voice. "Get away from him!"

Seeing the dark, winged form crouched over Valk's bed,

Klard charged. He extended his blade out ahead of him like a bull's lowered horn.

The creature's blazing red eyes barely had time to widen before the tip of the blade found its way through the stone-like hide and into its chest. With an unholy strength fueled by adrenaline and pure rage, Klard lifted the impaled beast from his brother's bed, using only the blade of the sword, and drove it towards the far wall of the cabin. He didn't stop pushing forward until the wall itself stopped them.

"You can't have him, Drak'nuul!" the words erupted from Klard's mouth, hoarse and cracking with rage. "You can't have him!"

The gargoyle thrashed its limbs and wings about. The creature's eyes blazed ever brighter, and its voice thundered in his ears, but Klard couldn't hear anything beyond his own hammering heartbeat. He kept pushing on the hilt of the sword until it punched through the beast's back and bit into the wood behind it.

Straining with all of his might to keep the creature pinned in place, he looked up into its eyes and realized that the deep, rumbling sounds coming out of its throat weren't words or cries of pain but laughter. Those eyes locked onto his and seared into him with their blazing intensity.

"YOU FOOL!"

Claw-tipped fingers reached up, one set of them wrapping around his throat and pulling him in closer with an undeniable strength. The other set extended a single, razor-sharp claw towards his forehead.

"YOU ARE AS MUCH MY CREATURE AS YOUR BROTHER HAS EVER BEEN!"

Unable to pull back, Klard cried out in renewed pain as the claw dug a deep furrow into the skin of his forehead. Sharp pain became pure agony as the claw moved in a circular motion, scoring so deep that it felt like the tip of the claw was grating against bone.

Klard gasped, helpless to stop both the pain being inflicted on him and the invasion of his mind.

::SEEKER, YOU HAVE SERVED ME IN WAYS THAT YOU ARE TOO WEAK-MINDED TO COMPREHEND.:: The voice invaded his mind. *::YOUR LITTLE MUSICIAN LACKS THE STRENGTH TO DO ANYTHING MORE THAN GRANT YOU A TEMPORARY RESPITE FROM MY INDOMITABLE WILL.::* Finishing its work on the sigil, the gargoyle shook with laughter once again. *::THIS SHALL SERVE AS YOUR REMINDER AS TO WHO YOU TRULY SERVE.::*

The grip around his throat loosened at the same time that the red light in the creature's eyes dimmed and the invading presence faded from his mind. The gargoyle gave one last, shuddering breath before all of its muscles released. It fell limp and silent, still pinned to the wall by his sword.

Gasping, Klard staggered backwards. He pressed his left hand to the wound on his forehead. It was as large around as the palm of his hand. Blood seeped through, dripping into his eyebrows and streaking down his already wet cheeks and into his beard.

Ignoring his pain, Klard turned towards Valk. His brother's chest rose and fell in a slow and steady rhythm. His heart lurched, however, at seeing three freshly-emptied vials of Valk's treatments lying next to his sweat-stained pillow.

"Wait," he muttered. "I didn't give you any of those..."

His own wounds forgotten, Klard dropped to his knees next to Valk's bed. Worried for what he might see, he peeled the sheet back. The wounds on his chest and sides were fading. The deep gashes from the tiger's claws were now little more than raw, puckered scars.

"That's impossible!"

Valk stirred, shifting his head on the pillow to look up at him with feverish eyes. His lips curled into a small, innocent smile but deep inside the pupils, Klard saw a hint of light: a faint red glow.

"Soon, brother," Valk whispered through gritted teeth. "I will be well enough to rise from this bed to serve our Master with you once again."

Klard's breath caught in his chest. He wanted to speak, to say something, anything, to his brother, but the words wouldn't come.

"You've been marked by the Master, brother." Valk's hand raised, trembling, to touch his forehead. He smiled. "You must've served him well."

Before the big man could find his tongue, what little strength remained in Valk failed. His arm dropped back down to the soiled linens, and his eyes closed. The loving smile, however, remained on his lips.

"No..."

Conflicting emotions — love and hate, fear and hope — swirled around inside of Klard, clutching and pulling at his heart.

"No!" Klard dropped his right hand down to the hilt of the dagger still sheathed at his belt. "I can't...I won't let him have you, brother."

...*promise me*... His mother's soft voice echoed inside of his head. ...*love him...protect him*...

His fingers tightened around the hilt.

A wave of nausea and weakness washed over him. His strength was fading.

Awash in despair, Klard yanked the blade from its sheath and raised it up over his head, ready to plunge it down into Valk's chest.

"It's the only way, Valk." His voice was soft and thick with love for his little brother. "I'm sorry I did this by taking you to the Seekers, but I couldn't bear to lose you!" Hot tears streamed from his eyes, mixing with the blood streaking down his cheeks. A heavy sob escaped his lips. "I didn't know what would happen to you...to us!"

Valk stirred. He opened his eyes to mere slits. He stared up at Klard, a smile on his lips.

"I love you, 'Lar."

Klard gasped. His throat tightened, and his heart swelled. He swayed on his knees, feeling dizzy and lightheaded. His thoughts were foggy.

Sounds echoed in his memory...

...his mother's soft voice singing a lullaby as she cradled his baby brother to her breast and rocked him to sleep...

...Valk's tiny bare feet slapping along the wooden floor accompanied by his childish giggles at being chased, then the breathless laughter of being mercilessly tickled when Klard finally caught up with him...

...of his father lecturing him on how to be an example for his impressionable younger brother...

...of Valk's labored breathing as he struggled for each and every breath as the Black Scourge brought him closer and closer to death...

Staring down into his brother's eyes, Klard summoned the last reserves of his strength, preparing to plunge the dagger down until a strange thought hit him, something he'd never contemplated before...

What would Mouse do?

"How...much...further...?" Mouse labored to form each word.

"We're close...lad...close," the orc wheezed out his answer between ragged breaths. "Just keep...moving..."

Mouse grunted. It took all of his concentration and most of his strength to keep placing one foot in front of the other. If Tra'al hadn't been there, supporting him with an arm under his shoulder, he couldn't have made it very far at all.

Each step sent fresh waves of pain surging through his body — from the tired and battered muscles of his legs to the incessant pounding and the uncomfortable pressure that was building inside of his already sore skull. He had stopped looking ahead after the shifting shadows created by the swaying lanterns caused him to stumble to his knees and convulse in dry heaves. Tra'al had only just managed to get him back up and moving again.

A fierce growl somewhere ahead brought Mouse out of his pain-induced reverie. Raising his head, he tried to focus on the shadow-drenched path ahead. Both wolves stood in the debris of the smashed door to the stable hold. Their heads hung low, and their tails were bushed out and extended straight back. The fur on their shoulders stood on end.

"What in the blazes?" Haddock's voice bellowed from the depths of the hold. "Two wolves? Stay back or by the Shards I'll shoot!"

"Shite!" Tra'al cursed under his breath before letting the bag fall from his other hand. He leaned his weight into Mouse, pushing him up against the nearest wall. "Stay here..." he wheezed, his eyes flashing, "until I...get back..."

Wincing from the fresh agony of a thousand tiny needles lancing into his back, Mouse exhaled and clamped his eyes shut. By the time he was able to breathe and open his eyes, the old Marine had his back to him, chugging down the last few feet between them and the wolves with an unsheathed dagger in hand.

"Stay back, orc!"

Mouse had never heard such panic in the First Mate's voice before.

"Easy now...matey."

Tra'al stumbled through the debris, pushing past both wolves. Holding his empty hand out, the old orc turned to his left.

"There's no...reason...we can't....work together...to escape..."

SNAP!

The end of the Serpent's Tongue lashed out, snapping around Tra'al's neck.

Both wolves jerked back at the unfamiliar sound, their lips curling up as their hackles grew even higher.

"Arrgh!"

Mouse shuddered in sympathy with Tra'al's choked cry of pain but that remembered agony gave him the strength and motivation to push off of the wall and stumble towards the hold.

Yanked to his knees, Tra'al struggled to jerk free of the whip wrapped around his neck, but it remained taut.

"I ain't spendin' another blazin' minute with any worthless orc!" Haddock snarled. "I had more'n my fill with your ilk durin' my time in the Marines!"

Gaining momentum, Mouse crashed through the splintered boards of the doorway with reckless abandon. He staggered between the two wolves and into the open space of the stable hold. Spinning around, his senses were assaulted by the smells and sights of the stunning carnage scattered throughout the hold.

Bulger's eviscerated carcass lay across the shattered remains of his stall, joined by the misshapen and crumpled bodies of at least two gargoyles. The body of a third gargoyle lay sprawled across the floor near Haddock, its claws still holding the remains of a human arm as it stared with unseeing eyes towards the rafters. He didn't immediately see where the arm came from, but he wasn't looking for that.

His head spinning, Mouse turned towards Tra'al and reached to loosen the grip of the Serpent's Tongue from his friend's neck. The throbbing inside of his head turned every movement into sheer agony, and the pressure inside his skull worsened.

"Mouse?" Haddock snarled as he snapped his wrist, releasing Tra'al and drawing the whip back for a second strike. "Ya let this bastard loose, didn't ya?"

Red-faced and feverish, Mouse stumbled between the orc and Haddock. He lurched around to face the man who'd inflicted more pain, humiliation, and suffering on him in the last six months than he had imagined was possible. His eyes flashed with unbridled rage.

Haddock stood taller and more imposing than ever, not six feet away. His bare, sun-tanned and heavily tattooed chest was covered in blood, although it wasn't obvious that it was his own. The handle of the Serpent's Tongue was held in his right hand — poised to unleash another strike — while his left aimed a cocked pistol in the direction of the wolves.

"Yes," Mouse spat at him, advancing despite the fact that the whip was undulating in preparation for another strike. "And we're getting off of this ship...together or not at all!"

"You're not goin' anywhere, you traitorous stower!"

Something inside of Mouse snapped. The pressure that had been building finally burst. As if a veil had been ripped from his eyes, the soundscape burst into view in all of its swirling, frenetic, and chaotic glory. He opened his mouth to yell out his defiance once again, only to have all of the anger and rage that he'd been suppressing explode out of him in a furious blast of sonic energy.

The First Mate was picked up and hurled backwards, thrown into the heavy reinforcing beams of the ship's side by the power of Mouse's cry. His head smacked into the wood, resonating with the same hollow sound a melon made when thrown down onto a stone floor. The forward momentum of the whip's iron tooth was stopped dead in mid-strike; both lash and handle fell harmlessly to the deck. However, the pistol remained in the man's left hand and the moment his body struck the wall, his finger constricted.

The impact of the hammer on the back of the gun reverberated throughout Mouse's being. Unconsciously and instantaneously, he turned that deadly sound into energy that enabled him to act.

Time slowed.

The muzzle flashed.

BANG!

Visible sound waves rippled outward from the barrel of the gun. The lead ball erupted in slow-motion from their midst, hurtling with deadly force towards the white-furred wolf. Unconstrained by whatever had slowed everything else down, Mouse threw himself into the path of the oncoming bullet.

Searing heat.

Breath-stealing impact.

Blinding pain.

Darkness descended.

CHAPTER 41

Seldy

Seldy's ears rang. Her nostrils flared, tickled by the acrid smoke in the air. A smattering of blood dampened the fur of her snout. She danced backwards on nervous paws, blinking and waiting for her eyes to adjust after the bright flash from the muzzle of the gun.

::*What just happened?*:: She projected her question to Shadowfang.

::*The Guardian slew the dark-skinned two-legs, but he has been hurt by the other's bang-stick.*::

She could feel the mixture of concern and admiration in the wolf's mind-voice. It was accompanied by a projection of the image of Mouse diving between her and the flashing muzzle of the gun.

::*It appears that he sacrificed his life for yours, Leafsister.*::

"Mouse!" Tra'al's voice was choked with emotion. He stumbled towards the fallen young man. "What've you...done?!?"

Stunned, Seldy watched the old orc stagger forward. A flood of raw and conflicting emotions overwhelmed her. Unbridled admiration for the young man's bravery wrangled with the terrifying fear that she wasn't worthy of such a sacrifice. The love she felt at seeing such selflessness wrestled with the anger bubbling up inside of her that he had been forced into such a choice in the first place.

Tra'al flipped the young man over onto his back.

"Blast it all...how are you...going to...survive this...lad?"

Tra'al pressed a hand against the wound, while reaching for the hilt of his fallen dagger with the other.

The moment she saw the gaping wound in Mouse's upper chest and the fountain of blood gushing between the orc's shaking fingers, Seldy snapped into action. She took a step forward, her body already undergoing the bone-crunching, muscle-spasming, and breathless transformation back into her normal form.

By the time she reached them, Tra'al had his dagger out and poised at the entry of the wound.

"Mouse...don't you...quit on me!"

"No, Tra'al!" Her voice shook as she pushed the orc's hand aside and moved between him and Mouse. "Let me!"

Without pausing to explain anything to him, she threw a leg over Mouse's torso and straddled the unconscious young man. She leaned in close, staring at the wound with a single-minded intensity that any of her fellow circus performers would have recognized in an instant. She focused all of her emotions — but most particularly the love that Mouse's music and recent actions had inspired — into her intention.

"But...the bullet..." Tra'al struggled with each word. "It has to...come out...and the...bleeding...has to stop."

Ignoring the strange look the orc gave her, Seldy simply nodded in acknowledgement before placing her hands on either side of the spurting wound. Once she had a good visual image fixed in her mind, she closed her eyes and opened herself to the thrumming vibrations coming from deep inside of her gut the pulsing green seed at the center of her being. Just as it had when

Layra was dying, the seed was responding to the urgency of her need.

Tha-throom.

At first, the sound wasn't all that different from the deep rumbling purr of a tigress, but that soon changed, becoming faster and more varied in its beat. The vibrations reverberated throughout her entire body — causing her to shake like a leaf in a windstorm — until she directed all of that vibrational energy towards the tips of her fingers. They felt white hot and full of energy. She plunged both hands into the gaping wound in front of her.

Mouse's back arched. A primal scream erupted from his lips. He writhed, trying to buck her off him with more strength than seemed possible. Having grown up learning to ride on the bare backs of a variety of circus animals, Seldy refused to be thrown off.

Tha-throom.

Tightening her knees around his hips, Seldy leaned down and pinned Mouse in place. She plunged her fingers even deeper into his chest. His pulse pounded against her skin. Blood spurted with each thrashing beat of his wildly pumping heart, weakening him further. Ignoring the panic that sought to grip her mind, she pushed through the gushing blood, torn muscles, ripped tendons, and broken bits of bone until she found the source of his trauma: a hot mass of foul metal that stung her fingertips as soon as she touched it.

Tha-throom.

Gritting her teeth against the burning pain stemming from touching the unclean metal, Seldy grasped the offending slug. It was no longer a round ball but was, instead, a misshapen and uneven mass wedged into and between bones. Pulling hard, she pried it free. Her vibrations grew stronger, deeper, and more powerful as she yanked the bullet from Mouse's chest and cast it aside with a wordless cry of triumph.

Blood fountained out of Mouse's chest. He convulsed beneath her, a rosy red froth bubbling up from his lips.

Tha-throom.

Tra'al shouted something. Shadowfang's mind was pressed against hers. Seldy ignored them both and reached with bloody fingers back into the wound. Already exhausted, she kept humming, even as the vibrations began to shift. By the time her fingers were in contact with his wound, she was no longer humming but keening a gentle and wordless song.

Tha-throom.

The connection that formed between them was instantaneous and far more intimate than anything she'd ever experienced. Image after jarring image came rolling through the connection into her, each of them accompanied by fresh waves of pain. At first, the images were just a confusing jumble of faces and conflict — faces of hard-eyed men with tattoos and piercings who struck at her without mercy, the bearded face of the captain carrying her, the red-eyed visage of the man who'd struck down Layra, the snarling face of a gargoyle with glowing red eyes as it struggled to catch her as she repeatedly slipped free of its grasp and ran around an office — until Seldy realized it wasn't her that had seen these faces and fought those battles but Mouse.

He's been fighting the Enemy! He's been fighting to help me all this time!

Tha-throom.

The realization hit her so hard that it took every bit of concentration and determination she had to keep singing so that the critical link between them could remain open.

Looking down at Mouse with fresh eyes, she didn't see his broken and battered body but the glowing radiance of his spirit. His aura was awash in vibrant colors that spoke to her, describing who he was and how he conducted himself.

Tha-throom.

The warm hues of kindness, curiosity, and love dominated his aura, with equally strong doses of determination and perseverance rounding out the mix. Beneath those clearly visible traits, however, she saw deep levels of self-doubt, loneliness, and...loss. She felt how — like her — he'd lost his parents in some way that had left him orphaned, alone and adrift in a harsh world. However, unlike her, he'd never experienced the unconditional love and support of an adoptive family. The yawning gulf of his loneliness was overwhelming.

Tha-throom.

Her voice caught in her throat. She stumbled over the notes of her song. They became strained as her confidence flagged.

Can I really save his life merely by touching and singing to him?

The moment she voiced that doubt in her mind, however, a memory of the Elder Spirits speaking about her ability to heal came rushing back to her.

As an immortal Fae, Seldirima, life-giving energy is constantly flowing through you from your surroundings. It is that energy that renews your body, that keeps you strong and healthy at all times, that keeps you safe from disease and the ravages of age, that prevents you from suffering pain and injury from natural sources of cold or heat. That is why the touch of certain metals, such as iron, steel, or lead, is painful and dangerous because those metals disrupt the flow of that natural energy. It is also why prolonged contact with any of them can be deadly to you.

As a Treemaiden, you can share that sacred energy with those who are closest to you, giving you the ability to heal deadly wounds, to cure terrible diseases, and to extend their lives beyond what is normal for their kind. Simply by being near you, mortals will be less susceptible to disease. For those you allow to have prolonged contact with your bare skin, they will gain minor benefits without any other conscious action on your part. They will experience relief from chronic aches and pains and gain energy and warmth — including the healing of minor cuts, scrapes, and bruises. But until your ta'ir is released, access to your true powers of healing is both very limited and extremely difficult to control.

In order to heal major wounds or acute diseases in others without the full power of your ta'ir, you will have to open yourself up in ways that will make you vulnerable to the pain and suffering of those you are healing. All magick comes with a cost, and that is the cost that you must bear in order to heal others of their life-threatening wounds. The more love you feel for those you are healing, the easier it is to access this power. But beware: the deeper your love and shared connection with the patient, the more vulnerable you will be to their suffering, and the more you will share in their pain.

Pausing, Seldy took a deep and restoring breath. She gathered herself. Her choice was clear.

I have to share his pain and connect with him. But, how do I do that?

Tha-

His heart skipped a beat.

A lump of hot panic formed in her throat, threatening to cut off her healing song before it ever truly began.

Tha-

Still connected to the dying young man through her fingertips in his wound, she felt his pulse weaken with each beat of his wounded heart. His aura dimmed, fading as quickly as his body was failing.

-throom.

"No!" she cried out. "You can't die!"

"Lass." Tra'al's hand touched her shoulder. "It's a...deadly... wound."

Tha-

"No!" Seldy shook the orc's hand off of her shoulder and pushed him away. "I won't allow it!"

Swallowing down her doubts, Seldy opened her mouth and began to sing to again. As she did, she invested herself — all of herself — into the music. She opened her heart, mind, and spirit with the intention of sharing whatever was needed of her own energy with Mouse — whatever the cost.

-throom.

The drain was as immediate as it was powerful. Waves of crackling energy rolled from her into him. Somehow, through the sheer force of her will, she directed that energy into his wound.

Broken blood vessels knitted themselves back together. Tendons and muscle fibers reconnected. The fragments of his shattered bones began to fall back into place and fuse. With each tiny improvement, his heartbeat strengthened, and his aura grew slightly brighter.

Yet, even as the healing energy continued to bind them together, images of what Mouse saw right before he was wounded and the emotions he felt in that moment washed back into her. The connection between them was so intimate, so personal, that she was unable to stem the flow of those feelings and images.

She experienced all of his aches and pains of his older wounds as he rushed past the blurry images of two wolves to rescue his mentor from his tormentor. She felt the building pressure inside of his head and how disoriented he was. She felt the rage he had for the man who had inflicted so much harm on him become an unstoppable torrent.

As all of that remembered rage twisted and erupted into a killing blow against the dark-skinned man, Seldy fought to remember who she was and what she was doing. Her voice faltered, almost fading away.

Tha-

Before her song failed entirely, however, a chord of the beautiful lullaby that Mouse had played in the face of the Enemy brought precious memories back to her. Fighting off the fatigue that threatened to overwhelm her, Seldy opened her heart even wider and deepened her connection with this remarkable young man.

-throom.

A flood of emotion cascaded through that shared connection as she re-lived the desperate moment when Mouse chose to throw himself in front of the bullet, sacrificing himself for her. The bravery of that act renewed her strength and her sense of self. Even as she was hit with the searing impact of the bullet into his body, the strength and vibrancy of her healing song returned full force. Pulling her fingers from the surface of the wound, she watched as his skin knitted itself back together into an angry, puckered scar surrounded by the torn remnants of his tunic and jacket, now drenched in pools of coagulating blood.

"By the Ancestors!" Tra'al's words were almost inaudible. "I've never..."

Shuddering with a combination of sheer exhaustion and the aftershocks of the pain she now shared with Mouse, Seldy collapsed onto his chest. Her own heart pounding, she pressed an ear to his chest, listening for the proof of success.

Tha-throom.

Darkness crowded the edges of her vision and fatigue pulled at her limbs, making her feel sluggish and weak as she inched her way up his body towards his face. It took almost all of her remaining strength to lift her head up in order to stare down at his bruised, battered, and bloodied face through eyes blurred with tears of love and relief.

"Thank you, my Guardian." She whispered her words, brushing a stray curl of tangled brown hair from his forehead.

Sighing, Seldy pressed her lips to his cheek in a soft kiss. "You are a true Guardian."

Exhaustion took its toll. She collapsed across his gently rising chest and fell into a deep and dreamless sleep.

Tha-throom.

Seldy awoke with a gasp to a pounding headache. Her heart thudded against her ribcage. She was shrouded in darkness. Her lips were dry and cracked. It felt like every muscle in her body was stiff and sore. Unsure of where she was or what was going on, she stilled her breathing and opened all of her senses hoping to figure things out before some new danger appeared.

The only sounds she heard were the rhythmic creaking of wood, the irregular snap and pop of canvas blowing in the wind, and the grating crunch of teeth gnawing on a bone. The room was dark and stuffy with the odors of musty canvas, wet fur, and rank body odor. She was curled up in a fetal position on a rough woolen blanket with her bare back pressing against the wood of a solid wall.

For the briefest of moments, Seldy imagined that she was back home and had perhaps fallen asleep in one of her tigress' wheeled cages as the *kumpania* traveled from one stop to the next in the circus tour. However, that thought passed almost as quickly as it came. Too many terrible memories came flooding back to entertain that illusion for long.

Blinking in the darkness, Seldy sent out a probing thought towards the source of one scent she did recognize.

::Shadowfang, where are we?::

The bone-crunching stopped.

::What's going on?::

::Leafsister.:: A welcome and familiar presence brushed against her mind. *::It is good to hear your mind-voice again.*

I was worried about you. We are riding in a smaller floating wooden den than the one we were in before. Much smaller.::

::*I don't understand. Do you mean a ship? Are we in a different ship than before?*::

::*Yes. Ship. Smaller ship.*:: The wolf's clipped response had a dry, bemused tone to it. ::*I care not for these...ships...with their walls and floors made from dead trees and foul smelling fire-stone. I long to feel good earth beneath my paws again. I ache to run and hunt and to sing out to the Shards of Luna.*::

Seldy couldn't help but smile at the wonderful images that Shadowfang sent with his thoughts. They stirred the same longings in her as they did with him.

::*Me too! But how did we get here? And where is Mouse? Is he okay?*::

::*The ancient two-legs, the grumpy old hunter, did it.*:: Shadowfang projected an image of Tra'al's face to her. ::*He moved you and the Guardian into this den, Leafsister. After you saved the young one.*::

He projected more images to her: of Tra'al opening a door in the back wall of the hold and then returning to retrieve first her and then Mouse. He wrapped each of them in heavy blankets before struggling his way through the back door.

::*I followed. I was eager to be away from that ship. It stank of fear and death.*::

::*So, are we safe?*::

She hadn't realized that she had been holding her breath until her lungs started to burn.

::*Yes. As far as I can tell. No more of the winged hunters have attacked, and the two-legs of the ship have not followed or bothered us.*::

Seldy exhaled a burst of stale air and took in another shuddering breath. She didn't want to ask the next question but needed to.

::What of the Enemy? Is he gone, too?::

::I have not sensed his presence since you slew him.::

::He's dead, then?::

::So it seems, Leafsister.::

Breathing a massive sigh of relief, Seldy pushed herself to her elbows. As she sat up, the woolen blanket that had been covering her face slid off, revealing that it was both lighter and cooler in this new ship than she at first thought. She blinked at the bright sunlight streaming in from above and looked around at her new surroundings. For the first time in far too long, her heart was brimming with hope.

The Enemy is dead!

The 'ship' they were in was smaller by far than the prison hold she was most familiar with and even smaller in sum total than the stable hold. The whole thing couldn't have been much more than twenty-five feet long and fifteen feet wide. The space was flat but relatively crowded, with waist-high wooden walls and heavy canvas panels extending up from the walls that ended as they arched into a tent-like ceiling. Thick iron ribbing provided the support the canvas needed to stay in place. A single, trunk-like mast arose from a solid iron socket imbedded in the center of the floor. It was tall enough to poke through the canvas tenting at its peak.

Looking across the way first, she saw Shadowfang stretched out across the floor, a couple of blood-covered, horse-sized bones laying between his front paws. A bucket of water was next to him. The wolf watched her with bright eyes as she surveyed the rest of the ship.

To her immediate left, Mouse had been laid out on his stomach. A blanket covered him from head to toe. From what little she could see of his hair, his head was turned away from her. Except for the slow and steady rise and fall of his back as he breathed, he wasn't moving. Beyond Mouse, Seldy saw the endless blue expanse of the open sky since there was no panel above the front wall of the tiny ship.

To her right, which seemed to be towards the back of the ship, Tra'al was seated behind a large wooden counter, but he was slumped over a sloped panel, seemingly asleep. Behind him was another open expanse of crystal clean air, although the back wall was higher than the rest of them. Most of the space between the front of Tra'al's counter and the mast was occupied by a set of barrels and crates lashed together, a stack of neatly folded canvas panels, several coils of thick rope, and a pile of stuffed sacks.

Standing up, Seldy let the blanket fall from her shoulders to pool around her feet. Stretching out her tired and stiff muscles, she reveled in the feel of the brisk, clean air flowing in from the front of the ship and across her bare skin. The headache was gone the moment she breathed in the fresh air. The stretch loosened all of her muscles. Pulling her hands back, she noticed that they had been scrubbed clean of Mouse's blood. Her face was clean as well, although some dried blood was still stuck in her hair, and her chest was covered in crusty red blotches of old blood.

Padding on bare feet over to Mouse, Seldy knelt and pulled the blanket back far enough to touch the skin of his neck.

His skin feels warm and dry. That's good, I think.

But even that brief, light touch revealed how badly he was still hurt. Pain and loss resonated throughout his body, washing into her. It didn't seem, however, that he was in any immediate danger. The blissful fog of sleep was preventing him from suffering from any of his older wounds. Pulling back, Seldy stood up again.

Her eyes were drawn to the front of the ship and the sense of boundless freedom and endless opportunities that beckoned. She wobbled a bit as the floor tilted and shifted beneath her with each gust of wind, but it didn't take long before she felt the warming rays of the bright winter sun shining down on her as she leaned her arms on the top of the waist-high wall. The contrast between the chilly air and the warm sunshine on her bare skin was beyond delightful.

The sight of so much sky both above and below her took her breath away. The lands of the Untere unfolded before her eyes, thousands upon thousands of feet below. Dozens of tiny blue ribbons and slightly larger expanses of sparkling blue water interspersed amidst large areas of green vegetation showed that the lands below her were fertile and teaming with life.

Seldy found a surprising amount of joy in the feeling of the stiff winds pushing and teasing through her hair, making it stream out behind her like a silver banner. However, what she loved most of all was the pervasive feeling of her freedom: the most cherished possession of the Freeborn.

I could change into my owl-form right now and fly back to the kumpania!

The temptation was so tantalizing that she could taste it.

But what about Mouse and Tra'al and Shadowfang?

Mulling that question over, Seldy turned around. She sucked in her bottom lip in contemplation. Pangs of guilt hit her hard in the gut.

I can't leave them behind! What if the Enemy isn't really dead and comes back? Or that evil captain and the rest of his crew come after them?

Strands of silver hair fluttered in the wind along both of her cheeks, streaming past her face. Biting down on her lip, Seldy weighed the urge to take to the air and truly be free with the desire to stay and help her friends. The memory of all the sacrifices that had been made for her freedom tugged at her conscience.

"Could I really leave Mouse?" Her whispered question was

snatched by the wind. "Or Tra'al? Or Shadowfang? After all that they have done for me? No. I can't. I won't leave them!"

Whirling back around into the teeth of the wind, Seldy leaned one hand on the top of the wall and raised the other in a clenched fist, shaking it at the empty sky.

"I am wild! I am free! I will not be caged again!" Seldy shouted her defiance out to the world. "And whoever tries to cage me or hurt those I love — you will be sorry!"

A FINAL NOTE

This story continues in Book Two of The Seeds of Hope: *The Seedling's Song* (available now), and in Book Three of The Seeds of Hope: *The Guardian's Quest* (in progress).

I would be so appreciative if you could leave a kind review on Amazon. I truly hope you enjoyed reading this book!

ABOUT THE AUTHOR

Douglas S. Pierce is a son, husband, and father who lives in the Metro Detroit area with his wife Patricia (of more than 25 years), two Shiba Inus (Suki and Akira), and a black cat named Harley. He is a proud veteran of the United State military and a practicing pagan. Raised on weekly trips to libraries and bookstores, Doug has had a lifelong love affair with the kind of stories that inspire hope, kindness, and love.

You can find him on Facebook at www.facebook.com/douglaspierce.author/

You can follow him on Instagram at: @douglasspiercebooks
Finally, you can find sample chapters on upcoming books, scenes and chapters that were cut from already released books, news of book signing events, and articles about the people and places of Sundatha by visiting Doug's Patreon account, where all of the material he posts is freely available: www.patreon.com/douglasspiercebooks

OTHER WORKS BY DOUGLAS S. PIERCE

The Maiden's Song, Special Edition containing Books One and Two of *The Seeds of Hope*
(2018, Sanhedralite Editing and Publishing)

The Hunted Maiden, Book One of *The Seeds of Hope*
(2019, Sanhedralite Editing and Publishing)

The Seedling's Song, Book Two of *The Seeds of Hope*
(2019, Sanhedralite Editing and Publishing)

The Guardian's Quest, Book Three of *The Seeds of Hope* —
Forthcoming in 2020

Omega Rising, An Agent Rusty Bones Novel — Forthcoming
in Fall of 2019

Omega Falling, An Agent Rusty Bones Novel — Forthcoming

Boneswolf, An Agent Rusty Bones Novel — Forthcoming

Selected stories that appear in the anthology: *Before the Moon
Fell, Book One*, by John Gorney
(2012, Wubba Productions)

Made in the
USA
Columbia, SC